Praise for David Keenan

'I sometimes think David Keenan dreams aloud. His prose has the effortless, enigmatic, unsettling quality of dream.'
Edna O'Brien

'Sit back and marvel at David Keenan's colossal ambition, at his singularity, at his monumental achievement.' *TLS*

'I wanted to live inside this book.' Kim Gordon

'At this stage of his game Keenan can make his books do pretty much anything.' *Irish Times*

'At times it feels a little like reading Yeats.' *Literary Review*

'David Keenan is a blazing, deviant, fearless force and just a total one-off.' Wendy Erskine

'A colossus of imagination.' Lenny Kaye

'David Keenan is the literary disruptor in chief.' *Spectator*

'Haunting, visionary.' *Guardian*

'A 21st century cult classic.' Salena Godden

'Remarkable . . . demented brilliance.' *i Paper*

'Keenan is a new kind of historian . . . extraordinary.'
New Statesman

'This is visionary fiction, occult in intent, brilliant in execution.' *Irish Times*

'David Keenan is one of the few writers I know who had to exist because we could never have invented him . . . a wizard, a true star.' Bruce Russell

'David Keenan's books are just off-the-charts mind-bogglingly brilliant.' William Basinski

'Every book by David Keenan is cause for revelry (at the hands of revelation).' Daniel Lopatin

'Read something by David Keenan and then come back with something as good as that – if you can.' Stephen Pastel

'One of the most exciting new writers around.' *Daily Mail*

'Buzzing with energy and manic idealism.' *Dazed*

'Keenan's hot streak continues.' *List*

'As raw, warm, bloody and poignant as it is intellectually engaged.' *Scotsman*

'If you are someone who's ever loved a small city local legend that got chewed up by the impossible-ness of their existence or evaporated in the mist of their own gorgeousness before they could become part of the bigger world, see (*This Is Memorial Device*) if at all possible.' Mary Gaitskill

'Brilliant.' Stewart Lee

‘The sound of young Scotland distilled forever.’

Andrew O’Hagan

‘Compelling, funny, furiously particular and often profound.’

Alan Warner

‘Utterly definitive.’ Irvine Welsh

‘Savage and tender and poignant and mad.’ Lisa McInerney

‘Demented brilliance.’ *Scotland on Sunday*

‘There are some writers whose books disrupt you so profoundly that to encounter them is to survive a life event. David Keenan is one of these beasts. Read him.’

Lara Pawson

‘Don’t tell me Keenan has done it again . . . another classic.’

Scotsman

‘*This Is Memorial Device* was my favourite book of the last decade.’ Andy Bell

Also by David Keenan

Fiction

This Is Memorial Device

For the Good Times

Xstabeth

The Towers The Fields The Transmitters

Monument Maker

Industry of Magic & Light

Non-fiction

England's Hidden Reverse

Volcanic Tongue

David Keenan is the author of six critically acclaimed novels: the cult classic *This Is Memorial Device*, which won the London Magazine Prize and was shortlisted for the Gordon Burn Prize; *For the Good Times*, which won the Gordon Burn Prize and was shortlisted for the Encore Award; *Xstabeth/The Towers The Fields The Transmitters*, which was shortlisted for the Dublin Literary Award; *Monument Maker*, which was a Rough Trade Book of the Year; and *Industry of Magic & Light*. He is also the author of *Volcanic Tongue*, which collects the best of his music writing, as well as *England's Hidden Reverse*, a history of the UK's post-punk and industrial music scenes.

First published in Great Britain in 2026 by White Rabbit,
an imprint of The Orion Publishing Group Ltd
Carmelite House, 50 Victoria Embankment
London EC4Y 0DZ

An Hachette UK Company

The authorised representative in the EEA is Hachette Ireland,
8 Castlecourt Centre, Dublin 15, D15 XTP3, Ireland (email: info@hbgi.ie)

1 3 5 7 9 10 8 6 4 2

A CIP catalogue record for this book is
available from the British Library.

ISBN (Hardback) 978 1 3996 2499 2
ISBN (Export Trade Paperback) 978 1 3996 2500 5
ISBN (Ebook) 978 1 3996 2502 9
ISBN (Audio) 978 1 3996 2503 6

Typeset by Input Data Services Ltd, Bridgwater, Somerset
Printed and bound in Great Britain by Clays Ltd, Elcograf, S.p.A

FSC www.fsc.org
MIX
Paper | Supporting responsible forestry
FSC® C104740

www.whiterabbitbooks.co.uk
www.orionbooks.co.uk

BOYHOOD

DAVID KEENAN

WHITE
RABBIT

Split the Lark – and you'll find the Music –
Bulb after Bulb, in Silver rolled –
Scantily dealt to the Summer Morning
Saved for your Ear when Lutes be old.

Loose the Flood – you shall find it patent –
Gush after Gush, reserved for you –
Scarlet Experiment! Sceptic Thomas!
Now, do you doubt that your Bird was true?

—Emily Dickinson

Here is the tree that never grew
Here is the bird that never flew
Here is the bell that never rang
Here is the fish that never swam

—The Four Legends of St Mungo

THE HIEROPHANTIC ROSE

Deeper, into flutter darkness. There is a tree. In a dark tunnel there is a black tree. A woman with the body of a bird points to the tree, which is silhouetted in the darkness, like crooked bones. There is something on the tree. There is something impaled on the tree. What is the obverse of Christ? The Precious Gift thinks to himself. The backside of Christ is a murdered boy. A bird is the dream of matter into nothing. Who said that? Now the birdwoman has alighted in his mind.

A small boy leaves Firhill Stadium, hand in hand with an older man. It is like The Precious Gift is viewing the scene from above. The man leads the boy, with almost impossible speed, up Firhill Road, before escaping onto the canal. For a split second they disappear under a bridge, then reappear on the other side. At one point they pass in full view of the crowd in the stadium, past a group of young men watching the match for free from the towpath. Later, when questioned, none of them will remember the young boy, and the shadowy older man, passing. There is a final bird.

Now they are high above Garscube Road. On their way home, is how it would appear, to passers-by. On their way home from the game. They pass the Highland Distilleries warehouse on Dawson Road. Beneath the pylons. They cut through the trees across from Speirs Wharf and into some shaded industrial wasteland where stones and debris and traffic cones and piping mark out the shape of Omega. And what takes place there at the centre.

THE ATTEMPTED RESCUE

1

Think of all the wee starving punters in Ethiopia, this older man, come out of nowhere, said to him, as they were nearing the finish line, and that was when Aaron Murray first met The Precious Gift, when he was struggling on a sponsored run to help the wee starving punters in Ethiopia, through Glasgow Green, on 25 May 1986, the last day of his boyhood, or so he thought, because he could never imagine doing a sponsored run again after that, because he got into literature and smoking pot straight afterwards, and, of course, espionage, thanks to The Precious Gift and his introduction to what he called 'remote viewing', which was a term Aaron didn't understand back then but grew to, after he was fifteen years old and left the old world behind him like a strange chrysalis, his father there crying in the street (it's true his dad was losing his marbles) after he left for Glasgow University when he was seventeen and moved into a top-floor flat on Cresswell Street just off Byres Road with two other boys named Dougie and Si, where they shared the living room together, all three of them (there were three single beds in there), and Si insisted on falling asleep to The Alarm's first album on cassette, the one with 'Sixty Eight Guns' on it, which was hardly falling-asleep music, and which often meant Aaron had to decamp to the kitchen and then creep back to bed once they were both out for the count (Si's brother Steven shared the other room with Tall Tommy), which meant that Aaron would spend most afternoons between lectures at the cafe on the top floor of the Queen Margaret Union, or playing pool in the bar, which is where he once met a couple of guys from The Undertones and their manager Craig who were drinking in there ahead of a concert they were playing as members of some new band they were doing and there was The Precious Gift all over again, he knew them from back in the day, he said, what were the chances, and Aaron said to one of The Undertones, your friend here propped me up when I was flagging trying to run the world for the wee starving punters in Ethiopia, and they said, that's just like him, The Undertones agreed, that's just like your man The Precious Gift, they said.

2

At the Glasgow Garden Festival there is an attraction called the Clydesdale Bank 150th Anniversary Tower. It rises like a UFO to a height of more than two hundred feet. Only today it's Scott Ruff and Aaron Murray in there and Scott is telling Aaron about all the women in his life – Scott is voracious – as he is sat back there among all the old women with his shirt unbuttoned to his navel he is talking about his chicks, the chicks man, he is saying, the chicks are out of hand, he is bemoaning, handsome Scott Ruff the gypsy, and he takes out a cigarette paper and he rolls it a certain way so that he can play it like a penny whistle, like a high keen penny whistle, and as the UFO rotates they can see all of Glasgow open up before them – it is a beautiful summer's day in 1988, just after the rain – and the clouds part as they look towards Govan in the soft sun, and Scott Ruff plays a lament, although afterwards he said it was 'Hot Legs' that he played, 'Hot Legs' by Rod Stewart, and all the old women in their headscarves marvelled at such a handsome talented boy and Scott asked one of them to take a photograph of them with his new Polaroid camera and Scott wrote a message to Aaron on the Polaroid and gave it to him and ever since then Aaron has had it framed on his desk, so even though it's all those years ago now, it still lives forever.

3

You've got to trap it. This is Aaron's father Donald speaking now. Aaron and his father are sitting on a bench in the Botanic Gardens in the west end of Glasgow eating cheese-and-ham sandwiches that Aaron bought them from a newsagent on Byres Road. Trap it and never let it go, he is advising Aaron. Don't let it fall through your fingers, he is saying. Hold on to it with all your might, he is underlining. He clenches both his fists in demonstration, like that. He is encouraging Aaron to start saving money. I wish I had a dad who told me that, he is telling Aaron as his father, that he wishes he had a father just like himself to repeat the things he says to himself. You're going to miss me when I'm gone, he warns Aaron. Then: you're not a fruit merchant, are you? What?! A fruit merchant, his father says. What's a fruit merchant, Aaron asks him, though he knows exactly what he means. A three-speed, his father says, by way of clarity. You know, a three-speed gear, a queer. What?! Aaron says to him. You think I'm a three-speed? No, I don't think, his father says, I'm just asking, because not that I'm against it, you understand, he is saying, Aaron's father sat on the bench there in the park, it's just that I wouldn't wish that kind of life on anyone, because it's tough, it's a challenge, and there is a lot of . . . what do you call it, he asks Aaron, what is the word for it when people don't like something? Prejudice? Aaron suggests, and then his father says, it's just these boys you live with. It's not ideal, Aaron tells him. I'll give you that.

4

Aaron Murray hates the sounds of skateboards in the night. He really can't stand it. It's a pet peeve. Don't ask him why. He is sat in the living room of The Precious Gift's flat. The sound of skateboarders in the night stirs his memory and gives him the fear that he will fall from this eighth floor into the summer of his boyhood, is why, perhaps. The soft summer in which his mum and dad and his brother Nemo are holidaying in the countryside, at Rose Cottage, outside Rothesay, on the Isle of Bute. And in the field beside them, there are ponies, or maybe just tiny horses. In the summer of his boyhood Aaron's father is lifting his brother Nemo onto the back of one of the wild horses and now it is running off. It is running off with Aaron's brother on its back, Aaron and his father in desperate pursuit.

5

To the sounds of wild horses in the night, The Precious Gift is educating Aaron in all the wonderful knowledge of the world. He is talking about one of his favourite books, which is the *Anabasis* of the soldier Xenophon. What does 'anabasis' mean? It can mean a lighting out, The Precious Gift says. Or a retreat. He is drinking wine while he says this, in the low light of the late-night apartment. The solitary lamp casts strange shadows on the walls. It can also mean a movement from the exterior to the interior, he says. What is the *Anabasis* of the soldier Xenophon about? It is about a battle between two brothers, The Precious Gift explains. Do you have a brother? Aaron asks him. Yes, he says. What happened to him? I went to war with him, he says. Aaron is hanging on his words as The Precious Gift lights a joint and puts the *Anabasis* to one side. The

Anabasis was written under a pseudonym, he continues. But I thought you said it was by the soldier Xenophon? It was written by Xenophon; it was a first-person account. But he chose to use a pseudonym. Why? Because he had to distance himself from the subject of himself, The Precious Gift says. And once more Aaron feels a strange sense of vertigo and a certainty that he will tumble into the past from this precarious vantage point in the air.

6

Do you know what remote viewing is? It is the ability to see anywhere in the world with your mind without travelling there. No, it's not astral projection. No, it's not ESP. This is what The Precious Gift did. He was part of a group of special remote viewers who helped solve crimes in Northern Ireland.

7

The Precious Gift lived in a flat on the Wyndford Estate off Maryhill Road, on the eighth floor of a tower block that was built on the exact spot where the high-ranking Nazi Rudolf Hess had been imprisoned during the Second World War, after he made a mad flight to Scotland to negotiate peace and betray Hitler, was what The Precious Gift told Aaron the first time he visited him, in this flat that was lined with books and with records and with encyclopedias. The Precious Gift was the kind to read an encyclopedia, like, for instance, *The Encyclopedia of Jazz*, alphabetically, from start to finish. He would bring up something like the Tree of Life and Aaron would say, what is the Tree of Life, and The Precious Gift would say, it is a dark tree peopled by angels. Or say he would say, like one time, he said, no one has ever listened to *Trout Mask Replica* by Captain Beefheart all the way through in one sitting, except for you and me, tonight. Make no bones about it, he said, *Trout Mask Replica* is the greatest album of the twentieth century. Though he had already said that about *Hex Enduction Hour* by The Fall and *Marquee Moon* by Television and *Fun House* by The Stooges and *The Modern Dance* by Pere Ubu and *The Modern Lovers* by The Modern Lovers and a bootleg cassette of Bob Dylan playing acoustic at Sheffield in 1966. As well as the first Suicide album. Or he would play Aaron what he called an 'environmental recording' of a rainforest in South America and light a candle and have them sit and listen to it in the dark. This is going to blow your mind, he would say. Make no bones about it.

8

Aaron Murray was becoming best pals with Scott Ruff, a flamboyant gypsy from a camp on South Street who always wore hats, like a battered old bowler, his old man's bunnet, a beret with a scarf, only but Scott wore it more like Keith Richards, a long flowing scarf down past his navel (he would have his shirt unbuttoned to the bottom in the summer with this scarf), his old man's bunnet at an angle, his old man who was known locally as the King of the Gypsies, or at least of the Glasgow gypsies, on account of the fact that he had won a bare-knuckle boxing bout, in a locked shipping container, in the pitch dark, parked on neutral ground somewhere in Bargeddie, against the King of Carntyne, who came out with brain damage and a skelly eye but who insisted, fair enough, it was a fair fight, he said, even though it was in the dark and no one could see a fucking thing, and here he was coughing up blood and saying it was fair enough, so it was, and that Dan Ruff, Scott's dad, was the

King of the Gypsies 'fair and square', Dan Ruff who had a massive head like a rhombus and who had once been fucked over the head with a fire extinguisher in a beer garden and his head didn't even move on his neck, Scott said, he just turned round slowly to look at his assailant as if he had been slapped by a girl, he said, Scott who Aaron first met in a record shop on Park Road in the west end of Glasgow that was a well-known front for swingers and a pick-up joint, when they both went to grab a second-hand copy (Aaron on the advice of The Precious Gift) of the double LP *Andy Warhol's Velvet Underground Featuring Nico.*

9

The first words that Aaron's dad Donald Murray forgot, the first words that slipped through the slow-widening hole in his head, were 'crowbar' (he used the word 'jackdaw' instead) and 'geraniums'. I know what I'm trying to say, his dad would say, pointing to the potted flowers that lined the windows of the extension at the back of their house, its fogged-up windows with blackbirds skipping past, the colour of autumn in the air, their warm, safe house whose name was Tara, in Mount Vernon, where Aaron grew up, and the abandoned sandpit next to it. It's just that the words have gone missing, he would say. Now hand me that jackdaw. Then: Nephew. Illiterate. Incline. Insole. Then: Son. Brother. Then: Nemo. In dreams Aaron is walking backwards to return these words to his father. He is walking backwards in order to piece him back together. His father's hand is shaking as he drinks soup from a flask and the hot soup runs down his chin. And now his short grey beard is dyed orange. On the bench in the Botanic Gardens, Aaron wants to ask him if he remembers. But memory now is a taunt, a goad, and he's better off out of it. Then his father says: Aaron was just a little boy. And Aaron says to him, but I'm Aaron, you mean Nemo. And all his father says is, yes. Yes, he was only a little boy. And now Nemo is come back to them. An angel touched Aaron on the head when he was born, his father says to him, and he nods, to himself, and still, it is Nemo, come back to them once more.

10

Between Aaron and his mum Elizabeth, it was T. Rex that was their bond. Or anything to do with Marc Bolan, really. They collected Bolan records and memorabilia as their hobby together and in the summer of 1984 the two of them took the bus to London and stayed in a hotel on Kensington High Street where they shared a room with two single beds. In the morning, they walked to Notting Hill Gate in the sunshine, to shop for Marc Bolan records at the Music & Video Exchange there. When they arrived, the Exchange had only just opened, and the guy behind the counter asked Aaron if he was starting work there that morning. He wasn't even old enough to be employed. He felt so cool. His mum was so proud. One day you could work in a record shop like this, she said. Together they bought an American pressing of *Electric Warrior* on Reprise Records as well as *Dandy in the Underworld* with the original cut-out sleeve and with a sticker on it saying 'FACTORY SAMPLE NOT FOR SALE' as well as a 7" single with picture sleeve of 'Ride a White Swan'. They were so excited to buy some rarities. Afterwards they agreed to split up (Aaron wanted to visit a record shop in South London near Clapham Common) and meet again on a bench in Kensington Gardens to have lunch together, later in the afternoon. His mum was so impressed with him being so independent and brave and taking the Tube on his own to a record shop. He had such an odd feeling, a similar feeling to when he had traded his children's library card for an adult one at Shettleston Library on the Wellshot Road, a sense of excitement tinged with sadness about all that he was leaving behind. Which made it all the more sweet when he got back to their bench in Kensington Gardens and saw his mum waving to him as she approached across the park in her long flowery dress and with her dark hair in a headband – her nickname among friends, he later found out, was Wonder Woman – bringing them tuna sandwiches that she had bought in the bakery, and two cans of Coke. Something about them being apart in London and then coming back together again was so wonderful. That night, while his mum had a shower, Aaron nipped over to the McDonald's across the road. There were no McDonald's in Glasgow until the summer of the Garden Festival, so it was a rare treat to order Filet-O-Fish and a Big Mac and two fries please – the dim lights in the night and the sweet smell of grease – even though the woman couldn't understand his accent and kept saying, fush, fush, which Aaron and his mum had a laugh about when he returned, just in time to eat their joyful meals in bed and watch a horror movie on TV. When she phoned his dad, his mum talked about how adventurous Aaron had been, and he fell asleep as Elizabeth sat up in bed smoking and with the TV on low, reading *The Women's Room* by Marilyn French. And now he is sat on a bench in the future, which is also the past, now, with his mum dead, and his brother disappeared, and his father a blank for a memory, and he thinks of that T. Rex song, the one his mum loved best of all and that she would play in the morning while getting ready on her old Dansette, the same one she'd had as a teenager, the one that smelled of burnt dust, that T. Rex song about dancing from the womb straight into the tomb.

11

I watched them advancing across the hills. Shadows, between the trees. Closer: whole battalions. Whole battalions moving stealthily through the forest, The Precious Gift is explaining. It was my first glimpse, is how he describes it. I was reading an account of the Maginot Line (which up until then might as well have been an imaginary line in my brain) when I saw them. I saw them coming through the impenetrable forest. The Ardennes. As a kid I was obsessed by war. But this was a vision (an invasion, I almost said an invasion, which is what it was, of course) that happened spontaneously. In an instant I glimpsed them, these soldiers, entering France. And I saw them from above. Like I was suspended above them. What is the angle of Christ in the painting by Dalí in the Kelvingrove Museum? That is where I saw them from. Pétain had declared the Ardennes impenetrable. The Maginot Line was the great fortification of its age. But still they came. Convoys of vehicles. It is 13 May 1940, Derry Library, in Northern Ireland – I was just a boy then – and I am watching the tanks advance across Europe like I've been nailed to the sky. That's how I discovered my gift, he says. Or rather, how it was revealed to me.

12

There was also the story of how he first met The Undertones. The Precious Gift. This was when he was working for the secret service. Back when he was stationed in Derry. When he would drink at The Alcazar, this notorious pub that was basically just two Portakabins nailed together on top of a bomb crater where the previous pub had burnt to the ground. The Precious Gift would drink in there with a co-worker named Jim Monaghan. You had to take a piss outside because there were no toilets indoors. Even in the snow. There's live music on. A band is loading in their equipment. Jim goes out for a piss. And never returns.

13

Can you see fear on their faces? The anticipation? Aaron asks The Precious Gift, about seeing the soldiers from above, live, as they moved into the Ardennes, back when The Precious Gift himself was just a boy. Can you make them out as individuals? Yes, The Precious Gift says. If you zoom in close enough you can make out the expressions on their faces. That's like God, Aaron says to him, if he cared to zoom in close enough. I doubt God zooms, The Precious Gift says. He is more like, what is the word? Omnipresent.

14

The Precious Gift sits there for a good five, ten minutes more. Jim is probably having a bifter and making small talk with the band, he's thinking. But after fifteen minutes there's no denying it. The Precious Gift walks outside and Jim is nowhere to be seen. He sees some guy lifting a battered amplifier out of the boot of a tan Vauxhall Viva. It's your man John O'Neill who – unbeknown to The Precious Gift at the time – played guitar for The Undertones. The Precious Gift asks him if he saw someone come out for a piss while he was unloading, tall thin fella about six foot two with a dose of acne and dark-black hair. Sure, I saw your man, John O'Neill of The Undertones tells The Precious Gift. A car pulled up and he got talking to the fella in the driver's seat and then he got in. Then what happened? They drove away. Did you notice anything unusual about the vehicle? Yeah. They were driving in the dark with no lights on. Then The Precious Gift asked John O'Neill if he needed a hand carrying the equipment into the pub and John O'Neill said that would be grand and so The Precious Gift helped The Undertones carry in their equipment and sat through one of their first gigs, and thoroughly enjoyed it, even though in the morning it turned out that Jim Monaghan was gone for good and that he would never return to work or to his family about which, The Precious Gift eventually came to realise, absolutely no one knew anything.

15

A blackbird hops past with a worm in its mouth. A woman with long red hair smokes a cigarette on the bench next to them. Now Aaron's father is telling him about his idea of *perfect heaven*. Do you remember, he says, the fox we found asleep in the long grass next door, when the neighbours had to leave their house? We climbed up on the fence. Do you remember me showing it to you? I don't remember, Dad, Aaron is telling him. I don't remember that at all. That's my idea of perfect heaven, his father is telling him, and Aaron can't even remember it. A fox asleep in the tall grass, and he can't even bring it to mind. Then he remembers the night their neighbours were burnt out of their house. Rab Biggart of the bad bastard family the Biggarts, who lived in the corner of the estate, soaked a cloth in petrol, lit it and pushed it through their letterbox. Then their garden became overgrown, and a family of foxes moved in. Aaron can't remember the fox asleep in the tall grass the way his father does. But what he can remember is much worse. Aaron and his friend Fat Gordon broke in a summer later. The family had obviously been living in complete poverty. The holes in the windows were covered with plastic bags. Plus, they were hoarders. In one room there was piled up all this old stereo equipment, some of which had melted in the fire. But the worst, by far, was the kitchen. They could smell something bad in there, but the door was blocked by the cooker, somehow the filthy old cooker had been moved and it was blocking the door, so it took them a while to manoeuvre it out of the way, but that's when they saw it. There was blood all over the walls. Stinking blood. Animal blood. All over the filthy white tiles and running down. A family of foxes had moved in and taken to tearing each other to pieces. The smell of warm animal blood like metal, hot from the boiling. The mad eyes, staring. The stinking breath. Stinking. The blood boiling.

16

The boy soldiers. Tracking through the forest. Making their way. There is so much strange fauna in the forests of the Ardennes, the German word for which is Tierwelt, a tiny world of tears. The boy soldiers are marvelling at the Tierwelt, as they move silently through the forest in tanks and in the beds of military trucks.

17

Jim Monaghan, who has just gone missing outside of The Alcazar, was involved with Project Deep Run alongside The Precious Gift, a secret project that was based in an ancient fortification in Derry, run under the front of being a team of 'topographical surveyors', and where they attempted to map, in real time, the movements of paramilitaries using remote viewing.

18

Back at the flat on Cresswell Street, and the police have turned up. They arrive just as Scott and Aaron are walking up the stairs. It's the police, the police shout at them, because these police are in plain clothes. What do you know about your neighbours? the fat plain-clothes cop asks Aaron. I know nothing about them, we're not long moved in, he tells them. Except they don't mind loud music and listening to The Alarm's first album every night, he says, and the fat plain-clothes cop says, holy Christ that's grim, and he shakes his head. What about that bloke's haircut, he says. What bloke, Scott Ruff says, there's more than one bloke with a murder haircut in The Alarm. I'm talking about the singer with the mad haircut. If you think that's bad, you should see the barnet on the bassist, Scott Ruff says. Scott Ruff is standing there with his shirt unbuttoned and his hairless chest. Is that right? the fat cop says, and he shakes his head. Mental, he says. Anyway, mate, the thin plain-clothes cop says, they obviously bailed before we got here. Your neighbours, he clarified. Not those cunts in The Alarm. Here's my card, he says. Get in touch if you notice anything untoward, he says, and he winks. On the card it reads 'Private Investigator Luke G.B. Caird'. In the corners are the signs for the four suits of playing cards: hearts, diamonds, clubs and spades. They're not even the actual police, Scott says when they get inside. What the fuck is that about? Pair of wide boys, Aaron says, the type of private dick that gets hired to follow unfaithful wives round Safeway, he says, and then they both forget all about it.

19

Attempts are made to locate Jim Monaghan. Remote viewings of Loyalist and Republican boltholes. The scanning of back alleys and waste grounds. The Precious Gift is warned not to return to The Alcazar. They could be onto us, he is cautioned. Make yourself scarce, he is told, and they send him on a holiday to Ayrshire, which stinks, there's too many Ulstermen in hiding down there, it's where everyone goes to make themselves scarce and The Precious Gift is getting the heebie-jeebies, and so he heads to Glasgow, where he secures a short-term rent in the east end in a tenement facing Tollcross Park where the flower beds are arranged in the shape of a great rose. That's when he hears John Peel play The Undertones on the radio. Wow. They're going places, he thinks.

20

But then I had to immediately travel back for a funeral, The Precious Gift says. Because they discovered Jim Monaghan's body. Although, at first, they didn't realise it. They found a body in the Prehen Woods. Project Deep Run. We regularly scanned the woods for bodies. As well as the back alleys and the lanes. And the rivers and the abandoned farms. And the bogs, the peat bogs. And the burnt-out cars. As well as the fields outside Derry, and the waste grounds near the small villages, the playparks there, which at the time were the run of a serial murderer dubbed the Vampire of Derry, on account of his draining the blood of his young boy victims, as well as his ability to evade capture completely. And someone spots this body. At first she thought it was a dead sheep. An animal carcass. Because it was bloated and in a semi-decomposed state. But when she zoomed in she could see it was a male. There's the body of a human male in the bushes there, the remote viewer said, her name was Helen, and she circled the position of the body on a map. So we passed it on to the army and they sent some of their boys out there and make no bones about it, it's the body of Jim Monaghan. I met his wife at the funeral. She said to me, what was he involved in? What is it that you do? She thought Jim was some kind of civil servant. She seemed to have no idea of what we were involved in. He had never squealed. I was impressed. I mean, I didn't have a partner at the time, I lived alone in the countryside out Carndonagh way, The Precious Gift explained, so there was no one asking what I was up to. But a lot of the viewers were married. I always thought that was weird. It's a young man's game, really. That's when you are at the peak of your powers. A young man's game, Aaron says. I love that phrase. Me too, The Precious Gift says. I wish it could be a young man's game forever. What age was Jim Monaghan when he was murdered? Twenty-three.

21

Aaron's father was a young man once. It seems impossible to imagine. Because his father grew up in a time before young people existed, in a time when childhood careered straight into adulthood, kind of like it is now all over again. Whereas Aaron was born in the once-time of the young, the window of the young, the gasp. When his father was a boy, he sold firewood door to door in the east end of Glasgow. Aaron's grandfather took Donald out of school and made him work, so he received no education. Early on, a customer, a retired teacher on the Shettleston Road, took Donald under his wing and told him about a thing called poetry. He said that one of the best things a boy could do in his life was to memorise poetry by heart. And so, every time he saw him, he taught Aaron's father one line from 'If' by Rudyard Kipling. His father remembered it all his life and used to recite it to him. For Aaron's sixteenth birthday, his dad bought him a scroll with the poem printed on it. I want to say that Aaron still has it there in front of him, next to the Polaroid with Scott Ruff. I want to believe it was so precious that it would live forever. But the truth is that Aaron threw it in the bin years ago. There is something heartbreaking in the transmission of masculinity from fathers to sons.

22

Can you hear or is it silent? You can hear. The sound of the wireless communications in the forest, The Precious Gift says. The crackle of the speakers. Later, I read that the average age of the German soldiers who crossed the border into France was twenty-three. Here is Josef Noth, a promising young gymnast from Wuppertal, stood in the turret of a tank travelling through the Ardennes in the early-morning light. It is 14 May 1940.

23

Scott Ruff is wearing a skintight T-shirt that is too small for him that says 'No One is Perfekt' on it for their night out. Aaron and Scott are going to a concert at Fury Murrys in Maxwell Street, down by the Clyde. Scott smells of sweat and musk; his blue eyes, his tight leather jacket. Who's playing tonight? Who cares.

24

Then I get a letter from Joyce, Jim Monaghan's wife, who I had met at the funeral. This is The Precious Gift in his eighth-floor apartment in the Wyndford. She was disposing of his estate, she says, and had come across what she described as a 'mysterious folder' containing what she said appeared to be maps. As well as some photographs that she didn't recognise. And the thing is, my name was written on every page. Right at the bottom corner there. My real name, from before I became The Precious Gift. On the front there was the word 'Welt', which is the German word for 'World'. She asked if I might want to take a look at it. I told her to post it to me. And to keep this strictly between ourselves. They had been married two years, eighteen months of which Jim had worked on Project Deep Run. Previously he'd worked for the RAC. Compiling guidebooks for the RAC. Which is how he discovered his abilities, I imagine, but I can't be sure because we never talked about anything personal, or anything in the past, or anything family-related. We didn't even talk about the job itself. Instead, we talked about music, books. The artists that we loved. Lou Reed. Bob Dylan. Picasso. Philip K. Dick. Charles Olson. Antonin Artaud. Jack Spicer. Steve Lacy. Clarice Lispector. Rilke. Jim was an art lover, a self-educated working-class art lover, always the most ardent, soaking everything up, asking about the flying buttresses on the Gothic cathedrals one minute, the plays of Samuel Beckett the next (which I never got on with) (the entire oeuvre is what I'm talking about) (never got on with any of it). He was also a keen birdwatcher and kept a series of quite detailed nature journals which I also inherited but which are hard to decipher because he used a strange microscript, with odd signs and symbols.

25

Everyone in the queue at Fury Murrys looks like the Ramones. Red Adidas T-shirts, too-tight leather jackets. Drainpipe jeans. Bowl cuts. Insignia deodorant. Aaron gets asked his age by the bouncer. He just waves Scott through, but he stops Aaron. Any ID, he says. Eh, I have my National Insurance card, Aaron pleads feebly, and the bouncer must have felt sorry for him, sorry for innocent Aaron back then, because he relents and lets him in regardless. Scott is already explaining his credentials to two girls with thick black eyeshadow and back-combed hair. We're the most underground guys in here, he is explaining. At this point we are so far underground we are basically moles, he is saying, pointing back to Aaron and himself. The support band are on. A guy who looks like an emaciated junkie is making up lyrics over drums, bass, guitar and bongos. The guy on the bongos presses his face to the drumskin as he plays and occasionally rants into his microphone. That guy's my new guru, Scott says. The emaciated singer asks for a theme. Someone give me a theme, he asks. Flight, Aaron shouts out. Flight. OK, flight. I forgot to say that someone is playing a turntable and scratching vinyl in the corner, but you can't see him for the PA. He makes some wiggly scratching noises, still unseen. Flight, the emaciated singer says, flight. He starts to sing, what is the difference between mind and flight, he is singing. Then he starts to sing about someone who is taking off, a pilot or a spaceman. Now he is singing about the angle of its rise, this flight of the mind, he is singing. Here, take this, Scott says, and he gives Aaron a little wrap of speed in a cigarette paper. Someone grabs Scott Ruff's hat off his head, he is wearing a cowboy hat. Don't fuck with me, Scott warns them, but the guy says, what you gonna do about it, mince me to death, you little poof? Don't fucking call me a poof, pal, Scott says, and Aaron joins in, who the fuck do you think you're talking to, he says, and one of the guy's pals steps up, they're just drunk thugs, what are they even doing here, looks like I'm talking to a pair of bum chums, this guy comes back at Aaron, and his pal is making jokes about gaylords and uphill gardeners. Leave it, Scott says to Aaron, fucking leave it, these guys are fucking retards, he says to him, let's go and get a drink, he says, and they walk off with these two doing wanking hand-signs and miming butt-fucking. Pair of dicks, Scott says when they get to the bar, and he shakes his head, but Aaron is a little shook up. I'm used to it, Scott says, don't worry about it, he says. Fucking Glasgow, he says. But then the headline band comes on and they forget all about it, both speeding and dancing manically until Scott Ruff clambers on stage and then leaps right off again, back into the audience, where he is lifted above their heads – what were they singing about flight, and about mind – and Scott closes his eyes and lies back and stretches out his arms, this pose like Jesus come down from the cross, as he is passed to the back of the room over the heads of all the revellers, and disappears from sight.

26

At first I thought that he had been spying on me, that's how it felt when I looked over the maps Jim Monaghan had made, this is The Precious Gift speaking now, which clearly plotted my movements to and from my favourite hills in the area round Carndonagh, he is explaining, my favourite vantage points, is how he puts it, as well as my movements around Derry, my back-and-forth to work, as well as my not infrequent journeys to Belfast. And the photographs too, photographs of me in *various situations*, is how The Precious Gift describes it. Photographs of me with *various characters*, is how he puts it. I thought I had been compromised. But then I had an uncanny feeling, he says, and I realised that Jim Monaghan had been literally watching over me *like an angel*. And that he had never betrayed me. Never once. Hadn't I ever wondered why we were given this gift of second sight? Wasn't all of this Troubles-watching and manipulating – and murder, let's face it, certainly witness to murder, make no bones about it – a bit beneath our abilities? When we could be angels for each other? This is what I'm thinking in the wake of the revelation of Jim Monaghan's angelhood. And it was a life-changing revelation. That without some kind of higher calling, some kind of holy purpose, what are we but glorified fucking camera obscuras. And that's when I began to realise the true nature of my calling, The Precious Gift says. Too late, he admits. For Jim. But still.

27

It's late. After the Fury Murrys gig. The pair of thugs from the club are waiting for Aaron and Scott in a doorway. They come up behind them. Aaron gets hit over the back of the head and remembers nothing. But they take one of Scott Ruff's eyes out. Beautiful Scott Ruff's eye. They take it out with one punch because the thug was wearing a studded ring that tore right through his beautiful eyeball (sapphire blue) and destroyed it forever.

28

There are butterflies in the forests of the Ardennes. How many days do butterflies live? A chalkhill blue alights on the finger of the promising young gymnast Josef Noth. Perhaps it's because his fingers are so supple, the pure white of his hands. The promising young gymnast who incorporated leaps and exaggerated floor moves into his sphere-juggling routines, even though for the German sporting bodies those kinds of moves were worth nil points. The promising young gymnast who, when he performed in Berlin, had become a cult sensation, enacting a kind of fantasy gymnastics that brought to mind quickly suppressed images of Berlin's magical fin-de-siècle dance troupes while still appearing, on the surface, to be a ritual of pure adulation of the male form.

29

Aaron visited Scott Ruff in the hospital, with his empty eye socket covered in bandages and gauze. Have you adjusted to your one eye yet, he asked him. No, Scott said, the world seems at least half smaller. Then he said, my dad is on the warpath. We're talking about the King of the Gypsies, Dan Ruff, as you well know. He wants to hunt them down and kill them, Scott said. The boys that did this to me. But how could they have any hope of finding them? Aaron went to say to him. But then he had an idea.

30

My friend Scott lost his eye in an unprovoked attack, Aaron said to The Precious Gift. Can you help us find who did it? That's impossible, he said. You don't even remember anything from the night, he reminded him. Scott Ruff says he has a vision of the guy that punched him frozen in his one good eye, Aaron told him. What good will that do, The Precious Gift said. There are over one and a half million people in Glasgow. Then Aaron had another idea. And now Private Investigator Luke G.B. Caird and his fat assistant have agreed to take on their case and to help them track down and bring justice to, though really rain down vengeance upon, the young men that took beautiful Scott Ruff's dazzling eyeball out.

31

There is a second Anabasis, The Precious Gift is telling Aaron now, in his eighth-floor apartment in the Wyndford Estate. At night, in the summer of 1988. Which is another favourite of mine, he says. There is a second Anabasis that I also highly recommend, and that is *The Anabasis of St-John Perse*, The Precious Gift says.

32

Private Investigator Luke G.B. Caird (and his fat assistant) revisited the scene of the crime down by the Broomielaw. Mate, that must have been murder polis for your man, the Elephant Man, eh? the fat assistant says, when Aaron meets them in a cafe on Dumbarton Road to go over their findings. What? The Elephant Man, the fat assistant says, your man with the *elongated cranium*. I was just reading about him, he says. For instance, did you realise he was in the Mensa? Who was? The Elephant Man. Very high IQ. Just goes to show you, the fat assistant says. What? Compensation, he says. You get a face like that, it balances out with some serious brains, he says. God moves in mysterious ways, Luke G.B. Caird says. That's one thing you learn from being a private investigator, he adds. Well, so what have you found out? Aaron asks them. Mate, there was a bloodstain there, reveals the fat assistant, whose name we finally find out is Mark C. Burl. That's some wound your man must have suffered, Mark says. For that amount of blood, he clarifies. So, is your man blind now? he asks Aaron. No, he's not blind, Aaron tells him. He just lost his sight in one eye. Half-blind, eh? Mark says. Mate, that's murder polis, he commiserates. Then Luke G.B. Caird plays his trump card. I found a tattered business card on the ground there, he says. At the scene of the crime, he elaborates. With blood on it, he underlines. And Mark C. Burl sits there next to him and nods slowly and says, that's right, mate. Seems like a lead worth following, Luke G.B. Caird says, as he hands the card to Aaron with the address of a garage in the east end on it, all blood-spattered. I know just the man to take a look, Aaron tells them.

33

What is it you can see? What can you see from above, Aaron is asking The Precious Gift, and he says, it looks like some kind of outhouses, some kind of stables perhaps? Horses? The Precious Gift hangs suspended as if by nails from the sky above a garage in the east end of Glasgow. Wow, horses, he is saying, in the back there are stables with the most beautiful horses, he is relaying, from somewhere up in the air. The two of them have a map of Glasgow spread out on the table next to a bowl of fruit. A model of a little wooden bird sits on the map. And suddenly, in a flash of vision, Aaron sees them too. The beautiful horses. There, in the east end. Beneath him. Like Christ in the Dalí painting.

34

The Anabasis of St-John Perse talks of colts being sacrificed on the graves of small children at the founding of cities, living things among us brought dead and still to honour the purity of young boys, the green parakeets among the pink roses that rise up in tribute to the old men, the purification of widows and the mutilation of adults between tributes of torn flags. It is a prophetic poem, The Precious Gift explains, which is a poem that is *spoken out of the air*.

35

Between his disappearance from The Alcazar on the night of The Undertones' show and the discovery of his corpse by a remote viewer a month later, Jim Monaghan was seen alive on at least two occasions. A pair of witnesses have emerged. We know that he returned home at least once, because a neighbour reported seeing him enter his house just after his wife had left for work and leave again four or five hours later. Another witness by the name of David Levy, a fellow birder, bumped into him on the street, in Derry. Where he was living or what his other movements might have been in the space between his kidnap and murder, we are left to imagine. But here he is on the street, by the cathedral, and he is wearing Vaseline on his face. It looked like Vaseline, David Levy said. That's what it seemed like to me, some kind of strange paste on his face. Plus, he was wearing some kind of animal-skin coat, some kind of animal hide, was how David Levy described it. In the bright sunshine, he added. And what was your relationship to the deceased? We were friends. I worked alongside him at the RAC, David Levy explained. We often went on birding expeditions together. Northern Ireland is the first landfall for migrating American birds and gulls blown off course. He loved to watch the migrations come in and we would do it together, he would call me when they were starting to arrive, he had good sources, he would tell me, and I would pick him up and we'd head out to Malin Head and watch for the birds over the water, where they would fly in as majestic Vs, like bombers, or sometimes broken letters, barely-held-together letters, confused letters, like birds trying to spell out sad human words. I don't know if he even recognised me. In the street there. I called out to him, and he put his arm up in front of his face, like that. He said that he was shielding himself from the sun. What? He was worried about the sun, was what he said, when I saw him in a state of some distress, it has to be said, outside St Eugene's Cathedral, in the rain and the snow, in a state of some distress and done up like a madman, I might add, which I had no idea would be the last time I ever saw him, like a madman with these huge sunglasses on and, as I said, Vaseline on his face, which he said was to *protect him from the rays*, and I said what, and he said that he had flown *too close to the sun*, was how he put it, and that now he was paying the price, which was to make him *preternaturally susceptible to the voice of the sun*, was how he phrased it, and of course he was wearing these ridiculous sunglasses in the very depths of winter. Who was your man, the angel that flew too close to the sun? David Levy said. Icarus, The Precious Gift said. Though he wasn't a real angel.

36

Scott Ruff has to wear an eyepatch now, but I think we can all admit it's cool as fuck. A black eyepatch like a pirate is cool as fuck, come on. Aaron is attempting to lift Scott Ruff's spirits, now he is discharged from the hospital with only one good eye left. It's like the world has lost all of its depth, is how Scott mourns it, even when Aaron takes him back to the Garden Festival to relive their memories, even when he takes him up in the Clydesdale Bank Tower that still spins like a UFO, even when the light from Govan that he will never see again with both his eyes breaks over the tenements, and the river, down below, even then there is no more depth, Scott Ruff mourns, and Aaron puts his arms around his shoulders and feels like crying but he holds back the tears so as not to break his friend's heart with sorrow.

37

By this point the convoy has crossed the Ardennes with very little military engagement. Outside of the forest now, Josef Noth is smoking a hand-rolled bifter and thinking of Paris, how it lies up ahead, once more. Josef Noth first travelled to Paris in 1937, at the height of his career as a gymnast, to appear at the International Exposition of Art and Technology in Modern Life. Paris in the wake of the factory occupations and the election of the Popular Front was a time for athletic displays, and theatre, and painting, and upheaval, and bacchanal, and dance. Fresh fish flown in from the coast. Barrels of wine come down the river. The German pavilion with its great eagle and swastika raised high, right across from the Soviet pavilion with its great hammer and sickle. The erotic dancers. The street cobblers. The great fountains and beautiful gardens. The smell of urine, and of open fires. The wild shanty suburbs. The flea markets with their broken gramophones and Chinese vases. The cafes with their delicate pastries. The perfume of the women. Their long dresses and kitten heels, their furs and their capes. And, of course, their pretty hats. The streets like a circus. The world's strongest man, the world's smallest dwarf. The world's most beautiful woman. Paris has the most beautiful women, Josef Noth thought when he was introduced to the ballerina Thérèse Barnier that night at the socialite Albert Azéma's top-floor apartment on Rue Lepic, with its views of the marvellous wooden windmills.

Theo van Gogh and his darling brother Vincent once lived just along the street, Thérèse told Josef as they stood out on the balcony drinking wine. I always dreamt I would marry a ballerina, Josef told her as they kissed. That first night they made love on a bed in a spare room.

38

Aaron meets Scott Ruff at the Equi cafe, at the Charing Cross end of Sauchiehall Street, on a Saturday afternoon. The walls are of dark wood, the old posters say things like 'Doon The Water' and 'Glasgow's Miles Better' (which features a grinning yellow Mr Men-style character). There are framed pictures of Sophia Loren and Italian boxers, all of which are autographed, above the booths. The booths with their ring-marked wooden tables and worn red leather seats. The lights, low; it is almost dark in here. In the background the radio murmurs something about the closure of the Kingston Bridge. They order a pot of tea between them, which is served in a chipped blue clay pot on which someone has scratched the name McIver, plus a Tunnock's Tea Cake and a wee apple slice. We need you to help identify your assailants, Aaron is telling Scott. Who's this 'we', Scott's asking him. Me and The Precious Gift, Aaron says. Aaron is telling him about how The Precious Gift has a form of second sight, how he is like an eye come out of the sky, and how he's been keeping watch over the garage from the bloodied business card found at the crime scene. Scott Ruff asks him whether he means remote viewing, and Aaron says, yes, I mean exactly that, how do you know about remote viewing? And Scott says, I read about it in a magazine about the SAS. Then he reminds Aaron of how he still has a perfect picture of his assailant 'in his mind's eye' and how he could easily recognise him from a description, only but then he says, don't tell my dad, though, cause then we will have a murder case on our hands. Aaron suggests they give The Precious Gift a phone and head over to his in the evening. But before that Scott brings up going to John Menzies on Sauchiehall Street for one of their favourite rituals, which is clacking through the huge posters in the racks that seem so large they loom down on them like gods. Samantha Fox, Sylvester Stallone, Harrison Ford, a woman's legs in heels sticking out the window of a Ferrari with the words 'No Other Lover' in neon, Linda Lusardi in a bikini, The Cramps. Have you heard The Cramps, Scott Ruff is asking Aaron, they're sick, is what he is saying on this perfect Saturday afternoon (for Saturday afternoons are the domain of boyhood, those carefree afternoons where every possibility seems to lie, tantalisingly, just up ahead, and the rest of your life beckons and you wonder about it all in the company of sweet friends), where later, maybe, they'll go for a baked potato and cheese, who knows. But before that they head to Flip on Queen Street, that smell of Flip on Queen Street is a whole other Saturday afternoon, that musty-basement smell that smelled like America might. Now Scott is trying on jeans with huge roll-ups. They are too baggy, Aaron is telling him, while shaking his head in disapproval. Aaron buys his first pair of cream-coloured chinos and a little tartan shoulder bag, as well as a book from behind the glass counter called *Roadside America*. Scott buys a green-and-white baseball jacket that he intends to wear with no top on. Together they walk up to Queen Street Station, where Aaron calls The Precious Gift from a phone box. I'm with Scott, Aaron tells him, can we come over this evening? Come on over, The Precious Gift says. I'm looking forward to meeting the legendary Scott Ruff, he says. It's a clear night, he says. Why don't we get the telescope out? But first Scott and Aaron go for that legendary baked potato, with cheese, in the basement cafe at Virginia Galleries, and have a sly look round the unit with all the mad Nazi memorabilia while they're at it.

39

Then there was the visit to the abandoned Magic-City amusement park to attend the drag ball at the dance hall on Rue de l'Université with the ballerina Thérèse Barnier and two of her friends, Ambassador Alexis Leger, Secretary General of the French Ministry of Foreign Affairs, and a man he introduced as an artist and composer who went by the name of The H and who refused to give his full name when asked. That is my full name, he said to Josef Noth. All around them were the abandoned rides, the hand-painted facades of the amusement park, now eerie, and melancholy, now that they were no joy to anyone, the great googly eyes and the strange row of teeth that Noth and his new friends were photographed behind, as if stood in the mouth of Leviathan.

40

It was the first time Aaron ever saw inside a crater on the moon, the night when The Precious Gift set up his telescope for him and Scott, in his flat on the eighth floor. You only need one eye for a telescope, he said to Scott Ruff, and The Precious Gift ruffled Scott's hair, and Aaron thought about the other meaning of Scott's name for the first time. They gazed in awe with their one eyes at the insides of marvellous craters, their shadows straying across desolate seas and awful cliff drops for no one but them right now, is how The Precious Gift put it, for no one but us, right now, was what he said, this particular moon that will never come again, as they took turns at this brass telescope stood on a tall wooden tripod, with the window open. Then The Precious Gift turned down the music (he was playing the first album by The Cramps, which Scott had requested for Aaron's edification) and they unfolded a map of Glasgow across the old wooden dining table. As before, they started by placing a small wooden bird on the target, or rather I should say Aaron placed it, Aaron placed the small wooden bird on the map at the exact place where the target was, being in this case the garage in the east end, just off the Baillieston Road. Then The Precious Gift asked Aaron to navigate for him, which meant taking down notes while he attempted to return there in his mind and report back. And that was the night that The Precious Gift said to Aaron, you are like Metatron, and Aaron said, who is Metatron, and The Precious Gift said, Metatron is God's recording angel, who notes down everything that happens, and who stands behind the throne of God, on his right-hand side.

41

At the drag ball beneath the abandoned Magic-City amusement park, Ambassador Alexis Leger, Secretary General of the French Ministry of Foreign Affairs, is talking about jazz and avant-garde composition and poetry and winters. In particular, he is bemoaning the awful winters in Paris. You should try a German winter, Josef Noth jokes with him, but Leger doesn't have much of a sense of humour. I don't intend to, he says. But I can't have any more talk about winters, with what's left of my life, he says, even though at this point in his life Leger is a young man of only fifty years. I need an island of summer, a southern coast, he is saying, to spend my days boating and writing poetry in eternal sunshine. I couldn't help but notice the sun symbolism in your display last night, he is telling Josef

Noth, and the ballerina Thérèse Barnier lets out a gasp as Noth admits that, yes, the weights he juggles with are modelled on the planets of the solar system, including Pluto. He's amazed that anyone would pick up on this, his secret conceit. I predict Pluto will have a short reign, Leger says to Noth, before becoming just another god of antiquity, he says, but nevertheless, he says, I picked up on the solar imagery, the solar . . . current, shall we say. And Josef Noth says, yes, I am the fixed point around which everything revolves, he says, and he talks about the harmony of the spheres and how everything is in its perfect place, thanks to God, and to gravity. The Juggler, Leger says to him. Isn't that the original name of The Magician in the Tarot? And now the ballerina Thérèse Barnier is mock-angry with Josef Noth and makes a scene of slapping him gently across the side of his handsome face with an opera glove. How many more secrets about you are there to be discovered, she purrs. And Josef Noth knows, already, there are many. Alexis is also a great poet, in secret, Thérèse Barnier informs Josef Noth. Anything I would know? Noth asks her. Probably, she says, if you are a fan of modern poetry, that is, and when Noth says, forgive me, but I'm not up on the latest developments in poetry, Thérèse Barnier says that surely he has heard of the great modernist T.S. Eliot, and when Noth replies, ah, yes, *The Waste Land*, I do know that, in fact I read it in the German translation, Thérèse Barnier reveals that Eliot translated a great poem of Leger's only a few years ago, but it was published under a pseudonym. And what was this pseudonym? St-John Perse, Thérèse Barnier reveals, and Leger takes a mock-bow as she announces him as the author of *The Anabasis of St-John Perse*, which at this point Josef Noth has never read. What is it about? Josef Noth asks him, and Leger – speaking now as Perse – tells him how he wrote the poem in a strange, deserted pagoda near

Peking in the 1920s. From there, Perse says, it was as if I could see forever. But what is it about, Noth presses him again, and St-John Perse says, it is about vastness, and about space, and about scale. It is about migrations and the founding of cities. It is about the ends, and the beginnings, of civilisations. It is about love and war. It is about the movement of people, across time. And you saw all that from a deserted pagoda in China, Josef Noth asks him, and St-John Perse insists, that was the *only* place I could see it from, he emphasises, and when Josef Noth asks, but what do you mean, St-John Perse says, because ever since then I have suffered from poetic myopia, is how St-John puts it. Which is why, once more, I am in search of the sun. St-John Perse: what kind of a pseudonym is that? Josef Noth thinks to himself, and inevitably he thinks about the apocalypse of St John, and about endings, and beginnings.

42

Lit up by a single floodlight in the rain, there are horses. The Precious Gift is viewing them from his apartment on the eighth floor of the Wyndford Estate in Maryhill. Their hot breath hangs in the air in front of them. The stables are silent, but for the muffled sound of reggae music, in this back street of Glasgow, lit up in the night. The horses stare out over the half-doors of their stables, in sad knowledge or incomprehension, who knows. Aaron is writing everything down. Wow, Scott Ruff says, wow, you can really see that, and he asks him, is there anyone around, is there anyone guarding the horses, but before The Precious Gift can reply, Aaron says, no, they are locked in the stables with no one else around, and The Precious Gift snaps open his eyes. What?! he says to Aaron. You can see them? And Aaron says, yes, I can see the horses, in the rain, locked in their stables, their hot breath hanging in the air in front of them. Wow, The Precious Gift says, you have the gift?! I can see the horses, Aaron shrugs. It happened last time too, he says. But why didn't you say anything? Because I thought I might be just imagining it, Aaron says. My dad always said I was a boy with imagination. Make no bones about it, that's incredible, The Precious Gift says. Right then a figure emerges from the back door with a flashlight and carrying a bin bag. The reggae music gets louder. That's him! Aaron says. That's the boy who took Scott's eye out. We need to get some of the boys from the flat together and head over there with a squad, he says. We need to head over there with a team and fuck this cunt up, he says. And that's when Scott Ruff makes the suggestion that changes everything. What if we just stole the horses? What?! What if instead of violent retribution, we just stole their horses? Scott Ruff says. Aaron almost bites through his tongue when he says that. Wild horses, he's thinking. Does he know, he's thinking. And that's when Scott Ruff reveals he is a dab hand at breaking horses and that he grew up racing them. And once again, it is as if Aaron might fall all the way into the summer of his boyhood, from this precarious point in the air.

43

You've never seen anything like it, Josef Noth, these queers, these fairies, these masked men in thigh-high heels impossible to walk in, and chained together, this madam is huge and bursting out of her dress as she leads a man by a dog leash round his neck. Someone is wearing underpants for a hat. Outrageous queens in over-the-top make-up parade past, as Thérèse takes your hand and leads you to a table that they have reserved especially. Alexis Leger, the ambassador, asks you what you think of the scene, and you tell him, I've never seen anything like it, it's wonderful, you confess. Thérèse slides her hand under the table and strokes your cock through your trousers as a naked man on stage with a huge erection sings a hymn to gluttonous pleasure. The queens move as if in slow motion on the dancefloor, from one pose to the next. The H makes his excuses and disappears into a back room. Now there are men in lipstick and nylons gracefully leaping this way and that. The bodies of the men, so poised and beautiful. And now there is a live sex show. On Josef Noth's return to his hotel that night, he makes love to Thérèse Barnier for six hours straight. He was only supposed to be in Paris for two weeks to perform at the exposition. But now he is making plans to extend his trip. Stay with me, the ballerina Thérèse Barnier pleads with him. I'm falling in love with you, she says, and she tells Josef that he can move in with her. She is appearing in a revival of Findlay Anderson's *Veneer* at Le Petit Théâtre. I want you to come to the opening night, she says. Alexis is going, we are using his poetry, she says, or should I say, St-John Perse's poetry. It's an avant-garde production, she tells Josef Noth. You will love it, my darling, she says. She calls Josef Noth her handsome darling. I think I'm falling in love with you too, Josef Noth tells Thérèse, and with Paris. I am Paris, she says, as she falls into his arms. It is two years before the outbreak of the Second World War.

44

Who fancies an adventure? Aaron, Dougie, Si, Scott and Tall Tommy are gathered around the kitchen table at the top-floor flat on Cresswell Street. Scott Ruff is making a presentation. The stables are in a back lane behind the garage, which is accessible via a locked gate, he says. Aaron has drawn a simple map on a sheet of paper in bold strokes of red and blue pen, which Scott Ruff points to. The route then runs up behind some bin sheds where there is a second locked wooden gate. Both simple padlocks that we can use cutters on. This second gate is the entrance to the stables which consists of a large courtyard with four separate wooden stables running along the fence on the right. That's right, Aaron, isn't it? Yup. The biggest problem is that they've become aware that the family that runs the garage, and that owns the horses, actually lives on the premises, in the filthy flat above the garage that has two windows looking out onto the stables. What are they doing with the horses, do you think? Tall Tommy asks. They'll be racing them for money, Scott Ruff explains, and then he asks everyone who has ever ridden a horse to put their hands up. Three people put their hands up. Dougie, Aaron and Si. I've only ridden a horse three times, though, Aaron tells Scott, just on holiday, like on a beach. Good enough, Scott says, we are going to be racing these horses through Glasgow at night so there's not much that's going to prepare you for it. Dougie and Si point out that they grew up in Fife and therefore are 'all about the horses' and Scott says, perfect, we have our four riders. I'll help you break in and keep the edge, Tall Tommy says, but then I'll be out of there. I'm too tall to ride a horse, he points out, somewhat implausibly. Will we be riding them bareback? Si asks, Si with his mad fringe hanging down over one eye and his permanent duffel coat, and Scott Ruff says, no, that would be mad, you would slide off in no time and the horses would run off and cause havoc. They have saddles at the stables, Scott Ruff says, we discovered during our reconnaissance that they do have saddles, but the horses will be locked up for the night, so we are going to have to bridle them ourselves, or I should say, I am going to have to quickly and quietly bridle all four horses myself. Then we're going to belt it back to my gaff, on South

Street. But isn't your dad Dan Ruff? Tall Tommy asks him. Won't he go mental and kill everyone if he finds out you have tracked down the thugs that assaulted you and stolen their horses from right under their still-breathing noses? True, Scott says, which is why we are going to say I won them in a bet. What?! You regularly win horses in bets? Gypsies win lots of things in bets, Scott Ruff says, he won't bat a fucking eye. What if we get stopped by the police? Dougie asks him. Of course he has his Alarm T-shirt on. Feign ignorance and say you're a gypsy, and that you're just doing what gypsies do, riding a horse through the Gallowgate, Scott says. Is that the route we're taking? Si asks him. Yup, we'll go right along the Shettleston Road and through Parkhead and the Gallowgate and then cut across Glasgow Green to the Clyde and follow that all the way to South Street. Also, there's these, Scott Ruff says, and he spread out his palm to reveal a handful of small sugar cubes. What's that, Tall Tommy asks him, and he says, it's a bunch of microdoses of LSD. What?! We're not going to take LSD and ride horses through the night in Glasgow, are we? Dougie says, and Scott Ruff says, no, don't be mad, they're for the horses.

45

It is the afternoon of the première of the revival of Findlay Anderson's *Veneer* at Le Petit Théâtre. Josef Noth is dining with Thérèse Barnier and Alexis Leger beforehand, alongside one of Leger's beautiful mistresses (for there are many) and the strange creepy composer The H, who is still giving Josef Noth the heebie-jeebies. Where did you get the idea for the libretto? Josef Noth asks Leger. Josef Noth is making small talk while playing footsie with Thérèse Barnier beneath the table at La Tige Noircie, in Montmartre. Oh, it's not a libretto, Alexis Leger contradicts him, or is it St-John Perse? It's very much a series of poems, he insists. Inspired by what? Josef Noth asks him. Inspired by a trip I took a few years back through Mongolia on horseback, Leger (we presume) says. Which was a descent – or perhaps an ascent, is a better way to put it – into a place of complete timelessness. On a horse called Allan, he adds. At which Josef Noth lets out a snort, and Thérèse Barnier kicks him, affectionately, underneath the table. A horse called Allan was your steed into timelessness, he jokes, but Leger is not laughing. Allan and I became one in that desert, he says, solemnly. Rider and horse became one, across those sands, he repeats. We travelled on instinct alone, he continues, across this endless desert, and sometimes we would come to a stop, and I would be aware that both Allan and I were somehow picking up on the same thing that was drawing us on. Like, for instance, we would both stare into the distance at the exact same empty point on the horizon. And so, I trusted Allan completely, to lead me where I had to go, in this featureless desert, in this timeless wilderness, is how he describes it, Leger, or St-John Perse. Suddenly, out of nowhere, we were able to orientate ourselves. There was what appeared to be a marker in the sand, just up ahead, and Allan began to make his way towards it without any encouragement from myself. Only as we approached, I realised what it was. It was the skull of a horse, the perfect archetypal skull of a horse, is the only way to describe it, buried in the sand as if the skeleton were still stood there, upright, beneath the dunes, its head exposed and still pointing the way. The skull was of such perfect dimensions, so perfectly bleached and so pure in its lineaments, that it seemed to me we were in the presence of the very ancestor of the whole horse race itself, as if it had come from the lineage of the Cheval de Przewalski, which I had long dreamt of encountering. Allan came to a stop right next to it and waited while I bent down and retrieved the skull, carefully lowering it, like the most precious art of antiquity, into a saddlebag. Straight away, I could smell the sea. In the skull of the horse? Yes, in the most perfect form of the equine skull I became aware of the smell of the sea, of the roar of the sea, more like, for this is what it appeared as, Leger continues, like a seashell that contains the whole sea within it, a skull that traced its own origins back to the very waters that had birthed it. And with that, gulls. What? that creep the composer everyone calls The H bursts. Gulls in the desert? That seems a little preposterous, even for you, he says. But no, Leger insists, I could smell and hear the sea and then suddenly: here come the gulls, and the swallows, he adds, and now the nomads, the trains of Mongolian nomads, passing by in a great convoy, their wagons seemingly rigged with great sails, and the camel drivers too, in the eyes of the camel drivers there was the echo of the sea also, Leger insists, it was uncanny, and I said to Allan, to my faithful horse Allan I said, but surely we are approaching the sea, and sure enough, Allan led us onwards, in this desert lacking anything approaching a sign outside of a perfectly bleached horse skull, a trail of wagons set sail on the sand, westwards, where the desert became a perfect sea, the infinite sands an ocean, and everything on it, floating, or drowning, or risen up. This doesn't sound like poetic myopia to me, Josef Noth says, and Leger says, ah, but it's all too much of me, I fear, and of my own experience, he bemoans. Don't you think it would make for such a great dance piece? Thérèse Barnier asks Josef Noth. Can't you feel the undulating rhythms of the sea in the echoing bone, in the dead skull left to bleach in the sun atop an upright skeleton in the sand? And it is true, Josef Noth thinks to himself, he can hear that music of undulating time, of infinite waves, and feel the dance of it too.

46

Do you know how Glasgow was founded? Aaron and Scott Ruff are visiting The Precious Gift at his flat in the Wyndford and he is telling them the story of the founding of Glasgow by warrior monks. Or maybe just straight monks, Aaron's memory could be elaborating. It was founded by St Mungo and his buds, The Precious Gift tells them. Glasgow began on the very spot where the cathedral stands, at the top of High Street, he says, and it became a place of religious pilgrimage, to a church built in the sixth century on the banks of the Molendinar Burn, which is now an underground river, he explains. Which is now a stinky river, he emphasises. Which is now a subterranean cesspit, he underlines. Make no bones about it, Glasgow came from the Anabasis of St Mungo, who christened it the Dear Green Place, and who fished there, in peace, for most of his days, that is when he wasn't welcoming religious pilgrims or laying stones or wandering in the ancient woodlands, which back then was Glasgow. Did you know that to this day Glasgow has more parkland per head of population than any other city in Europe? The Precious Gift asks them. No, they did not know that. Everyone thinks it's a concrete nightmare, Scott Ruff says. Let them, The Precious Gift says. But how did he settle on this precise spot? Aaron asks him. Originally, he came from Fife, The Precious Gift says, and his family name was Kentigern, though everybody called him Tommy. He was given the name Mungo, which means The Precious Friend. One night, being such a precious friend, he was visiting another monk who was on his last legs, and when he died Mungo had his body strapped to a cart pulled by two wild bulls. Then he spoke to the bulls at length in the language of the beasts, which he had mastered, and asked them to convey his dear friend's body to the place of the Lord, and he followed on as the bulls crossed the central belt, these bulls from the beginning of time, was how it felt like, that he had yoked the body of his friend to the first animals of creation, which were a pair of bulls, followed by a pair of eagles, followed by a pair of black lions, followed by the first humans – male and female – and these bulls from the beginning of time took the body of his dear friend to a spot hard by a river where they spoke the word 'Glas-Gu' in smoke from their nostrils, and Mungo, The Precious Friend, buried his friend on the very spot that Glasgow would grow from, which was the all-used-up heart of his dear friend, from which grew a tree with two birds, and a great stone cathedral, and a pair of fishes that sang like silent bells. Which is the Anabasis of St Mungo, The Precious Gift says, and the founding of the city of Glasgow.

47

The opening night of Findlay Anderson's *Veneer* at Le Petit Théâtre is a night that Josef Noth will remember for the rest of his life. It was when he first heard the poetry of St-John Perse, which was to hear poetry for the first time, not just to have it enter the auditory canal, not merely to have it bounce around your brain in search of analogues and ideas, but to experience a moment of perfect timelessness, where everything is speaking, in that same thunder of beyond-the-days (was that a phrase he fastened onto in the text?), this same moment dissolving as the words *assassin meaning*, that's what it feels like at the words of St-John Perse, to enter the stream of the first words, sounded, in that same thunder, and in that pure space someone is dancing, beneath the thunder of words, Thérèse Barnier is dancing in a great desert, and waving her hands in the air, her silhouette is like smoke, going up, or a beautiful woman's hair, hanging down, as Josef Noth turns in his seat to look at the politician Alexis Leger, whose eyes are closed, whose eyes are shut tight as someone else sounds the works of his other, his twin self, his beautiful mistress beside him, as well as the foul-mouthed and foul-tempered H, as Thérèse Barnier undulates – it's the only word for it – as she undulates on stage there to these syllables of sand, these repeated syllables, and now her shadow makes of her a pair of dancers, as they rise up, like a puff of smoke, in these years before the war, and disappear, like that, in language. Wow. That's some of the best shit I have ever experienced in my life, Josef Noth says to Thérèse Barnier afterwards, and that is exactly how he puts it. Thérèse calls him her handsome angel and tells him how precious he is to her, and he shakes St-John Perse's hand and looks into his dark eyes that can see for miles and for the first time *knows poetry*, which is the knowledge of his ship of fate, leaving. What was the name of that piece? Josef Noth asks St-John Perse in wonder, and Perse says something that he doesn't quite catch – he thinks he said, it is the name of a bird, the last sound of a bird, but he's unsure even of that, and besides, what bird? – before Leger is swept away by a gaggle of dignitaries and admirers. Afterwards, at the reception, back at Leger's apartment, Josef Noth asks Leger if there is a German Anabasis and Leger tells him, why yes, there will be, that in fact his friend, the philosopher and critic Walter Benjamin, is working on a German Anabasis as we speak. In the meantime, he says, if your French is up to speed, there's this, and he takes down a copy of the French edition of *The Anabasis of St-John Perse* and dedicates it to Josef Noth 'from beyond-the-days'. Josef Noth sits down at the table in Leger's study and enters the legendary space of his poetry. Some time later he overhears someone in another room ask Leger about how advisable it is to have 'a German' in his quarters and Leger silences him by saying that Josef Noth is a man, not a German, and even though, or more truly, precisely because, Josef Noth has entered the legendary space of his poetry, Noth thinks to himself, no, St-John, I am a man *and* a German, as you well know. Because poetry says so.

48

Aaron Murray's little brother Nemo disappeared at a football match in the autumn of 1979. Partick Thistle were playing Aberdeen at home at Firhill Stadium, in Maryhill, in Glasgow. Nemo was five years old. The boys were there with their father. They had already been to the toilets together, once, but Nemo needed to go again. Aaron's dad told him to take Nemo to the toilet. Why didn't he just go in with him? Instead, Aaron told him that he would wait right here for him, but as soon as Nemo went in, he wandered down the tunnel across the way to watch a little more of the game. By the time he got back, Nemo had disappeared. Aaron waited outside for a little longer, then he went in to get him. But there was no one there. He went back out, presuming he had missed him, and that he had headed back to their seats with their dad, but when he got back his dad said he hadn't returned and that's when Aaron's heart dropped. They both ran out into the corridor and asked the woman at the food stand whether she had seen an unaccompanied blond child walking past. She may have been the only witness. She said, yes, that she thought she had seen a young blond boy, walking hand in hand with an older man. What way were they headed? Out. What did the man look like? I can't remember, she said, tall, she said, dark, she said, thin, she said. This was the only description they were ever to get of Nemo's kidnapper. He might as well have been the Invisible Man. They ran outside. Small crowds were starting to drift off. Aaron's dad shouted out: my boy has been taken! His boy, shouted like that, his boy. Groups of people began turning around. What does your boy look like? they are asking. He's blond, he's only fucking five years old, Aaron's dad says to them, and he is shaking with emotion. He lights a cigarette. We're going to murder this bastard, he says. Spread out, someone shouts. We're looking for a young blond boy who has been taken by a man! There are shouts from a street away. But it turns out to be nothing. People are running this way and that. At the stadium they put out a Tannoy announcement. A young boy has gone missing, they say. Please look out for a young blond boy that has gone missing from his dad.

49

The boys made their way to the east end on foot. Aaron, Scott, Tall Tommy, Si, Dougie. They had to do this right. They went up past the cathedral and paid their respects to the stinky ghost of the Molendinar Burn and of course Scott and Aaron thought about those two bulls who spoke the first Glasgow. It felt like they were walking back in time as they made their way eastwards, beneath that yeasty smell that hangs over the east end like a curse (for the gods of the east end are bread and booze), and along Alexandra Parade, holy Alexandra Parade (for the soul of Glasgow is Alexandra Parade) (and its complement, Dumbarton Road, in the west, which together plots the winged figure of Glasgow with the lightning scar in its belly). Aaron's father worked in a shoe shop there, back when it was a street of working men, early in the morning, committed nine-to-fivers in hats and long coats. And who doesn't love a parade? Didn't Walter Benjamin write something about a parades project, or was it arcades? The parades are the arcades, in Glasgow, and the gypsy camps, huddled against the railway line there. And on through Carntyne to the Shettleston Road with Tollcross Park on the right in the dark, the shops with their hand-painted signs, inevitably misspelled, the cemeteries with their toppled graves, the windowless bars, the occasional drunk, clinging to a lamp-post on his impossible way home, the glow of the late-night buses. Look: this newsagent, lit up orange in the night, just before the corner there, is the place where Aaron bought scraps with his mother when he was a young boy with a scrapbook, and not a horse rustler, as we pass his old school, Eastbank Primary, where his mother would pass him comic books through the fence at playtime. Are we really walking backwards in time? Only to thieve horses in order to return? Because Aaron has licked that LSD-laced sugar cube; they all have. That way they will have perfect empathy with the horses themselves, on their way back home.

50

Roses. Golf. Quality Street. Pizza pie. Kettle. Knife and fork. Extension. Draft excluder. Sausage dog. Aerial. Immersion heater. Hot-water bottle. Electric blanket. Transistor radio. Coal scuttle. Video cassettes. Teabag. Blanket. Body warmer. Slippers. Bunnet. Carbolic soap. Hot chocolate. Signet ring. Aftershave. Behind the words, there are silences. Pigeon. Aaron's dad is struggling to name a pigeon. The . . . the whatchamacallit . . . he says . . . Aaron's father is pointing at the pigeon like it has been abandoned by language altogether and is now nameless. Why does he never forget 'whatchamacallit'? His arm shakes in front of him as he points. What do you call these spiky things? he asks Aaron. He shows him his chewed nails. These spiky things on the ends of my fingers, I know I chew them to bits, he says. I don't think there is a name for the spiky bits of chewed nails, Aaron tells his dad, as Donald looks at his nails in disbelief, as though once there was a world of infinite detail, lost, now, to language.

51

It's 2 a.m. when they arrive at the Old Manse Road. Oh wow, Tall Tommy says. I know this road. Me and my dad used to go for walks here, back when I was a kid and my dad was teaching me about trains and the weather and the moon, he says. In fact, it's where I first saw a rag-and-bone man, complete with a horse-drawn cart, coming right down this very lane. There's a feeling the whole night that they have been walking straight into the past. OK, Scott Ruff says. Stay towards the shadows. When we get to the gate, we check the scene. All being well, I'll cut the locks and go straight into horse-whispering mode. We feed them the sugar cubes, we lead them out into the lane, we get you all mounted, then we belt it back to mine. Tommy stays outside in the lane until we are gone, and then you make yourself scarce, Tommy. Understood. Here, Scott says, bally up. What? I've brought us balaclavas, Scott Ruff says. So as not to facilitate easy identification, he explains. I feel like a fucking paramilitary, Si says, this is so fucking good. But there's a light on when they get to the gate. There's a light on in the flat above the garage. Shit, they're still up, Scott Ruff says, and Aaron sees him pat the waistband of his trousers. I don't know if he even realised he did it, it was involuntary, but Aaron says to him, wait a minute, what is that stuck down the waistband of your trousers, that's not a gun, is it? Scott Ruff says, yeah, it's a handgun. You think

I'm turning up for a run-in with the cunts that blinded me without a piece, he says, and it's like he has turned. I don't like this, Scott, Aaron says to him. This is way beyond what any of us were expecting. Is that right? Scott Ruff says, and he turns to Si and Dougie and Tall Tommy, and he asks them if they would really have a problem if he 'plugged' the clown who blinded him. Si says, an eye for an eye, you can't argue with that. Dougie just shrugs and says, I believe in vengeance, so . . . and just kind of shrugs again. They are all tripping balls on LSD. Scott Ruff turns to Aaron, and he says, actually, I think *you* need to look after the gun. Then he holds the gun out to him in the flat of his palm, like a dare. If I get caught with a gun, on the back of a horse, riding through the night in Glasgow, I'll go to jail, Aaron says to him. And Scott Ruff says, in that case, don't even think about it. Just do it. Go on, he says, we've fucked about enough already, and after what feels like an eternity but is probably only a few seconds, Aaron takes the gun and slides it down the waistband of his jeans. Scott Ruff looks at him for a second, with his one good eye, and that eyepatch of his, and Aaron knows right then that he would blow the bollocks off anyone who fucks with them that night. Scott Ruff turns and cuts the chains on the padlocks – it goes through them like butter, wow – and they approach the invisible horses, the invisible horses in the dark, while Tall Tommy stands outside, keeping his eye on the window that casts an unearthly glow over the stables, while this music comes from inside, this awful reggae music, it might be UB40, as they feel between themselves this dangerous new sense of brotherhood, this sense that everything depends on what is happening right now. What a feeling.

52

What a feeling: Josef Noth is walking arm in arm with his sweetheart, the ballerina Thérèse Barnier, through the charming arcades of Paris. They pass a drinking fountain in a grand square where young boys are tossing coins and sailing beautiful model boats. How long can we hold on to this, he asks nobody in particular. Rather, he addresses the air, the moment, the times. Isn't it ours forever? beautiful Thérèse in her ballet pumps and her blossomy dress says to him. Already it is as if she is speaking from beyond a great distance and Josef Noth is bidding her farewell. I mean Europe, he says, this dream of European capitals, he clarifies. How long can we hold out? he asks her. There is a force set on destroying everything we have achieved as Europe, he says to Thérèse. The times themselves are under assault, he insists. Is there a war coming? Thérèse asks him, and Josef Noth says, let it come down. Josef Noth quotes Shakespeare on the coming storm, and he says, perhaps there will be an awakening from this trance of time. Thérèse asks him if he is quoting St-John Perse, but no, this trance of time is more the feeling I get from his poetry, Josef Noth says. It has electrified me, Josef Noth insists, like a monster brought to life. I feel reborn on this trip, Thérèse, he tells her, reborn as a *full participant*, is how he puts it. Then he describes himself as *a player in the show*, though perhaps he is quoting Shakespeare once more. I have to go back, Josef Noth tells his sweetheart. I must return to Germany. Leger believes there will be a war, Thérèse Barnier tells him, he says he can see it in Hitler's eyes. But why are we fighting? Because we are brothers, is what Josef Noth tells her in return. Isn't that what the Anabasis is about? Fighting like brothers? You talk about it like it's sport, Thérèse Barnier says to him. Oh, it's much more than sport, Josef Noth says.

It is destiny, he says. Aren't we destiny? she says to him, and Josef Noth takes her in his arms, and he says, we're perfect, and he kisses her on the lips, and he lifts her up into the air. We will never grow old, he tells her. And our love will never die.

53

Terry Wogan. Who was the man your mum loved to listen to while she was getting ready in the morning? Aaron's father is asking him, all the way in the past now. The Irish fella. It is Terry Wogan. It is names and things and places that defeat him, never the structure of a sentence. It is so strange. It is so strange to remember Terry Wogan as a disembodied voice in the mornings on the radio. All together in the oval dance, Aaron's dad sings to himself, and he nods. That was a good song, he says. That was a song your mother loved, he says. She didn't, Dad, she really hated that track. What do you call them, the vinyls, the small vinyls. Seven-inch singles, Dad. The guy with the big hair and the braces. Leo Sayer. The woman we met at the garden party. Princess Anne. Though we just waved, we didn't actually meet her. Who was the woman that gave us the horse skull? What horse skull? The skull we had hanging above the door of the old house, Aaron's father says. Do you mean the antlers? Aaron asks him. Do you mean the antlers you bought that Mum wouldn't let us hang up in the living room or in the kitchen, so we hung them in the loft? Yes, it was a horse skull, Aaron's dad says. I bought it in an antiques shop run by Lady Diana's mother. Or was it the mother of the newsreader, Sue? Sue Lawley? Yes, Sue Lawley, the mother of Sue Lawley, did I meet her in a car park that time? The places with the levels. A multi-storey car park? Yes, we bought a horse skull from Sue Lawley in a multi-storey car park, that was great, he says. He is so far away from Aaron, sat there next to him like a little boy. Then he asks Aaron about Rose Cottage. Do you remember Rose Cottage? he says.

54

In the dark, to the muffled sounds of UB40, beneath a single window, lit up, the young boys are feeding sugar cubes to the invisible horses.

55

On the delightful terrace of a Parisian cafe on the Champs-Élysées, in the autumn of 1937, the gymnast Josef Noth is talking poetry with St-John Perse. There are doves feasting on the crumbs beneath the tables. Have you ever dissected a bird? Perse asks Noth. I did at school, Noth tells him. Then you know what any schoolboy knows, Perse says to him, as he tears off a bit of baguette and scatters it on the ground in front of them, that the body of a bird resembles a great ship, complete with a hull, a keel, an oarlock and a stern. It seems more designed for the water, than for the air. Yet it is lighter than a feather when taken up on the breeze. Birds have no fealty to any single element, Noth says. Their body is the territory, neither land nor sea nor air. When did you start talking like a poet? Perse asks him. Something has changed in me, Alexis, Noth says, and he uses Perse's given name, his birth name that Alexis, too, has only limited fealty towards. Thérèse tells me you are returning to Germany, Alexis says. I have to, Josef Noth says. Why? Because poetry says so, Josef Noth says. There will be no more poetry, if Germany has its way, Leger says. And Josef Noth says, what of the conquerors of the Anabasis? Are they not in the place of poetry also? Well, I made it so, Alexis, speaking now as St-John Perse, says. Exactly, Josef Noth says. Just as I intend to make it so. Is there poetry in the rape of Paris? Alexis asks him. Is there poetry in the conquering of a Mongol horde? Josef Noth asks him in return. I think, Alexis, Josef Noth addresses him, that for you, perhaps, poetry is something that is retrospective. Whereas for me, thanks to your poetry, ha ha, thanks to the revelation of your poetry, I should say, for me true poetry is found in the rapture of what is. *In the flaming heart of the moment, man is immortal.* Is not every young man's anabasis taking place right now? Josef Noth says, and he gestures all around him at the scene that is unfolding. Or are your values not the values of poetry? Yes, for St-John, Alexis says, his values are exclusively poetic. But as a man, and a diplomat, and a loyal Frenchman, right now, my values are political and cultural. Why St-John? Josef Noth asks him. John the Revelator, Alexis says. Exactly, Josef Noth says. And Alexis Leger has to smile. At which the doves, suddenly startled, rise up like a flotilla of ships. You're asking me if there is poetry in the obliteration of the world, St-John Perse says. And Josef Noth says, exactly. At which St-John Perse offers Josef Noth his hand and says to him, good luck, my brother. It is the last time Josef Noth and St-John Perse ever meet.

56

Rose Cottage is outside Rothesay – was outside Rothesay, for it has since been demolished – on an estate with an old stately home and a Victorian greenhouse that the owner, Julio, was in the process of renovating. It was the Murrays' first and only family holiday to the Isle of Bute, back when Aaron's mother was healthy and well and looked like Wonder Woman still. At that point Aaron was deep into collecting badges and he bought endless Adam and the Ants badges at a shopping arcade on the seafront with his holiday money, as well as a 7" single of 'Being Boiled' by The Human League that melted before he could even play it, because he left it lying in the window of the cottage that warm summer. To this day Aaron can't see a copy of *Starlog* or *Fantastic Films* without it taking him back to Rose Cottage, because that was all he read that summer, copies of magazines gone yellow from the light of an old newsagent's window. In his memory there is a fortress out at sea, a haunted old fortress with no doors or windows risen up from the sea, an impenetrable fortress lit up in the night as they walk along the promenade, his mother arm in arm with his father in what seems like a perfect dream now, with all that was about to happen to them. But even then, there were omens, dry runs for the future, like the time the tide caught Nemo's legs while he was wading in the sea, and he was swept off, and under, and Aaron screamed that he was drowning, and his dad ran and grabbed him. Aaron tasted his first beer with his dad. There's a photograph of it that Aaron's mum took to mark the occasion, his father is sunburnt from the crazy golf, sitting with his shirt unbuttoned at the table, smoking a cigarette and drinking a beer on this barely imaginable holiday long ago. Nemo eating an ice cream sundae as big as his head. The leafy gloaming of the estate where Aaron and Nemo played swingball and Frisbee and kicked around a football. The dusky evenings where Nemo played on his skateboard while Aaron watched TV. The time when they met a family next door whose young son was a pogo-stick champion. The time when they saw a buzzard for the first time, while out walking secret paths around the estate; their father pointed it out. The time Aaron saw his mum and dad on the couch, his mum lying in his dad's arms, watching TV on this tan leather couch late at night, when

Aaron got upset and couldn't sleep and came in to tell his mum and dad that he couldn't sleep because he was crying about death in his mind, and he asked his dad if it was true, that we all really had to die, and his dad told him that was nothing to worry about just now, that it was a long way off for all of us, and Aaron cried some more because in that case his dad admitted that we all had to die. The time when the wild horse ran away across the field with Nemo on its back. And then when they were leaving, and loading their suitcases into the car, their dad said to them, that's us, we are leaving Rose Cottage. Leaving Rose Cottage. The way he said it. Yes, his father says to him, yes, he says, across the years now, from this bench in another world completely, he says, yes, but the blind fortress was at Douglas, on the Isle of Man, and not at Rose Cottage, he says, this fortress that rose up, out of the waves.

57

In the dark, the horses are moving. Four figures stand in the shadow of the stables. One by one they are leading the horses out into the lane. A single figure stands guard. The first-floor window casts a tunnel of light. There is music in the background, soft reggae music illuminates the scene. Then a car appears. A car with its lights on turns into the lane just as the figures are mounting the horses. It comes to an abrupt halt. The horses and their riders, illuminated in the headlights. A figure emerges from the car and runs towards them. It looks to have some kind of improvised weapon in its hand. One of the horses rears up in panic. Somehow the rider stays on its back. Another figure appears from the back door of the garage. The music cuts completely. The riders turn the horses and run them in the opposite direction, up the Old Manse Road, which is the direction that the past came from, in Tall Tommy's telling. At this point Tall Tommy, who was on lookout, disappears into the estate on the other side of the lane and is impossible to track. Then the car restarts. The driver is gunning the car straight towards the horses. This cunt will kill these horses rather than let us escape, someone says, a shadow on a horse. Then one of the riders pulls a gun. One of the riders pulls a gun and lets three shots loose through the windscreen of the car. Once more, the horses rise up, like in an old action movie, but the riders stay in place. The car comes to a dead halt. The windscreen is completely shattered. It's impossible to know if anyone is left alive inside as we track the horses up the Old Manse Road, past the backs of the houses, through the abandoned industrial buildings, beneath the flooded railway bridge, by the side of the old Sandymount Cemetery, turning at Barlanark, onto the Hallhill Road, towards Shettleston, via Budhill Park, on an unplanned route, now, straight into the past.

58

Josef Noth's final night in Paris is spent making love to the beautiful ballerina Thérèse Barnier with the aid of a trunk of sex toys that Thérèse brought in an ornate leather suitcase to the luxurious hotel room in Le Meurice, on Rue de Rivoli, and to the reading of the poetry of Rilke together. Yes, Rilke, who, it turns out, also fell under the spell of *The Anabasis of St-John Perse*. Yes, it is true, Thérèse is telling Josef Noth, as they lie in bed together, covered in sweat, and with the bedclothes rolled down and soaking too – Thérèse still wears her ballet pumps, Noth's cock is prodigious – Rilke intended to translate the Anabasis, she confirms. But he could not. He could not because he said that he *did not have the time*. Which means that he understood the

Anabasis perfectly, Josef Noth says, and Thérèse Barnier says, yes, and so, in that spirit, he passed it on to his friend Walter Benjamin and urged Benjamin to make the first German translation himself. I think it will come to pass, Josef Noth says, that the imagination of the twentieth century will be haunted by the Anabasis.

59

The dark horses are moving in the night. In the ink-black night the dark horses are moving down the Shettleston Road beneath their young riders. In this strange silence the dark horses appear to float above the ground. This mare is liquid, in the night. As the boys hold tight to the horses that might well take off into the air, it is like holding tight to a dream. This dream of boyhood runs the length of the Shettleston Road in the dark. It is haunted by the illuminated garages of the east end. In the smoke from the horses' nostrils is spoken the word: Glas-Gu, Glas-Gu!

60

Mate, did you know that in the olden days people thought that memory was stored in the tonsils? Mark C. Burl asks Aaron, at the Equi cafe, on Sauchiehall Street, on a blustery evening in Glasgow, with the streetlights illuminating the booth in the window. Can you imagine what they would have thought of all these young people having them yanked out at the first excuse for anything, he says, and Aaron has an uncanny feeling right then, when Luke G.B. Caird says, the fact is, memory exists nowhere. What? Nowhere. Then how can I remember at all? Aaron asks him. I read this thing, Luke G.B. Caird says. This scientist, or maybe he was a Buddhist, said that you can only remember what arises in the moment, and that is a gift, Luke G.B. Caird says. There is no memory in the body, is what he is saying, there is no store of memory in the blood or the brain cells or the organs of the body themselves. Something else is remembering. And even then, it is not remembering, it is presenting. So what we call memory is as present, and as real, as our own bodies, Luke G.B. Caird says. Imagine we could remember at will, Mark C. Burl says, imagine we could rescue anything from the past, by force of will alone, and return it to the present. Is it possible, Aaron is asking them, is it possible to rescue someone from the past, is it possible for the past to be present, all over again, and that's when he tells them about his brother Nemo, how he was kidnapped in the past and how he only returns in dreams, in strange prophetic dreams, now, where he is being taken by the hand by a tall shadow and led over an impossible horizon.

61

Josef Noth returns to Germany and prepares for war. He signs up for an infantry division and begins intensive training. He spends his weekends alone, at his hut in the woods, swimming, and boating, or writing poetry, because now Josef Noth has taken up writing poetry in the style of the early twentieth century, echoing St-John Perse and T.S. Eliot and Rainer Maria Rilke and Blaise Cendrars (who lost an arm to poetry in the First World War, Noth noted) and Guillaume Apollinaire and Gérard de Nerval (another pseudonym, this time a stand-in for Gérard Labrunie), whose novel about an unrequited love that had consumed his youth, *Aurélia*, had an uncanny effect on Josef Noth, as did Keats, of course, the favourite of doomed youth, and Rimbaud, inevitably. He occasionally visits his mother's house, where she calls him by his boyhood nickname,

Achilles. The ballerina Thérèse Barnier writes him beautiful love letters, and when she talks of the coming war, which is inevitable by this point, she talks about the back of the war, the other side of the war, as though behind the war itself was the peace that humanity had been fighting for, forever, only now it is just up ahead, this final reckoning, on its way from the very beginnings of history. And something else is beginning too, as the ballerina Thérèse Barnier reveals in a letter to Josef Noth that she is pregnant with his child, whom she intends to name Achilles, if it is a boy, because who knows if we will ever see each other again, my darling, is how she puts it, as Josef Noth imagines a place from which all of history is visible, which is the place of poetry, perhaps, he thinks to himself, as he returns to his family home for the last time.

62

Look, Aaron's father says, he is pointing to a shrunken man in the Botanics, sat on this same bench now, where his father is literally shedding language, he is pointing to things that no longer have names in awe and confusion, like midgets. Aaron knows the word his father is looking for is 'midget' and he is glad he cannot say it, because the midget is walking right past them, and Aaron's father Donald is saying, look, it's one of them, one of them _______, he is saying. Eskimos, he says. It's one of them Eskimos. Your mother got smaller as she died, he tells Aaron, in the wake of the midget. She died from a wasting disease, he says, as if he is updating a complete stranger on the course of his life. Near the end she was like a little child, he says. It's true that Aaron's mum Elizabeth was tiny already, and that in the end she disappeared, almost completely. As she died in her bed Aaron and his father sat next to her and spoke to her. Because they say that hearing is the last to go. Spoke to her over the terrible rattle that announced her transubstantiation into light as air. And when they took away the body, now no longer her body, but the property of the nameless dead, Aaron's father called him in and said, look at this, and he pulled back the duvet and pointed to the smallest indentation in the centre of the mattress where his mum had died and there was a terrible yellow stain there where Elizabeth had gone on herself, and his dad said, it looks like a fox curled up to sleep. By this point none of them had even cried. Aaron was waiting for his dad to start, it was all caught up inside of him, so as when he said this thing about the fox curled up asleep, Aaron burst out crying, he started sobbing, one slow great sob at a time, and his dad looked at him in confusion, as if it was the poor fox and not his tiny disappeared mum who had literally pined away in front of them through the trauma of losing her youngest boy, and the affairs that his father was having, that he was crying for, sobbing, really, just sobbing there with his dad's stupid expression on his face and his stupid comment about the stupid fox curled up there.

63

The dark horses spill into Tollcross Park in the night, like ink into water. The young riders hold tight to their steeds, like horses into war. They cut across the great rose garden, itself in the shape of a rose, and along the Tollcross Road in the dark. Watch me, one of the boys commands the others, as he stands up on the back of his horse. He is stood in the figure of Christ, now, and as they enter Parkhead and pass Celtic Park a silent cheer goes up, for these bold young boys, illuminated there. The night is electric, in Glasgow. The city is completely denuded of people, and the streets are for racing horses in, and for thieving, and for bold displays. Just as Glasgow has always been, as they turn back time on the city. Just by racing horses through it, they arrive at the very beginnings of Glasgow, where Mungo's twin bulls first dragged the body of his friend. And the smoke from the horses' nostrils is the same word spoken by the first bulls, as they cross the secret underground river of the Molendinar Burn, they speak the first words and refound the city. Glas-gu! Glas-gu! – dear green of boyhood forever.

64

As an engineer in a previous life, a life before dance and gymnastics and poetry and Paris transformed it, Josef Noth is assigned to a Panzergruppe for training. There are boys from many walks of life here, a fellow engineer, Rudolf Naz, aka The Nazz, tells him, as he gives him the guided tour of the barracks they will be living in for the next few months. This is the ablutions block, he says, and Josef Noth thinks, what a word, 'ablutions', and he thinks of that carbolic smell, that smell of men, of young boys, together, and how much scrubbing it takes to even suppress it. The Nazz has keys to all the main buildings in the camp – trainee recruits are only starting to arrive – and there is something perfect and untouched about the classrooms with their desks piled high with brand-new radio receivers and oscillators and short-wave devices. The tanks parked up on the verge are pristine and smell amazing. It feels like the beginning of a great adventure, Josef Noth says to The Nazz, who says, it's so quiet, though, he says, it feels more like a ghost story. Written on the blackboard in chalk, at the back of the room, are the words (who wrote it there, weren't we waiting for everyone to arrive?) 'Die Welt'. The World, it says.

65

Now one of the boys is singing that song, 'Sixty Eight Guns', that song from The Alarm's first album, that song about how uprisings will take place forever, about how they will never die, and how they are pure joy, as the young boys sing on the horses in the night, as the Clyde is slate grey and opaque, and so is the perfect mirror for the movement of the dark horses, who appear impossibly tall on the waves, and as they pass the Jamaica Bridge (someone is asleep on a bench dreaming of horses in the night) the towers are craning to see the dark horses, as moonlight drives the boys home, to a gypsy camp in the shadow of the shipyards, where the horses come to a puzzled stop, and look around to see where they have escaped to, like they have somehow run out of land. And then a light goes on and a figure bursts from a caravan. It's only fucking Dan Ruff, the King of the Gypsies, bursting out there like something out of a myth, or a children's book, because what exactly is the difference, and he says, who the fuck is it on them there horses (is that a fucking shotgun in his hand?), and Scott says, it's me, Dad, it's me and the boys, we stole some horses and raced them through the night along the empty streets of Glasgow, sure we did. Scott just comes straight out with it, and his dad Dan Ruff says, I'm proud of you, son, I'm proud of you for riding them horses, he says, you remind me of my old da, he says, my old da broke horses, he says, riding them through the night like that, and so who did you steal them from, he says, and Scott says, I didn't want to tell you, Dad, because I wanted to do it myself, but we found out where the guys that took my eye out were from, we tracked them down, and these are their very fucking horses, and Dan Ruff looks like he is about to murder the world, but then he takes a hanky, he takes an elaborate hanky from his back pocket that he always wore there like a foxtail, and he dabs his eyes, and now he is crying, Dangerous Dan Ruff right in front of the boys there is shedding a tear, over his son righting his own wrongs, and after Dan Ruff composes himself, he goes over to a pony and he puts his hand against its belly, this great hand like a shovel, up against its great pulsating belly, and he turns to everyone and he says, this is a pregnant pony. You did well, boys, he says. You did well to bring these horses here.

66

Aaron's father's affairs went like this. His mother would meet her friend Sheila Black at the Ubiquitous Chip every Sunday afternoon – until Sheila unexpectedly married a Texan, name of Big Joe, that is, who shot a snake and blew its head off in his own front yard, the story goes – and that was when his father Donald's latest flame would ring the phone three times and hang up for code, and then if the coast was clear his dad would call back for real. Nemo was too young to know what was going on, but Aaron used to sit at the top of the stairs and listen to their love talk. Or rather, his father's love talk, where he would talk about taking them both to Paris, his girls. Would you like to join me in Paris, he would say, on one of my trips, on one of my upcoming trips there, he would insist, his father who worked in a shoe shop and who had only, as far as Aaron knew, been to Paris once, and that was on his honeymoon with Aaron's mum, on an epic drive to Italy, their first and last, and even then they were only passing through. But on the phone calls to his lovers Aaron's father was always offering them romantic getaways in foreign lands – should we go to Mexico, I'll take you to the Yucatán – as if he were an urbane novelist or jet-set playboy. Who knew he dreamt like that, till then. In those phone calls Aaron heard all of the lives that his father would never lead, spoken to complete silence. To no response. Picture him now, sat there, dressed in a suit – he always dressed well, but he definitely dressed for the phone calls – the receiver to his ear, sat at the old telephone table with a green velvet cushion and a tatty phone book, smoking, speaking from this secret part of himself that saw him arm in arm with a beautiful young woman on the parades of Paris, in the autumn. That saw them falling in love in street cafes and spending all of his money on his new young love – and Aaron knew they were younger because of the way he spoke to them, and the way he would joke about his age in relation to them – and then it comes out that one time, one time we can say for sure, he did actually take a young woman to Paris, in the autumn, and spent all of his money on her, just like he said he would. It was after Nemo was taken from them, when Aaron's mother was bedridden and dying.

67

The next day it is all over the papers. Man in critical condition after being shot during attempted horse heist, is how the *Evening Times* runs with it. It wasn't attempted, what the fuck are these clowns on about, Dan Ruff says, when his big mate Paul Vickers shows him the front page. It was fully fucking realised by my boy and his brave pals, he says. You know what this means, Dan Ruff says to the boys the next morning. He's sat there on the steps in the sunshine, in a short-sleeve shirt with his massive coupon and his arms all covered in mad tattoos. No, Scott says, what? Tell him, Paul, Dan says, and he nods towards the boys, but Paul says, I'm not exactly sure what it means myself, to be honest, and Dan shakes his head and says, it means we are going to have to (and here he holds his hand over his mouth so the horses that are stood around eating the grass can't hear him or see the shape of the words he is mouthing) *euthanise the horses*. What?! We're going to have to shoot them, and bury their bodies, he says, whispering now. But one of them is pregnant! Si says. We can't shoot a pregnant pony! Sure, keep your fucking voice down, Dan Ruff says, horses are sensitive animals, especially when they are carrying a baby. Sure, it's a cold heart that would murder a pregnant pony, Dan's big mate Paul Vickers says. Everyone is looking for these fucking horses now, Dan Ruff says, they can never be seen in public again. We could shoot them and throw them in the river, Paul Vickers says, and Scott says, fuck me, a second ago you were bemoaning the fate of these poor fucking horses and now you're ready to dump their bodies in the fucking Clyde. Keep your fucking voices down, the pair of you, Dan Ruff says, what did I tell you? This is a delicate situation, and we don't want to spook the horses. Can't we at least wait until it gives birth? Can't we at least keep its little foal? Aaron says. That wee guy had nothing to do with the heist. What would be the harm in that? Nobody would ever recognise him as he grows up. Big Paul, Dan Ruff says to him, how far off is the birth, do you think, and Big Paul Vickers goes over to the pony and looks in its eyes, and then feels its belly, and then he wraps his hand in a plastic bag from Safeway and sticks his hand inside – it slides in so easily – and the pony just looks back at him, calm as you like, and he says, any day now, boss. OK, Dan Ruff says, we wait for the birth and then it's crrrrkkk, he says, and he mimes drawing a blade across his throat with his back to the horses. And we're not dumping them in the fucking river, he says. They deserve a proper burial, these rescued horses that came so happily to us, is what he says, and he goes over and pats the black pregnant one, with its long mane parted in the middle. Beautiful girl, he says.

68

It is the autumn of 1986 and Aaron's father Donald is in Paris with his secret love, Mindy Sparrow. Mindy is a lipstick model and works in a shoe shop, but in a different shoe shop from Aaron's father. Donald has told his wife that he has to attend a 'sales conference' in Paris and that he will be gone for just under a week. He meets Mindy at the airport. She is wearing a headscarf like Frida Kahlo. Mindy is a burlesque dancer in her spare time. She has long red hair 'like fire'. Her brown eyes are perfect pools with 'endless depths'. This trip is Aaron's father's secret poetry. They are booked into Le Meurice, on Rue de Rivoli. Donald has been fiddling the tills especially for this trip. They get lost on the Paris Metro but eventually make it to their hotel. They have a suite on the top floor with doors that open out onto a miraculous balcony. Mindy showers and appears in a white robe with a bottle of champagne and two glasses. She tells Donald to pour them both a glass while she gets changed. When she reappears, she is wearing one of her burlesque outfits. I've been in love with you since the first time I saw you, Donald tells Mindy. He curls her hair behind her ear, and he slides his hand down to her mouth, and he parts her famous red lips, and slides a finger inside, which she bites down on. He pulls her panties to one side and slides two fingers inside. She is so wet; she is so wet already. As they kiss, Mindy runs her sharp nails down Donald's chest, his shirt unbuttoned. They both gasp, as he takes her tits from her black bra, and spits on them, then takes them in his hands, and sucks on them. Mindy is moaning with pleasure – 'purring like a cat' – as she climbs up onto the bed on all fours and takes Donald's cock in her mouth. He slides her black panties down, scrunches them into a ball, has her open her mouth, and stuffs the panties in there. And now she is repeating his name. Don, Don, Don. She is gagging on his name. Don, it's so weird to hear her say that, as he slides two fingers up her ass and dilates her asshole as he is fucking her. She comes so hard her body buckles, so hard that she pushes him off and he tumbles to the floor from the high bed as she vibrates in ecstasy and cannot be touched. It's too much, you're making me dizzy, she says, as Donald stands up, and strokes his cock, and comes all over her beautiful burlesque outfit, or what is left of it, as Mindy just lies there, vibrating.

69

It is April 1938. Thérèse Barnier gives birth to Josef Noth's son, Achilles. It is September 1939. The Nazis have entered Poland.

70

The boy is dead. Aaron killed a boy. He shot him three times through the window of his car. The boy slipped into a coma in hospital and died. Do they know it's us? Do they suspect his life was taken in revenge? So many questions. But Dan Ruff knows what to do. I've spoken to a friend who has an allotment in Maryhill. He says we can shoot the horses there and bury them in his allotment. In the meantime, they are keeping the horses in a shipping container until the colt is born. The dead boy's name is Brian Hamilton. Aaron is shaking at the news. The rest of the boys have split back to the flat in Cresswell Street, so god knows how they are feeling. Don't worry, son, Dan Ruff says to Aaron, we've all been there. I remember the first fella I ever killed. Sure, do you recall yon fella, Odd Billy, he asks Big Paul Vickers, and Paul Vickers says, coupon on him like the Elephants Man. It's the Elephant Man, not the Elephants Man, Scott Ruff says, how does that make any sense, but Big Paul Vickers says, it makes sense because he had a coupon that would fit in with the elephants, big fucking trunk like that on his face. Anyway, Dan Ruff says, the point being, when I killed him in a bare-knuckle scrap inside one of these pitch-black shipping containers and everyone was taking bets, no one bet on death. A bit of brain damage, maybe, but the cunt wasn't all there in the first place, so a few more brain cells was no great loss. Wait, Big Paul Vickers says, are you talking about yourself or the Elephants Man? Ha ha ha, don't come the cunt, Dan Ruff says. The point is, I got a fright when I killed him. Even though that's exactly what I was trying to do, in the moment. But I wasn't trying to kill this boy, is the point, Aaron says to Dan Ruff. I just wanted to stop him ramming the horses with the car. He was coming straight for us. Plus, excuse me, but there's the fact that he took my fucking eye out in an unprovoked attack and now I'm half-blind, Scott Ruff says. We were out for revenge, and they started it. Look, son, the world's better off without him, we can say that much, Dan Ruff says, and he makes a wee cross sign in front of himself in the air. Right, he says, clapping his hands and bringing this meeting to order, let's take a drive up to these fucking allotments and scope out Terry Johnstone's plot for the burying of these damn horses. But then they saw a picture of the boy Aaron had killed in the newspaper, and it wasn't the boy that attacked them at all. Turns out it was his brother they had murdered.

71

Josef Noth is sat inside a Panzer II, scanning across short-wave bands as the convoy moves through the forest of the night. French voices break through and then recede. They are running radio drills. The voices of the platoon command tanks are running map co-ordinates. They are driving blind in the dark night with the aid of maps and radio signals. Words appear from out of the air. Artillery. Flak. Machine gunners. Butterflies. There is an epidemic of butterflies in the Ardennes. Everyone is making jokes. Omen. Sign. How do these fucking guys get inside the tanks, someone asks, from out of the air? Josef Noth holds out his finger. There is a butterfly with a splotch of deep blue on a single wing fluttering around in here. Now it has disappeared. The tracks of the tank are hypnotic. The smell of warm metal. Like animal blood. The churning mud. Somewhere someone is singing. Somewhere someone is singing a song about a famous German whore whose name is Estelle. The song is called 'Ich Bin Die Beste'. I am the best. The song is about how many men she can accommodate. It is a song about the mystery of the human body, it occurs to Josef Noth, as this ribald voice like a ghost comes over the speaker and reverberates in the tank, as the rhythm of the gears seems to match it. It is a song of used-up bodies in joy, Josef Noth thinks to himself, as he wonders about what's up ahead, and what might be about to happen.

72

Is Aaron, perhaps, his father's angel? In these last days, on this bench in the Botanic Gardens? Is he becoming the author of this tale, through his newly acquired powers? Sole witness to his father's secret trip with Mindy to Paris, where they took the famous one-hour cruise along the Seine, in the rain? It was the autumn, after all. The warm October of that year. And Père-Lachaise Cemetery, where Mindy is wearing one of her pale-blue oriental-style robes, with her red hair and brown brogues. They are holding hands while taking a tour of the haunted cemetery where the ghosts of the past still live. Where they look at the graves of Jim Morrison ('the singer from The Doors') and Oscar Wilde and, of course, the composer Chopin, whose heart, the tour guide explains, was interred in another country altogether, due to his fear of being buried alive. Having your heart torn out is surely worse than being buried alive, Mindy says to Aaron's father Donald, who looks handsome and sophisticated in his houndstooth blazer and with his sharp haircut. There is a ghastly wall, the site of a mass execution, and now it has a terrible pained figure emerging from the stone forever. Mindy isn't sure of the wisdom of touring a cemetery but then Donald reveals the next stop on their itinerary: the famous catacombs, the underworld city of the dead – oh no! But first, lunch, where Donald eats snails for the first time and draws out their bodies with a hook, which is so satisfying. Donald lies and says he has done it before. Mindy is grossed out, as she eats her steak and frites. They are sat out on yet another beautiful terrace that could only be Paris, as people all around them are coming and going and stopping to light cigarettes or to wave for a taxi with a rolled-up newspaper or to drop in for an espresso coffee in an old blue raincoat. Afterwards, as Mindy and Donald stroll arm in arm by the river, saying nothing of consequence, in the autumn fog, the leaves the colour of blood and pumpkins, they stop by a street artist, who offers to draw Mindy for free, on account of her being so beautiful. Do me a favour, the artist says, when he hands them this drawing of Mindy that looks like a saint in an ancient fresco, the way she is looking up, and out of the drawing, towards something outside of the frame, the way her eyebrows arch like simple birds, her lips like the dream of a final destination. Do me a favour, he reiterates, this Parisian artist in the autumn. Make love tonight.

73

Now Aaron is remembering when his mother died. On the morning of her death, she was called on by an 'old friend'. Aaron's mother wasn't someone who had many friends in her life. She was focused on family, and being a mother, until she wasted away. But on this last day a stranger turned up on the doorstep and said she had come to pay her respects to Elizabeth. Aaron's father Donald cautioned her: she might not remember you. Her mind is going. This was a woman much older than Aaron's mother. A very graceful woman with long dark hair who was dressed quite eccentrically in a striped woollen poncho. But when she walked into the bedroom, Aaron's mother reacted. Aaron's mother Elizabeth, who had been alternately sleeping or catatonic for weeks, looked up and said, it's you. Yes, the woman said, it's me. Then the woman asked my father if she could have a little time alone with Elizabeth. Of course, he said, and they closed the door and left them together in the room. From the kitchen Aaron and his dad could hear the low murmur of the woman's voice, his mum's old friend, who had a lilting voice like she was reciting poetry, or singing, softly. Is she singing to your mum? Aaron's dad asked him. Is she singing her one of her favourite songs? They couldn't tell. But then Aaron tiptoed over to the door and put his ear against it. Listen: *Angels of heaven, descend without delay!*

74

Tall Tommy is moving out of the Cresswell Street flat. I'm doing a runner, he tells Aaron. Fuck this. We're wanted men, he says. This is a fucking nightmare, he adds, now that he is no longer tripping on LSD but instead marching up and down the kitchen and holding his head in his hands dramatically. Si too. Si and his brother Steven are moving back to their mum's in Coatbridge before they get done for assisting in manslaughter, is how Steven puts it. Dougie – well, Dougie is still high, he can't stop tripping cause it turns out he ate half his sugar cube, and right now he is marvelling about how fucking good The Alarm's music sounds on LSD, but by the end of the month he will be doing a runner himself, back to Perth, or wherever the fuck it is he came from, and that's when Aaron asks Scott if he can move in with him.

75

Do you remember, Dad, do you remember when Mum's old friend turned up and sang her into death? It was the day Mum died, do you remember? That was Sheila Black, Aaron's father says to him, as they are sat there in the park, with the birds gathering all around them. Aaron has brought the two of them dried mealworms so they can try to get the robins to eat out of their hands. The carer has said to create memories, to keep his father engaged. Aaron's dad is sat with his arm outstretched, with the dried mealworms in his hand, while he is talking. You can put your arm down, Aaron says, but his father ignores him. That was your mum's old friend who moved to America, he says. The woman whose husband shot a snake in their garden in North Carolina, that was her, coming to say goodbye, he says. But Sheila never returned, Aaron wants to say to him, she never came back to Scotland after she emigrated, although her son did, once, as he and Aaron had become pen pals. He came over to visit one summer and everyone laughed when he said that his ambition was to write the 'Great American Novel', and it became a funny story in the family.

76

Every time he dices an onion, Aaron thinks of Scott Ruff. Scott taught him how to dice an onion and he said to him, now every time you dice an onion you will think of me. There he is, through the window, cooking on his little hotplate in their shared caravan now, off South Street, in the shadow of the huge grain silos, as gulls flit in the summer light. Those silos are overrun with rats, Scott warns Aaron. It's a big problem. They are listening to a cassette of the third Neu! album, *Neu! '75*, dubbed for them by The Precious Gift. The vocalist, Klaus Dinger, is singing about how the only crime is money. Then Scott says, OK, watch me: first, cut the onion in half through the root. He is wearing a beret and with his eyepatch he looks like a French pirate. You look like a French pirate with a cutlass, Aaron says to him. Peel the skin off both halves, Scott says, ignoring him. Now put the cut onion face down and cut vertical slices into the onion from top to bottom but don't cut through the root, let it stay in one piece. Now, put your hand on top of the half to hold it in place (and here he takes Aaron's hand and holds it in place) and, holding your knife flat, cut horizontal layers through it without severing the root. Finally, chop through it from top to bottom, all the way to the root now, getting perfect little dice. Then do the same with the other half. And now every time you dice an onion you will always think of me, Scott Ruff says. Plus, this way you won't cry when you dice an onion, because it's a magic way of avoiding tears, he says. But it's not true, Scott. Aaron still cries when he dices an onion, almost every time.

77

It's the night before they shoot the horses and bury them in a mass grave in an allotment in Maryhill and the rain is fucking biblical. Of course it's fucking biblical. Earlier today the black pony gave birth to a foal. Sure, it's a good thing, this fucking unfortunate downpour, Dan Ruff says. This way we have the allotments to ourselves. But there's a problem. You're never going to fit four horses in a garden this size, Terry Johnstone, who owns the allotment, says to them. I thought it was just the one horse youse were trying to dispose of. Everyone looks at each other. The cunt's got a point, Big Paul Vickers says. Who you calling a cunt, Terry Johnstone says to him. A good cunt, I'm saying you're a good cunt, don't be so fucking touchy, Paul Vickers says to him. I'm a fucking accessory to the crime at this point, Terry says. I'm putting my fucking arse on the line. A bit of respect should be fucking shown, Dan. Look, you're a good cunt, that's all he's saying, and you are a good cunt, it's true, Dan Ruff says, and he puts one of his massive hands behind Terry Johnstone's neck and squeezes it, in order to remind him he could snap his head off like a fucking alligator if it came down to it. And then Dan Ruff says, wait a minute, I've got it. We'll just bury the horses standing up, he says. We'll dig it deep enough that they can walk down these planks into the ground and then we'll shoot them standing up, in the grave, and fucking bury them like that. Job done, he says, and he hands Aaron a spade. Your turn, son, he says, and Aaron climbs down into the ground like Yorick, or whoever the fuck it was in Shakespeare, and starts digging in this fucking pishing rain that is turning the walls to mud and the grave into a cesspit. Something fucking stinks in here, Aaron says, and Dan Ruff says to him, here, it's probably some kind of sewage, just smoke a fucking bifter, it'll kill the smell, he says, and he lights Aaron a cigarette and passes it down to him, Aaron who has only ever smoked about five fags in his life. And now he is hacking his lungs out and bent over there on his knees in the grave, and that's when he sees it. There's an animal carcass in here. There's a dead fucking dog in here, a half-decomposed dead fucking dog, Aaron says. That'd be my dog Barry, Terry Johnstone says. What?! We're burying horses in the grave of your own dog? How do you think I got the idea for the horses? Terry Johnstone says to them. I had to get Barry put down because he bit some bird in the allotments and she ran out into the road in a state of some distress and ended up getting sideswiped by a car. I shot Barry with an air rifle so the police couldn't inject him and then I buried him in my plot. Your dog was called Barry? Dan Ruff says to him. What the fuck kind of a name for a dog is that? It was a boy, it's a boy's name, no need to come the cunt, Terry Johnstone says. Oh, so it's alright for you to call Dan a cunt, is it, Big Paul Vickers says to him. Aw, no, no, he's a good cunt, is what I'm saying, Terry Johnstone says, so that everyone has to laugh. Cunts in Glasgow, Big Paul Vickers says, it's a fucking minefield. By the way, I got those videos for you in the car, Terry Johnstone says to Dan Ruff. Talking about cunts. I watched one of them last night. This black guy fucking this blonde bird. You should see the amount he comes on her face. You could have shampooed a buffalo.

78

The tank tracks in the mud in the night of the forest of the Ardennes. Occasionally: houses, farmsteads; lit up in the night. Surely word has gotten through. Surely the enemy will be upon us. Josef Noth drifts off as the cycle of the tracks becomes hypnotic. In a state between sleeping and waking, Josef Noth is dreaming words from out of the air. Is that voice from the radio, or is it inside his head? Something is speaking in a strange sibilant e-l-o-n-g-a-t-e-d voice. It is speaking your name, Josef Noth. I am spoken for, Josef Noth says to the driver, Konrad, as he blinks awake. What?! Sorry, Josef Noth says. Sorry. I think I was dreaming. What about the butterflies, he says to Konrad, what about that, huh, and Konrad says, butterflies, what are you talking about? The butterflies in the tanks, Josef Noth says, you saw them, they must have come through one of the sight-holes, he says, and Konrad asks him, are you on drugs? Just a metaphor, Josef Noth says, backtracking. I was just making the point of a metaphor, about young boys into war, he says, and Konrad says, well, the time for poetry is behind us, he says. But Josef Noth can't help but feel that the time for poetry is just up ahead.

79

The night they bring the horses to their death. Go slow, Dan Ruff says to Big Paul Vickers. They'll be getting flung about all over the shop in the back there, he says. There's music on the radio, Ph.D., 'I Won't Let You Down', a miserable song that no one can bear to hear again, and Big Paul Vickers says, so what does Ph.D. stand for, and Dan Ruff says, Physically Handicapped Danceband. What the fuck do they know? They are improvising knowledge as they drive through Maryhill. The singer was at one of them special schools, Dan Ruff says. That's how. They pull into the car park of Garscube Allotments. There's Terry Johnstone sat in his car with the lights on. They lock the gates behind them so they can't get surprised, then they lead the horses up the hill, the sad, innocent horses now, because they are forlorn but don't know why. Past the observatories on the neighbouring hill. One of the domes is open and the telescope is out, to another planet maybe, where men are leading horses to their death, probably. I've never buried a horse before, Terry Johnstone says. No shit. The silhouettes of the tumbledown huts in the dark. Two planks lead down into the earth. Once more they have done that mad gypsy thing of giving the horses LSD to calm them down. Aaron strokes the once-pregnant pony, and then Scott, and it snorts and nods, and Aaron takes it by the reins and walks it down the planks and into the grave, like one of those guides through the underworld. It follows in complete trust and surrender. Scott leads a second horse down, Dan Ruff the third and fourth, but it's clear that they have fucked up. The fourth horse is far too tall for the grave. Sure, it's entire back will be above ground, Big Paul Vickers says. That's gonna look mental. Did nobody think to measure these things? When we shoot them, they'll collapse on top of each other, Dan Ruff whispers to Aaron and Scott. I wouldn't worry about it, he says, with his hand over his mouth. But they're packed in like sardines, Big Paul Vickers says. There's no room to collapse. Watch your mouth, Dan Ruff says to him. These horses are sensitive creatures. Here, he says, and he hands Aaron, Scott and Paul Vickers a handgun each. We're going to (and here he mimes pulling the trigger) at the same time so no one is spooked or put through unnecessary suffering, do you understand me. Yup. Oh shit. But, yes, yup. Aaron has a gun in his hand for only the second time in his life. They are sat on the edge of the grave, the four of them, facing the horses. Stroke their heads and whisper something powerful, Scott Ruff says, and they do just that, and at Dan Ruff's signal they put their guns between the horses' eyes and blow their fucking brains out. Only they stay right where they are. The horses. Big Paul Vickers was right. They're packed in too tightly. The horses just stand there, upright, next to each other, with four exit wounds streaming ghastly horse stuff. Ah, fuck, Dan Ruff says. Someone run down to the van and get me my sledgehammer, he says.

80

Josef Noth is returned to France, finally, as the tanks break from the forest at the point of the Meuse river at Sedan. Small formations of Luftwaffe aircraft criss-cross the sky. The sound of machine-gun reports and ground-to-air artillery. The tanks are late, held up in convoy in the heart of the wood. The German air assault has been going on for five hours now, five non-stop hours of daring dive-bombing raids of the French defences, which seem half constructed, or are they already half destroyed? They are bringing down the antennas on the command posts, sweeping in low, like heroes of the skies. The poetry of war, Josef Noth thinks to himself. Because man has been travelling towards the graves of his companions ever since time began, Josef Noth thinks, as he bears witness to a Stuka pirouetting through a great arc above the near horizon. It drops and descends – a high diver – this lusty surrender to violence and gravity – as the pilot pulls out at the very last minute and an explosion goes up. There is lightning in the black cloud, the very forge of the gods, as a voice comes over the radio, the voice of the lightning, the first forked tongue, and it speaks of certain co-ordinates that have to be, that have got to be, as Josef Noth relays them to Konrad, the driver, whose mother was a ceramicist, when she existed, which is more poetry to be had, and Konrad turns the tank off the road, and down a steep wooded hill, where the trees have been torn apart by the tanks and the gunfire, like the declarative rhythm of a perfect sentence.

81

I have something to tell you, Aaron's father says to him on this bench, in the Botanics, on this perfect autumn day. I came here with something to tell you but now I've forgotten, he says to Aaron. It'll come to me, he says. Wait, I know what it was, he says. Did you hear that they sentenced the killer? What? What killer, Dad? Aaron gets a fright then. Does he know, does he somehow know? The killer who strangled the young boys on TV, his father says. You mean Dennis Nilsen? Yes, that's him. I meant to tell you that they caught him and that he murdered lots of boys and dissected them and took out their organs. That's what you came here to tell me? What? No, don't be silly, Aaron's father says. I'm just letting you know that they caught him. He e-jac-u-lated on his victims, his father says. Dad! Aaron says to him, do we really need to be talking about this? And then he starts crying. Aaron's father starts crying on the bench. My boy, he says. My boy, he keeps repeating through the tears. Your mum was a real bookworm, his father says to him, after he has stopped crying and forgotten what he was crying about in the first place. That's one thing about your mum, he says. She loved her . . . What do you call the outer-space stuff? Science fiction. That's right. She loved her science fiction. It's true, Aaron's mum loved Isaac Asimov and Arthur C. Clarke, that's how Aaron got into it himself. But her favourite was

Bob Shaw. Bob Shaw who wrote *Other Days, Other Eyes*. And now Aaron is remembering slow glass, the idea of slow glass that Bob Shaw came up with, and how his mother would talk about it as her favourite thing ever. Slow glass is glass so thick that light takes years to pass through it. So that you are always seeing something right now that happened long ago.

82

The French line is broken. Josef Noth's panzer convoy speeds through open country. They are headed for the coast, for the English Channel. The intention is to sunder the Allied forces, to drive a wedge between the armies in the south and the north. Radio reception is patchy and sometimes Josef Noth loses touch completely and they are become a ghost column. Where is the enemy, as they pull into the valley of the Somme, at this perfect moment in history, and Konrad agrees. The miracle of the Somme is perfect valley for this ghost column.

83

It's quiz night at the gypsy camp on South Street. This week it's Dan Ruff that is hosting in his caravan. Scott and Aaron are there, as well as Big Paul Vickers and his silent friend The Wee Sponge. Big Paul reads out the first question. What is the biggest carnivore in Great Britain? Wait, Dan Ruff says. I know this. It's not the Pleasure Beach . . . Wait, it's Alton Towers! What the fuck are you talking about? It's a badger. It's a fucking badger that is the biggest carnivore in Britain. Who knew? That's how you get the phrase 'rough as a badger', The Wee Sponge whispers to himself, so as no one else can hear. Question two. The gold from Spanish bullions was melted down for which famous London statues? Wait, wait, Dan Ruff says. I know this one: Greyfriars Bobby! The fuck you on about. Question three. Who are the biggest bookmakers in the UK? Ladbrokes! No, no, wait, William Hill! Question four. Which famous philosopher was buried in a London cemetery in 1883? Marx, Scott says. Aye, but which one? Dan Ruff says to him. What do you mean, which one? Karl. No, no, it must have been Groucho or Harpo, Dan Ruff says. No, it was fucking Karl Marx, Scott says. The one that nobody knows, the one that was just normal? Dan Ruff asks Scott. It was defo Groucho or Harpo, though. It was Karl Marx, Scott is right, Big Paul Vickers says, and Dan Ruff says, you know what? Shove your quiz up your arse. Youse think you know it all, he says, and he storms out of his own caravan in a rage while The Wee Sponge asks everybody how was the Marx Brothers a philosopher and no one pays him any attention whatsoever.

84

Mate, I heard about that boy that got shot in the east end, Luke G.B. Caird says to Aaron. The one with the horses, he clarifies. Then: wasn't that the same place that was listed on that business card that we found? It sounded like the exact spot, Aaron says to him in return. Then he says to Aaron, you wouldn't know anything about that, would you? And Aaron says to him, obviously not. Quite fortuitous, though, innit, Mark C. Burl says. I guess the universe is always making these little adjustments, just to balance things out, Aaron says to him, and he says to Aaron, adjustments, aye, mate, always, mate, he says.

85

The body of a boy is discovered by Project Deep Run. The body of a poor murdered boy is discovered on some waste ground outside Bridge End, near Derry. His genitals have been mutilated with a semi-blunt instrument, possibly a pair of scissors. The boy is naked except for his Action Man underwear, which is twisted around his bruised ankles. Later he will be identified as Thomas Meighan, eight years old, last seen playing in the fields near his home a few days earlier.

86

Josef Noth enters occupied Paris, on leave. It is the same momentous week when the Führer arrives and has those incredible photos taken in front of the Eiffel Tower where even he can hardly believe what has happened, and how easy it has been. Thérèse Barnier has fled the city. Josef Noth visits her apartment only to find it abandoned. There are the ghostly outlines of framed paintings on the walls. In a drawer he finds baby clothes, and he puts them up to his nose and he smells them. He smells his own baby for the first time in its mother's abandoned apartment. Achilles. He goes through the rest of the drawers, as well as Thérèse Barnier's dresser, but fails to uncover any photographs. He still has no idea of what his son looks like. Or, indeed, if either of them are still alive. He decides to visit the apartment of his old friend the Secretary General of the French Ministry of Foreign Affairs, Alexis Leger, aka the poet St-John Perse.

87

The circus is coming to town. Or rather, Dan Ruff and the gypsies are setting it up, on waste ground by the Clyde, between the camp and the Garden Festival, a medium-sized Ferris wheel and dodgems and a shooting gallery, plus a haunted house and a ghost train and a sad old hand-painted merry-go-round with its harnessed horses turning in the same circle forever. Families are arriving from all of the camps in Glasgow, from Carntyne and Milngavie and Shettleston and Easterhouse, to help set it up. The rides have paintings on them of Marilyn Monroe and red Ferraris and of a lizard-creature from *V* in a red jumpsuit and a wrestler with a mullet and mirrored sunglasses and, of course, Shakin' Stevens. It'll be like an unofficial extension of the Garden Festival, Dan Ruff says. We're gonna make a killing. Sorry, he says to Aaron and Scott, that's an unfortunate choice of phrase, considering, he says. Can't believe you got this past the council, Big Paul Vickers says to Dan Ruff. Pulled in a few favours, didn't I? Dan Ruff says. And then he says, wanna meet the star of the show? Dan Ruff takes the three of them into the shipping container, where their beautiful young colt is asleep in a bed of straw. Check this out, he says, and he sits down on the floor next to the colt and it wakes up and looks round at Dan Ruff, at all of them, and Dan Ruff whispers something in its ear. He whispers something in its ear, and it reacts. It gets to its feet, and it looks to Dan Ruff, and Dan Ruff says, come on, let's hear it, he says, and the colt turns back to the three of them and it says, yessss, it neighs, yessss. What?! Yessss, Dan Ruff says, yessss, I have taught this beautiful colt to say 'yes', he says. And that's only the beginning, isn't it, he says to the colt, and the colt just says again, yessss, it neighs, yessss, and it shakes its head from side to side.

Just like dogs, horses understand words. That is why they are man's best friends, Dan Ruff explains, and he shrugs, like it's only natural. Did it actually say anything, though, or did it just make a noise that sounds like 'yes', Big Paul Vickers says, and Dan Ruff says, did you just use words, or did you just make sounds that sound like words, and while you're at it, he says, can you explain to me exactly what the fucking difference is? Make no mistake, this beautiful wee colt is talking. This wee guy is gonna be the star of the show, Dan Ruff says, a magic talking baby-boy horse called Willy. Willy?! What the fuck is going on, Aaron says to Scott Ruff right then, but Scott just shakes his head from side to side and says, yessss, yessss, ha ha.

88

But Alexis Leger has also fled Paris. All that is left are the papers of St-John Perse. Josef Noth has been given special permission to enter the apartment and to inventory his papers. In case of information that could speed the conclusion of the war, which, Josef Noth has decided, is the speed of poetry. On the bookcase there, a copy of St-John Perse's first book, *Éloges*, with its hymns to boyhood. On the mantelpiece, a framed photograph that looks to have melted onto the glass. It shows Leger on horseback, posing for the camera. He has his irritating moustache like Hitler's. He is wearing jodhpurs and riding boots with a buttoned-up tweed blazer, white shirt, black tie and black gloves. In his hand he holds a flail. He looks like a Tarot card, Josef Noth thinks to himself. Josef Noth, who has always identified with The Juggler, thinks that St-John Perse, perhaps, appears as The Chariot. Astride a black horse in a white leather harness, he seems like a vessel for something, something that even now is dimly rising inside of Josef Noth. Josef Noth decides to move into St-John Perse's apartment for the length of his leave in Paris, which is in upheaval and feels like heaven. The first night, on the advice of his Unteroffizier, Josef Noth visits a prostitute at a local brothel and they get wasted together on good French wine and cocaine before he fucks her up her voluptuous arse. Her name is Erithena. Afterwards he says to Erithena, do you know the story of the Nephilim in the Bible, which inevitably Erithena does not. They were giants who were the progeny of human females and angels. He has been reading about them in the papers of St-John Perse. Fallen angels, he reiterates. Better watch you don't get pregnant, he says, and Erithena says, not likely up my voluptuous arse, which is so sexy, in French.

89

In French, it is so sexy, don't you think? Aaron's father Donald is with Mindy in the Paris of his dreams. How come the French are so stylish, he says to Mindy, Aaron's father is really marvelling, they just know how to live, the French, he says, we've got it all wrong back in the UK, he says, here they spend hours over lunch, drinking wine in the afternoon, having naps and reading literature and having great romances and talking about philosophy in cafes, just like we are doing, he says. They've got it all figured out, he says, and he shakes his head and marvels at all of the folly going on back home. Aaron can't ever remember his dad talking about philosophy or having a three-hour lunch. But there he is. Now he is saying that they should head to the Louvre, that they have to see the paintings in the Louvre, but Mindy complains that all they are doing is visiting the same tourist traps. Where is the real Paris, she asks herself, and no one in particular, and Aaron's father says, it's right here, it's here on the streets, and it's in the great galleries and museums also, he says, so let's go and find it. Mindy doesn't seem quite so interested. Museums are boring, she says, and Aaron's dad says, we've got to see the *Mona Lisa* in real life, you can't come to France and not see her famous smile, he says, and he folds a newspaper under his arm and offers his elbow to Mindy, who mutters something that no one can pick up and that Aaron's father is oblivious to anyway. Never mind the *Venus de Milo*, his father says as they get out of their cab on the other side of Paris; he is still talking about the wonderful highlights just up ahead. He gestures towards the building. The greatest art of humanity, he announces, right here. And he walks off without paying, so that Mindy, who thankfully can speak a little bit of French, is left to sort out the fee. Is this the most beautiful woman in the world? Aaron's father Donald asks, stood in front of the famous *Mona Lisa*, in Paris, at last. Mindy says, no way, no way is she the most beautiful woman in the world. But that smile, Donald says, what about that smile? You have to admit that is an enigmatic smile. Doesn't make her any more beautiful, Mindy says. Her skin is sickly, it has a sickly radiance, she says. She looks like an evil witch. No way, Donald says, no way, this is a masterpiece, he says. What is a masterpiece, Mindy says, what does that even mean, a masterpiece? It means the best of the best, Donald says. It means it's the perfect art and nobody could do any better, he says. Surely somebody could do better than painting a sick old witch with an awkward smile, Mindy says. That's a woman who's sat there knowing she is dying, Mindy says. How is that supposed to be a masterpiece? In that case you are not going to like the *Venus de Milo* one bit, Donald says to her, because she has no arms. Can't we go out to a nightclub? Mindy says. Who cares about all these dead and dying masterpieces. How about some glamorous nightlife? OK, Donald says, you mean like a jazz club? I mean like a discotheque, Mindy says, and Donald agrees, but on the condition that they get to visit *The Raft of the Medusa* and *Liberty Leading the People* before they leave.

90

Someone has been brought in for questioning for the murder of Jim Monaghan. The Precious Gift called Jim's wife. Joyce, he said. It's me. And she said, for god's sake, what are you all mixed up in? What's the story with the guy they arrested? The Precious Gift asked her, and she told him that all she knew was that they had arrested a young man with paramilitary connections who was known as The Mole by MI5 on account of the fact he was a double agent and had penetrated deep into the Red Hand Commando. Shit, really? The Precious Gift said, and when Joyce said, what do you mean, he backtracked and said that he was only concerned that it was going to make it difficult to bring this guy to trial. Exactly, she said. My fears exactly, she said. And then he said to her, do you have any reason to believe that a paramilitary organisation would want to kill your husband? and she said, to tell you the truth I have no idea because as far as I knew when he was alive he was a civil servant with a normal job but now it is coming out that he worked in some kind of secret capacity spying on paramilitary targets, so yes, I now think there probably are loads of people that would have killed him had they known, yes. You worked alongside him, she said to The Precious Gift. Surely you know better than any of us. I realise that I barely knew him, The Precious Gift said, yet it appears he knew me so well. Can you think of any reason they would want to kill him, Joyce asked him, rack your brains, she said. He was a good man, my Jim, she said, and The Precious Gift said, he really was. He was an angel, he said. Who knew?

91

Mindy is dressing for her night out with Aaron's father Donald in Paris. She is laid on her back on the bed trying to wiggle into a pair of tight maroon leather trousers. She has on a rock 'n' roll T-shirt that says 'CBGB' on it. She seriously cannot believe that Donald has never heard of CBGB. It's where punk was born in New York, she informs him. Now she is putting red lipstick on her famous lips. She runs a brush through her long red hair. She is wearing the French perfume that Donald bought her, Élégance. Before they go to the restaurant, they stop in for some cocktails at a dimly lit bar on Rue Commines. The handsome bartender comments on Mindy's T-shirt, which she is wearing with a short black leather jacket. A-ha, he says. The Ramones. Patti Smith. Television. Are you into punk rock music? Mindy asks him, and he says, oh yeah, Tom Verlaine is my god. Donald hasn't got a clue but attempts to salvage the situation by asking if Tom Verlaine wasn't named after the famous French poet and Paris habitué (he actually uses that word) Paul Verlaine. Yes, he was, the bartender, whose name is Achilles, confirms. He used to live about fifteen minutes from here, he confirms. Achilles, Mindy marvels, as the bartender fixes their drinks with sexy, flourishing movements. That's an unusual name, she says. I'm the son of a sea nymph, Achilles jokes, what can I say. And, obviously, a great warrior, he says, and he does a mock-flex of his arm muscle so that it is all that Mindy can do to hold herself back from reaching over and squeezing it right there in his tight T-shirt. So, what are you two youngsters up to tonight, he asks Mindy and Donald. Don is taking me to a disco, Mindy says. Achilles says, don't tell me, you are going to Éternité, he says to Mindy, and she giggles and says, wow, how did you know, and Achilles says, I knew it, I knew it, it's just that my friend is a DJ there. Who is your friend, Mindy asks him, and he says, DJ Pierre. No, Mindy says, that's who we have tickets to see! Donald makes some feeble joke about how you don't actually get to see a DJ, I mean they're not much to look at, are they, he says, it's just about the music, he adds, though no one, at this point, is listening. Tell you what, Achilles says. I can get you into the VIP area if you like. No! I just have to make a call, he says, and he hands them their cocktails, two French Connections, and shrugs his muscular shoulders like it is no problem at all.

92

Dad, have you heard of remote viewing? Never heard of him, he says. No, it's a thing, not a person, Aaron says to him. What's it mean? It means you can see anywhere in the world right now from where you are sitting. With your eyes? You can see it. But more like with your mind. I know what I would do if I could see anywhere in the world. What? I'd go back to the day I married your mother and relive it all again. And before Aaron can say, no, Dad, it doesn't work that way, there are limits to what you can see, his father is stood at the altar waiting for the entrance of his bride. Only he is wearing a pair of dark sunglasses, and the priest isn't happy about it at all.

93

And now Aaron's dad Donald is joking about all the reasons you might wear shades to a wedding with his best man, Steven Tate. The wedding is out of doors, in the summer, in a gazebo next to a river. Guests are sat in wooden chairs on the grass. There's Big Billy Schumer and his strange silent wife. Aaron's gran and grandfather, on his mum's side. Aaron's grandfather on his father's. The Collins kids. Jim and Jackie Veitch, from up the road. Uncle Andrew and Aunt Jean. And now the bride appears, and it is that same moment, that same moment of Aaron's mother returning to him in the park in London, all over again. His mother in a vintage white wedding dress with her sister behind her, holding her train, and her friend and bridesmaid, Kathy. It is so strange to see them so young. They are just kids, these two, getting married. A female photographer has been hired to document the wedding and she circles the bride as she approaches. Wow, Aaron's father Donald says, look at that beautiful woman, and Steven Tate makes a joke and puts his hand up to his eyes and stares into the distance and says, where? Aaron's father reaches out with both hands towards his wife-to-be and they look into each other's eyes. By this point even the photographer is crying. The love between Aaron's father and mother right then is so real. They have a cool priest who is dressed down for the occasion. They have agreed to mention God in the vows, but not Jesus, 'so as not to throw the baby out with the bathwater', is how the cool priest put it. For a moment Steven Tate can't find the ring, but it's in his trouser pocket all the time. The priest pronounces them man and wife and they kiss, and everyone cheers, and then they lead everyone to a dining hall at the bottom of the garden where a buffet has been prepared. But not before the speeches. Steven Tate reads a poem, written by Aaron's father. Who knew his father wrote poetry? It is a poem he wrote about his young bride, about when they first met. Aaron's father is acting embarrassed. I didn't know he was going to do this, he protests. The poem is titled (cough) 'A Feather on the Breath of God'.

94

Wise Crow is on the phone. Wise Crow who is in charge of Project Deep Run. Get your arse over here, she says to The Precious Gift. The Mole is singing, and they want operatives from Project Deep Run to assist in the interrogation. I put your name forward, she says, told them you were my trusted right-hand man. And also Ruth Prior. You remember Ruth, Wise Crow says, and of course The Precious Gift remembers Ruth, because she was a completely unremarkable old woman, aside from her visionary abilities, that is. What the fuck, The Precious Gift thinks. How to play this? We have a week or two, Wise Crow says, the three of us. Book your ferry. The Precious Gift hangs up and immediately calls Joyce Monaghan. Joyce, he says, I'm coming to Derry. I'm on the team questioning The Mole, he says. And she says, bury him, bury that fucking bastard Mole and do the right thing for the memory of my angel Jim, is what she says.

95

You should see the state of this funfair, it's an absolute tragic joke, this fucking funfair. How is a half-rusted rollercoaster with a painting of a clown that looks like John Wayne Gacy and a single loop-the-loop going to compete with the Coca-Cola Rollercoaster next door? How the fuck does it look like John Wayne? Big Paul Vickers says. John Wayne Gacy, I says, Scott Ruff says, he's a serial killer that dressed like a clown to rape and murder young boys. Fucking hanging is too good for these bastards, Dan Ruff says. Giving fucking clowns a bad name with children. Are you sure you actually have permission from the council for this? Scott Ruff says to his dad, Mad Dan Ruff. Why would they let us set up in direct competition to the Garden

Festival? The crowds are here anyway, is Dan Ruff's logic, it's not as if we're attracting them somewhere else. It's just spreading the flavour, he says. Anyway, he says, it wasn't permission so much as they said they would turn a 'blind eye' if we set up. I says to them, youse need to include the gypsy community in this multicultural celebration, and what better way than letting us do what we do best. Which is risking people's lives on barely functioning fairground equipment. Only joking, Dan Ruff says, some of it works fine. And besides, he says, we're the only ones with a talking horse. I've written to the *Guinness Book of Records*, he says. I says to them that they should send someone over to verify the first-ever talking horse. How is that a record, though? Big Paul Vickers says. What do you mean, Dan Ruff says, it's a talking fucking horse, that's record-breaking right there. How is it a record, though? The first person to run a mile isn't a record, it would be the person who ran it the fastest that would be a record. You would need to have lots of horses start speaking and then one be the best at it. The first person to run a mile the fastest is the same as the first horse to ever speak, that means it beat all the other horses to it, Dan Ruff shrugs, like it's that's simple, before yelling at some kids to get down off that fucking scaffolding before someone gets hurt.

96

Achilles has made the call. I'll no doubt see you there, he says, after I finish work. Have a great evening, he says, as he waves Aaron's father Donald and Mindy off, while ferociously shaking a cocktail mixer. That guy was so cool, Mindy says. And what a name, she says, Achilles. I'm sure like the original Achilles he has his own fatal flaws, Donald says, and Mindy says, well, he did say he was half

German. It is raining as their taxi speeds through Paris towards Éternité, so that all of the lights look fuzzy and underwater, like they are already remembering this trip that they will never forget. The nightclub has a rope and red carpet outside. Just like in old Hollywood, Mindy says. This is so my style, she says. It's such an odd feeling, to be remembering something as it unfolds: the man on the door with a pencil moustache and beautiful cologne and a clipboard who confirms their names and then escorts them to another beautifully dressed young man with a dark-blue suit and a quiff like Elvis, the young Elvis, the hungry Elvis; the thick curtains that open onto blinding white light, just like the club promised; the roped-off area, raised, next to the dancefloor, and with another handsome man in a waistcoat and rolled-up sleeves standing guard. The waitresses are in dress shirts and leather miniskirts with high heels and crimped hair with coloured headbands. Mindy is in her element. They are playing Donna Summer, 'I Feel Love'. Before she sits down, Mindy makes this move, this one move that Donald will never forget, you can see the way he looks at her as she puts her arms in the air, her handbag around her shoulder, and swivels and pops her hips to the music, her eyes closed, for that split second she is transfigured, he is in the presence of the primal energy of the goddess, the first one to ever pop it in celebration of herself, and with it she has driven a little kink into reality, so that it will never be the same again.

97

The body of a boy is discovered by Project Deep Run. He is laid in the snow like a starfish. His clothes are strewn artfully around him. The snow is streaked blood-red. It looks like a painting, from above, The Precious Gift says. Or more like an assemblage. What the fuck's an assemblage? Wise Crow asks him. It comes from Joseph Beuys, The Precious Gift says. Even though I don't rate Beuys's assemblages like I rate George Herms's or Wallace Berman's or Bruce Conner's, he says. Beuys asked, how fine could you draw the line? Between what? Wise Crow asks him. Between art and real life, how fine can you draw the line? And one answer was assemblages. Assemblages are poetic combinations of found – or, more properly, discarded – objects which were put together in such a way – sometimes in a box or in a window – that created a sort of uncanny delight in proximity. Like what? Like, say, a small brass model of a hare, and a marble. In a box. Confronting each other. In a shabby box with all of its patina streaked and fading. Or, like, a bunch of rusty nails tied with old string and hung from a painted metal hook. It is something akin to resurrection, was how Beuys described it. Beuys said: art aspires not to immortality but to eternity. Or, like, pieces of an old fire alarm mounted in a wooden frame just so. Or like a strange, mummified doll, its bandages confused with cobwebs, sat in an old wooden highchair. Or. Or a faded calendar stuck to a thick piece of wood with splotches of old paint and oil stains like it had lived on the wall of a garage in the east end for a lifetime. Or. Or a poor murdered boy in the snow, his belongings scattered this way and that? Yes. A boy whose name is Peter McKenna who disappeared while making his way home to Pennyburn, in Derry. A boy who was anally raped in the snow and whose eyes were put out with sticks, whose eyes had broken sticks in them. A boy who was stabbed thirteen times in the chest in a frenzied attack. A sadist, Wise Crow says. Or a naïve artist, The Precious Gift replies. And Wise Crow just stares at him, like that.

98

Josef Noth spends his days lounging round St-John Perse's apartment and reading his poetry (of which there are cratefuls), his evenings fucking and drinking and drugging with Erithena (who has no clue about poetry whatsoever), and his nights in fevered dreams of rivers, of being pursued to the banks of uncrossable rivers, though when Josef Noth wakes up he recalls them as inconsolable rivers, as if the rivers were crying tears from the beginning of time and could not be solaced, rivers as wide as the Danube, and as treacherous as the Meuse, and that he was being pursued to their very limits. One night he discovers a false bottom in a crate labelled with a piece of paper with a single handwritten word on it: 'Monde'. Inside, there is a map. A map of China. Circled is the location of a Taoist pagoda, outside Peking. He lets out a gasp and for some reason goes to the window and looks this way and that into the street, as if at any moment he might be discovered. Nothing but soldiers carousing with their sweethearts and the movement of legions through the streets. He thinks of the *Anabasis*, these movements across time, the endless cycles of conquest and defeat, and he has to wonder whether the Taoist pagoda, outside Peking, isn't, in fact, the very pagoda where Perse wrote his *Anabasis*, and from where he claimed you could see all of the world, all of time and space, as though stepping outside of it. Whether in fact this map doesn't reveal the exact location of the centre of the world. And he makes up his mind, that after all this war is over, he will travel there, and recall all of this, from that same still point in tranquillity.

99

The Precious Gift arrives in Derry and checks in to a hotel under the name Lucas Black, a pseudonym. At reception there is a drunk man with a bottle of white wine that he needs a corkscrew for. What do you mean, you don't have a corkscrew, he is saying, this is a hotel, you must have a corkscrew. The guy has no top on, bare feet and a pair of pyjama bottoms like he has come straight from the bed in his room. The receptionist, a blonde with a sunbed tan and heavy make-up, is explaining that the kitchen is closed and locked up and that she has no access to a corkscrew. What about the bar? There is no bar in this hotel, she explains, as you well know, and she bends over to take some sheets out of a photocopier. Her blouse has come untucked, and it rides up her back. The Precious Gift gets a glimpse of a tattoo, some kind of Native American symbol, it looks like. It is sexy and cheap. The drunk turns to The Precious Gift. What a fucking joke this place is, he says. I've got my girlfriend up the stair, he explains. The Precious Gift asks him to give him the bottle. I'll open it for you, he says, and he takes one of his boots off. He slides the bottle into the boot and taps it forcefully against the wall six or seven times. When he takes the bottle out, the cork is half popped and he puts it in his mouth, draws the rest of it out with his teeth, and spits the cork in an arc across reception. Genius, the drunk topless guy responds. You've saved my weekend, he says, and even the receptionist applauds. Now, what can I do for you, she says. I'm booked in under the name . . . Lucas Black, he says, nearly giving himself away. That's fine, she says. In the distance the voice of the drunk guy echoes along the corridors: Arlene, Arlene! You should've seen it! The receptionist wears a badge that says 'Michelle' on it. You're staying with us for a week, is that right? That's correct,

Michelle, The Precious Gift says, and he feels devious using her name without her offering it. And what are you in Derry for, might I ask, Michelle says, business or pleasure? Hopefully a little bit of both, The Precious Gift can't help responding, and Michelle laughs a cute little laugh. That was some display, she says, where did you get your skills, she says, and The Precious Gift says, a friend taught me, I never knew it would come in so handy in Derry. Mind you, she's from here, he says to Michelle, so she would know. Yeah, that's the kind of skills they prize round here, she laughs. Do you need a map, she says, and The Precious Gift says, yes, I'll take one, he says, although I used to work here, he says. She gives him his key. Second floor, she tells him, the stairs are over there, she says. Reception is open till eleven p.m., she says, breakfast is served seven till nine a.m. What are your plans tonight? The Precious Gift can't help from asking. Nothing, why? Michelle says. Just wondering, The Precious Gift says, but then he puts it out of his mind and takes the stairs to his room, a small room with a stained blue carpet, two single beds and a window that looks out on an abandoned pub across the way. The Precious Gift looks closer. In the window of the pub there appears to be a dead bird. It looks like a raptor, a falcon, lying there, dead, in the window. I hope that's not a terrible omen, he thinks, and he picks up the phone and calls Joyce Monaghan and invites her out to dinner. In the room next door, through the wall, someone appears to be watching the horse racing. They are repeating the name of the horse. Pegasus, Pegasus; isn't that the horse that flies? Then he sits down at the desk facing the window, unfolds the map that Michelle gave him, and runs his fingers over it like it's Braille, like he can feel the very brogue of the streets, the very cut of their jib. So that he appears as an angel above them.

100

Steven Tate reads 'A Feather on the Breath of God', a poem by Aaron's father, at the wedding of Aaron's mum and dad outdoors, next to a river, a river where they might even have caught the salmon for the cold salmon mayonnaise on the buffet, his father's favourite dish, which he said should always be eaten by a romantic river, this poem about how love is so light on its feet and which references the twelfth-century German mystic the Sibyl of the Rhine, the Prophetess of the Great River, Hildegard of Bingen, who believed herself to be, or longed to be, a feather on the breath of God. All the while the band are setting up in the background and they are noisy and joking around and already eyeing the wedding cake and casing the buffet and generally upsetting the atmosphere. Donald worries that they are drowning out his words, the words of this immortal, forgotten poem, now, but his new wife just holds his hand and stares into his eyes, and says, poetry, wow, I didn't know you wrote poetry, and he says, it was mostly before I met you, Steven and I thought we were poets in our twenties, he says, think about it, poets in their twenties, he says, and he rolls his eyes, he is awkward, he didn't know Steven was going to do this, but Elizabeth says, it was meant to be, look, and she points to Steven, who is folding the poem neatly and replacing it in his top pocket, and the friends and family all around, sat out on the grass on folding chairs, all of whom are applauding, and the wedding photographer, who once again is fighting back tears, and it is as if the poem was written for precisely this moment, or more, as if this very moment could not exist without the writing of this poem, it is as if all writing were prophetic, and necessary, is what is dawning on Donald, thanks to Elizabeth, at the moment of their marriage, co-arising, is that the word, Donald thinks, a Buddhist term, back then when all sorts of words were available to him, or more interested in showing up for him, put it that way, sat on this park bench with him, now, here where he is left with the very dregs of vocabulary, the smallest words, the most superficial descriptions, the broken building blocks of ingress, is what it sounds like Muntu is singing, 'the broken building blocks of ingress', again and again, like Muddy Waters, as the band soundcheck, a black blues band that Aaron's mum and dad loved and went to see a few times when they first got together and liked to party, called Ensemble Muntu Blues Band. The first dance – the band have learnt it specially – is 'Forever Young' by Bob Dylan.

101

The Precious Gift arrives at the restaurant early, which is one of his foibles, of which there are many, including never wearing shoes (boots only) because he hates to expose his ankles, and only wearing brown boots, or tan boots, never black, even then. Only wearing slightly flared trousers. Never straight-leg. A scarf, regulation, de rigueur, always. Or at least most of the time. Never wearing T-shirts, only shirts. Never being late, always early. Having a bath every evening at 6 p.m. Never a shower. Red wine only, never white. Never owning a TV. Hating curtains. Blinds only. Never draining a bottle of milk. Always leaving dregs. Always reading omens too, which is why that damn peregrine falcon, is what it turns out to be, that damn corpse of the peregrine falcon in the window of the abandoned pub across the way, is really getting to him. How did it get in there? And how did it die? The Precious Gift crossed the road to view it up close before he walked over to the restaurant, an Italian joint called Tony's, Tony's Trattoria, and the falcon lay there, stiff, staring up at him in the dusty window of this abandoned pub that looked like it had been abandoned since time immemorial, and the falcon, the bird that The Precious Gift identified as a peregrine falcon, appeared to have no wound on its body whatsoever, as if it had somehow got itself trapped in there and flown around in despair until it finally keeled over and died through the promise of all that now-inaccessible sky. Joyce Monaghan enters the restaurant as if she is escaping a storm, as if she is seeking desperate shelter, is how The Precious Gift reads it, at first. She looks around the restaurant, trying to spot him. There he is. She visibly relaxes. She is wearing a black leather dress with a zip up the front. I didn't know there were two Tony's Trattorias in Derry, she says to the guy at the door, who takes her coat, and who turns out to be Tony himself. There's only one Tony's Trattoria, he says. How could there be two Tony's Trattorias in Derry, he says. That makes no sense, he says. I just went to it, she says. I got a taxi there, she says. Nonsense, he says. Anyway, he says, as if dismissing the ramblings of a lunatic, you're here now. At the one and only Tony's Trattoria, he says, this guy who looks like a beefy John Travolta who has been dragged through the divorce courts. I'm not kidding, she says – sorry, hi, so nice to see you – I'm not kidding, she says, I went all the way to the other side of Derry to the wrong place. I like to be early, she says. I'm sorry if I kept you waiting, she says. The Precious Gift leaps up and pulls out her chair and seats her like a gentleman. Me too, he says, and she says, no, you went to the other Tony's Trattoria as well?! No, The Precious Gift clarifies, I like to be early. Me too, she says. I hate latecomers. What are you drinking? she asks The Precious Gift, and he says, it's Bushmills. What's that, Joyce asks him. It's Irish whiskey, he says, secretly delighted at how naïve Joyce is. I'll have one, she says. I've never had an

Irish whiskey, she says. The Precious Gift finds it attractive. Your husband liked a drink, he tells her. Then he retracts that and says, he was a good man to have a drink with, is what I mean, in order to clarify that he is not suggesting her husband was some mad boozer. He never drank at home, she says. He liked to be 'up with the birds'. He was a hell of a man with a hangover, she says. Forget it, she says. So, The Precious Gift says. Are you happy they caught him? And Joyce Monaghan, whose silhouette is playing, huge, along the wall of this Tony's Trattoria, flickering across the wall of this mysteriously doubled restaurant in Derry, thanks to candles, and the setting, and the subject matter, and the time of day, and the position of the stars, inevitably, who knows, the widow Joyce Monaghan says, I no longer think it is possible to be happy. But I do think it is always possible to be unhappier, is how she puts it, as this shape like a witch or a spider, or even worse a falcon trapped behind glass, rises up on the wall behind her.

102

It's the night before the grand opening of the funfair when The Lark starts talking for real. Willy is no name for a horse, Aaron said, so Scott Ruff came up with The Lark from a poem he had read. Aaron and Scott Ruff are sat with him by the edge of the Clyde, passing a joint back and forth, The Lark stood there staring off across the water, implacable, the way that horses are, the dark, stinky water of the Clyde. That little patch on his nose. What must it be like, Scott Ruff says, when you hit that water for the first time. A suicide leaping from a bridge, I mean. When it catches you in its current, and you know that's you. Done for. No way back. What do you think happens? Are you conscious and for how long? How cold must it be? Maybe if you're lucky you get your head smashed off some piece of industrial debris and you don't remember a damn thing. Don't they say something about a moment of clarity? A peaceful moment when the water is outside you and inside you perfectly? After the choking and the feeling like your lungs will burst, you would imagine. This strange feeling of equilibrium, you would think. Thinking about this kind of stuff is like invoking fear, Scott Ruff says with a shudder. I'm still living in fear, Aaron admits to Scott Ruff. I'm still living with the fear of god that I'll get done for murder. We would have heard something by now, Scott Ruff says. Unless, he says. Unless, what?! Aaron says to him. Unless they're playing the long game, he says. Don't say that, Aaron says to him. Unless they are watching us right now. Don't the police have these remote viewers working for them? The police don't believe in them, Aaron says. The public wouldn't take them seriously. Plus, you get enough aggro when you suggest sticking up a camera in the street, never mind this all-seeing eye. Remote viewing is for the more esoteric arms of the secret service. You have nothing to fear, a voice says. What? Aaron asks Scott Ruff, what did you just say? I didn't say anything, Scott Ruff says. Again: you have nothing to fear. Holy shit. Did The Lark just say that? Did your dad teach him to say that? Then The Lark says, unmistakably: you did. Did it just say, you did, Aaron asks Scott Ruff, because they are so freaked out that they can't bear to turn their heads and look at a colt talking like a terrible human. You made me speak, it says, The Lark says, again, and Aaron and Scott Ruff look at each other and slowly turn their heads towards this talking horse. See if my dad has put it up to this, Scott Ruff says, I'm going to fucking murder him. How? Aaron says to the horse, to The Lark, now. How did we make you speak? By performing the appropriate actions, it says, in this awful, elongated voice that is still, unmistakably, human, even as it sounds like it is coming into being one terrible syllable at a time. What actions? The sacrifice of a child, it says. The conceiving of a foal, it says. The murder and burial of four bright horses, it says. You mean like in a ritual? Scott Ruff says. You mean like in a satanic ritual? Essentially. What a weird way for a horse to talk, Scott Ruff says. 'Essentially'. Fucking hell, that means magic is real, Aaron says to this talking horse. What about losing an eye? Scott Ruff asks it. Is that part of it? That is irrelevant, it says. This horse is a wise guy, Scott Ruff says. But the horse doesn't even deign to respond. Then it says, tell me what you want to know. What? Tell me what you want to know, it says. Otherwise, why summon a prophetic horse, it adds. So much, Aaron says, to this talking foal named The Lark, stood there in front of this tormented river that runs through the heart of Glasgow. So much, Aaron says, to this inexplicable talking horse.

103

Aaron's father orders champagne, a cooler of champagne, and he sticks some francs in the waiter's side pocket. Add a rose, he says, under his breath, but Mindy isn't listening anyway, she is in heaven, gazing around her at the beautiful and fashionable crowd that dances on the top floor of Éternité. It just smells heavenly, don't you think? Thank you, Don, she says. I'm having the time of my life, she says, and she leans over and kisses Donald on the cheek and leaves a perfect lipstick shape there. The warm-up DJ is playing new-wave classics. Wait, this is my favourite song, Mindy says. Dance with me, Don, she says, and she grabs him by the arm and leads him onto the dancefloor, where they squeeze their way past dancers in turquoise off-the-shoulder dresses and satin shirts and silver heels, through clouds of perfume – it is true that it smells heavenly – in order to dance to the music. The song is 'Teenage Kicks' by The Undertones.

104

The band strike up the first chords of 'Forever Young' by Bob Dylan and invite the newlyweds to the centre of the dancefloor. As Muntu leans into the microphone, he says, that looks like some fine cake, be sure to leave me some, y'all. And then he says, this is a song about eternity, he says. Then he purses his lips and blows into the microphone, softly, as if he is snuffing out a candle, and making a wish.

105

Are you into chakras? Joyce Monaghan asks The Precious Gift, after the waiter takes the menus away. Joyce has ordered linguine alle vongole with melon and Parma ham to start. The Precious Gift has ordered veal saltimbocca with minestrone. Chakras? Yes, they're energy centres that run up and down the spine, Joyce says. I know them, The Precious Gift says. Well, I'm really into them, Joyce says. Sometimes they can become blocked. Or confused, more like confused, muddied, really, might be the best word. My chakras have been in a mad state, as you can believe. Like a filthy aquarium, she says. Aren't the chakras related to the planets? The Precious Gift asks her. Yes, she says. Like, Saturn is your third eye and Jupiter is your crown. The sun is your solar plexus, obviously. At the base of the spine, it's Mars. Typical, Mars, at the base of everything, The Precious Gift says, and Joyce says, what, what do you mean? She is naïve, this Joyce, The Precious Gift is thinking, it's easy to see how you could fall in love with her, he is thinking already, either that or she would drive you mad, he thinks, and he says to her, war, the god of war, at the bottom of everything, and she says, oh, right, I get it, she says, it's certainly at the bottom of Derry, I'll tell you that. And at the bottom of my husband's murder. So, does it look like he was killed by paramilitaries or by the government, in this case, do you think? Did you ever go birdwatching with your husband? The Precious Gift asks her, why did he ask that then. Changing the subject. I did when we first met, Joyce says. We went on some birding and camping trips together. But I hate spiders, so that was a problem. I hate sleeping outdoors like that. To me it's a torment. I preferred to just go on a walk with my Jim. My Jim, she calls him. And not to be stopping every two minutes to identify some bird in a bush. So it became a solitary thing for him, in the end. Or sometimes with friends. Male friends. Like yourself. I never went on birding trips with Jim, The Precious Gift says to Joyce, and Joyce says, that's a shame, even as The Precious Gift is thinking, well, it's a shame you didn't go on more of them yourself, but instead he says, I think Jim had a remarkable impact on many people's lives, so many people we will never even know. Right then some clown in a red jumper stares in the window from the street. He casts his eye around the restaurant, then walks away. You mean through his job, Joyce says. Yes, The Precious Gift is forced to pretend, yes, he says, through his job, he says, keeping it vague. That's some consolation, isn't it, for a small life lived. It is, The Precious Gift says, and Joyce says, god, this melon's lovely, as the restaurant dims the lights. This is so lovely, Joyce repeats. I've missed this, she says. The waiter brings the wine. I don't know anything about wine, Joyce says. Do you think that's bad? What? Not knowing about wine. Not at all, The Precious Gift says. No one can know everything about everything. Everyone has to specialise.

That's the thing, though, because outside of chakras and astrology and archiving I've never really specialised in anything much, she says. Sometimes I feel that I need one of those electro-shock therapies. Why? To shock me back to life. I'm just finding it harder to feel, or to have enthusiasm, as I get older, Joyce admits. Even with my Jim, she says. There was a day when if you told me this would happen to me, how my life would be torn apart like this, I would have told you that I could not survive something like that. Now I am the proof all too well that I can, she says. It's disappointing to know that nothing can completely destroy you, she says. Look at me, she says. Enjoying this lovely melon, she says. What chakra might be responsible for that? The Precious Gift asks Joyce, and she looks to the side while she chews her food. They're all mixed up, she says finally, they're all confused. My Mars is in Uranus, she says. And then she says, sorry, you see what I mean? I'm awful. This is the best veal ever, The Precious Gift says, as they tuck into their mains. Isn't veal cruel? Joyce asks him. Isn't it something about a cruel process? she asks him. And then she laughs and with her smoky made-up eyes she says, what do I care, what do I care about cruel veal. Listen to me, she says. Ridiculous. The guy with the red jumper appears outside on the street again, and this time he is shouting, he is screaming and shouting into the night, Eleanor Rigby, you bitch! Everyone in the restaurant, which is really just a handful of tables, but still, everyone bursts out laughing. Eleanor Rigby, Joyce says, that's a good name for a song. What the fuck is going on, The Precious Gift is thinking, and are you even serious, but he just keeps laughing all the harder despite it. Do you think if you are born a woman, you will come back as a man? Joyce asks The Precious Gift. Joyce is drunk by this point. The Precious Gift asks Tony to call them a taxi. What's your address, Joyce, he asks her. I can drop you off on the way. Can you smell that? Joyce asks him in the taxi. That crazy smell, she says. Like lemons. It's true now that she says it: The Precious Gift can smell lemons. The driver, a young man with short greasy hair and a black tracksuit, puts on a cassette and starts to nod along in an unexpectedly syncopated style. Is this jazz? Joyce asks him. It's jazz, yes, Ornette Coleman, the young man says. I don't get it, Joyce says. What? Jazz. I don't get it. What's to get? the young man says. You're only creating barriers that don't exist, he says. I'm from Derry, she says. Of course I am. And the young man says, that's a good one, and he laughs at that. The car pulls into a cul-de-sac of bland modern houses. I'm just at the end, Joyce says. Then she asks The Precious Gift if he wouldn't like to have a cheeky nightcap, is how she puts it, and The Precious Gift agrees. That's for the jazz, Joyce says, as she insists on paying for the cab herself. The living room is so ordinary. Did an angel really live here? A cream leather couch and a single cream leather armchair next to an electric fire. A TV on top of three retractable white plastic tables. Cream curtains. We know how The Precious Gift feels about curtains. Above the fireplace there is some framed sheet music for a piece entitled 'Dark Lochnagar'. Take a seat, Joyce orders The Precious Gift, and he does as he is told and sits down on the leather armchair. When Joyce reappears, she is holding two clear plastic dildos in her hand. Here, she says, and she hands them to The Precious Gift. Then she lowers the straps on her leather dress and takes her tits out, and holds them there, displaying them. Her nipples are dark brown. She has freckles on her chest. Beneath one of her breasts there is the beginnings of a tattoo. Then she puts the knee of her right leg between the legs of The Precious Gift and puts her tits in his mouth. The Precious Gift closes his eyes and kisses and licks these perfect tits, these amazing tits, it has to be said. Then Joyce stands up and unzips her black leather dress, from the bottom to the waist, and pulls her skirt to one side. She isn't wearing any panties. Her beautiful black bush. She spreads her legs, still standing, while The Precious Gift fucks her with one dildo, then the other, bigger one, until she comes, trembling. Then she takes the dildo in her mouth, and she says, tastes like lemons, from the Mediterranean.

106

The body of a boy is discovered by Project Deep Run. In the grass by the river. In the grass by the river in Derry there is the body of a naked boy with a pair of tights over his head. Why is there a pair of tights on his head? Why is there a hole in the side of his body? Why is his leg broken and the bone protruding? Why is his shin at a terrible angle to his thigh? Why are his teeth missing? Why is his underwear balled up in his throat? Why are his genitals bloody? Why has he shat himself? And why has no one come forward to claim him? Why has he never been named?

107

Josef Noth applies for a transfer to military intelligence so that he can remain in Paris. He makes his case at a meeting with his Unteroffizier, Fritz Weizel. Isn't this incredible, Fritz says to him as they make their way to a small cafe for drinks and to talk it over. The streets of Paris lined with swastikas, Fritz marvels. Didn't Hitler say he went to his fate with the certainty of a sleepwalker? Josef Noth says. The fate of the Führer and the fate of his people are one, Fritz agrees. Europe is ours, he says, as they take their seats. They are in full uniform, and a young French girl brings them menus. Fritz asks for 'good French wine' and 'good French cheese' and then he says, the French whores are the greatest in the world, we should ship them all back with us, he says, that's a war worth fighting right there, he laughs. To think we have been putting up with German whores this whole time. If war hadn't broken out, we might never have known. I mean, don't get me wrong, he says. German whores are filthy. In the best possible way. And if that's your taste, then fine. But with French whores there is an art of love, not the simple debasement that the German whore offers. I couldn't agree more, Josef Noth says. French women are the greatest lovers, he says. But then, I knew that already. I had a lover in the city, he tells Fritz. Before the war. She gave birth to a son that I have never seen. So, you want a post in intelligence in order to track your own family down? No, no, Josef Noth reassures him, not in the slightest. I have discovered the most remarkable archive in the home of Alexis Leger and I believe, if given time, the consolidating of this archive could seriously contribute to the war effort. After all, he says, Leger was a major figure in the French government up until yesterday. That's how it feels, doesn't it, like only yesterday Europe was a hodgepodge of sovereign states, Fritz says. Now, already, it is a Reich. My big worry is that, along with the Germanisation of France, Josef Noth says, we might see the homogenisation of the French whore. That would be a tragedy, Fritz agrees, and he laughs and says, now I see your motivation, you want to be around for the twilight of the French whores. He laughs again. I mean, it's understandable, he says. Right then the young French girl arrives with a selection of cheese and a baguette and the two men turn silent, as they watch her open the bottle of wine with a little knife she has connected to the thin belt on her skirt with a piece of string. Her skin is so pale, her hair so dark. What is your name, Fritz asks her, and she says, Justine, and Fritz mishears and says, Justin, a boy's name, Justin, and she says, no, Justine, as in the Marquis de Sade, she says, as she pours Fritz a little wine to taste. Wonderful wine, he says. Pour away. He stares at her in fascination. What did she say about this marquis, Fritz asks him once she is gone, and Josef Noth says, he was a writer, and a libertine, who experienced joy through pain and suffering, and Fritz bursts out laughing and says, see, already, the Germanisation of the women has begun, and Josef Noth laughs too, or at least pretends to, because his laugh is stifled, his laugh feels like the kind of laugh you might fake when you're really not sure what you think about anything anymore. Who in their right mind would ever want to see the world remade in their own image, he thinks, as he looks over at the French girl named after a book by a famous sadist, while she slices fruit with such concentration, as she carves delicate curls of orange peel that she then threads through green olives to serve on a toothpick in a cocktail, and he cannot imagine, for a second, what her interior life might be like, and for a terrible second, a second that feels like being suspended over endless depths, he asks himself if there is any interior life at all, and if perhaps the spaces between us are gifts, merciful gifts, that this other, that we seek to vanquish, or incorporate, in love or in war, was the only thing stopping us falling, tumbling, into the empty mirror of ourselves.

108

There had been constant arguments as to how to bill the funfair. The Authentic Funfair Experience was at first favoured by Dan Ruff, who made the point that travellers had invented funfairs, not banks and corporations or Scottish local councils. Then why not call it The Original

Funfair Experience, Big Paul Vickers suggested, but Dan Ruff nixed it, no, 'authentic' is deeper, he said, it's the real thing, but then he said, wait a minute, it's coming to me, and he said, The First Garden, he said, you know, like the Garden of Eden, that'll draw them in, but when Big Paul Vickers pointed out that there were no garden attractions per se, Dan Ruff said that he took his point, he did take his point, and so what about . . . True Gypsy Funfair, and Big Paul Vickers said, go easy on the 'gypsy', I say, because a gypsy funfair is synonymous with a dangerous funfair, a fly-by-night funfair, a mechanically unsound funfair, a potentially litigious funfair, let's face it, and Dan Ruff said that he took his point, fair point, he said, what about The Lark's Playpark? Not descriptive enough. OK, fair point, in that case how about The Lark's Old-Fashioned Funfair? Nah, Big Paul Vickers said, sounds like it'll be coconut stalls and a raffle. What about The Lark's Garden, you have to admit that sounds like a good time? It's not descriptive enough, Big Paul Vickers said. We need to have some kind of intimation of what they might expect, not just a garden, and Dan Ruff said, I don't know, I'm beginning to think a poetic approach is the way. You're a literalist, he said to Big Paul Vickers, you need some poetry in your soul, Dan Ruff said to himself, as much as to anyone else, and then he said, The Lark's Pleasure Garden, come on, who could resist that? And Big Paul Vickers said, it sounds like a whorehouse, and Dan Ruff clapped his hands and said, now we're talking. A bunch of birds on the game, Dan Ruff said. The perfect complement to the Garden Festival.

109

Mindy and Aaron's father Donald return to their table to find a bottle of wine and a rose, a single red rose in an elegant thin vase. It's for you, baby, Donald says, and he pulls out Mindy's seat to let her sit down. A server brings them the menu and asks if they will be dining tonight. In that case here are our specials, he says, and he sits a small blackboard on a chair next to the table on which the specials are written in chalk. How wonderful, Mindy says. I've never seen that before. That's how they do it in Paris, Donald says. They know how to live, on the continent, he adds. Fancy some oysters? Donald asks Mindy, but she says, oh no, I can't eat oysters, she says. You never know with oysters. Plus, their texture, she says. No. What about snails? Donald says. What about snails in their shells with garlic butter, he says. That's what it says right there, he says, and he points to the chalkboard where it says 'Escargots en Coquille au Beurre à l'Ail'. No, not for me, Mindy says, and the way she takes her hair and tucks it behind her ear means that Donald will forgive her anything – those beautiful lips from the adverts, that smile – even her conservative tastes, which in real life, and not in Paris, Donald actually shares. OK, he says. You choose. I like it when you make decisions, Mindy says, and he says, in that case, steak frites, how about we just get steak frites served in a little pool of pink blood, he says, what about that, some moutarde on the side, he says, and she says, great but only I can't have my steaks rare, I like it at least medium, and Donald goes to say, this is France, they will laugh you out of the restaurant for overcooking a steak, but instead he says, OK, honey, OK, sweetie-pie, if that's what you want, after all, this is our trip out of time, he says, as if they have literally entered a parallel dimension for which there is no measurement of duration, as if this little trip is a kind of side-hall off eternity, as opposed to Éternité itself. Different rules apply, Donald says, and you can see he is chiding himself, he is chiding himself for importing judgement and taste and manners into the vestibule of eternity, where no words and ideas, except the very heaven of what is, should apply.

110

The Precious Gift returns to his hotel in the early hours of the morning. Joyce asked him to leave. She said that she was weird about waking up with people in the morning and being seen fully naked. There's no one on the streets at this time. The Precious Gift crosses in front of a betting shop with metal grilles on the windows. He cuts over some waste ground and then nips through a residential area, a scheme. Derry is taking shape in his mind once more. It is becoming the shape of his brain. He remembers this park, up ahead, a park where he would sometimes take lunch and visit the church next door, and he remembers how unhappy he was in Derry, working that job, sitting in that church, the things he had seen, or, more properly, the things he had turned a blind eye to. Right then he hears a car approaching. He looks around and sees it is approaching with its headlights off. It is so silent, in the dark, it is almost as if it is gliding. The car matches pace with The Precious Gift, staying just behind him. He looks back several times but can't make out who is in the car or how many. Keep walking, he says to himself, you're a few minutes away tops. No matter what you do, don't run. He turns onto the street where his hotel is, at the corner with the abandoned pub. He stops to look in the window, to check that the dead, perfectly preserved peregrine falcon is still in the window. It is. He crosses at the lights and as he unlocks the hotel door the car stops outside, for just a second, not long enough for The Precious Gift to look round, before accelerating off. Probably an opportunist paramilitary patrol, he thinks to himself, his old Derry way of thinking is returning too, so that when he gets to his room he slides the desk up against the door and then creeps to the window, where he parts those hated curtains just an inch, and looks out on the empty street. No one there. No one but this dead raptor on its side staring at him with glassy eyes and without a hint of putrefaction. He lies back on his bed and strokes his cock while thinking about screwing Joyce Monaghan in her leather dress, he strokes his cock in a desultory fashion, it has to be said, before falling asleep and dreaming of a goddess with bird feathers and talons and a vagina stuffed with twigs and twine and soft foliage like a nest. In the morning, he can still smell her on his fingers. He wakes in time for breakfast and as he is crossing reception he spots Michelle behind the desk. How long has that dead bird been lying there behind the window of that pub across the way, he asks her, and she says that she has never noticed it before. I've no idea, she says, and she shrugs her shoulders. There is a television behind the desk that appears to be showing aerial footage of Northern Ireland accompanied by the sound of fiddles and pipes. What are you watching? he asks her, and she says, I'm not watching it. It's a tourist thing. For the tourists, she says, and then she says, it is beautiful, though, this country, you have to admit, she says. A savage beauty, he says, and Michelle doesn't respond. In the dining area there are five hotplates: eggs, bacon, sausages, mushrooms and beans. Cold toast in a rack. There is also a soup. Soup for breakfast, The Precious Gift thinks, why not, and he helps himself to this clear broth with herbs that actually tastes wonderful. There is one other person in the room, sat at a table on his own, an old man with a bald head covered in liver spots, who is reading a book while burping and eating a plate of the really watery eggs, to which he keeps adding ground pepper. There's something oddly familiar about him. Some nagging sense of recognition. The Precious Gift tries to catch a glimpse of the book he is reading. It is titled *Tunnel Warfare in Vietnam* and for a second The Precious Gift imagines a network of tunnels, set beneath Derry, undermining the whole city completely.

IIII

Josef Noth is reading Alexis Leger's letters, in Leger's abandoned Parisian apartment, late at night. There is so much street noise outside. Paris sounds like a revel. A Nazi revel. Erithena is working at some kind of Nazi banquet, or debauched orgy more like, for the upper echelons of the Nazi Party in France. Are we really at war? I used to be jealous, as a young man, Josef Noth thinks. Now look at me. He is reading a letter to an unnamed Irish woman that Alexis Leger has kept a copy of. She is evidently planning to visit him in China. But Leger warns against it. Don't do it, he says. Besides, he says, I am leaving myself. The letter is dated 17 March, 1921. He talks about China as a country. It has the skinniest hips for birth, he says. It is not voluptuous, he says. Instead, he suggests an itinerary touring Spain, on her own, on horseback (or, failing that, Morocco), an itinerary that he says should take in Aragon, Catalonia, the Castiles and Asturias. He says China has a look in its eyes of complete forgetfulness. That a time in China will age an occidental woman prematurely. He laments the short stubby legs of the Chinese horses, far from the wild mares and graceful stallions of Ireland. He talks about the nature of time, in China, how it is languorous and set for daydreaming and for opium and for a sort of forgetting of history, he suggests. And then he tells her that there is no hate in this world. There is no hate, he says, there is only being less than life, he assures her, this ex-lover, we can imagine, this old Irish flame, who once made plans to travel halfway around the world to be reunited with her lover, Alexis, who refused her. Still: you cannot make a mistake, Leger assures her. Except through lethargy, and forgetfulness, and sloth, he says. You cannot make a mistake by pressing on, he writes, even as he, himself, is pressing on. Josef Noth is reading Alexis Leger's letters from China alone at night in Leger's abandoned apartment in the newly conquered Paris, is how Josef Noth sees it, even as he reveres the Paris of old, French Paris, the Paris of only a few months previous. He moves to a chaise longue by the window, upholstered in a lustrous shade of deep blue. Outside, some drunken soldiers are singing German songs about Fräuleins with tits like udders and arses like heifers. In an apartment across the way, an old man sits at a table by the window, with no top on, and repeatedly runs his hand through what's left of his hair while muttering to himself and staring into thin air. It is hot in Paris. Why is it so much hotter in Paris, Josef Noth asks himself, is it closer to the sun? On 10 May 1921, Alexis Leger writes to André Gide, the French author of *The Immoralist* and *The Return of the Prodigal Son* and *The Counterfeiters* and, even better, *The Fruits of the Earth* and *The Attempt at Love*. He talks of friendship and how it has so many silences. He talks of China like the surface of the moon, a place where space and time are confused and left behind, especially in Peking, he says, which he describes as the astronomical omphalos of the world, its belly button even, this umbilical into space running all the way through time. Unlike with his unnamed Irish sweetheart, he urges Gide to visit. You must, he insists. Leger talks about living in the desert and how voluble the desert is. Although you might not think of it, the desert is overflowing. The desert is overflowing with signs, he insists. Leger lived in the Gobi Desert for a month, he says, and he points out that this is the beginning of Asia, that desert comes first and, once across the desert, on a camel or on a horse, who knows, distance itself is not real, or rather it has the endless, ephemeral quality of time, and Josef Noth pictures horseshoes, camel trails, whole caravans, erased by the dust and the wind. Alexis Leger makes a gnomic point about geometry, then talks about a return to Paris, and the difficulties that might present, for a man who has toured Japan and the South Seas, a man who has looked back from a vantage point beyond the accumulation of moments. And then he says that love itself has no connection to time. That love, perhaps, he hints, more than states, is itself liberated from time. And then he talks of an eternal day, a single day to live, like a butterfly or a pupa, and he greets Gide once more, from back of time, in silent friendship, and excuses himself, finally, this time to take a boat across the sea to America.

112

DJ Pierre arrives in the DJ booth and Achilles is with him. Look, Mindy says to Aaron's father Donald – the two of them are dancing to 'The Magnificent Dance' by The Clash – it's Achilles! Mindy waves to him and he waves back and then says something in Pierre's ear and points to the two of them. Pierre plays 'You're the One for Me' by D Train and he turns on the mic and dedicates it to 'Don and the beautiful Mindy'. Donald's dancing is awkward in the spotlight. Let's take a seat, he suggests, damn, I need a rest, he says, but Mindy says, no, and she pouts, we have to dance now, he's picked us out, she says. I just want to dance, she says, and she runs her hands through her hair and rocks from side to side and it is so sexy. I'll dance on my own, she says. I don't care. OK, Donald says, I'll order us another bottle of wine, and he heads back to their table. Let her dance, he says to himself. The club is rammed and filled with eccentric characters, like a guy in a leotard dancing with a black guy in a glitter top with massive silver sunglasses. At this point Mindy does a little sexy pirouette and is swallowed by the crowd. Donald can't catch the eyes of any of the waiters. It is like he is shrinking right there on the spot. He can't see Mindy anymore, but he can see DJ Pierre and Achilles, signalling and making hand gestures and winking to the women in the crowd, no doubt, and he thinks about the kind of action these clowns must be getting on a nightly basis. And something clicks in him. Or something breaks in him, more like. And he asks for the bill. He makes a big deal of raising his arm in the air and clicking his fingers demanding the bill. Then he explains to the waiter, who looks like Harvey Keitel gone to seed, or who is that handsome actor but with a piggy nose, he explains to him that he is clearing the bill but that he wants to 'keep the table open', is how he puts it, and he takes out a wad of cash that he must have saved specially for the trip, and he gives it to the waiter, who it turns out isn't even French, who is German, and Don says to him, when Mindy returns, leave this key for her on the table, he says, it's the key to our room in the hotel, he says, and the Harvey Keitel German looks at him with a look of infinite pity, his arched eyebrows like the Buddha's, heartbroken to learn the truth under a damp tree, and he puts his hand on Donald's shoulder and he says, you got it, brother, and Donald nods and puts on his Aquascutum overcoat and heads for the door. It's past 4 a.m. when Donald feels Mindy creep silently into bed. In the morning, neither of them brings it up. They dress in silence and make small talk – the whole air smells like croissant and coffee in the morning, in Paris, don't you think, is Mindy's sole contribution, or maybe a croque-monsieur, she adds – and then take breakfast on the terrace of a cafe near the Eiffel Tower. Mindy has forgotten to take any photographs on the trip. How could I have been so dumb, she says. And she snaps a portrait of Donald Murray, for the first and last time, beneath the Eiffel Tower, at the end of his tether. Afterwards, they climb the famous tower, and, arriving at the top, Donald stares out, over the whole of Europe, and then the Baltic states, and then Russia, Mother Russia, Donald thinks to himself, and he sounds it in his head, four syllables, and he asks himself where a country ends and another begins, where an age ends and another begins, and the same thing with another person.

113

Dan Ruff gets up in this caravan by the Clyde where he has lived on his lonesome for some years now, ever since his wife died of cancer. He looks out his window at the rising sun lighting up the grain silos across the way. It is so melancholy, the way the sun plays across the old industrial buildings and the endless rows of tenements, in Glasgow, something sad about the way it bathes these buildings in an eternal torpor, he thinks, a phrase that he got off a documentary that he watched on the television last night, 'torpor', only there it was applied to hibernating bears. Next to his bed there is a table with a lamp on it and an old-fashioned clock that ticks continuously and disconcertingly. Who can live with a ticking clock? There is a book on the nightstand, too. *The Art of Horsemanship* by Xenophon. A wooden cupboard stands at the foot of the bed. Apart from that, the room is entirely bare and wood-panelled on all sides. He climbs into the shower, a white plastic shower with mould which he has built inside a cupboard. Dan Ruff is the type to sing in the shower. What is it about showers that inspires song, he thinks to himself, and he wonders if Xenophon ever sang in the bath or the shower. Probably. He was a volatile guy, like myself, Dan Ruff thinks to himself, prone to excitable passions, he thinks. On the subject of that, Dan Ruff doesn't think about having a chug in the shower anymore. No. That's yesterday's news, he accepts. And when he does, when he checks in down below to see how the old waterworks are bearing up to age and confusion and the death of his libido, it feels perfunctory and unnecessary. Worst of all, unsatisfying. He thinks about the proximity of the river, the River Clyde, how could he not, this stinky river flowing past in full force. Instead, he sings 'Fat Bottomed Girls' by Queen. He sits down at his breakfast bar and has his customary bowl of cornflakes with milk and a mound of white sugar, while a pot of tea stews on the cooker. He has his tea with toast and marmalade, or sometimes toast and salmon spread, or sometimes even smoked mackerel. He thinks about all the responsibilities of the day, which will involve, without doubt, dealing with inter-family disputes in the camp – he rolls his eyes – warding off threats and intimidation from other camps – he shakes his head – running the funfair and making sure all these bastards pay their money, promptly, and in full – he cracks his knuckles – and dealing with the police, making sure they are paid; he nods his head, solemnly. Introspection is for people with time on their hands, he thinks to himself, and thank fuck. Because Dan Ruff is missing so much and cannot bear to think about it. He slips into some jogging trousers and stays in the white vest he slept in, slides his feet into a pair of flip-flops, and crosses the camp to the blue metal container where The Lark has been sleeping. As he draws back the door, he sees it rise to its feet, this silhouette with its great mane, rising on its rear legs first, wow, that mane is really growing, it's like a Mohican, Dan Ruff thinks. The smell too. Hello, The Lark, he says, and he holds out a handful of raisins, which The Lark eats quickly and awkwardly. He looks into The Lark's black eyes like ink in a river and remembers how Xenophon pointed out (or was it Xenophon?) that horses' pupils are rectangular, and not round. Which must be like gazing out of a coffin, he thought to himself, in bed at night on his own, reading that. Thank god for globes and for round vision, he said to himself then, and he shuddered. But then he reasoned that, if you're born with it, you can probably get used to anything. He strokes The Lark's head, with its little dapple of colour. 'Dappled', what a word, it is lovely to say that, and he says it out loud to The Lark, dappled, he says, there's a word for you, little boy. Now, he says, any words for me? Is there anything lonelier than the inter-species divide? That two hearts beating in proximity to each other, that two pairs of eyes seeing themselves in each other, still cannot speak in the same way. But you spoke before, didn't you? Dan Ruff says to The Lark, as he strokes its head. You spoke to me before. Is there no word now? he asks this young colt with liquid coffins for eyes. Are there no more words for me anymore? After they sit there together, in unworded silence, for what feels like an eternity, but is probably only about fifteen minutes tops, Dan Ruff leads The Lark out into the sunshine, and ties him to a post with some grass, and heads over to see Melissa, The Nippy Sweetie, as she is known, an alcoholic clairvoyant who when she is drinking keeps the entire camp up, night after night, when she is drinking and out on her porch, prophesying vengeance, or doom. Something needs to be done, and as usual it is down to Dangerous Dan Ruff to do it. In the distance there is all the joy of the Garden Festival.

114

Private Investigator Luke G.B. Caird is at his office on Dumbarton Road, up a close above a dentist called Veitch who looks like a Nazi surgeon in hiding. Caird makes himself some Nescafé Gold in a Styrofoam cup while heating a bowl of Chunky Chicken soup in the microwave. Outside, it is pouring, and people on Dumbarton Road are rushing this way and that in the evening gloom, either that or sheltering in doorways and beneath awnings. A train passes over Partick Bridge and the whole building vibrates. Caird takes the soup back to his desk in the next room, a room he shares with Private Investigator Mark C. Burl. They've spent the morning unsuccessfully following a woman who is having an affair with a client's husband, only she spotted them in Safeway and confronted them and asked them if they were private investigators and if they were following her. What a bitch, Caird says. I can't believe she clocked us, he says. She's minging, Burl says. Who would sack off Sandra Meaghan for a minging bitch like that, he says. Maybe she's frigid, Caird says. Good-looking is one thing. Filthy in the sack is another. Good point well made, Burl says. Burl actually has a pencil behind his ear. Mate, you're the only person I know, outside of my uncle Jim when he was a joiner, who puts a pencil behind his ear, Caird says. Mad, innit, Burl says. Who was the first person to think, wait a minute, I can store this pencil tucked in behind my ear? He must've looked like a tit, at first. Now he has the last laugh, Burl says. Even though he doesn't, cause no cunt knows who the fuck he even was. And here's you, still repping, Caird says. I love this Chunky Chicken, Caird says, as he tucks into his steaming bowl. Tell me about it, Burl says. The rain is running down the window in sheets now. What you up to this evening? Burl asks Caird. Got a date,

Caird says. That bird that's the air hostess? Burl asks him. The very one, he says. Top notch, Burl says. You can't beat those birds, mate. Up there with birds that work at perfume counters. And sexy estate agents. And strippers, obviously. Obviously, Caird says. Top notch, he agrees. Pulling an air hostess, mate, that's life goals right there. How did it happen again? I did nothing, mate; it was all about her. This gorgeous bird from Georgia. Not the American state, she says to me, Russian Georgia, Caucasus Georgia, Black Sea Georgia, she says to me. I was eyeing her up already, I can't lie, this is on the flight to New Zealand, where I did that conference. Right, Burl says. I can see her down the front of the plane, she has her hair tied up in a bun, dark eyes, dark skin, everything about her is saying that her soul is in the mountains, you know what I mean, her soul is in a wooden gaff in the mountains, but here she is, come down from the mountains and with all of the glamour of someone newly arrived in the city, who has fallen for it completely. Do you get me? Course I do, mate. And she is so good with children, she is a real mother-to-be, if you know what I mean, she is picking up the young baby boys in her arms and kissing them and whispering god knows what in their ears, and then she is looking at me, she is whispering to them and then looking over at me, like it's my younger self and she is setting me up with instructions to fall in love with her forever. And then she comes over to me. What are you travelling for? she asks me. What a question. I tell her that I am travelling to a conference, to a festival, to a literary festival, that I have been invited to appear on a true crime panel, I tell her. Wow, she says. Crime, she says. And then she says, well, when are you travelling back? And I tell her three days, I tell her it's a flying visit and that I will be returning in three days' time, and she says, wow, that's tough, that is a schedule like an air hostess, she says, and then she says, so you are flying back on Sunday? And I tell her, yes, I am, Sunday. And she says, me too, I'll be on that flight too. And then she says, are you going to buy me some chocolates? No! Yes! And of course I say, yes, yes, I am planning on buying you some chocolates, and she says, my name is Tamar. And she asks me mine. I say it's Luke G.B. Caird. OK, Mr Luke, she says, I will see you soon. And then she goes back to kissing baby boys and parading them round the plane and rocking them in her arms. It's too much. Tell me about it, Burl says. What are you supposed to do? So, we do the true crime convention, it's boring, there is some boring ex-gang member who has reformed and now he is speaking out against violence, boring, some fat Māori gangster, boring, some female reporter, boring but a little attractive in an obviously unhinged way. I'm nodding off on the panel. I go back to my hotel, with glass windows down to the floor, looking out over Christchurch and that weird winter light they have in the summertime, and I call my friend Bruce, I end up getting a taxi to Bruce's place in the morning, and we basically cook and drink and eat in front of the stove in his basement for the next two days solid, all the while he is playing me music, Big Star, Alex Chilton, Alan Vega, Iggy Pop, as well as NZ jams like Toerag (legend, Burl says), Wreck Small Speakers on Expensive Stereos, Look Blue Go Purple, the good shit, all the while eating beautiful home-cooked food, pork-and-mushroom risotto, you name it, until suddenly it's time to go home, and he drives me to the airport, we hug and I depart, but not before sinking a few beers in the departure lounge. And when I get on the plane, I see her. It's true, she is working the same flight. I don't know if she will really remember me, and of course I forgot to buy her any chocolates, so I kind of just go about my business, settling in, when she spots me and comes over and says, Mr Luke, that is what she says, Mr Luke, how was your visit, and I tell her it was good, if exhausting, and I ask her what she got up to, and she says, I went to see the famous stones. What famous stones? I don't know, she says, some famous stones. And then she says, you are a lover of literature, did you say? And even though I didn't say, though I might have hinted at it, I nod and I say, yes, I am, for sure, and she says, do you know the book, or rather it is a poem and a book – prose poetry, I ask her? – and she says, yes, prose poetry, it is called *The Knight in the Panther's Skin*, by Shota Rustaveli. Do you know it? No, I explain. I don't know it. We were taught it at school, she says. You must read it. And then she starts reciting it from memory. In Georgian. No! Yes! We have our own language, she says, and she ravishes me right there with verse after verse of Georgian poetry, impossible to understand, but for the command of her tongue, this tongue that might as well be speaking from beyond the beginnings of time, in the first language, designed, specifically, for the beautiful mouths of young Georgian girls. I'm in a trance, I am set spinning, at the sound. And then she says: let me write it down for you. And then she says: wait, let me give you my phone number. No! Yes! And then she says: call me, call me once you have read it and let me know. And now she's in Glasgow for the weekend. But have you read it? Burl asks him. Have I fuck, Caird says. How the fuck am I supposed to find a copy of that? And anyway, it's just a ruse, isn't it, just an opening for romance, after all, don't you think? I think you should read it, Burl says. Anyway, I got to make a phone call, Burl says, and he heads next door to the 'conference room'. Burl picks up the cream telephone with little bits of earwax around the speaker, why does he always notice that and yet do nothing about it, and he calls The Gimp, that's his name for him, and he urges him to 'turn the screw', to 'increase the heat' and to 'squeeze this bastard dry'. Don't worry, you'll get your fair share of whatever we make, he says, and then he hangs up the phone and walks back into the office. What you working on? Luke G.B. Caird asks him. A little something on the side, is all Mark C. Burl says, and then he tells their secretary Yvonne that he will be out for the rest of the afternoon. Just some lowlife scum, he says, as he heads out into the rain.

115

The Precious Gift is on the blower to Wise Crow. What is the significance of a peregrine falcon? he asks her. A falcon, eh? she says. A fucking peregrine falcon, is it? What is? The Precious Gift asks her. The falcon, she says. You're asking me about a fucking peregrine falcon? Yes, I am, he says, and he remembers how much the people of Derry swear. Mid-sentence, mid-breath; as soon as their minds drift. And then she says, guilt. What? Guilt, shame, regret, she says. And what if it is lying dead on its side? The Precious Gift says. You do the fucking maths, she says. Where is this fucking peregrine falcon? Across the road, The Precious Gift tells her. Dead in the window of an abandoned pub. What is the significance of an abandoned pub? she says. I don't know, The Precious Gift says, what is the significance of an abandoned pub? How the fuck would I know? she says. Anyway, she says. Enough of these signs. Come over to the jail, she calls it, though it's actually a subterranean police interrogation cell. Come over to the jail for eleven a.m. We have an hour with The Mole. Then she hangs up. The Precious Gift has a shower, in this shower stall that smells of urine, like it all flows into the same pipe. Michelle is back at reception when he makes his way down for breakfast. Hiya, darling, he says. There is Irish dancing on the TV screen. Then: what the fuck is that sound? There's a roaring sound, a rending sound, coming near, something outside, coming in the air, and it's all The Precious Gift can do not to duck, although Michelle doesn't seem to react at all, and that's when he realises, it's the fucking helicopters, it's the fucking military choppers, how do you ever get used to that, he thinks, but of course you fucking do. In the breakfast room the same bald dude with, now that he looks closer, some truly awful facial acne, some horrible scarring actually, is reading another book, this time titled *Improvised Traps of Vietnam*. Imagine if it was a novel with a title like that, The Precious Gift thinks to himself, as he helps himself to streaky bacon and a fried tomato and two sausages and some mushrooms and scrambled egg, but no toast, it gives him indigestion, this guy couldn't be more of a plant if he tried, this guy is so obviously . . . a mole, he thinks to himself, ha ha, and of course he thinks about guilt, and about regret, and about his previous life, is how he thinks of it now, how he rationalises it, and all that he did there. As he passes the bald guy's table he makes a joke, he is feeling provocative. Bit of light reading there, mate? he says. And the guy with the quite awful facial scarring actually, who looks as if his face was once set on fire, now that he turns and The Precious Gift gets a good look at him, that his head was, at one point, consumed by flames, says, no. He speaks with a German accent. It's not light reading, he says. In fact, it is completely harrowing, he says. The ingenious barbarity of man towards man, he says. And he looks The Precious Gift in the eye, only the German's eyes are yellow, his eyeballs are a sickly yellow, like someone who is drinking themselves to death. And he goes back to his reading. The Precious Gift takes a table facing away from him, facing out towards the abandoned pub with the dead falcon on its side, and he says to himself, under his breath, almost inaudibly, he repeats the words, guilt, shame, regret, like a mantra.

116

Wasn't there an experiment where they taught dolphins to speak? Scott Ruff asks Aaron Murray. To communicate, not to speak, Aaron says. What's the difference? They didn't use words, but they could understand words, and they responded in sounds. And how did it turn out? The woman that trained them fell in love with the dolphin, Aaron says. I think we were just stoned, Scott says. I think that's it. I think we just read words into the sounds. Or remember, we gave its mother LSD before it was born, could it have caused some kind of weird evolutionary development? Or like it said – or did it – that we had somehow unwittingly recreated a kind of magic ritual. I'm spooked, Aaron says. Me too, Scott says. There's my dad, he says. Dan Ruff wanders over in his vest and flip-flops. Any more words from The Lark? Scott asks him. I swore it spoke, Dan Ruff says. I swore it said something, But since then, nada, he says. Zip, he underlines. I was planning on exhibiting it, he says. It was gonna be the star of the show. Better to keep a talking horse quiet, Scott says. I mean, we don't want to bring down the heat on our heads, he says. And then Dan Ruff says, uh-oh, look who's here, subject of heat, and he points, aggressively, to a group of three men in suits walking into the camp. Shabby suits, creased dark-blue suits, like mid-level accountants. Sunglasses, cheap sunglasses. Side-lacing shoes, ghastly grey side-lacing shoes. A man as dangerous as you in charge of a funfair, the one in the middle says. What could possibly go wrong? I hear you're opening this afternoon, he says to Dan Ruff. This is never gonna fly, he says. It's right next to the Garden Festival. This is private property, Dan Ruff says. And I suggest you don't have permission to be here. I'm here to ask some questions, the middle man says, that's all, questions you would do well to go along with, and then he says hi to Aaron and Scott and introduces himself as a councillor, Councillor Andrew Lethal, he says, nice to meet you, boys. Are these your fucking bodyguards, Dan Ruff says, and he snorts and runs his eyes up and down the pair of them. I'll eat my way through your fucking faces, he says to them, but they don't even react. What do you know about horses? Andrew Lethal asks Dan Ruff, and Aaron and Scott freeze, and Dan Ruff says, everything that you need to know, he says. I learnt from the best, he says. And who would that be? From your man Xenophon, Dan Ruff says. And who's he when he's at home? The author of the definitive work on horsemanship, Dan says. You fucking ignoramus, he adds. We can't all be as cultured as you, Andrew Lethal says, and he lets out a snigger. Forgive my ignorance. So, what does this Xenophon have to say for himself? Read the book, you illiterate son of a bitch, Dan Ruff says, and Andrew Lethal makes a big deal of getting a pen from his top pocket and pulling out a notebook and licking his lips and exaggeratedly lolling his tongue out the side of his mouth and writing down the words 'HORSEMANSHIP BY XENOPHON' in slow capital letters like a retard. Then he says, you see, Dan, he says, putting away the notepad, I've been speaking to the Bollands, the Bollands of the east end, I think you know who I mean. Horse-racing gypsy bastards. This is about a shooting. A shooting that took place in the east end over the theft of some horses. Well, as you can imagine, these horse-racing gypsy bastards are the top suspects. Number one, he reiterates. Only they fingered you. What the fuck do you mean fingered me? Dan Ruff says. They come anywhere near me with one of their fingers and I will force it up their own arseholes, Dan Ruff says. They maintain that you had, in fact, come into receipt (was how this Andrew Lethal continued) of a fleet of horses right about that time. And then it is like a clumsy zoom shot in a

B-movie accompanied by a power chord as simultaneously everyone turns and looks at this colt at the exact same time, like it has been beamed out of nowhere for precisely this moment, this Lark tied here suddenly to a tree on a pathetic island of green amid all of the tarmac and abandoned junk and all of this rubble, staring back at them. And what about its coffins for eyes, Dan Ruff thinks to himself, frozen in its frozen gaze, as if it could still all of time – well, of course it can, of course a talking horse can still all of time, is the message that Dan, and that Aaron, and that Andrew Lethal also, receive right then, but not Scott, and not this pair of faceless goons, who are all too busy thinking about crime and legality.

117

In his spare time Andrew Lethal is a writer. A creative writer is what he calls himself, if anyone asks, which is rarely, working as he does for the council. But in his spare time, he is writing a novel. A novel that he is workshopping at The Warehouse, a creative writing hub in an old gymnasium in Springburn that encourages ex-cons and other marginalised people in order to turn their impulses to art. A novel that is set during the discovery of Mexico. And in the present day. A novel that consists of a series of 'translations', Andrew Lethal calls them. 'Translations', like that, because they are not strictly what a translator would recognise as a translation. Because they are translations into the same language. They are English translations of English translations of Spanish texts. Specifically, the letters the conquistadors wrote home during the conquest of 'New Spain'. Andrew Lethal is very interested in the discovery of the Americas, and what they found there. As part of his hobby, he is also interested in the Aztecs. And in the Mayan codices. And in Mexican food. And in Mexican myth and lore. And in Mexican whores, if we're being honest, in Latina honeys, truth told, which is what has got him into trouble, time and time again, his propensity for prostitutes, especially Latin American prostitutes, his trips to Tijuana, the trips he saves all his money for, the beautiful chicas with their dark hair and dark eyes and dark skin, who have looked like that since the beginning of time, Andrew Lethal believes, not forgetting their asses, the most voluptuous asses in the world, he believes, the transmission of their immortal asses across time is an obsession, and on full display at the Hong Kong, in Tijuana, his favourite strip club in the world, not to mention human sacrifice, Andrew Lethal is just as interested in the phenomenon of human sacrifice, as well as human trafficking, inevitably, this being Mexico, and in gangs, and in gangland rituals, and in migrations, and in refugees, and in marginalised communities, in gangsters living in improvised shanty towns in Mexico, just like they do in Carntyne and in Whiteinch and in Shettleston, in Glasgow, which is his area of speciality. His deep rapport, he flatters himself, with the traveller communities, is what marks him out as a councillor. Start him talking and you will find out that he is particularly obsessed with the story of the cracking of the Mayan codices, which is the story of Sylvanus G. Morley and Benjamin Lee Whorf, of Yuri Valentinovich Knorozov – who looked like a demonic Chet Baker or Artaud's half-mad brother and loved Siamese cats – of Sir Eric Thompson and David H. Kelley, of the brilliant Russian who defined her age, the unassailable Tatiana Proskouriakoff, of the German grocer-turned-epigraphist Heinrich Berlin (whose lowly station, and lonely passion, and amateur status, give Lethal hope, and succour, in his own work), and of course Merle Greene Robertson and Lethal's contemporary Linda Schele, with whom he occasionally, and tetchily, corresponds. Andrew Lethal is also interested in alchemy, in the turning of shit to gold. Which is something that he also 'translates'. Mexico is the country of alchemy, he will tell you, if you ever think to ask him such a thing as, what is the country of alchemy? And if you were to say to him, well, in that case, what is the city of alchemy, then he would surprise you and say, Glasgow, he would tell you, Glasgow is the heart of alchemy, and Mexico is the musculature of alchemy, he would say. And then he would explain that together they make up the *body of the conquistador*. And before you could quiz him and say, well, what about Spain, what about Prague, where is the brain of alchemy, he would assail you with his pet theory regarding the Mayan glyphs, how he 'takes issue' with Knorozov – normally when he is on his own and drinking and muttering to himself late at night in his library in the front room of a tenement facing Tollcross Park in the east end of Glasgow, a room with a view over the beds that are arranged with flowers in the shape of a rose, beds of roses, in the shape of a great rose, a rose of roses – and he would pooh-pooh and guffaw and generally deride Knorozov's idea (as well as Ezra Pound, the poet Ezra Pound's lame-arse idea, he would spit, to no one but himself) that the Mayan glyphs were perfect ideograms – that historical shaggy dog, that perfect literary phantom, that complete fucking myth, as mythic as snuff movies or satanic abuse – that a sign, a letter, a word, could both stand for and literally be the thing-in-itself. That finally with the Mayans, or rather, primarily with the Mayans, they had seduced the symbol (there was always the hint, the idea, the hunch, that perhaps it went hand in hand with ritual, with the practice of human sacrifice, that this repeated enacting of ritual murder is what made the scales fall from the eyes, and symbols, of the Mayans) and left the bride stripped bare.

Bullshit. Lethal believes, rather, that the Mayan glyphs were phonetic, and stood in for sounds. That the Mayan glyphs were, in fact, a vast musical composition intended to be sung. That the ruined Mayan civilisation was, in fact, the tomb of a song.

118

The Precious Gift makes his way to the police station in Derry, a police station that does, in fact, look more like a jail, a high-security jail with tall metal fencing and barbed wire and multiple bombproof doors. He rings a buzzer, and a voice asks him to state the reason for his visit. I'm here for the interrogation of The Mole, he says, and he is buzzed through to an outer courtyard that is littered with cigarette butts and what seems to be dog shit, dog faeces all around. How grim is dog shit on concrete, he thinks. How sad and unnatural, he thinks. What an awful metaphor, he thinks, and he remembers that Situationist quote about how beneath the paving stones there is a beach. He imagines policemen on their tea break smoking while their attack Alsatians squeeze one out. Couldn't they at least clean up after them? On the roof of the station there is an observation tower where two men are passing a pair of binoculars back and forth. There's a click and a second metal door swings open. A man with a small moustache, wearing one of those dark-blue military jumpers with the patches, asks him to take off his jacket and to remove the contents of his pockets. Then he pats him down. They're waiting for you in holding room number five, he says, and he points The Precious Gift to a stairwell that descends into the ground. Follow the yellow line, he says. This is more like a nuclear bunker, The Precious Gift thinks, as he descends into the bowels of the earth. Holding room number five is at the end of a featureless corridor with strip-lighting that flickers on and off like in a movie. He knocks on the door. Enter, a voice commands, and he opens the door to the sight of Wise Crow and Ruth Prior sat on one side of a table, both of whom are smoking and drinking coffee from Styrofoam cups. Look what the fucking wind blew in, Wise Crow says, and she gets up and gives him a hug. Ruth offers him her hand. Nice to see you, Ruth, he says. How have you been keeping? You know, she shrugs. Getting by. Wise Crow has no make-up on and is wearing a chunky white polo neck. She has her hair pulled back in a severe ponytail. It is like stepping back in time. To Project Deep Run. To how things were. Before. Before what? Before the murder of Jim Monaghan. Want a fag, Wise Crow says, and she flicks her finger against the pack of twenty Embassy small in an expert way so that a single cigarette pops out. I'm OK, he says. So, what do we know about this goon? Wise Crow says, and she picks up a sheet of typed paper. His name is Davey Brennan. Aged twenty-six. Originally from over the border in Burnfoot. Shitehole, Ruth Prior says as she lights a fag with the tail-end of another one. Arrested at the age of twenty-three during a shoot-out with police, he has been singing like a fucking canary ever since, Wise Crow says. A trusted source, it says here. A reliable witness, it says. Embedded deep within the Red Hand Commando, it says. What ties him to the murder of Jim? The Precious Gift asks her. Someone squealed, she says. He was named, she says. Privately, she says. On the wires, she says. How's he pleading? Not guilty, of course. Then the door opens, and Davey Brennan appears, in handcuffs, and flanked by two policemen, a fat one and a thin one. Fucking Little and Large, Wise Crow jokes, once they have handcuffed him to a chair and left them on their own. Fucking Laurel and Hardy, Brennan agrees, and rolls his eyes and asks for a smoke with his one free hand. A pair of fucking comedians, alright, he says. And then he says, and who the fuck are you? Special Branch? And Wise Crow says, we're the true secret service, sunshine. You don't fuck with us, she says. We handle the special cases, she says. Plus, this is personal, she says. So I'll be deciding exactly what level of humour is appropriate, considering we are quizzing you about the death of a friend and colleague. I hear you asked for access to the library when you were brought in, she says. What the fuck was that about? Brennan makes the point that in the movies there is always a library in prison, and that he was simply asserting his right to access literature. Only this is a police station, and not a jail, Wise Crow says. That's what fucking Cannon and Ball said, Brennan says, and The Precious Gift realises who he reminds him of. It's Robert De Niro. Robert De Niro in *Taxi Driver*. Robert De Niro on the loose in New York rounding the scum up from off the streets. But before he shaves his head into a Mohican. So, you're a literary type? The Precious Gift asks him. I like to read, he says. Like what? Speculative fiction, he says. What's that? Ruth Prior asks him. It is literature that has to do with the problem of the future, he says. Like who? she says. Jules Verne, he says. H.G. Wells, he says. Bram Stoker, he says. What does *Dracula* have to do with the problem of the future? Ruth Prior asks him, and he answers her with just one word. Vampires, he says, and he looks straight at The Precious Gift, like that.

119

Late at night, in the apartment of St-John Perse, in occupied Paris, in mid-century Europe, in the heart of the war, Josef Noth is sat by the open window reading Perse's letters to his mother, and he is moved by their love. By the quality of their love. Which seems deep, and sincere. The kind of love only an archetypal son could feel for an archetypal mother, in a way that isn't often spoken, that isn't often acknowledged, that – damn it – isn't often experienced by sons of the West, Josef Noth has to admit to himself, and he feels this great lack then, and he thinks of tribes and traditional societies and the status of motherhood around the world and whether we robbed ourselves of it, all these independent women, all these tough-guy men. But poets, he thinks to himself. That's something else. St-John Perse tells his dearest mother that there is no suffering. There is no suffering, dearest Mother, in my life, he writes. After all, he says, I have the companionship of horses. Don't you worry. He talks about the size of his chest and about animal magnetism, how it is a tragedy. He writes about wild mounts and how he can control them with his gaze, using those eyes bequeathed to him by his mother, he is quick to underline. He has a horse called Allan that hates foreigners so much it turns its nose up at the smell of his Scottish tweeds. Hilarious, Mother. He doesn't know how ugly he is, this horse, Allan, he writes. He is so ugly that I must cover all of the mirrors in case he catches a terrified glimpse of himself, he writes, and he is so clumsy that he regularly falls on the floor, he adds. St-John Perse boasts of his mastery of Asiatic horses. Just so you know, Mother. Also, dogs, he writes, and – he asks his mother to repress a chuckle – mosquitoes, also, bow to me, in brotherhood, and friendship. In tragic acceptance of my mastery, Mother, he writes. Tragic acceptance of my mastery, Josef Noth repeats it under his breath. Then St-John Perse brings his mother up to speed about an armistice, a resignation, and a resumption of hostilities. Dearest Mother, he writes. I love you, dearest Mother. Josef Noth moves to the open window and sees the same guy with the thinning hair across the way, running his hand across his head and muttering to himself in the hot night, the sound of the whores and the servicemen down below, the clatter of people, the lights of Paris, suspended in the very air, it seems, the sound of bells, it feels like, a great hymn, 1940, rising, inside or outside of him, who can tell. I love you, dearest Mother, he says, to no one outside of the air.

120

Mindy gets back to her flat late on a Saturday night. She and Donald flew into Edinburgh from Paris, and after a twenty-five-minute search for their car, which Donald had insisted on parking in a cheap, out-of-the-way car park, right next to the motorway, they drove home in silence, until Donald said, well, that was a lovely trip, thank you for your company, and Mindy said, thank you, Donald, it was a memorable trip. Then a road was closed, and they had to take a diversion, so in order to break the awkward silence Mindy asked if she could put on a cassette. Good idea, Donald said, they're in the glove compartment, and Mindy flicked through a bunch of cassettes including the greatest hits of Frank Sinatra until she came to *Picture Book* by Simply Red. Can we listen to Simply Red? she asked Donald, and of course he said yes, and they both listened to the album as they drove home in the dark, both alone with their thoughts after what was, let's face it, an aborted romance, a failed dirty weekend, the setting sun on Aaron's father's dream of a romantic life of sophistication with a glamorous young woman somewhere else. He could see Mindy's reflection in the window of the car, in the dark and in the rain, those famous lips, and those eyes, so faraway now and already in another life without him. When they pulled up outside her flat in Athole Gardens, in Hillhead, Mindy just offered him her cheek to kiss and he kissed her and said, I'll call you, and she said, sure, even though they both knew that was that. The next day she sleeps in late and checks the mousetraps that she had set under the sink because the landlord did nothing about pest control, and of course there is a mouse there with its eye popped out and she steels herself and shudders as she picks it up in a plastic bag and throws it in the bin. Then she runs herself a bath, in the bathroom that she has painted herself and which features what Mindy called 'Mindy's murals'. As she lies there in the foam she runs the showerhead between her legs while she rereads the note that Achilles had given her, the note that simply said 'Astonish me' and then gave his address, Achilles' address in Paris, and Mindy couldn't help but think how the 'A' in Achilles was written to resemble a phallus, a tumescent phallus, was the phrase that came to mind, as Mindy brings herself to a climax in the bath and quite honestly never thinks about Donald Murray again. That afternoon her upstairs neighbour Gina calls in to see her and to return her spare set of keys and they spend an hour after lunch making hippy-style hanging baskets for plants – her neighbour is a hippy girl from Hungary who enjoyed arts and crafts as well as vegetarian cooking and meditation – and once she leaves (but not before leaving Mindy with a hand-rolled joint and some joss sticks she had made) Mindy sits down at her desk in the bay window of the living room and writes a letter to Achilles Noth, in order to astonish him.

121

What was all that about? Wise Crow said, and she turned to The Precious Gift and Ruth Prior in holding room number five, with a look of confusion and astonishment and, it has to be said, a little bit of awe. He talked for an hour without saying a fucking thing, Wise Crow marvelled. Either he is a genius or an idiot savant, she said, and Ruth Prior said, what's an idiot savant, and Wise Crow said, kind of a spectacularly wise idiot, she said. And Ruth Prior said, wow, exactly. All that shit about *Dracula*, she said. He talks as if it's real. Vampires. If he's talking metaphoric vampires, then, yeah, in Northern Ireland there are many, Wise Crow said. Plus, there's the actual Vampire of Derry, Ruth Prior reminded them, if we're to believe that all of these murdered kids were killed by the same man. And to stop them may take a stake through the heart, Wise Crow said, though I doubt garlic would work. The Precious Gift admitted that he was shaken. There is something not right about that boy, he said, and then he said, what's that line about staring into the abyss and the abyss staring back at you? Isn't it Nietzsche? Wise Crow said, and Ruth Prior said, who's Neatsy, and Wise Crow said, Friedrich Nietzsche, he was the prophet of the superman, the race of overcomers, which was the next step for man, he believed, if only weak people don't destroy them from resentment, she added. He went mad when he saw a horse get punched in the street, she said. But that abyss, that abyss that gazes right back at you just as hard, that abyss right there sat in that damn chair and not just gazing right back but talking, talking non-stop madness for the best part of an hour. It's enough to give you vertigo, The Precious Gift said. You seem agitated, Ruth Prior said. What is it that's getting to you? He kept hinting that he knows more than he is giving away, The Precious Gift said. Plus, he has no fear. He never once denied the killing, Wise Crow said, do you realise that, he simply said things like, I wasn't there, he never said, like, I didn't do it, he would simply say, I have no idea, or he would duck back into this thing about vampires, as if to say, what are you gonna do, there are vampires behind the scenes. What an idiot savant,

Ruth Prior said, and she, too, sort of marvelled. Afterwards, The Precious Gift calls Joyce Monaghan and arranges to meet her at Tony's Trattoria, the same Tony's Trattoria, he feels the need to point out, that we were in previously, he says, and not the mysterious double you went to by mistake. I'm not a complete dummy, Joyce says on the phone, and then she laughs. In the event she is twenty minutes late, for which she gives no explanation. You didn't take the taxi to the wrong one by mistake, did you? The Precious Gift asks her, and she just says, no, what, no. Then she says, I'm absolutely gasping for a pint, to be honest, she says. Do you think you could order me a beer? What beer would you like? The Precious Gift asks her, and she just says, oh, I don't know, a pint of 'heavy'? The Precious Gift waves Tony over, who has a tea towel over his shoulder and who tonight looks like a martial arts master as he has a sweatband on his head and is wearing a tight grey vest. Alright, Jackie Chan, The Precious Gift almost goes to say, but he thinks better of it. Tony, can we get two pints of heavy, he asks him, and Tony just says, coming right up. I could low-key fall in love with you, Joyce says to The Precious Gift right then, as soon as Tony walks away. She is doing that thing where she has crossed her legs and has slipped her shoe off and is balancing her sandal on her big toe. Who doesn't love that move. What did you just say? The Precious Gift asks her, and she says, nothing, and she laughs and says, how was your day? Mental, The Precious Gift says. And of course I can't talk about it, as it's ongoing, he says. I know, she says. But tell me anyway. Seriously, he says. But I will tell you one thing. The suspect is clearly insane. Of course he's fucking insane, Joyce says. Keep your voice down, The Precious Gift says. Walls have ears. And eyes, also, he adds. When the beers arrive, these sudsy, hearty, brown frothing beers in dappled-glass tankards, Joyce picks up her glass and says, cheers, big ears, and necks half of it in one go. Now she has a little frothy moustache. She lets out a belch and then creases up with laughter. I can't handle my beer, she says. I warn you. The food is good. There are only two other couples in the restaurant, and they eat by candlelight, and no one stares through the window or screams in the street this time. Wanna come back to mine? Joyce asks The Precious Gift when they were enjoying the digestivos that Tony had foisted on them. I'd love to, he says. I want to show you something, she says, and The Precious Gift thinks, wow, considering what she showed me last time this could be a spectacular night, he thinks, but instead he just says, sure, I'm into it. By a miracle they get the same taxi driver as the first time taking them back, though it was just a minor miracle because after all Tony uses the same firm every time and they only had about five drivers max. The jazz driver, Joyce says, what's on the menu tonight, and he says, it's Albert Ayler, it's the late great saxophonist Albert Ayler who was known as the 'Holy Ghost', he says, and whose body was found in a river after he went mad staring at the sun, and both Joyce and The Precious Gift look at each other and ask him to repeat what he just said, and the boy, whose name was Joseph, Wee Joe, as he was known, says that Ayler became involved in a sect called the Sun Watchers who stared right into the sun and who eventually burnt their eyes out, and that near the end of his life he was wandering the streets of NYC wearing a fur coat and covered in Vaseline because he claimed that the sun had turned on him and that he was being inundated with solar rays. Wait, what?! Then he plays the music. A tune called 'Truth Is Marching In'. And Joyce says, this doesn't sound like jazz at all. And The Precious Gift says, this sounds more like a marching band from hell. And Wee Joe says, that's because Albert said he had lived more than he could express in bop terms alone. It's an amazing quote, right, Wee Joe says. He sounds like he is crying, Joyce says. It sounds like he has lived so much that all he can reasonably do now is cry into his horn. Amen, sister, Wee Joe says. True believer, he calls her, as he drops them off at Joyce's house in this nondescript cul-de-sac in Derry. As soon as they go through the door, Joyce says to The Precious Gift, this is really getting weird, isn't it, and then she says, come upstairs with me, and The Precious Gift begins to imagine a dungeon, a first-floor sex dungeon with leather swings and sex toys and perhaps even plastic coverings on the beds for all of the fluids they are about to expend on each other, but instead she opens the door onto what looks like an artist's studio. All around the walls there are wooden shelves piled high with paints and glues and brushes and knives and piles of old newspapers and cardboard boxes and screws and nails and jars of what appears to be hair, jars of human hair, is what it looks like, or dog hair, or animal hair, who knows, and is that a jar of nail clippings, and bird feathers, assorted bird feathers, and birds' eggs too, boxes of birds' eggs in sawdust, and butterflies, and insects too, jars of petrified insects, and The Precious Gift tries to appear unfazed, tries to take it all in his stride, and he says to Joyce, your man was an artist, huh, he says, your man was an artist in secret, he says, and she points to the table in the centre of the room, the wooden table which has something hanging underneath it, like a terrible nest, like a nest grown down, and sagging, or like terrible testicles, or udders, but then when he gets closer he sees, no, it is not some fleshy appendage or terrible nest, it is a fortress, an upside-down fortress, a castellated abyss, that Jim has been building, underneath this table, and suspended from it, what was it Nietzsche said, right there, staring right back at the two of them. He was absolutely fucking mad, The Precious Gift thinks, and Joyce says to him, this is Jim's studio. He was building a reverse diorama, she says. Then she asks him, what is the vision of the fortress?

122

Luke G.B. Caird is on his way to meet Tamar, the Georgian air hostess, at her hotel. She is staying at the Hilton in Anderston. He jumps on the subway at Partick and gets off at St Enoch's. *The Knight in the Panther's Skin*, he thinks to himself, what a title. A guy with a white face mask and a white boilersuit with telephone cords stitched to it so that he looks like a robot is body-popping to a ghetto blaster at the bottom of Buchanan Street. There are the usual drunk bums gathered under the bridge at Central Station. Tamar is waiting for him at the bar on the ground floor where she is drinking a flamboyant cocktail. Mr Luke, she greets him, and she waves from across the room. Her long black hair hangs down over her shoulder in gorgeous kinks. Wow, I almost didn't recognise you with your hair down, he says to her, as she gives him both cheeks to kiss and smells so delicious. What do you mean, that you're not in love with me anymore? Wow, Luke G.B. Caird is taken aback. Uh, no, not at all, he says. In fact, I think you look even more beautiful. You are such a tease, Mr Luke, she says, and she giggles and puts her hand over her mouth and looks to the side in a way that is already driving Luke G.B. Caird mad with desire, so much so that he finds himself getting an immediate hard-on. He can't remember the last time he popped a spontaneous hands-free erection, and he pictures her mouth, her beautiful red lips, balls deep around the shaft of his penis. Luke G.B. Caird orders a whisky 'with one ice cube' and Tamar asks him if he got the book she recommended him, *The Knight in the Panther's Skin*. Luke

G.B. Caird thinks again about what a great title that is, but says, no, unfortunately I haven't been able to track it down. Tamar says, that's actually great news, because I got you an English translation for a present. Luke G.B. Caird is embarrassed, he hadn't thought to get her anything, not even some chocolates. That's so lovely of you, he says as she hands him a copy tied up in a red bow with a card that says 'Just For You'. It's a hardback copy, with what looks like some Eastern Orthodox priest imploring the heavens to stop it all raining down on him and him alone on the cover. Luke G.B. Caird flicks through it and it turns out that it isn't prose poetry at all, that it's just straight-up poetry. What's it about, then? he asks Tamar. It's a medieval epic, she says. It's about a knight, she says. A mysterious knight who disappears to live in a cave because he cannot find his true love, she says. When he leaves the cave, obviously it's a mistake. He is immediately hounded by women. Hounded by them, she reiterates, and she rolls her eyes as if to suggest we all know too well about being hounded by women, that god knows there is nothing worse under heaven, and she says, to make matters worse, this strange knight, whose name is Tariel, by the way, finds out that this woman who desires him was actually harbouring his true love for him, in fact was on her way to deliver his true love to him, when his lover was captured by a demon and imprisoned on an *island of demons*, she says, and she opens her eyes wide, dark eyes from the beginning of time, as if all of history had conspired to bring forth these beautiful dark eyes right now, wide as if to suggest that the one thing worse than being absolutely hounded by women day and night is being unexpectedly imprisoned on an island of demons. And then what happens? he asks her. Ah, for that, you will have to read the prose poetry, she tells him, and he doesn't even bother to correct her. So, she says. How is your literary career, may I ask?

Well, I don't really have a literary career, he says. I'm a private investigator, most of the time. Wow, that's amazing. What is it that they call them in the American movies, Tamar says. A private dick? Ha ha, he says. Yup, I'm a private dick, he says, and Tamar says, that sounds so sexy, in Scottish. You are so mysterious to me, she says, and she mock-slaps his arm. She has a long split in her skirt, and it rides up her thigh to reveal perfect flesh. Unblemished flesh. Original flesh. The first thigh ever bitten by man. Luke G.B. Caird is so horny. But you are a writer also? This is when Luke G.B. Caird starts to lie. Yes, I'm a writer, he says. A private writer, as well as a private investigator, and, of course, a private dick, he says. You are outrageous, Tamar says. Maybe you could read me some of your prose poetry, she says. You know I would love that, she says. Sure, he says. At some point, he says. And then she says, would you like to make love? What, Luke G.B. Caird says, but then he adds, yes, sorry, yes, I would love to make love to you right now actually, should we order a bottle of champagne and take it up to your room? And Tamar says, why don't you finger-fuck me right here. What? Why don't you finger-fuck me right here in the bar, she says. Uh, OK, Luke G.B. Caird says. Then she takes control. Slide your chair over next to me so that your back is to the bar, she says. Luke G.B. Caird is worrying that he is just going to spontaneously ejaculate, and it'll be all over. Has she done this before, is this something that she does, how does she know the drill? he is thinking, but who fucking cares. There are a bunch of business types standing around the bar proclaiming about fucking this and fucking that. The barmaid is chopping limes for cocktails and is completely immersed in the process. Pull my panties to one side and slide two fingers in, Tamar says, and she slides her split skirt up to reveal turquoise panties. And they're wet. God, you're so wet, Luke

G.B. Caird says to her. You've soaked your tight panties, he says, and she groans as he pulls them to one side and inserts first one finger and then two. Deeper, she says. Go deep, she whispers, and she arches her back. He feels like he is lifting her up, like if he could hold her by the neck, he could raise her on his fist. She is half his size. And then it feels like she will take off, like she will take off into the air and shoot through the ceiling of this bar, she is coiled like a snake, what is it they say about the serpent power, Luke G.B. Caird is wondering, what is it they say about chakras, he is thinking, what is it they say about panthers, when she says to him, you're going to make me come, you're going to make me come, she whispers in his ear, I want you balls deep, she says, like she has read his mind, even as she is looking over his shoulder, at the assholes pontificating, at the woman absorbed in her task at the bar, at the traffic passing by outside, and she comes a thick cream, a thick beautiful cream, it is all over his fingers, and she says, you can wipe that on my thigh, but instead he puts his fingers in his mouth, and he tastes it, like lemons, like lemons from the Caucasus.

123

The body of a boy is discovered by Project Deep Run. Looks like the Vampire of Derry has struck again, Wise Crow says to her colleague Ruth Prior. He's in some state, Ruth Prior says. The Vampire? Wise Crow asks her. No, the boy, she says. There's a great hole in his neck, Ruth Prior says. His head is literally hanging off his body. Is he naked? He's naked there, yes. What else? The body has lain there so long it has started to decompose. The corpse is bloated. There is foam, strange foam, coming from its mouth and nose. It is like ectoplasm, Ruth Prior says, you know like in those old photographs of séances? Only this is the opposite of a séance. Not really, Wise Crow says. We're hoping the dead can speak. I keep thinking about what The Precious Gift said, Ruth Prior says. About what? About how it could be artistic. About how a murder, how the very placement of a corpse, could be artistic. An assemblage, wasn't that what he called it? Sometimes it feels like everything is speaking, she says. In this job, I mean, she clarifies, and Wise Crow says, only to a psychopath. What? Only a psychopath feels like everything is speaking. Or a schizo, a schizophrenic, that's what they feel like, not an artist. But you just said that we are hoping that even a dead boy can speak. A dead boy laid there in the shape of a swastika, almost, when seen from above, or a thunderbolt, Ruth Prior thinks to herself, or even a letter. And she wonders what word these poor boys might be spelling, laid out on the ground there, for only God, and herself, to read.

124

The cunt's bluffing, Dangerous Dan Ruff thinks to himself. There's no way the Bollands could have fingered us, he thinks. He's walking along South Street in the sand and the sticky willows. Where does that sand come from, he thinks to himself, is it coming off the Clyde? Is it coming from across the sea? Are tiny particles of Egyptian sand travelling on the waves all the way across the Mediterranean and out into the Atlantic and up the Clyde estuary, tiny particles blown off the pyramids and carried down the Nile, washing up on South Street like a fucking desert? He imagines the snack van half buried in the sand like those old photos of the Sphinx, with a painting of a hotdog jutting above the surface. Archaeologists wouldn't know what the fuck to think. They'd probably think it was a shaman's wand.

There's Sadie sat out front. Alright, darling? Aye, good. Aye, it's going well. To be honest, it's mobbed. We'll be bigger than the Garden Festival, Dan Ruff predicts. Do us a bap with ham and cheese, would you, love, he asks Sadie. And a wee coffee, love. Black, two sugars? That's the ticket. I'll just sit here and eat it. Dan Ruff takes a white plastic seat and draws it up to the white plastic table that is covered in stains and fag burns. In the distance there are the sounds of children screaming with joy and elation and just a little bit of terror, he thinks to himself, on this beautiful summer's day, the kind of day where everything is right with the world, where there is not a cloud in the sky, he thinks to himself, and under his breath he says, thank you, Lord, thank you, Lord, for this beautiful day that I am alive to see, this beautiful day that is so perfect we can afford to indulge in a little terror, in a little danger, all the same. All the fun of the fair, he thinks to himself, and he decides that if the Bollands really have grassed him up, which now he is not so sure about, that he will bring down a rain of terror, or a reign of terror, right then Dan Ruff can't decide which is the most appropriate term, whose visitation they will regret for the rest of their physically compromised lives. And that's the lucky ones, he thinks to himself, exactly like a gangster in a movie. Do you want your horoscope, Daniel? Sadie asks him, when she brings him his bap and coffee. Sure, love, he says. Gemini, right? Might be, he says. And he laughs. Fucking Gemini, Sadie says. Right. Duty calls. But the question is, who does it call? Sometimes your left hand doesn't know what your right hand is doing. It is more than a father's embrace. Orient yourself towards the future. Then choose. What the fuck is that supposed to mean? It's gnomic, Sadie says. It's Gnomic Astrology. That's how he always writes. Who's he? Tam Coyle: 'the stars are his foil'. Anyway, he says. How's your maw? Och, she's fine. No idea where she is or who I am, but happy nonetheless. I'd be happy if I had no idea who I was, Dan Ruff says. As it is, I've got the weight of the world on my shoulders, he says. The weight of the gypsy world, he says. Which is the heaviest world imaginable, he says. Why's that? Sadie asks him, and he says, because it has no fixed location on earth.

125

Andrew Lethal gets up in his flat that overlooks Tollcross Park and, as he does every morning, he switches the radio on. Radio 3, with its pleasing mix of classical recitals, the arts and current affairs. He cracks the window in his kitchen and lays out some bread for a pigeon he likes to feed and who he flatters himself is in love with him, whom he has named Clara. On the walls of his kitchen there are tapestries with Mayan glyphs on them. A squat character runs backwards across a bridge of fire emerging from the mouth of a monstrous head. A monkey with wings hangs suspended from the air. A girl with long Rapunzel-like hair. A character imploring three floating heads, impaled by three bright feathers. The kitchen door is draped with a hand-sewn tapestry of Our Lady of Guadalupe that he bought in Coyoacán Market, in Mexico City. He sleeps in his underwear. Stood there in his pants that have seen better days, he makes a mug of decaf tea with a single teabag. He suffers from hypothyroidism and despite the desiccated animal thyroid he takes in place of the pills, which he refuses to touch, he can't do caffeine anymore, because it sends him hyper and half insane. He nearly died and was only diagnosed when he fell asleep in the shower. As a result, he has gained weight and is as almost as pudgy as he was when he was a young boy. Only now his hair has started to fall out. He lives on his own, though he had a live-in girlfriend for a bit, a Mexican girl named Ramona who he met in Mexico City on a trip he organised with the idea of twinning Mexico City with Glasgow and so mutually boosting ties and tourism between the two metropolises. That lasted three months before she could no longer stand the darkness and the constant rain, she said, and went back home. He takes his tea and wanders into his study, which is lined with books and eccentric plants. He has a typewriter set up at a desk in the bay window. He rereads a draft of a letter to Linda Schele, the founder of the Maya Hieroglyphic Workshop, who famously decoded the hierophanies of Palenque, and revealed them as king lists, and who established that the Mayan's principal obsession was with royal dynasties, and total war, and human sacrifice. As opposed to magic, and shamanism, and spirit-flights. Or was it? Andrew Lethal argued for the presence of the sacred, of hierophanies, in violence, in the eruption of the terrible, in blood and still-beating hearts offered up to the unwavering gaze of the sun. Though Schele has yet to respond. Still, he is trying again. My interest in Mexico is indomitable, he tells her. Although he admits he is just an amateur. A passionately engaged amateur nevertheless, he reminds her, and by dint, the entire community of Mesoamerican archaeologists. Which isn't very large. He takes the letter out of the carriage and feeds in a clean sheet. He reaches for a pamphlet. *Three Tracts* by Eleazar of Worms. Published by the Tree imprint in 1975. An imprint run by the poet David Meltzer. A text of Kabbalistic alchemy. He rereads the text, and then he starts to write.

126

In the response Mindy received to her letter to Achilles Noth, Achilles mentioned his love for the great cathedrals of Europe, the French cathedrals in particular, he insisted, were the absolute peak, and he labelled their style as 'medieval psychedelia' and Mindy swooned. That is so cool, she thought to herself. He was so cool. How do you astonish someone who is this cool? First, Mindy picked out some famous cathedrals in France. Next, she looked into flights and visited a travel agent on Great Western Road who specialised in French jaunts and who alerted her, strictly off the record, that is, because after all they were there to sell package holidays and to favour official hotels and holiday resorts, but still, if you're on a limited budget, she said, a young woman of similar age to Mindy, then you should know about the phenomenon of couch surfing in Europe, she said. What is that? Mindy asked her. She said it was a guide, updated annually, and with reviews, about people who let you come and stay in their spare room or sometimes, even, literally on their couch, for free. I went through Europe couch surfing last year, she said. Let me tell you, it was an experience that I am not likely to forget. Why? Because this way you experience the real city, she said, not the tourist bollocks, she said, she was really warming to her topic, this girl Jenna, it said on her badge. Didn't you meet some headcases? Mindy asked her, and she said, course I did. That's part of the fun, she said. Believe me, she said. Nothing that I couldn't handle, she said. If you know what I mean. Mindy nodded like she knew exactly what Jenna was on about. Where can I get this guide, she asked Jenna, and Jenna opened a drawer in her desk and said, here, you can borrow mine. It's last year's edition. But still. I doubt that much has changed. This is Europe we're talking about, after all. Then Mindy dropped in at Hillhead Library and borrowed a book on the great churches of Europe, as well as a *Reader's Digest Atlas of the World*, and went home and worked out that she could fly straight to Paris from Glasgow in order to view Notre-Dame and take it from there. She revealed her astonishing plan to no one. She went through the phone numbers for Paris in the couch surfing book. Her rule was simple. If they couldn't speak English, then what was the point. The first English speaker was a man named Simone. He said, yes, that he still had a spare room and, yes, that he would be very happy to host. He asked her if she could describe herself to him. So that he could meet her at the airport, he clarified. That's very nice of you, she said. I'm a five-foot-two burlesque dancer with red hair, she said. And he said, wonderful, wonderful, that sounds adorable, he said. And then he said, what brings you to Paris? And Mindy said, I am coming to be astonishing.

127

Andrew Lethal is in his office at the City Chambers on George Square when he receives a phone call. He watches the phone ring for almost a full minute before he picks it up. A voice on the line says, why didn't you pick up the phone, it's me. I was walking into my office, Andrew Lethal lies. And then he says, this is harassment. You're the harasser, the voice says. You're the pest, it says. You're the lowlife scum, it adds. Fuck you, Andrew Lethal says. Fuck me, is it? the voice says. Give me the word and I'll fucking ruin you, it says. If you're not willing to play ball, just let me know, it says. Then it says, go ahead, make my day. Andrew Lethal rolls his eyes. You really are a two-bit gangster, he says. Make my day, he says, give me a break, why don't you come up with something original instead of parroting movies, you illiterate son of a bitch? OK, the voice says, while I'm off trying to come up with original lines with which to seal your fate, I'll go ahead and post the stash to the relevant people. Andrew Lethal hates that term, 'the stash'. Do you know what karma is, you dumb son of a bitch? Andrew Lethal says to him. Oh, I know all about karma, it says. And you're about to be visited by a shedload of it. This won't end well, Andrew Lethal says. For you, the voice says. Listen, Andrew Lethal says, what have I ever done to you? Fuck-all, the voice says. Which is part of the problem. Tell your boss Alec Bolland I'm not scared of him or of any of his fucking family, Andrew Lethal says. Who the fuck is Alec Bolland? the voice says. He's the one that's orchestrating this, isn't he? Andrew Lethal says. Don't think I don't know, he says. And after all I've done for his community. Fucking nerve. I've no idea what the fuck you are talking about, the voice says. Then it hangs up. Andrew Lethal walks to the window and gazes out on George Square. A group of women in bright-coloured saris are feeding the pigeons. In the far corner, the police are putting on a display with their attack dogs. Some guy in a special outfit is pursued by a snarling Alsatian. It bites his costume and brings him down. Everyone applauds and takes pictures. My appetites will be the end of me, Andrew Lethal says to himself.

128

Dan Ruff calls round to Paul Vickers' caravan and asks him to 'put together a squad' and to 'get tooled up'. Get fucking tooled up, he says to him. We need to go see the Bollands. And scare the living shite out of them, he says. Big Paul Vickers cuts through the crowd and walks over to the ghost train that has a painting of Elvis Presley being operated on by aliens from Roswell and tells Stevie Shaw to put his little brother in charge. You're needed, he says. Get your tools, he says, we need to pay a team a visit in the east end, he says. Then he crosses over to the hall of mirrors and says the same to Wee Boab who is leaning against the entrance eating a roll and square sausage. Can I at least finish my bap, he says to Big Paul Vickers, and Paul Vickers says, aye, no bother, meet us at Dan's bit in ten minutes, he says. OK, Dan Ruff says when he has his whole team assembled, including Scott Ruff. War council, he says. Then he opens a book and clears his throat and starts to read, slowly, stumbling over the words and mispronouncing them, but still. The first duty is to sacrifice to the gods, he reads, and pray for them to grant you the thoughts, words and deeds likely to render your command most pleasing to them and to bring yourself, your friends and your city the fullest measure of affection and glory and advantage. He looks up to blank expressions all round. Xenophon, he says, as if it's fucking obvious. So, what do you think would be a suitable sacrifice to ensure that today, as we go into battle, he says, that the gods are on our side? No one says anything, at first. Then Wee Boab says, semen. What?! You know, he says. Have a chug, sacrificing all of those babies. Don't be disgusting, Dan Ruff says, and Big Paul Vickers says, this bastard is going to bring down the wrath of the gods on our heads with this kind of talk. Any other ideas? Dan Ruff says, rolling his eyes, and Stevie Shaw says, what about cold hard cash, and Dan Ruff says, now we're talking. Everybody put in a pound note, he says. Fuck sake, Wee Boab protests, but he does it anyway. Then Dan Ruff takes an ashtray and puts the five quid in it and lights it on fire. Fuck sake, Wee Boab says again, as Dan Ruff stands gazing at the flames with a mad look like Mephistopheles. No greater sacrifice than burning money, he says. Except for your own life, he says, am I right, except for burning up your own life for the gods, he says, which is something we are also willing to do today, am I right, boys, he says, and the two kids just sort of say, yeah, I guess, while shuffling from one foot to the other, and Dan Ruff says, no guessing, the gods are watching, he says, they can hear every fucking thing, he warns. We need to be resolute and determined. In the eyes of the gods, he says. We're paying the Bollands a visit, he says, and I don't want to have to do it twice. Put your tools in that blue Adidas bag, he says. And let's go. With the blessing of the gods, he adds, and he looks up at the roof of the caravan and crosses himself. Then he winks, up at the air, like that.

129

I want to be alone. Donald Murray is sat on the bench with his son Aaron in Glasgow's Botanic Gardens. I want to be alone, he repeats. And then he says, that's what Martina Dietrich would say. I want to be alone, he says, only this time in a feminine German accent. Any other sayings? Aaron asks him. No, he says. Just that one. John Wayne, he's another one. Another what? But his dad just stares into space. A little bird alights on the arm of the bench as a woman walks past with a pram. Dad, Aaron says to him. Do you want to know what happened to Nemo? Who's Nemo? he says. Nemo, your son. Nemo, my brother, Aaron says. Nemo? Is that you? Donald says, and he turns to Aaron as if it is Nemo come back to him. No, it's me, Aaron, Aaron says. How do you know about . . . Nemo? he asks Aaron. A little bird told me, Aaron says.

130

Luke G.B. Caird is making his way along Dumbarton Road in the early-morning gloom. The sky is low and grey, the pavements are damp. He's eating a bacon roll as he goes. And thinking of the events of the night before. Inevitably. He sees Drunken Duncan across the road, always a good omen. Drunken Duncan, who leaps into puddles with great joy while singing and listening to his Walkman. There he goes. Luke G.B. Caird waves to Charlie McCann, the manager of the shoe shop on the corner. Then he heads up the stairs to his office, through the tiled close that smells of ammonia, Caird & Burl. Mark C. Burl is already at his desk, as is their secretary, Yvonne. Alright, mate, Burl says. Yvonne says, hi Luke. I heard you were out on a date last night with a glamorous air hostess who recites poetry, she says. I was, he says, as he hangs up his bunnet and takes off his scarf and hangs his dark-blue Crombie next to it. Well, Yvonne says. Don't keep us in suspense. How did it go?! Oh, it was great, he says. A great night, he says. She's lovely, he says. Then he says to Mark C. Burl, can you come into the conference room with me for a second, and Mark C. Burl says, sure. Once they are behind closed doors Luke G.B. Caird says, you won't fucking believe the night I had, mate. Burl offers him a fag from his pack. Give me all the lurid details, mate, he says. She literally wants my babies, mate. Hot to trot, huh, a real nympho, Mark C. Burl says, as he sparks one up. Insatiable, he says. I know the type, he nods. We've all been there, mate, he says. Lucky you, he says. No, Luke G.B. Caird clarifies. She literally wants to have a child with me, he says. She's a fucking fast mover, Mark C. Burl says. At least she's up-front about it, he says. Not like some bitches, he says. But I mean, she *is* totally insatiable, don't get me wrong, Luke G.B. Caird says. Check this out: she had me finger-fuck her in the bar at the hotel. You finger-fucked her at the bar in the Hilton? The very one, Luke G.B. Caird says. Fuck me, Mark C. Burl says. That's like the inverse of the Mile High Club. The Mile Low Club, Luke G.B. Caird laughs. Mental, Mark C. Burl says. Did she instigate it? Yeah. Get this, Luke G.B. Caird says, she just asked me straight out, would you like to make love? No way. Seriously. And then she suggested that I finger-fuck her right then and there. Wow. Did anyone notice? No idea, mate. She's not going to get too many babies from your stumpy tips, though. Well, obviously we took it upstairs and I fucked her senseless on the bed afterwards. At one point I had a dildo up her ass, in her pussy, and down her throat at the same time. You brought a bag of dildos, mate? Legendary. No, she did. She poured them out on the bed and told me to 'plug' her. Fuck me. I know, mate. Did you take her up the arse, mate? Obviously. Nice one, Mark C. Burl marvels. She's beautiful, mate, smells amazing. Dark eyes. Got this tattoo of a pair of feathers beneath one of her tits. So hot. We're lying in bed afterwards. Her make-up is all smeared and there is cum in her hair. Love it, mate. We're lying there smoking, and she says, the minute I saw you, I thought, here is the father of my children. Can that happen, mate? You believe in that, mate? I believe in fate, Luke G.B. Caird says. I believe in poetry, he says. More so than ever, he clarifies. I believe in destiny, he says. Why not, he says. And then she says: I want to be inseminated with the spunk of a literary man. That's what she said, mate? Word for word, mate. The spunk of a literary man? Seriously. Inseminated? Seriously. I hate to break it to her, mate, but you're a private dick, not a literary man. I know, mate. Funnily enough, that's the word she used. Literary man? No, private dick. She thinks I'm literary because she met me on a plane going to a book festival. Didn't you tell her you were a private dick? Of course. But then she goaded me into saying I was a writer in secret, that I was a novelist *behind the scenes*. A crime novelist. She thinks crime novelists have the spunk of literary men? Mark C. Burl asks him. Mate, she's from Georgia, Luke G.B. Caird says. Give her a break. Ha ha, nice one, mate, Mark C. Burl says. Then Mark C. Burl says, you know what I am going to say, don't you. I know exactly what you are going to say, Luke G.B. Caird says.

Luke G.B. Caird and Mark C. Burl have exactly this type of relationship. A symbiotic relationship, is how they describe it to clients. Plus, they are both trained to be suspicious, and to question everything. That it's a honey trap, Luke G.B. Caird says. Boldest honey trap ever, mate, Mark C. Burl says. Then he says, nothing would surprise me. Except this, he admits. Except how mad this is, he clarifies. What you gonna do? he asks Luke G.B. Caird, and Luke G.B. Caird says, I'm gonna follow the leads, he says. Just like I did in the bar of the Hilton. And they both crack up laughing, like that.

131

Josef Noth gets the word he was waiting for. The Wehrmacht have found a post for him as a short-wave radio operator in military intelligence. His new boss is Alexander Bärnighausen. My father was a judge, Bärnighausen tells him, as they walk the endless corridors of a subterranean vault beneath a bank in the eleventh arrondissement. He speaks it like a thin-lipped threat. There is something reptilian about Bärnighausen's appearance, something chthonic about his thin lips and bulging eyes, his ghastly skin that almost glows in the dark. It is like he has risen up on two legs from the primordial swamp a bare few generations ago. He tried many famous cases, Bärnighausen says. Perhaps you have heard of the Vampire of Düsseldorf? No, Noth says. Peter Kürten, Bärnighausen says. A monster who drank his victims' blood and stabbed young children through the heart and through the genitals with blunt scissors and pounded them to death with hammers and ejaculated while he did so. It was my father who sentenced him to death, Bärnighausen says. Justice, he says to himself, as much as to Josef Noth. Kürten was a conscript in the German army, stationed in Metz, Bärnighausen tells him, when he committed his first crimes. Can you believe it. That's so weird, Josef Noth says. I never visited Metz, he tells Bärnighausen. But my father owned a picture book about it. I would stare at the pictures in it when I was young. They come back to me so clearly now. A cat sat in a deserted street outside a tall building with crumbling masonry. A traditional chimney-sweep in a top hat on a roof somewhere. The beautiful cathedral, of course, towering over the neighbouring apartments. The esplanade in front of the Palace of Justice. Exactly, Bärnighausen said. Justice. Two kids playing in the river, Noth says. The sound of blood made him come, Bärnighausen says. Can you believe it. My father ordered that he be guillotined and now what do you think of this: Kürten thanked him for the sentence. Unbelievable. But there's more. At his execution Kürten asked the prison psychiatrist who accompanied him to the gallows whether, once his head was cut off, he would still be able to hear, even for a brief second or two, because he said that the pleasure of all pleasures would be for him to hear the sound of his own blood gushing from the stump of his neck. A German soldier in France, Bärnighausen says. Can you believe it.

132

By the time Aaron arrives at the camp, Dan and the boys have left to see the Bollands. Aaron pushes through the crowds at the sideshows. It's mobbed. People are eating candyfloss and kids are screaming. There are queues for every ride. Loud music is pumping over the Tannoy. 'Never Gonna Give You Up' by Rick Astley is once more, inexplicably, the sound of the summer. Aaron spots young JB manning the dodgems. Where's Scott? he asks him.

Didn't you hear? JB says to him. They've sent out a war party. Who has? Dan Ruff. Dan and Scott and some of the boys have gone over to have a word with the Bollands about unsubstantiated rumours of stealing horses. Ah fuck, Aaron says. Don't worry about it, JB says. They'll just give them a fright, that's all. Haw you, JB says, no standing up on the dodgems, get your arse back in that chair, ya womble. Aaron slips off. This is his chance. He heads for the shipping container where they keep The Lark. He lets himself in through the gate and tries the door. It isn't locked. There's something religious about the scene that greets him. The light is the light of a manger, Aaron thinks. The set-up is Euclidean, geometric, uncannily perfect. What is the word? Speaking. In its precise arrangement, the scene is speaking. The light of a single high window illuminates the straw on the floor. To the left there is a wooden water trough up on legs. On the wall behind there are leads and blinders and crops. To the right, a simple blanket, folded, on a low wooden table. In the corner there is an old lawnmower with a towel draped over it, so that it resembles a man in a gown, or a vestment, more like, bent over towards the centre of this reverse diorama, this nativity scene, as The Lark rises to its feet, first on its hind legs, and then onto all fours, and turns its gaze towards Aaron. Its coffin gaze. Everything is in place, it seems. Then Aaron says: I have come to talk to you about my brother. I have come to ask you whether or not you know what happened to my brother Nemo. And The Lark speaks. It speaks in a terrible elongated voice where it is as if every letter, every syllable, were originally travelling at tremendous speed and through impossible force had been slowed to a smear – the bare tail on a comet – this light that has been travelling towards us from the beginning of time, held in abeyance, barely, by an animal that talks, an animal that talks in a voice like a high breathless scream and that now speaks the word: 'es-ca-polo-gist'. What?

133

Why didn't you tell me about this? The Precious Gift is quizzing Joyce Monaghan. He is pointing at this fucking crazy-looking upside-down construct that is hanging from beneath this wide wooden table like a reflection in water of an invisible fortress. What was all that nonsense about giving me that single folder and telling me that was all you had uncovered? A folder that, it turned out, quite coincidentally, I'm sure, had a map of where I was living and a record of my daily fucking movements inside it. What was that about? The Precious Gift reiterates. He has lost his fucking cool. If something is going on you need to be up-front about it now because we are in a really dangerous position, he says. In fucking Derry and all, he says. I know nothing, Joyce says. And then she says, I just wanted to know if you would tell the truth. The truth about what? About what you and my Jim were up to. And what really happened to him. You know more than I do, she says. You are at an unfair advantage, my friend, she says, and she makes a big deal about winking in an over-the-top fashion. Then she suggests that they go downstairs and have a drink. The Precious Gift takes a seat at the breakfast bar. Joyce turns the radio on, low. Sorry, she says. I just like to have music on low like that. That way it seeps into the room, she says. She cracks open a bottle of vodka. Fancy a voddy? she says. The Precious Gift doesn't refuse. He can see his own face reflected in the dark of the window, in the night. What is that thing upstairs? The Precious Gift asks her, as she pours the vodka into special chilled shot glasses from the freezer. He told me he was working on a new model, was what he said. He said that he was getting into modelling landscape. He said it was his new hobby and of course it was no surprise to me, because Jim was always modelling ever since I knew him because he was into his wargaming and his Dungeons & Dragons. But this wasn't for any kind of game, this time, he said. This time he said that he wanted to see if he could create a reverse diorama. What does that even mean, a reverse diorama? Well, he never actually explained what it was. He said that he had seen it in a vision. In a 'waking dream'. The vision of the fortress was how he described it. How long had he been working on it before he died? Mmhh, about three months. He actually made it upside down. Like, he didn't make it on the top of the table and then fix it upside down like that. He would lie underneath it and build it up above him. I would bring him his tea and his sandwich, and he would be down there on his back, and all I could see were his legs sticking out, like that. Like Michelangelo, The Precious Gift said. What? Like Michelangelo in the Sistine Chapel, he said.

134

Mindy takes the bus from Buchanan Bus Station to Glasgow Airport. On the bus she listens to her Walkman. A cassette of the soundtrack to *Death in Venice*, the 1971 film by Luchino Visconti about falling in love with a young boy there. Because she couldn't find any French music in the library. Will I fall in love with a young boy in Paris, she wonders, as she listens to this sad music, this music by Mahler, which she is guessing must have come at the end of the movie, once love is lost and all we are left with are memories. Yet here Mindy is, right at the beginning. She has told no one of her plans. Not even in her response to Achilles Noth, where she talked more about her job in the shoe shop and how the long-haired manager was always pestering her for a date and also about Glasgow and Scotland, because Achilles had never visited, and he imagined it snowbound and everyone living halfway up the mountains like in the Alps. My father was German, and my mother was French, Achilles wrote, so I understand the mountains and the forests, as well as the village and the city, he wrote. Mindy had to disabuse him. She told her mum that she was attending another sales conference in France, and her mother said, you have such a jet-set lifestyle with your job, it's wonderful. But watch out for French men, she warned her. They are forward, but in the end they only care about their mothers. Believe me, she said, like she had previous experience of their amorous ways. Mindy arrives at the airport three hours before her flight and so treats herself to a toasted cheese-and-ham sandwich, which she convinces herself is the equivalent of a croque-monsieur, and a glass of red wine, while she reads a book, a book entitled *How to Read a Cathedral.* It describes the structure of cathedrals and their features in a way that a layperson can understand, because Mindy has never gone to church in her life and her mum is a hardcore atheist. On the flight she sits next to an older man who compliments the pilot all the way to Paris, pointing out what a smooth take-off it is, his use of the gears (which he describes as 'textbook'), even his reassuring tones over the Tannoy. Think about it, he says. In the end it all comes down to him keeping his cool. If he breaks his cool? At this he shakes his head at the chaos that would no doubt ensue. Once again, when he asks Mindy what she is travelling to Paris for, she tells him it's in order to be astonishing. And what does that involve? he asks her. We'll see, she says. When they disembark at Charles de Gaulle Airport, after a landing that the old man describes as 'flawless', Mindy waves him away and wishes him all the best, only afterwards realising that she didn't ask him a single thing about his own journey. When the door at Arrivals slides open, her host is stood there with a card that says 'MINDY' on it. He looks older than she thought he would. He has dark thin hair, swept back over his head, over a little bald patch. He is well dressed, in a white dress shirt with rolled-up sleeves and a pair of dark slacks. He has a nice tan. He wears round designer glasses, like John Lennon. Mindy, he shouts when he spots her, and he waves. The legendary Mindy, he shouts, as if he has known her forever. It's me, Simone, he says. He kisses her on both cheeks. He smells of French cologne and cigarettes and leather. Your chariot awaits, he tells her, and he grabs her suitcase and whisks her off to the taxi rank. I thought you were picking me up in your car, Mindy says to him. I thought you had a car. There was no need to go to so much trouble, she says. But Simone dismisses her. Nonsense, he says. On the ride into the city, he points out interesting monuments and places where he grew up and where historical things took place. He is a retired historian, he informs her. Roll down the window, he says. Breathe in the roses, he says. The smell of roses mixed with the smell of decay, he announces. Eros and Thanatos, he says. What? Eros and Thanatos, he repeats. The god of love and the god of death. The god of life and the god of putrefaction, he says. Locked in a love embrace, he says. Wow. Mindy sticks her head out of the window and her long red hair trails in the wind. Breathe, she says to herself. Breathe deep, Mindy, she says, and with that she feels sure that she will be OK.

135

What the fuck was all that about? Wise Crow says, again, at the end of their second morning of interrogating The Mole. This guy is inscrutable, she says, and Ruth Prior agrees.

The Precious Gift suggests a pub lunch to talk it over and they all head to a pub in the Waterside, the Golden Gate. They only do cheese toasties here, Ruth Prior warns them, but that's cool with everyone. A cheese toastie and a pint of Guinness, you can't beat that, Wise Crow says, as they settle at a table by the open fire. In the corner there are some old boys playing the traditional music. He's right, you know, The Precious Gift says. In what way is he right? Wise Crow asks him. He's right that unless we charge him or release him soon he's going to be fatally compromised. It might look like he's squealing. If so, it's all over when he gets out. What was it he said, 'the cause that was there before any of us'? What did he mean by that? He knows something, The Precious Gift says. I think he's guilty, he says. Make no bones about it. I say we propose that they release him. I say we propose that they release him and then we track him. I'll track him. But before we even get into that, The Precious Gift says, I need to ask you both something. And I need you to be as honest as possible with me, he says. What is the vision of the fortress? What? I think it might be connected with Jim's death. I think he was modelling it at home. What is the vision of the fortress? But before they can answer, some guy bursts from the toilets in a balaclava and shoots one of the old boys in the band. He shoots your man on the hand drum at close range so that his brains are blown out across your fiddle player there who is covered in his blood and brains and the fella walks out the bar calm as you like while this fiddle player is screaming and shaking and the drummer falls to the ground in slow motion, he slumps over to the side and then he tumbles to the floor, with all eyes on the falling man, there's something balletic to it, The Precious Gift thinks, but then he feels bad, it's a poor old fella with his brains blown out, come on now, and he runs over to him, and he kneels beside him, and your man is dead, and he looks up at the fiddle player who is paralysed and whose hands are gripping the sides of the chair so tight that it will take a team of paramedics to prise him free, even as your man on the flute immediately does a runner, and splits the scene, and the landlord calls the police, and they all wait to make their statements, and then they're taken away in a police van, via the back door, just in case.

136

At night the light is eerie, in the catacombs, which is what the Wehrmacht operatives have nicknamed it, this bank vault where they have set up countless short-wave radios, the tombs where Wehrmacht operatives sit hunched over their desks, in their own sphere of light, with headphones on, scanning the frequencies for irregular activity, for French or for English voices, and for codes too, and for call signs. Alexander Bärnighausen introduces Josef Noth to his nearest neighbour, a young German named Thomas Tebaldi, or Tab for short. He also provides him with a logbook where he records the precise frequencies scanned and the exact time a transmission is intercepted. Wait till you come across a numbers station, Tab says to him. Creepy as fuck, he says. What's a numbers station? Josef Noth asks him, and he says, it's a station that just broadcasts numbers, for a certain duration, according to a strange schedule. In a voice like a robot or a far-away child, he adds. Creepy as fuck. They have little musical intros that sound like they are made by robots or children, he adds. What is the point of them? Josef Noth asks him. No one knows for sure, Tab says, but the best guess is that they are broadcasting codes to secret operatives. Who is? They all are, there are numbers stations in all sorts of languages, he says. Including us? Including us. Then why don't we know anything about them? Cause they're secret, Tab shrugs. Cause if we knew the truth behind anything it would scare the living daylights out of us, Tab suggests. But wait till you hear them. Tab shudders. Ugh, he says. But everything sounds creepy when it's far away, everything ghostly, he says. Welcome to the catacombs, he says. Welcome to the graveyard shift, he says. Will you take a smoke, he says, and he offers Josef Noth a cigarillo. Thanks, Josef Noth says, and they both spark up as Josef reaches for his headphones. It's the music of the spheres, out there, the song of the solar system, Josef Noth thinks to himself, as he turns up the volume and thinks about how he used to juggle the whole damn system himself, in another world now. He closes his eyes, and it is like he is floating in a sea of solar frequencies, a dark invisible sea that is nevertheless speaking all the same. There are gods in the ether, he thinks to himself, as he hears those first voices, voices in French, at first, a weather report from Fontainebleau that makes the villages that orbit the forest sound like sweet constellations, Montigny, Cugny, Grez-sur-Loing, Villiers, La Genevraye, Bourron-Marlotte, how delightful is an amateur weather report on the airwaves, then German, a German channel is playing classical music, is that Mahler, and now English, two English women are discussing making 'reconstituted potatoes', by which they mean instant dried potatoes where you rehydrate them in water, they are discussing how remarkably delicious they can be, someone somewhere is playing a flute, or is it an oboe, that high reedy sound, wow, he thinks, it is like St-John Perse, he thinks to himself, it is like my old friend St-John Perse sat at the very heart of the world, he thinks. Two people are having a conversation, in French and in German. It is the vaguest conversation imaginable. They keep referring to 'a certain thing' and to each other's knowledge of this 'certain thing'. And to how it will become necessary to deal with this 'certain thing'. Josef Noth details it in his logbook, and he slides his headphones off and asks Tab, do you often come across illicit lovers on the short-wave, and Tab says, why, yes, all of the time.

137

Luke G.B. Caird is back home after a long day mostly trailing unfaithful husbands and wives across Glasgow. Why does anyone get married? he thinks, as he runs himself a bath and walks over to the window to smoke a cigarette and look out over the bowling greens and tennis courts and across to the University of Glasgow, illuminated in the dark there. The Kelvin Way has been closed off by police after a hit-and-run. The lights of the police cars flashing between the dark trees. He does a few press-ups on the bathroom floor, a few sit-ups, then he looks at himself in the mirror. He has a paunch, for sure. How do women put up with men's bodies, he asks himself. How can this be attractive to them. But thank fuck they do all the same, he thinks. Ugh, he says to himself, as he lowers himself into the bath, a tiny claw-footed number that means he has to bend his legs. By this time Tamar will be in Texas, he thinks to himself. She has three days off in Houston. I wonder if she has a man in every port, he thinks. I mean, she's a glamorous air hostess, how easy is it for glamorous air hostesses to pick up paunchy mugs like me, he thinks. He dries himself off, pulls a T-shirt on, a Bob Dylan tour T-shirt he bought at a concert a few years ago, and makes himself a mug of mint tea. He climbs into bed, though really it's just a bunch of wooden pallets on the floor with a mattress on top, and switches his reading light on. He reaches for his copy of *The Knight in the Panther's Skin* and opens it at the introduction. He reads that it is an allegory, a thinly veiled allegory. That the whole poem is, in fact, an ode to Queen Tamar. What the fuck. That Queen Tamar quite possibly commissioned the poem herself in order to mark the era of cultural enrichment, not to say peace, stability, wealth and glamour – a true renaissance, is how the introduction phrases it – that she presided over in Georgia. The first woman to rule Georgia oversaw its golden years and was called Tamar. Luke G.B. Caird sits there in silence. It's so quiet at night at this end of Sauchiehall Street. Sometimes all you can hear are the foxes, fighting in the park. She has gifted me a love poem in which her namesake is praised as the most beautiful queen and which details all of the disguises that it takes to woo her, he thinks. This chick is blowing my mind, he thinks, and he falls asleep with the book open on his chest like a pair of loving arms. In the morning, before work, he heads to the Mitchell Library and asks for books on medieval Georgia. That pest Sarah is working at the desk. Luke, she says, we never see you! Who is this 'we', Luke G.B. Caird is thinking. Her and her pathetic husband? Why don't you come over for dinner sometime, she says. Sure, he says. We need to get that in the calendar asap, he says. You always say that and then it never happens, Sarah sulks. What can I say, Luke G.B. Caird says, it's always just so mad at work. Sarah brings him a bunch of books about medieval Georgia, and she sets them up for him at a long table near the window. Those mad Mitchell carpets are enough to give you a migraine this early in the morning. Luke G.B. Caird opens this one huge book like a medieval manuscript and there, on the first page, above an inscription that reads 'Queen of Kings and Queens, Glory of the World, Kingdom and Faith, Champion of the Messiah, may God increase her victories', is a painting of Tamar. A painting of Queen Tamar, yes, but also a painting of Tamar, Luke G.B. Caird's Tamar. She looks exactly like her. The weight of her dark eyes.

The kinks in her long dark hair. Her skin is lightly tanned. And those eyebrows: a simple bird in flight. And those lips: impossible entrance to heaven. I knew this would happen, Luke G.B. Caird says to himself. What the fuck is going on.

138

Dan Ruff takes out a crowbar from his blue Adidas holdall and bangs it on the locked metal gates of the Bolland compound in Sandyhills. A hatch slides back on the door and a gormless face looks out. Fuck you looking at? Dan Ruff says to it. You're the one banging on my gate with a crowbar, it says. What the fuck do you want? Is there a particular reason youse have yourselves barricaded in there like fucking Nazis in South America? Dan Ruff says to this face. It's for your own safety, the face says. You know the way you would keep killer dogs behind high walls, it says. I'm here to have words with your man Alec Bolland, Dan Ruff says. Tell him I'm here. It's Dan Ruff, the King of the Gypsies, tell him. Dogs or not, he adds. The hatch slides shut, and you can hear footsteps receding into the distance. Keep your cool, Dan Ruff warns his boys. No tools, unless I says so. Then the face comes back and unlocks the gate. Go on in, it says. Alec is waiting for you in that caravan over there. Stood outside the caravan there is a team of six or seven boys just staring. Keep your cool, boys, Dan Ruff instructs his boys. When he gets to the other team he says, youse boys stay out here with these thugs, I'm going in to speak to Bolland, and one of Bolland's boys says, who the fuck you calling thugs, and Dan Ruff says, what the fuck you talking about, I was talking to you, I was saying that youse can stand out here with my thugs while I speak to your man Bolland, and the bloke says, I'll be having that, he says, and he motions for Dan Ruff to hand over his crowbar, here, Dan Ruff says, and he throws it spinning through the air to Big Paul Vickers, who makes a big theatrical deal of catching it behind his back, so that the whole thing feels like some mad acrobatic set-up. Inside the caravan, Alec Bolland is sat topless behind a small foldaway table where he's eating a microwave meal straight out of the container. He wears his hair in a salt-and-pepper quiff and with lots of chains and jewellery. This better be fucking important, Bolland says. Cause I'm trying to watch *Neighbours*. What a fucking coincidence, Dan Ruff says. Because I've come on neighbourly business. Ever read Xenophon? Dan Ruff asks him. As a matter of fact, I have, Bolland says, while never removing his gaze from the TV, like something out of an updated book by your man Xenophon exactly. I know what you are going to say, Alec Bolland says to Dan Ruff. You're about to point out the inadvisability of internecine strife, am I right? I'm glad we're on the same page, Dan Ruff says, you, me and Xenophon. Do you know his book on horsemanship? Dan Ruff asks him. Alec Bolland scrapes out the rest of his chilli con carne and white rice, still without looking away from the TV, and he says, no, I don't believe I have read that one, he says. It's a classic, Dan Ruff says. And, inevitably, about so much more than horsemanship. Alec Bolland doesn't respond. There's rumours about horses doing the rounds, Dan Ruff says. Rumours that are rumoured to be coming from you, I might add. And what is the substance of these rumours, Alec Bolland croaks, for that's how he speaks, in a low croak like a devious gangster toad. That we stole some horses, and that we shot a poor kid in the face just to get them, Dan Ruff says. Doesn't sound like you, Alec Bolland says, without looking round. Why would you be out here in the east end shooting young kids for horses? Why spread the rumour, then? I didn't, Alec Bolland says. And I'm disappointed to see you come charging in here about it. You know me better, he says. I'm not a gossip. And I don't believe in internecine conflict. Who told you I was spreading a rumour? A trusted source, Dan Ruff says. He's bullshitting you, Alec Bolland says. He's playing you like a fucking canary, Alec Bolland says, just as *Neighbours* finishes and the theme tune begins. Here, Alec Bolland says, pass me that remote. He still hasn't looked round once. Dan Ruff picks the remote up off the chair and hands it to Alec Bolland, who presses a button without even looking. The BBC news comes up. They are interviewing a group of ex-offenders at some kind of book festival they are having in Springburn. What do you know? Alec Bolland says, and he nods towards the screen. It's our friend Lethal, he says. Andrew Lethal is being interviewed on screen by Mary Marquis. He is talking about 'naïve art' and about how well the ex-cons have done, and now he is looking to the camera and advising anyone who 'feels crime coming on', that's how he puts it, I would advise anyone who 'feels crime coming on' to channel that same energy into art, he is saying, don't end up behind bars, he is saying, put those same energies into creation, he is advising the viewers at home, which right now is Alec Bolland and Dan Ruff. See when I hear the word 'art', Alec Bolland says to Dan Ruff, without looking round once, that's when I reach for my crowbar.

139

Yvonne takes a phone call at Caird & Burl. It's Aaron Murray. Hi Aaron, Yvonne says, how are you? I'm fine, he says. Can I speak to Mark or Luke? he says. Luke's not in today, I'll put you through to Mark, she says. What's up, bud? Mark says to him. I have a name, he says. What? I have a name I need you to look into. Regarding what? he asks Aaron. Regarding the disappearance of my brother

Nemo. Fuck, Mark says. Where did this name come from? Let's just say a little bird told me, Aaron says. Fair enough, Mark says. Give me the name and we'll see what we can turn up. The Escapologist, Aaron says. What? That's his name. Or his nickname. Or his codename. Who fucking knows. I don't have anything beyond that. It was hard to make out but I think that's what it said. It? They, I think that's what they said. Can't you be sure? I asked it – sorry – I asked them for a name and it said, Escapologist. And then it stopped speaking, they stopped speaking, sorry. It sounds like you were at a fucking séance, mate, Mark C. Burl says. Listen, Aaron says, do you think the dead can speak? Do you think the restless dead can communicate to the living by proxy? What do you mean, by proxy? Do you think they can take possession of other things in order that their deaths can be avenged? Like what things? Like, say, animals. Do I think the dead use talking animals to plead their case? Is that what you are asking me? Sort of, Aaron says. Can't ghosts speak? Mark C. Burl asks Aaron. I mean, if they can't on their own, wouldn't it be easier to possess a human who could actually talk than a mute animal? Well, humans have souls, maybe two souls cannot occupy the same body, Aaron says. So, you think animals don't have souls? Mark C. Burl says. Well, in your opinion, are there horses in heaven? Aaron asks him. Mark C. Burl has to think about that one. It's a good point, Mark C. Burl says. Maybe not. In that case, where do you think animals go when they die? Into the soil? Mark C. Burl suggests. And then he says, wait a minute, did a horse tell you this? Did a fucking talking horse say that an escapologist did it? Fucking Noah's Ark had nothing on this, mate, Mark C. Burl says. Then he says, what if he is talking about your brother? What if he is hinting, somehow, that he escaped?

140

Simone shows Mindy around his beautiful apartment in Paris, up a claustrophobic set of stone steps and right next to the Seine. He shows off his 'open-plan' kitchen and living room, and then he shows her to her room. This will be your room, possibly, he says. What do you mean, possibly, Mindy says to him, is there another option? There is, Simone says, but we'll get to that. Then he says, I am happy to cook for you most nights, but we must try the restaurants too. I can take you to my favourite restaurants, he says, because the soul of Paris is in its cooking and in its haunted courtyards way off the tourist drag, he says. Would you like that? Yes, I'd love for you to show me around, Mindy says. I have some things I need to do on my own, though. Such as? Such as visiting certain cathedrals on my own, she says. It's part of a ritual, she says. That I can't go into, she adds. Mindy, you are a very mysterious woman, Simone says. You really do appeal, he says. And then he shows her the bathroom and how to work the shower. Mindy asks if she can have a shower and freshen up and Simone says, of course. I have to finish some writing myself, he says, and then he suggests that afterwards they walk over to the terrace of his favourite restaurant where he will 'treat her' to dinner. Sounds good, Mindy says, and she disappears into the bathroom with her toiletries bag and a change of clothes under her arm. Simone puts some music on, the first album by Altered Images, and Mindy showers and changes into a tight black spangly dress that zips up the back. Dah-dah, she says, when she walks back into the kitchen for the big reveal. Simone gets up from his desk in the living room where he is writing on an electric typewriter. Are all Scottish women as stylish as you? he asks her, and she says, god no, I am the most stylish by far. OK, he says, let me grab my jacket and we'll take a walk. But as soon as they are out of the door Simone insists that they sit down on a bench. Before we go any further, he says, I think it's prudent to ask. Would you like to make love? Wow, Mindy thinks to herself. This guy is outrageous. Outrageous and attractive. She is already starting to feel astonished, and astonishing. No offence if not, Simone says, before she can reply. But you've got to ask, haven't you? he says. To tell you the truth, I don't go on dates as a rule. I tend to just sleep with the women who come and stay with me through couch surfing, he says. I thought it best to be up-front with you. Just to clear the air. But fear not, he says (his English is cute), if you're not interested, I won't bring it up again and I can guarantee you that you will remain unmolested (!) the entire time you are under my roof. And Mindy says, yes. Yes, I would like to make love, she says. In fact, I think that what we should do is go right back to your apartment and make love right now, she says. When they get back to the apartment Mindy announces that she is going to change into something a little special, and she goes into the bedroom that she now knows she won't be sleeping in for a single night and changes into one of her favourite burlesque outfits, white panties, white stockings, a white corset that pushes her tits up, and she puts on her favourite silver heels – she brought this outfit for precisely this kind of eventuality – and reveals herself to Simone, who is already buck-naked and laid out on the bed with a substantial hard-on. Wow, he says when he sees her. Are you real? And Mindy bends from the waist and takes his cock in her mouth and then she gets down on all fours and takes his cock deep in her throat before he lifts her up and throws her onto her back on the bed where he proceeds to devour her. Oh my god, Mindy says to him, you are devouring me, devouring me, devouring me, she says to herself, as he brings her to a climax and then slides his considerable cock inside her. Fuck me with your big daddy cock, she says, and he absolutely ploughs her to another screaming climax. Afterwards they lie in bed together and watch porn on a VHS that Simone has, where the girl in the film is wearing all-white lingerie just like Mindy. She's very talented, Mindy says, as the girl tongues the man's asshole while stroking his cock. You're very talented, Simone says to her, and they go at it all over again, only this time just like in the movie.

141

The decision is made. The Mole can go free. They're releasing him the next morning. Then it's down to The Precious Gift to track his movements and to keep him under surveillance. They've let him go, The Precious Gift explains to Joyce Monaghan, over a pint at the Golden Gate, which didn't even close for a day before reopening after the murder that took place there. The Precious Gift compares it to falling off a horse. If you fall off a horse, he says to Joyce, you get straight back on it, otherwise you might never get back in the saddle, he says. And Joyce says, do you think there is a psychic imprint? What? Do you think that when terrible things happen in a certain place, they leave a psychic stamp? How would you detect this psychic stamp? The Precious Gift asks her. It's a vibe, she says. It's a feeling. You can't articulate it, she says. Anyway, she says, why would they release him? We have nothing to pin on him except for hearsay, except for speculation, The Precious Gift says. Plus, he's an asset. The intent is to release him and allow him to incriminate himself and then send him down for life. Or not, he adds. Because he might be completely innocent, for all we know. But from now on he is going to be monitored. Closely, The Precious Gift adds. So don't worry. I had a weird dream last night, Joyce says. I dreamt of a bull that was getting its throat cut. Yes, I dreamt of this great heavenly bull that when its throat was cut it poured out onto the earth its blood and it fructified the earth. Fructified? Yes, that was the word that the man who cut its throat used. I went to stop it, to wade into this abattoir and stop this senseless slaughter, and the man, a muscular man with no top on, held his hand up to stop me in my tracks and said to me, with the blood of this bull we fructify the earth. What does 'fructify' mean? To make something fertile, The Precious Gift says. Bull's blood as a libation that makes the earth fecund. What does 'fecund' mean? Fertile, The Precious Gift says. All these euphemisms, Joyce says. For what? For sex, dummy, she says. Anyway, she says, I wish it was true. What? That death is the price of life. That would be something, at least, wouldn't it? They walk over to Tony's Trattoria, and there's Tony, out front, arguing with some drunken arsehole. The Precious Gift recognises him as the Eleanor Rigby guy. He is squaring up to Tony for a fight. Calling Tony a spic bastard. Then he whips his top off. Fuck me, The Precious Gift says, it's your man with the bull. The Eleanor Rigby guy whips his top off and puts his fists up at Tony like he's going to box his ears. Fucking Julius Caesar bastard, he is calling Tony. He turns when he sees Joyce and The Precious Gift approach. These are the same cunts that put Jesus to death, he says to them, pointing at Tony. This is Rome, he says to them. And The Precious Gift reels at this, he reels and he staggers slightly, as if Rome was something that could be conjured out of the air and across time, and he thinks of that psychic stain, even as Tony tells them to duck into the trattoria and that he'll be with them in a minute, even as two boys from the kitchen run out with tools, mops, hammers, and one of them fucks the Eleanor Rigby guy over the head and Tony drops onto the fallen nutcase's chest on the ground and pins him down by his arms and says,

Rome will make you a martyr should you ever attempt this one more time, he says, and Eleanor Rigby spits in his face and Tony responds by punching him, hard, right in the eye with his gold rings on, and Eleanor Rigby screams out, and Tony punches him again, and then says to him, I'm going to let you go, he says. I am going to let you go but if you fuck with me again, I will murder you, he says. And sure enough, Eleanor Rigby is subdued, subdued and with a bleeding eyeball, it looks like, as he staggers off, saying nothing. Sorry about that, my friends, Tony announces when he walks back into the restaurant, and he says, prawn cocktails on the house. André Breton said that Mexico was the home of surrealism, but truly it is Northern Ireland, The Precious Gift says as they sit down at their table. Who's André Breton? Joyce asks him, but The Precious Gift just says, never mind. Joyce orders clams in cream-and-vodka sauce. Clams, she says. I just love that word. It's exactly what it is, 'clams'. It has the sound of the thing-in-itself, she says. Clams, she says again. And she cracks up laughing to herself. The Precious Gift has ordered lasagne. Love a lasagne, he says. Can't be arsed making it in the house, though, he says. Then Joyce says to him, well, I'm going to ask you again. What is the vision of the fortress? What? What is the vision of the fortress? Where did you hear that? The Precious Gift asks her. I read it, she says. I read it in Jim's notebooks. He said he was haunted by the vision of the fortress. I don't know, The Precious Gift says. I don't know what that might be, he says. But I think it must be related to his creation of this reverse diorama. Quite, Joyce says, which is something she would say as she started to get drunk and glaze over. Quite. Against all the odds – though, as we have established, the odds are not substantial – once again they get the free jazz taxi home. Alright, troops, he says, and The Precious Gift says, what do you mean by that, and the free jazz driver says, it's just a phrase, it's just a term, he says, don't mean anything by it, he says, and then he says, back to the usual, and The Precious Gift and Joyce both laugh at how quickly they have established a routine together, as if they were lovers, lovers at the speed of light, and the free jazz taxi puts on John Coltrane, this is John Coltrane live in Japan, Wee Joe the free jazz taxi driver says, and he plays this music of suffering and abandon, this music of ecstasy and rage, and who knows whether it is set and setting, but everyone marvels, everyone in the car marvels. The Precious Gift says, how do you do that, how do you make that kind of music, how is that humanly possible to understand, that music, like the mind of God, he says, they are both drunk, but still, and the free jazz driver says, theta states. What? Theta states, he says. It's a state between wakening and sleeping. Just between the two. When you are at maximum receptivity to everything that is not you, he says. The theta state, he reiterates. Coltrane is in the zone, brother. It's also how remote viewing works, he says. Or so they say. And he looks at The Precious Gift in the rear-view mirror, like that.

142

Andrew Lethal is in a meeting at the City Chambers talking about some bullshit or other. In his mind he is in Mexico. In his mind he is floating down a river in Mexico on a boat named *Gabriela* with his girl Ramona. In his mind they are paying some destitute guy with a canary to pick out their fortunes from a set of cards by a lake and then eating seafood cocktails at Coyoacán Market with ketchup in them and now they are frantically scrubbing the water out of Ramona's kitchen during a flash-flood and Ramona is laughing at the two of them and comparing them to *Annie*

Hall, that scene in *Annie Hall* where Woody Allen and Diane Keaton are trying to cook lobsters and having so much fun and are completely in love right then. What are your thoughts on this, Andrew? Anne-Marie asks him. I think it's fine, he says. What's fine? Anne-Marie says. The situation, he says. The situation as it is, he says. It's fine, I think. So, you're saying we shouldn't replace the original lamp-posts with modern ones? Yes, he says. Exactly, yes. I'm against modern replacements in general, he says, and of course he thinks about human sacrifice, about how the original way of dealing with shite like this was to murder the whole room and trust in God to pay back in kind. And there were no fucking minutes taken either. Next on the agenda are the gypsy camps, Anne-Marie announces. In particular the volume of complaints we have received about this funfair running back-to-back with the Garden Festival. It's all about inclusion, innit? Andrew Lethal says, and he leans back in his chair and flicks his fag into a bin. The Garden Festival should be an opportunity for everyone, including marginalised communities, he says. The people from the Garden Festival say it's bringing down the tone, Anne-Marie says. You know what, Andrew Lethal says. Straight-up FUCK the people from the Garden Festival. The girl taking minutes dutifully gets it down. Come on, Andrew, Anne-Marie says, as the rest of the people sat round the table feign outrage. That kind of language is unnecessary. Who are these people policing on behalf of the Garden Festival? Who are these people deciding what's classy enough? How does this reflect Glasgow? I'm sorry, Andrew Lethal says, but I will continue to stand up for my traveller communities (he calls them his own) and ensure that they have a voice no matter what. Call it the Alternative Garden Festival. It's a boon, not a problem. Tell them that if they're not into diversity then they can tongue my— Andrew! Anne-Marie says. It's understood, how passionately you feel about these communities, just, please, watch the language. And Andrew thinks to himself, cunt.

143

Although Josef Noth doesn't know it – and which of us could ever hope to know the moment that something we loved and took for granted will never return again – it is the last time he will see his Erithena. He invites her to St-John Perse's flat and he reads her some of Perse's poetry. She stares at him with her big liquid eyes like they aren't anywhere near big enough for all of the wonders of this world. They make love with the window open, down on the floor on one of Perse's best rugs, which is now cum-stained forever and not just that. Then they walk out to a restaurant for some good T-bone steak, is what Josef Noth is demanding tonight, and fine red wine, dank red wine, village wine, he elaborates, and Erithena is all for it. You're my good-time girl, he says to her, and she squeezes up close to him, in her fur coat and heels, she smells so good. The moon is hanging so low over Paris that it is a sickle balanced on the top of a building, a comedy moon. That moon is so funny, Josef Noth says, he is more than a little drunk, and Erithena starts to sing a song called 'Moon, Don't Come Up Tonight' and that's when Josef Noth spots him. Wait, isn't that The H? The H who he visited the Magic-City amusement park with, for that strange, dark, unforgettable ball, in the days before the war? The H with whom they had attended the première of Findlay Anderson's *Veneer* with Thérèse and St-John Perse, the very night that Josef Noth first understood poetry? The H? Josef Noth says, and the man looks up at him in fear and in terror. It's me, Josef Noth says. It's me, Josef Noth. Josef Noth? The H says. Josef Noth, you are a soldier? he says to him. Yes, Josef Noth says, pointing out the obvious, after all he is in full uniform, yes, I'm a German soldier. And then The H says to him, in that case I have something to tell you. I have something cataclysmic to tell you, The H says. Your old girlfriend, Thérèse Barnier, is dead.

144

Luke G.B. Caird gets a call from Tamar. She is in Dubai and has returned from her stay in Houston, Texas. Oh, darling, it was fantastic, Tamar says. I should love to take you to see it. We viewed a house made out of beer cans! Tamar says. No! Yes! A house made out of beer cans that they call the Beer Can House. Then we went to the Orange Show, an adventure park created by someone obsessed with oranges. And then we went to a museum. Do you know the food they call Tex-Mex? she asks him. Luke G.B. Caird says, is it like fajitas? It is kind of like fajitas, but also tortillas and burritos, plus they have whole dishes that are just crisps served with sauce, Tamar says. Sounds like Glasgow, Luke G.B. Caird says. I knew you would love it, Tamar says. And Luke G.B. Caird says, so, is it true that I am addressing a queen? Ha ha, Tamar says, have you been reading my prose poem, she says (she calls it 'her prose poem'). I have, my queen, Luke G.B. Caird says to her. And she says, in that case you know just how to seduce me, she says. I do, Luke G.B. Caird says. Phone sex. Oh god, yes, Tamar says. Oh god please tell me you are stroking your cock as you speak, she says. I am stroking my big cock as I speak, he says. Tamar gasps. I am toying with my asshole, she says. Now I'm slapping my swollen pussy through my panties for you, she says. Luke G.B. Caird gets off in no time, and Tamar says she came too. Then he asks her, so, when will I see you next? And she says, in three weeks' time. In three weeks' time, I can come to Glasgow. Come and stay at mine, Luke G.B. Caird says. Really? I'd love that, Tamar says. Then she asks him how the writing is going. It's going good, Luke G.B. Caird says. Working away, he says. I can't wait to read it, Luke, Tamar says. You have such a way with words, she says. Luke G.B. Caird gets off the phone with Tamar and calls Mark C. Burl at home. What's up, mate? Mark C. Burl says. What's up with you? Luke G.B. Caird asks him. Just watching the telly, he says. Listen, Luke G.B. Caird says, can you remember that writing class that they were sending offenders to? That writing workshop or whatever that was, getting people out of jail early and teaching them how to write? Yeah, mate, I do, Mark C. Burl says. Why? I'm thinking of taking a course in creative writing myself, Luke G.B. Caird says. To impress the bird, mate? Mark C. Burl asks him, but Luke G.B. Caird says, no, no, it's something I've always wanted to do. Maybe Tamar has just awakened the bug, you know what I mean? Awakening the bug, mate, is that a euphemism for your cock? Ha ha, Luke G.B. Caird says. So, do you remember what the name of it was? Yeah, it was The Warehouse, in Springburn. Cheers, bud, Luke G.B. Caird says. I'll give them a call. Then Luke G.B. Caird crawls into bed with a herbal tea and opens *The Knight in the Panther's Skin* at random. 'They were both fit to be ranked as suns, or as the moon in heaven, cloudless, spreading her rays on the plain beneath. Compared with them the aloe-tree was of no worth; they were like the seven planets; to what else shall I liken them? They kissed each other, they were not bashful at being strangers; they opened the rose.' This is a true romance, Luke G.B. Caird tells himself. Why be bashful strangers, he says to himself. He feels inspired to become a writer; inspired by Tamar. That way the world will open to him like a rose.

145

Everyone is silent in the van on the way back. You really believe Bolland when he said he had nothing to do with it? Big Paul Vickers asks Dan Ruff. It didn't seem to me like he was bullshitting, Dan Ruff says. But mind you, the cunt didn't look me in the eye once the entire conversation. He was fucking glued to the telly. And guess who was on there. Jason Donovan and Kylie Minogue? After them, who was on after them. You tell me, Big Paul Vickers says. Wee Boab interrupts them. See as we're driving down the Shettleston Road, can we stop in and get a pie? Sure, son, Dan Ruff says. Pies all round. Youse did well today. Well, who was it? Big Paul Vickers asks again, and Dan Ruff says, that cunt from the council, Andrew Lethal. Lethal was on the telly? Yeah, he was getting interviewed about some writing project for ex-offenders in Springburn. You think Lethal is the one that's bullshitting? Big Paul Vickers asks him. He works for the council, Dan Ruff says, he bullshits for a living. Why, though? They pull up at the butcher's on the Shettleston Road. Butcher, are they pies warm? Wee Boab asks the butcher. They'll have cooled down by now, the butcher says. I'm not supposed to heat them up after they're made, he says. How come? Regulations, the butcher says. What regulations? Council regulations. About what? About the illegal heating of pies. What next? Dan Ruff says, and he slaps his massive forehead. What madness will this fucking council inflict on us next? Don't ask me, the butcher says, and he shrugs. But it'll definitely be madness, he says. You can bet your arse on that, he adds. You've got a fucking microwave right behind you there, Wee Boab points out. What the fuck's that about? Staff only, the butcher says. It is used strictly for the reheating of food to be consumed by the staff at their own risk. Then Stevie Shaw joins in. Where's the fucking staff? he says. It's just fucking you on your lonesome. So you're allowed to have a hot pie and no cunt else is? Alright, the butcher says. Alright. Pull that door over and lock it, he says. Staff lunch break, the butcher says. And then he says, how hot do you like your pies? Piping, Wee Boab says. Alright, the butcher says, five piping-hot pies coming up. And I'm charging you for the electricity, he says. By the way. Then they all sit around on a bunch of crates on this red linoleum floor that is covered in sawdust and eat their pies. Fucking unbelievable, Wee Boab says, and the butcher says, you taste that amount of pepper? That's my twist, he says. Aye, it's peppery as fuck, Stevie says. Right enough. Got any brown sauce? Scott Ruff asks, and the butcher says, here, try this, homemade brown sauce, vinegary as fuck, he says, and it's true it's fucking brilliant. Ever heard of a cunt from the council called Andrew Lethal? Dan Ruff asks the butcher. No, mate, he says. Sounds like one of they action heroes. Ha ha, could not be further removed, Dan Ruff says. What's his game? Internecine conflict, Dan Ruff says, and the butcher shakes his head and says, Xenophon, say no more.

146

In his writing room in his flat overlooking Tollcross Park, Andrew Lethal is composing yet another missive to his fellow Mayanist Linda Schele. He is writing with his thoughts on the frescoes in Bonampak, in the north of Chiapas, near the Lacanja river, a temple that is close to Lethal's heart because it was uncovered through love, through the love and devotion of an American conscientious objector named Carlos Frey, who went to live in exile in the forests of Chiapas and fell in love with the way of life of the Lacandón Indians and with a beautiful Lacandón woman, so much so that he married her and was welcomed by the men of the tribe, who one February took him on a mysterious male-only pilgrimage where they paid tribute to Kananka, a god of the forest, in an abandoned temple which, thanks to the humidity of the forest and the isolation of the temple, had miraculously preserved frescoes on the walls. What a thrill it was for Andrew Lethal to visit the site just last year, with a guide and with his girl Ramona, and although the frescoes were streaked with water where the colours had run, there was something about the primary colours – outside, inside, day, night – and the bold outlines of the figures, and the way they depicted dance as unmoving, and violence, as ineluctable, and the warrior king, as glorious, as he speared someone through the neck, and cast to one side a decapitated head, and kidnapped and bound sacrificial victims, all to this still music of shakers, drums, turtle shells and goat horns, that made it seem as if the temple had only been vacated a few decades previous. They had gone there with a guide, Chico Velázquez, aka The Hippo, who looked exactly like the men in the frescoes, with his large head and his pupil-less black eyes like a boar, like a black pig, which was his other nickname in Spanish, El Cerdo Negro. And the painting of the tongue that El Cerdo Negro pointed out, the painting of the warrior king running two cords of thorns through a hole in his tongue while the blood collected on a piece of burning bark. And the actors playing gods, some of whom had single letters in their blank eyes like El Cerdo Negro, or sometimes with antennas in front of their mouths, as if broadcasting this song, this song of violence and joy, across the ages. That night they returned, haunted, to Lacanja Chansayab, where they were staying, and El Cerdo Negro took them to a bar to sample some 'conquistador shit', a special rum drink that had been specific to the region ever since the Spanish brought sugar cane to New Spain, and they sat in this bar and talked, and although El Cerdo Negro's English wasn't great – he said he learnt English through watching *Cheers* on American TV – they were able to communicate with each other just fine. No one does us death like us fucking Indians, El Cerdo Negro said. Us live with it, he says. Daily, he says. Death is us father, he says. Us god, he says. Us who walks like a man, he said. Then he said, Ramona is very beautiful, yes? Addressing Andrew Lethal even though Ramona was sat right next to him. She is, Andrew Lethal said. My baby, Andrew Lethal said, and he put his arm around her, and she creased her nose in that way that she would do, with cute joy. Maybe you marry her, he said to Andrew Lethal. And even more will be revealed. Ramona just laughed. Then he told them of the time he robbed a grocery store where no one was at the checkout of six cans of beer, only it was a police set-up, and because he didn't have enough money to pay them, they dragged him into the back of their car and put a hole punch through his tongue. Fuck, did it heal? Andrew Lethal asked El Cerdo Negro and El Cerdo Negro stuck out his tongue so that they could still see the scar, which was like a tiny little 'x'. This shit never changes for us, El Cerdo Negro said, and then, just as abruptly, he said, I intend to make love to my girlfriend, and he grabbed his leather waistcoat with the animal fur and headed off. That night, after Andrew Lethal made love to his Ramona back at the house they were renting, she forced her sharp fingernails into his Jap's eye till it bled, and stared at him while she did it, in silence, except just for once, when she said, you have a big hole, I'm glad.

147

The Precious Gift walks back to his hotel. He still hasn't spent the night with Joyce. Each time they make love she makes a big deal of offering to phone him a cab straight afterwards, but it's walking distance to his hotel, and as long as he is back there by 2 a.m., when the clubs get out, he feels safe walking the streets, these damn streets that he got to know so well from above, when he worked for 'counterterrorism' as part of Project Deep Run. That peregrine is still in the window of the abandoned pub across the way, its dead body miraculously preserved, as if the pub were a mortuary, or an embalming tomb. He opens the front door with his key and takes the elevator up to his room. There is no one around. The hotel is as silent as a hospital in the dark. He can't be bothered to take a shower, so he washes his cock in the sink. That's another thing about The Precious Gift, he worries about fungal infections, even though he never bothers using protection. He lies naked on top of the bed and flips through the TV channels. There's an old sci-fi movie on, *It Came from Outer Space*. He turns the volume down to silent and lies there in this alien black-and-white glow. Then he falls asleep. He wakes a few hours later and, before he gets fully under the covers and turns the TV off, he is drawn to pull the curtains back and to look out of the window. And that's when he sees it. A huge bird, an impossibly large bird, on the pavement opposite – but no! It's someone in a bird costume. What the fuck. It is surreal and terrifying, this uncanny figure. This birdwoman who is dressed as a bird completely, only her round face is exposed. Her round face is exposed within a tight hood of bird feathers and bird legs and bird wings. Her face is like a human death mask on a bird, and at the sight of The Precious Gift she flees, this birdwoman flees across the road towards the hotel and then disappears down a side road. The Precious Gift is shaken. He tries to pull himself together, to remember the topography, to cast his mind back to the layout of the streets, but it's no use, he can't picture it, he lies down on the bed and he tries to rise into the sky behind the hotel and to follow this birdwoman into the night. But it's no use. I'm losing it, he says to himself. I'm getting old, he confesses. What the fuck is this birdwoman stood outside my hotel room in the night, he thinks to himself, and it can only be prophecy, or sign. The return of the repressed. In the morning, he calls Wise Crow to see what happened with The Mole. They let him go yesterday, she tells him. When exactly? Last night. But what time? They let him out close to midnight, apparently, just to fuck with him, Wise Crow says. The Precious Gift can barely repress a shudder as he hangs up the phone and showers and gets dressed for breakfast. Is The Mole onto him? He has arranged to take a drive with Joyce, out to his old stomping ground of Carndonagh. At the car hire he bumps into your man John O'Neill from The Undertones. John, he says, I presumed you'd be living in London these days, and John says, sure, I'm visiting family and I thought I'd hire us a car so I could take my ma on a wee jaunt, he says. What brings you back, John asks The Precious Gift, and The Precious Gift just says, business. Sure, did you ever find out who kidnapped your man? John O'Neill asks him, and The Precious Gift says, this is actually Jim's wife, he says, and John introduces himself to Joyce and says, I'm so sorry about what happened, that was terrible, so it was. Thank you, Joyce says. So where are youse off to? John asks them, though now he's looking at the two of them, like that, and Joyce says, he's taking me for a wee spin out Carndonagh way, she says, a wee escape, she says, and John says, lovely. And he thinks, what a caring person your man The Precious

Gift is. Then The Precious Gift asks John how the band is going. Sure, we're grand, John O'Neill says, we were on the telly the other night. Sorry I missed that, The Precious Gift says, and Joyce says, are you a famous rock star and John says, hardly, and The Precious Gift says, this guy is The Undertones. Sure, I've never heard of them, Joyce says. Not even 'Teenage Kicks'? The Precious Gift asks Joyce, and she shakes her head, and John says, here, we made a new demo tape, youse can play this in the car on the way. The girl behind the desk says she has a special on convertibles where you can roll the roof back and seeing as it's a lovely day – and now they even have a new album to play – they go for the upgrade. The music kicks in, this teenage music, and there isn't a cloud in the sky as they leave the city. I've booked us a room in my favourite wee bed and breakfast upstairs of a pub, The Precious Gift says to Joyce. Which is why I told you to bring an overnight bag, he says. Luring me into bed, huh? Joyce asks him. I thought it would be nice, if you were up for it, The Precious Gift says, but Joyce neither confirms nor denies, just shrugs her shoulders and goes back to listening to the music. What kind of music would you call this? she asks The Precious Gift. Melodic punk music, maybe, he says. Indie music, maybe. What does 'indie' mean? Independent music, music not on big labels, he says. That's a sound? Joyce asks him. It kind of is, he says. It's a bit of a catch-all term, he admits. Is the name of the band Alvin Lucier? Joyce asks him. No, what, The Precious Gift says, this is The Undertones. Sure, I was looking at the wrong side, so I was, Joyce says. I don't like this music, Joyce says. Let's try Alvin Lucier. She flips the tape, which has the words 'I Am Sitting in a Room' written on it in biro, and rewinds it to the beginning. She reads the title aloud. I am sitting in a room, she says. God, she says, that reminds me of that quote, that quote my mindfulness teacher would always say to me. You have a mindfulness teacher? The Precious Gift asks her. Used to, she says, used to have a mindfulness teacher. What happened to her? There was a schism, Joyce says. A fatal schism. That's the thing that is making me remember this quote. It's something like, all man's problems would be ended if he was only able to sit silently in a room on his own. That's what she would say. There's some truth to that, The Precious Gift admits. I think it's garbage, Joyce says. Really? Really, I do. There's a reason man is not able to sit in a room silently on his own. Because he's a man. Or a woman. Men and women are not meant to sit alone in rooms in their own head. Why teach a tiger to live in a cage? she says. That's Ireland, The Precious Gift says. That's Ireland talking right there, he says, as this music starts up, this music of sitting on your own in a room, this music which Alvin Lucier says will consist of him playing a recording of him sitting in a room and talking about it into the very same room again and again, until the shape of the room is revealed in the meaningless rhythm of his confused words. See, Joyce says, even he couldn't sit in a room in silence for a minute. He had to fill it with talk. Is this bastard Irish? she asks The Precious Gift, and they both crack up laughing.

148

The next morning Mindy rises early and changes into a green robe with flowers and jungle artwork on it and immediately puts lipstick on her famous lips and then picks a book off the shelf to read, a collection of short stories by Silvina Ocampo translated into English. Because Simone is retired, he likes to sleep in, and so he gets out of bed an hour later. He walks naked into the living room, where Mindy is curled up on a chair. What a night, he says, with his substantial cock just hanging down there. You are my favourite guest, he says, and Mindy says, I bet you say that to all of your guests, and he laughs and says, only to the ones that tongue my asshole, and then he says, Ocampo, huh, she was an Argentinian surrealist. What do you think of her? he asks Mindy, and she says, the stories mostly seem to be about terrible children doing perfectly awful things. Ha ha, Simone says, I like that. So, what are your plans, he asks Mindy, and Mindy says that she is going to spend the day photographing Notre-Dame. I have it all planned, she says, and Simone says, great, I'll just mess around at home and tonight maybe I could cook you dinner and we could open an expensive bottle of wine, he says, and Mindy says, ideal. Mindy has chosen a special outfit for her visit to Notre-Dame, right down to the panties that she will wear. When she comes back into the room, she looks ravishing. Wow, Simone says, let me slide it inside you all over again. A few strokes, he says, please? Because when he sees her famous red lips with the bright-red lipstick, her eyes in the shape of leaves in the autumn, her dark eyes combined with her dark lashes, her black nylons, her heels and her fur coat, it's all too much for Simone, and he wants to fuck her so bad, like a memory of every woman he has ever fantasised about, come real. But Mindy says, no, no you can't, she says, you'll mess up my make-up, and she pushes him away. I did it specially for my visit, she says, and then she says, but you can kiss me on the cheek before I go, and Simone kisses her on her powdered cheek and tells her that she smells so good, my god, you smell like a woman, he says. What should I pick up for a snack on the way, Mindy asks him, and Simone suggests getting a croque-monsieur at the place just along the street. The place just along the street is a single room made of ancient concrete like a cave with a scatter of tables outside and a lovely arched entrance with broken tiles. Mindy finds a seat outside and takes a couple of trial shots with her camera. Vous êtes photographe? the server asks her when he sees her, and she says, yes, I am a photographer, though really she imagines herself as a photograph, the way he says it, the way he says it she pictures herself out in the world on her own, like in a bold photograph from her past that she is looking at with pride and satisfaction over a life lived with no regrets. She orders a croque-monsieur and a coffee, she says, an espresso – she is young enough to delight in being in Europe on her own – and she lights a cigarette and crosses her legs in her heels and takes a floppy sun hat out of her bag to shield herself from the sun. She thinks of Achilles. If only he could see her. If only he knew. If only he could look down from the heavens and see her now in this scene from above. What a surprise he would get. Imagine if he walked past? But she has kept her trip a secret from everyone. When the server brings her an espresso he asks her, you are Scottish? Yes, I am, she says, and he tells her that he used to live in Glasgow. No! Yes. Bishopbriggs, he says. I had a flat in Bishopbriggs. Square sausage, he says, and he shakes his head. What a way to live, he says. And then he walks away. He brings her a delicious authentic croque-monsieur. Now someone is playing a flute from an open upper window. It sounds like a European folk tune, a mournful European folk tune about never returning to the landscape of your youth. Mindy lingers a little after lunch, smokes another cigarette. She is unwilling to leave this perfect moment. This perfect moment of self-will and decision, she tells herself. And she feels like the artist of her own life, for the first time. What caused it? Achilles? It's hard to say. But something of Achilles' passion, of Achilles' suggestion of astonishment, set fire to something inside of her. And now here she is. Sat outside some Parisian cafe like a great artist at the start of her career. Vous êtes photographe.

149

Josef Noth gives Erithena a wad of cash and pats her on the ass and says, I will meet you later at the restaurant, wait for me there, he says, and she asks him, who is this Thérèse Barnier who has died, and The H interrupts them and says, she was one of the greatest dancers of the age, he says, and Josef Noth says, yes, and the mother of my son, he says, and though Erithena's feelings are hurt and she pouts a bit, she says that she understands and she agrees to meet him in an hour's time. Let's get a coffee, he says to The H, and they cross the square to a small Parisian cafe like a cave with outdoor seating, where a bunch of Nazi soldiers in high spirits are smoking and drinking wine. Josef Noth recognises some of them and greets them as he takes a seat. What happened? he asks The H. She died fleeing Paris, The H says, or rather, she was killed fleeing Paris. By who? By you, The H says. By your soldiers. Where did she die? In a village in Normandy. She fled to Normandy with Achilles. What happened to Achilles? No one knows. He disappeared from the face of the earth. How do you know this? Josef Noth asks him. I know because I was with them, The H says. What?! Look, he says, and he raises his right hand to Josef Noth and it is crab-like and contorted. I was shot in the arm and my hand is paralysed. I can compose, but I can no longer conduct, he says. Thérèse had a cousin in Normandy, and we believed the Nazis would never make it to the coast, The H continued. And if it looked like they would, then England would surely invade. But no one expected your impossible victory, The H says. This victory that took the life of the mother of your child, he adds, and he stares at Josef Noth with something deeper than hatred but just as silent. How did she die? She was shot too. Why were the Germans shooting? Josef Noth asks. They were an invading force, and they were out of control, The H says. I was in Normandy, Josef Noth says. What?! But we barely fired a single shot, he says. They went door to door in the village of Thérèse's cousin, the widow Marceline, The H says. Raping and looting. No, Josef Noth says. I have never heard of this, he says. But already Normandy is becoming impossible to recall. What did I do in Normandy, Josef Noth is asking himself, what took place there and why can I not recall it? Was Thérèse raped? Josef Noth asks The H. Have you ever raped anyone? The H asks him in return. Of course not, Josef Noth says, and The H says, no, thankfully no, she was not raped. They simply shot her and her cousin dead on their doorstep and thought that they had killed me too. When they left with a bag of valuables and all the money we had to our name, they dragged the bodies to the back garden and then went on their way. They dragged me half-alive round to the back garden, and they didn't even notice that I was still breathing. That's how drunk they were, The H says. They were drunk? Legless, The H says. Then what happened? I waited a while to be sure they were gone and then I examined the girls to see if there were any vital signs. They were both stone dead. Their bodies contorted on the grass the way they had been dumped there. Do you know what army group these boys were associated with? Josef Noth asks The H. Of course not, The H says, I have no idea. And now here you are, The H says to him, the very reason we decided to flee Paris in the first place. And what about Achilles? He had been lying in his basket on a table in the back garden, in the sunshine, The H said. But when I came to, he was gone. Both he and the basket, disappeared. Was he taken by the drunk Germans? I don't know. I made a search of the garden, feeling apprehensive that I was going to stumble over the dead body of a little one, but I found nothing, nothing at all. I buried the two girls in the back garden and I holed up in the house in fear of my life, but the Germans never came back to our little ransacked village, and eventually I walked back to Paris. How long did that take? A week, The H says. A week that I will never talk about, he warns Josef Noth, and then he says, listen, I have taken up enough of your time, I know you must be eager for the rendezvous with your young whore, he says, and Josef Noth says, where can I reach you? I am at the same studio, I am living there now, he says, sleeping on the floor, he says. Though I don't know why I should ever have to see you again, he says. I will avenge their deaths, Josef Noth says. I will find out who was responsible and kill them with my own bare hands, he says. And The H says, I very much doubt it. This is wartime, The H says. And you started it. Some soldiers at the next table are starting to look over at The H. Goodbye, Josef Noth, The H says. I sincerely hope that we never meet again, neither in this life, nor the next. After he leaves, Josef Noth lights a cigarette and just sits there for a bit. One of the soldiers from the other table asks him if everything is OK and whether 'that Jew' was bothering him. He's not a Jew, is all that Josef Noth says in response. Then he makes his way to the restaurant where he has arranged to meet Erithena. But she's nowhere to be seen. Now Erithena has disappeared from the face of the earth.

150

Alec Bolland calls his best man in, Mekon. Fuck was that about, Mekon asks him. Someone is trying to stir up internecine conflict, Alec Bolland says to him. Can you turn down that telly, Alec, Mekon says to him, I can't hear a fucking word you're saying. Alec turns it down just a notch on the remote. Internecine conflict, Alec Bolland repeats, and Mekon says, what the fuck does that mean, and Alec Bolland says, it is conflict within communities as opposed to conflict between different communities. And who's fanning the flames, Mekon asks him, fucking Dan Ruff and his wee boys? No, not fucking Dan Ruff, I don't believe so. Do you know who I think it is? No idea, Mekon says. Do we need to keep shouting over this TV, he says, but Alec Bolland just shouts, your man Andrew Lethal, your man from the council. Remember, there was all that fuss about us expanding the camp to the other side of the railway. He accused us of having a vendetta against him. He really thought we were expanding the camp just to fuck with him. He takes everything so fucking personally, Mekon says. He thinks it's all about him. But Lethal's whole thing is he is the champion of travellers, Alec Bolland says. Maybe there's some fear in that too. Maybe the reality is, he's shit-scared of us. But kind of attracted to us at the same time. To our outlaw way of life, let's face it. The fucking fellaheen, that's what he calls us. What's the fucking fellaheen when they're at home? Mekon says, and Alec Bolland says, they're very rarely at home. They are the marginalised, the spit-upon, the put-upon, the vagrant and traveller and bum. That's us, Mekon says, and Alec Bolland says, that's right. See when I was talking to Dan Ruff in here, Andrew Lethal appeared on the telly. What? What do you mean, appeared? Like a vision? It *was* like a vision, Alec Bolland says. There he was, on *Reporting Scotland* with Mary Marquis, getting interviewed about some fucking thing, right when Dan Ruff is telling me that through the grapevine some cunt is spreading rumours that Dan Ruff and, as you so rightly called them, his wee boys, were involved in the death of that poor wee Hamilton kid what got shot and got his horses stole. Brian Hamilton,

Mekon says. Aye, that'll be Brian Hamilton, he says. I used to train with him at The Griphouse in Barlanark. Oh, really? Alec Bolland says. Did you ever know his brother, Findlay Hamilton? A wee bit, Mekon says. What was Brian like? Good fighter. Decent enough guy. Not the sharpest pair of pliers in the box, mind. I suggest we pay a visit to his brother. With what in mind? Mekon says. With getting to the bottom of what went what, Alec Bolland says. What? Mekon says. What went what? That's what I said, isn't it, Alec Bolland says, and Mekon has no clue if that's definitely what he said because Alec Bolland has turned the sound right back up cause *Blankety Blank* has just come on.

151

And then there was Mindy, Aaron Murray's dad Donald says, on this bench which feels like eternity, now, is how it feels to Aaron, like they are perched on the edge of a precipice in eternity and having some final reckoning, which is exactly what it is, even as the conversation is circular, elliptic, even as Aaron is trying to guide his father home, to the central unspoken fact of their relationship, to the blank at its heart, which is Nemo, which is poor kidnapped Nemo, and his dad says, what is that song, that song by your man? Of all the girls I've loved before, he says. Of all the girls that shared my life, he says. There was a . . . what do you call it, like a tick box, like a . . . A questionnaire? Aaron says. Yes, like a *questionnaire*, done somewhere, he says. And the biggest regret people had at the end of their life was that they didn't sleep with more people. That was the biggest regret? Aaron asks him. And Donald says, yes, outside of if you murdered someone, he says. Obviously. But what about Mum? Aaron asks him, and he adds, now that we are finally able to have these conversations, he says, only because you are a complete stranger to yourself, never mind me, Aaron says, but his dad is completely oblivious. He just starts repeating names, and counting them on his fingers: Barbara, Samantha, Mindy . . .

152

Mindy takes photographs of the rose windows and a piece of the true cross, and a nail from the crucifixion, and the crown of thorns worn by Jesus himself, and St Denis with his head lopped off, and the great organ, and also the angels that are musicians in heaven. She lights a candle, and she prays to God to keep her safe in her adventure. Then she sits on a pew in silence. The sound of people's feet, echoing. There is a woman appeared before the altar. An elderly woman appears as if from out of nowhere dressed in the church itself, as if she is robed in the thin air that hangs like glass in front of the paintings and sculptures and busts of Notre-Dame. And she starts to sing. In Latin, which feels like a time tunnel. Mindy closes her eyes and is transported by the music to a time when young girls ran to kiss icons in ecstasy. Then the woman disappears. It hadn't felt right to take a photograph, but as soon as Mindy is outside, she is already doubting whether it even happened. She gets lost in the maze of streets that Paris presents to her. She comes across the most perfect square, the most adorable plaza, where young lovers are sat around in the sweet sunshine and courting in the summertime. Some handsome chefs are cooking food on a grill over an open fire. They wave her over and offer her samples of what they're cooking, which is seafood grilled to perfection. In their manners they are so gentle. They are only here for the day, one of the handsome chefs tells her. It is a special day, he says, in his beautiful wonky English just for her. Right then a bell rings. A flight of birds takes off and circles the square. The sound of their wings. A church bell rings and some newlyweds emerge from the tiny church on the corner and it starts to rain flowers – where have they been hiding all of the flowers until now – and they seem to fall in slow motion, like feathers, and someone hands her a glass of white wine, an older, sophisticated woman with shoulder-length grey hair who says, congratulations, honey – was it bad English, who knows – but she appeared to say, congratulations, honey to Mindy, who can only clink glasses with her while wondering how everything could be speaking so perfectly at a time like this, and of course when she gets back and tells Simone about it, about the magic of her day, he has no idea of the square or of its whereabouts, even though he has lived here for years and has almost bankrupted himself through buying books on Paris and its history, and after dinner they make love, and Mindy does a special striptease and a 'fan dance' using two brushes from the kitchen, and then they watch porn and make love all over again.

153

Luke G.B. Caird is on the phone to The Warehouse. He is enquiring about the possibility of signing up for a creative writing course. You need to speak to The Dragonfly, the woman on the phone informs him. The Dragonfly? Yes, he's in charge of running the courses, she explains. He'll be in later this afternoon. Tell you what, Luke G.B. Caird says, I'll drive over and see him in person, I have some business out Springburn way. I'll tell him to expect you, she says. Luke G.B. Caird tells his secretary Yvonne that he will be out for the rest of the afternoon and drives first to Ruchill Park, one of Luke G.B. Caird's favourite Glasgow parks, where he pulls up next to the rusty green gate and walks to the top of the hill and takes the path that runs up to the flagpole. Is it the highest point in Glasgow? He remembers taking photographs of an old girlfriend here, years ago, and he takes some photographs of the view, of what can be seen from here, and of the curving path itself, and then walks over to the other side of the park where he takes more photographs of the view, you can see out to the hills, so much of Glasgow stands revealed, as well as the motorway that runs through it, which from up here sounds a constant drone. The park is completely deserted, as usual, and haunted, this is a haunted park, he says to himself, as he thinks of old girlfriends of long ago while making his way back to the car. Then he heads over to Springburn, to The Warehouse, which stands near the tall flats at Viewpoint Place, the tall flats that actually, definitely, are the highest point in Glasgow, come to think of it, and Luke G.B. Caird recalls the old boyfriend of his sister's that used to live in these flats, the self-published poet, Seán, who wrote lines like 'all the great poets are motherless sons' while dating Emma and selling his poetry books at the Third Eye Centre. The Warehouse looks like a working men's club, or a boxing gym, or an abandoned bingo hall. He knocks on the door and the letterbox opens and a pair of eyes look through. I'm here to see The Dragonfly, Luke G.B. Caird says. I called earlier. Sorry, the voice says, come in, it's me you spoke to earlier. I'm Susan, she says. Nice to meet you. Sorry but we have been attracting the wrong sort of attention since we were on the telly, she says. People think it's just a bunch of criminals got out of jail early and all conspiring in the one place, Susan says, which it kind of is, only we're channelling that energy into creativity. Are you an ex-offender yourself? Susan asks him, and Luke G.B. Caird says, no, but I've been involved in rehabilitation. Good for you, Susan says, now let's find The Dragonfly. What kind of name is that, Luke G.B. Caird is thinking to himself, but he says nothing. Susan knocks on a door and a voice says, two minutes. Susan and Luke G.B. Caird stand awkwardly outside the door listening to the sound of something being hurriedly cleared away into a desk. Then the voice says, come in. Sat behind the desk there is this corpse-like man in a purple suit with thin dyed hair and he is all bent over and in on himself and he says, Luke, nice to meet you, in this unexpectedly deep voice full of sexual vibrato, thank you for your interest in what we are doing, did you see us on the telly, he says, rising from his seat and walking towards Luke G.B. Caird like a cadaver. You think I look weird, don't you, The Dragonfly says, and before Luke G.B. Caird can say anything he says, I had tuberculosis when I was a boy, fucked me up, he says, but it's what made me dangerous, he says, in this mad deep voice that is supremely seductive, and then he just says, revenge, know what I mean, and he shrugs and offers Luke G.B. Caird his hand. Susan leaves them to it. Where did you get your nickname? Luke G.B. Caird asks him. In jail, he says. We're all jailbirds here, he says, most of us. Though we have some recovering addicts, and alcoholics, and just fucking straight-up mentalists as well. So, you're a budding author yourself? The Dragonfly asks him. What is it you do? For a job? I work in rehabilitation, Luke G.B. Caird lies. That makes two of us, The Dragonfly says. What you interested in? The Dragonfly asks him. Prose? Fiction? Memoir? Non-fiction? Poetry? Crime? Fiction, Luke G.B. Caird says. I'm interested in fiction, primarily, he says. What writers? The Dragonfly asks him. What writers are you interested in? And Luke G.B. Caird draws a blank. Kafka, he says, off the top of his head. I would have to say *Kafka's Diaries*, he says. *Kafka's Diaries* was the self-published poet Seán's favourite book (his favourite album was *Harvest* by Neil Young) and it's all that Luke G.B. Caird can think of right now. Surely a diary is non-fiction, The Dragonfly says. Or is it? is all that Luke G.B. Caird can come up with, and The Dragonfly laughs at that, good one, he says. Then he says, we have a fiction workshop starting in three weeks' time, he says. It's run by a writer that goes by the name of The Escapologist, he says. Really? Luke G.B. Caird says. That's what he's called? You know The Escapologist? The Dragonfly asks him. No, Luke G.B. Caird says. No, he confirms. It's just a mad name, he says. The Escapologist's the best teacher you could ever have, The Dragonfly says, and Luke G.B. Caird says, sign me up.

154

The Precious Gift pulls into the car park of the pub they will be staying above, just outside of Carndonagh, near Trawbreaga Bay. The views are unbelievable, at night, The Precious Gift says. Wait until you see the views, he says. We're in the attic room that has skylights on all sides. They walk into the pub, where a fire is going, and a group of men are drinking at the bar. The barman spots The Precious Gift and says, sure, it's yourself, how are you doing, it's good to see you, but no one else is particularly friendly. Sure, I'm grand, The Precious Gift says, and this is Joyce, he says. I'm Gerry, the barman says, introducing himself, and he grabs some keys and leads them up to their room. It's true, they are in the slope of the roof and there are windows on all sides. Told you, The Precious Gift says. I'll leave youse two lovers to it, Gerry says, and he heads back to the bar. Two lovers, Joyce says. Is that what we look like? she says. That's what we are, The Precious Gift says, and he comes up behind her and puts his arms around her tight and kisses her neck. She closes her eyes. No, she says, eventually, and she pushes The Precious Gift away. I want to have a shower and go for a walk, she says. The Precious Gift lies on the bed and flicks through a photobook on the nightstand where some artist has photographed grottoes and holy shrines around the north-west of Ireland. Joyce dresses in jeans and boots and with a long coat and a scarf on and says that she'll meet The Precious Gift in the bar when he's ready. The Precious Gift jumps into the shower. He combs his thinning hair in the mirror and changes into walking boots and a Crombie before heading downstairs, where Joyce is in conversation with the previously surly men at the bar. As The Precious Gift walks in he hears her say, and that, my friends, was that. Absofuckinglutely, she says, and a few of the once-surly men laugh. She has her legs crossed on a high stool in a way that is emphasising all of her sex. Look what the wind blew in, she says, when The Precious Gift walks into the bar. The men look round and leer and think less of him, it feels like, even though is it even bad or an insult. The Precious Gift asks Joyce if she is ready to go, to which she says, I'll see you boys later. Something about it drives The Precious Gift mad with shame and desire. They get in the car and drive out to Malin Head, at the request of Joyce. Can we go to see where my Jim used to do his birdwatching, she asked him, even though it seemed absurd that she only wanted to do this now that he was dead. When they get there, they take a walk along the cliff but somehow lose their way in the mud and end up having to climb a barbed-wire fence which catches The Precious Gift's long coat and tears it. They walk with the waves to their right, crashing on the slippery rocks. It's not hard to imagine one or the other of them tumbling to their doom and never being found ever again. As they round the headland, they climb up to a great precipice with gulls down below, and there, sat on the edge of the cliff, stock still, is a real live hare. It doesn't move. It just sits there. Wow, Joyce says. I've never seen a hare in real life before. Then it darts across the field in the gathering gloom. Sometimes, don't you think, it's the past that is more frightening than the future, Joyce says to him, staring out at the waves, crashing, and the gulls in the air, swift scribbles on the sky. And The Precious Gift has to admit that, yes, it really is. And then she says, do you have anything to confess? And when The Precious Gift says, no, what do you mean, what are you trying to insinuate, she changes her tack and she says, I mean, there's no chance it was an inside job, is there? and she looks The Precious Gift in the eye. You know, collusion, she says. Infiltration, she says. And then she mutters something under her breath. What was that? Nothing. Nothing. Though The Precious Gift could have sworn that she said v-a-m-p-i-r-e.

155

Davey Brennan aka The Mole, age twenty-six, resident in Kinsale Park, Derry, where he lives with his mother, dressed in a tracksuit and with a shaved head and the ever-present scowl on his face, the same as in the photos, alongside this harried look, this look that works with the scowl to give the impression that Davey Brennan is constantly being pursued by a thing that he has complete contempt for, leaves number 28 with his dog on a leash, a poodle, I think it's the mother's, and enters Kilfennan Valley Park. It is 11.14 a.m. He stops to let the dog squeeze out one of those awful poodle shites, awful for their tiny size compared to the terrible effort of a filthy white poodle squeezing one out, its white hair almost the pink of bald flesh, its ugly overbite, and of course he doesn't bother to pick it up. This is a park of dog shit, and of shady characters. Someone pulls up to him on a bicycle. The cyclist is wearing a hooded ski jacket. The bike is a racer, a Raleigh racer. The pair shake hands, and the ski-jacket guy says something and Brennan shrugs. Then he cycles off. There is a woman sat on a bench. Brennan makes his way over to her and sits next to her. At first she doesn't appear to react but, wait, look closer and you can see that they are actually talking, they are speaking to each other only they are looking forward, never looking at each other, so as from far away it might appear that they are not communicating at all. The woman has dark hair in a short bob. Older than Brennan. Then she makes this move. She does almost a mime where she mimes removing some kind of crash helmet, some kind of invisible space helmet, from her head, and resting it on her legs. She's wearing leggings and a pair of trainers – black-and-white trainers – and now with this invisible helmet or headpiece sat on her lap. Then she hands him something. It appears to be a carving of a small wooden bird. What the fuck is that about? Who are these people? At this point a third figure enters the scene. He is walking a dog himself. He comes to a stop in front of the two of them on the bench and lets his dog, another filthy white dog, a West Highland Terrier, sniff the poodle, which is highly strung and obnoxious and is hiding under the bench and snapping at the Westie, while the owner has a conversation with Brennan, but not with the girl, who sits there, impassively, like these two unknown guys have just invaded her day with no feel for her personal space. After the stranger leaves, the two of them sit there talking on the bench, but looking forward just the same, for another fifteen minutes or so. And then the woman gets up and walks off. In the opposite direction from which Brennan came. Brennan sits there for a little while longer. He lifts the filthy poodle with its dirty arse up into his lap and he kisses its leprous skin. Wait, someone else is approaching. Someone else is making a beeline for the bench. It's an older female, with her hair in a kerchief and a long coat. She wears a large scarf with sunglasses. It's hard to get a proper view of her. It's like she is flitting in and out of the scene, it is like she is wearing some kind of cloak of disguise. Wait. It's Wise Crow. I'm sure that's Wise Crow, flitting in and out of view. Which must mean that Wise Crow is in on it. And that the whole thing is a set-up. And that's when The Precious Gift decides that The Mole has to die. And he knows just the team to do it.

156

Andrew Lethal is on the phone to his one contact at the British Museum, a multimedia guy who works on their live presentations and in-person events, whose nickname at the museum is The Janitor but whose name is Roy Pearson in real life and who has his own theories about the Mayan script and the simple genius of the Mayan people. And by simple I don't mean basic, I mean primary, The Janitor says, and Andrew Lethal thinks, he is quoting the literature, he is passing off someone else's ideas as his own, but he listens in silence, because it's a fucking fact that Mayan studies are in need of some serious iconoclasm in order to smash through the same old tired interpretations, and to move away from this whole ethos of the Mayans as being led by shamans, that every indecipherable figure must be a stand-in for a god, because, after all, where were the gods in our own letters, and of course, if they were to dig out a contemporary cinema, a bingo hall, a theatre, in future millennia, they would palm it off as a relic from a more enlightened time, a ritual space, a space of magic, a pyramid to the gods, even though, no, both The Janitor and Andrew Lethal are in agreement, this Maya was a straightforward place of triumph and violence, of losers and winners, and was never upside down. It's kings' names, The Janitor says.

It is dates and kings' names, he insists, talking about the Mayan scripts, and that's all it is, it is names and dates, it is winners and losers, and he mentions a dinner with an up-and-coming Mayanist, the young French explorer Achilles Noth, whose writings and investigations of Chichén Viejo have done so much to embolden both Pearson and Lethal's belief in the warrior-king hypotheses, if not Lethal's pet theory of the song, the song set in stone by Mayan hieroglyphs. Noth says that the ancient Maya were the most perfectly at peace with what is, and, therefore, what it is necessary to embody, of any of the ancients, Pearson says on the phone. There is only one country in the world where the Day of the Dead is celebrated, Noth said to me, Pearson says. Think about it, he said. Yes, Andrew Lethal says. Yes, exactly this, he says. Breton said it was the land of the surrealists. In that, Pearson says, he was so wrong. It is everything else, Pearson insists, it is everything else outside of the Yucatán Peninsula, he insists, that represents a divergence from the real. Then: I am being blackmailed, Andrew Lethal tells his friend Roy Pearson aka The Janitor. I need you to acquire something for me, he says. I need the intercession of angels.

157

The body of a boy is discovered by Project Deep Run. Don't worry, Wise Crow says. We're closing in. The trap is set. We're in the hands of the angels now, she says. And Ruth Prior nods, like that.

158

At the funfair the children get to ride on The Lark's back all the way around the site for 12p. Aaron Murray watches the kids' delight as the little colt breaks into a trot and the parents fret that it will run off with their child. Aaron thinks of his brother Nemo. And of Jesus on a donkey on his entrance to Jerusalem. Only here it is The Lark that is like Christ, with his knowledge of fate and of certainty. Aaron is sat on a deckchair outside Scott Ruff's caravan. Loud music is blasting over the camp from the dodgems. 'Smooth Operator' by Sade. What a track. Scott Ruff comes out of the caravan with no top on and with his bare feet. It must be eighty degrees. Scott, Aaron says. Something is happening to me, he says. What do you mean? Something is happening to me, I am developing powers, Aaron says. Frightening powers. You mean the remote viewing you and The Precious Gift have been getting into? I don't know that it isn't something far less controllable than that. Think about it, Aaron says. I killed a man, then we slaughtered some horses. It's like one of those magic rituals. Like a pact with the devil. Did you know that a man's sexual peak is at the age of twenty-three? Scott Ruff asks Aaron, as he throws him a cold can of Irn-Bru. A woman's is thirty-two. Where's the justice in that? Scott asks. What has that got to do with my pact with the devil? Aaron says. What age are you now? Scott asks him. Eighteen. Well, maybe you're approaching the peak of your powers in every way. Maybe vision peaks in boyhood too. Maybe psychic powers have their peak there. Maybe it is all to do with libido. I have a name, Aaron says. I have been given a name in connection with the disappearance of my brother. What is the name? Escapologist, or The Escapologist, or something to do with that. What kind of a name is that? That's the name I have been given. By who? By Caird and Burl, Aaron lies. You're not still using those clowns, are you? Scott asks him. I am, Aaron says. I can't give up on Nemo, if I have a lead, and the actual police are hopeless. It makes sense, Aaron says. The Escapologist. I've been thinking about it. In what way? Swiftness. The speed with which he spirited Nemo away. The Escapologist. Elusiveness. How no one saw him. How he was never caught. Not as if you can just look him up in the phone book, though, is it? Scott Ruff says. Sounds like a gangster to me, Aaron says. A gangster or a jailbird. Who else has a name like that? Pop stars, Scott Ruff says. Or maybe like the nickname of an athlete, of a sprinter. We're the same mystery, Scott Ruff says. Think about it. To the family of the boy we killed, we are the same mystery as The Escapologist. It's beautiful how Scott Ruff always says 'we', when it comes to the murder, and not 'you', Aaron thinks to himself, and then he says, I feel capable of something terrible, Scott. If I discover who The Escapologist is, we'll kill again, he says. Imagine the kind of powers we will have then.

159

Josef Noth slides his headphones back after a shift on the short-wave. Thomas Tebaldi, aka Tab, offers him a chocolate biscuit. I've got a question for you, Josef Noth says to him. How would you go about finding out all of the various divisions of the Wehrmacht that went through Normandy on the initial assault? Why would you want to do that? Tab says to him. Weren't you there yourself? I believe the mother of my child was killed in cold blood by drunken Germans as they passed through Normandy, Josef Noth says. And I intend to murder them. What the fuck are you talking about? Tab says. You can't go about talking like that!

This is fucking wartime, you can't go about reporting your fellow soldiers and murdering your own side. There's a code of war, Josef Noth says. Who are you kidding, Tab says. I'm sorry for your . . . well, she wasn't your wife, right? No, Josef Noth says. We were never married. War turns father and son against each other, Tab says. Girlfriend and boyfriend, husband and wife, he says. She is French? Yes, Josef Noth says. She was French. And still you signed up to go to war against the French? I did, Josef Noth says. Well, what does that say? Tab says. I went to war because of a poem I read, Josef Noth says. And now I have my quarters in the apartment of the man who wrote it. My son is disappeared, Josef Noth says to Tab. My son Achilles is disappeared and his body has never been found. It is in the nature of war to disappear everyone, Tab says. How old was your son? Achilles was just a baby, Josef Noth says. The two of them switch off their desk lamps and pack their bags and together they walk along the dimly lit corridor of the lowest bunker of the bank vault, in the eerie green light of undersea. What you up to tonight? Tab asks Josef Noth. Quiet one, he says. What about you? Going to see my favourite whore, Tab says, and Josef Noth says, in that case I will accompany you, as I want to check in on my own favourite. When they get to the brothel there is pandemonium in the bar. It is Saturday night in occupied France during wartime and everyone is committed to the bacchanal. Josef Noth finds a madam and asks after Erithena but she says that she hasn't been back to work since Josef Noth last saw her in the company of The H. When he looks for Tab he's nowhere to be seen. Josef Noth heads back to the apartment of St-John Perse. Feeling no need of poetry, he goes straight to bed.

160

From Paris, Mindy Sparrow takes a train to Autun, where she has arranged to couch surf with an older woman who is a florist and who intends to put her to work at the various events she supplies flowers for in the town. She has upgraded her seat to first class for a treat. The train takes four hours, and Mindy looks out at a Europe that seems endless right then. The earth is flat, Mindy thinks to herself, in Europe, to all intents and purposes, or maybe it is just a feeling, maybe the feeling that the earth is flat is the prerogative of young girls in Europe in the summertime who feel they can see forever. A woman sat across from her says something in French and offers her a magazine. I'm sorry, Mindy says. I don't really speak French. You're Irish? the woman asks her, in perfect English. Half Irish, Mindy says. My father was from Belfast and my mother was from Glasgow, she explains. I knew it, says the woman, who introduces herself as Madeleine. I knew it, she says. I'm just back from a wake, she says. Well, she says. A private wake. But it was just like one of those Irish wakes where everyone gets drunk and gnashes their teeth and then starts laughing and singing and lamenting history. Only it was just me there, Madeleine says. Just me doing that, ha ha, she says. Like a mad Irish bird, she says, and she laughs some more. I threw my husband in the Seine, she says. All that was left of him. Back there, she says, and she gestures back towards the opposite way the train is running. Back there in Paris, she means. Did you get drunk? Mindy asks her. And Madeleine says, I had to get drunk, a little bit. Just so I wouldn't cry, she says. Really? Mindy says. I cry more when I'm drunk, Mindy says. When I am drunk emotions overwhelm me, Mindy admits. What happened to your husband? Mindy asks her, and Madeleine says, he was mauled by a lion. What?! Yes, really, he was mauled by a circus lion during his act. He was a circus performer? In later life, yes, he ran away to join the circus, but only because he had nowhere left to go. What do you mean? My husband was an MP, once, Madeleine says to Mindy. He was an MP involved in a scandal. Sex, drugs, prostitution, the old French way, Madeleine laughs. I can laugh about it now, she says. We split up, my husband Michel and I. You won't have heard of the Engrand Affair, you are blissfully Irish, Madeleine says, but at one point it was the talk of France. I moved out. I couldn't stand to sleep in the same bed and swim in the same pool and eat at the same table on which he had fucked all of his women and snorted coke from their armpits. He snorted coke from their armpits? Not just their armpits, Madeleine says. He was blackmailed by a rival politician who paid the women to talk. To give all of the lurid details. I loved my husband. I thought we had almost the perfect relationship. I thought he was a good man, and a good politician. A man of the people, with their best interests at heart. His fall from grace was spectacular. I went to live with a girlfriend in Switzerland. In a tiny house in Switzerland across the lake from Küsnacht, where the famous psychoanalyst Carl Jung lived and built his tower, though really I think of him as more of a mystic, wouldn't you agree? I don't really know anything about Carl Jung, Mindy admits. Except that he was something to do with Sigmund Freud. His student, Madeleine nods. For a time. But Freud believed in the existence, or should I say in the persistence, of the unconscious. Whereas Jung believed in the persistence of the gods. Anyway, I lived there with my Irish friend Joyce and sometimes we would sit out on the porch in blankets beneath these great mountains that rose all around us to snow-capped peaks which felt like the gods in silent judgement as we both wept over our bad decisions and all that we had lost in this life, because Joyce's partner had been kidnapped and murdered in Ireland and she had been forced to relocate. I met her at a fundraiser in an art gallery in Basel back when my husband was the darling of the European social scene. And sometimes Joyce and I would pass a pair of binoculars between the two of us and check in on Jung's tower, this blind tower that he built with his own hands, stone by stone, on the far shore of Lake Zurich, and thank God that he made men like that: solid, methodical, solitary, obsessed. Then word came to me that my husband had joined the circus. And not only that. That he had become a lion tamer. Yes, he had become a lion tamer with the Caliaris, the famous gypsy circus whose patch mirrored my husband's old social scene when he worked in foreign affairs, travelling across the north of Italy, as well as Austria and Switzerland, and the Balkans. I was impressed. And I was even more impressed when I heard from some people who had witnessed his act, this was in Bern, in Switzerland, who said that he performed a dance with a male lion, that the two of them danced together, this great lion up on its hind legs like a man, this great man embracing this beast like a lion, and then, to top it all, the dance would end with Michel putting his head into the mouth of the lion and holding it there. Against this urge. Against this virile animal urge to bite down and masticate and to enjoy. What a dare, I thought. And I fell in love with my husband, almost, at a distance, all over again. What faith, I thought. What faith to willingly invite your own destruction, night after night. It was such a taunt. Such a taunting of everything that had happened to him, of everyone who had conspired to destroy him. And then one night it tore his head off. Yes. Clean from his shoulders. The lion dragged his bloody corpse around the circus sands while it swallowed his head. In chunks, in bitesize chunks and not in one go. That's terrible, Mindy says. Well, Madeleine says, I'm not sure if it was. It was ghastly, undoubtedly, but I'm not sure it was terrible. And so, his body was cremated, and I travelled to Paris to a reggae bar by the Seine that he loved, in order to sprinkle his ashes there. There is a reggae bar by the Seine in Paris? Mindy asks her, which for some reason seems to her the most astounding detail of the whole affair. Yes, the Family Man's, after Bob Marley's bassist, Madeleine says. We had so many fun, drunken and stoned experiences there, she laughs. And so, I left him at his final resting place, she says, in the water just next to the Family Man's, and she has a little cry and so does Mindy, who is starting to think that maybe as soon as you become astonishing the whole world falls into line. She takes a note of Madeleine's number and promises to call her once she is settled in Autun.

161

Josef Noth travels to the studio of The H in an area of Montmartre that is lined with swastikas. He opens the great metal gate and climbs to the second floor where he knocks on an old wooden door and waits. What do you want? The H says when he sees that it's Josef Noth. I want to visit the grave of my lover, Josef Noth says. Can you give me the address where you buried her? The H tells him to come in and he sees The H's makeshift bed, a thin mattress atop some old wooden boxes piled high with blankets, and the scores, the handwritten scores for his compositions, that line the walls. Picasso continues to paint, The H says, as if anticipating Josef Noth's questions about art and war and futility and composing with one hand. So must I, he says, and he adds what look like the remains of a chest of drawers to the large metal stove in the centre of the room. I will paint you a map, The H says. Then, to himself, he says, an artist in wartime. He uncurls a sheet of paper like parchment or dead skin, and he picks up a brush in his one good hand. First, he draws a river, with three curling lines. First there is a river, he explains. Then there is a moon, he says, and he draws a half-moon. Moon-sur-Elle, he says. Then there is a bridge, he says. You turn left across this bridge, he says, and he paints a bridge in a single arc. You turn left and you follow the river, keeping it on your left-hand side, he says, and he paints a series of arrows. You come to the hamlet of Le Caperdu. He paints a sign with the words 'Le Caperdu' on it. There is a row of houses set back from the sandy road, he says, and he paints a row of houses set back from a sandy road. In the back garden of the third house with the name Ferme Rouge on it (he paints the words 'FERME ROUGE') you will find the grave of your lover and her cousin marked with two simple crosses. And now he paints an 'X' and an 'X' again, in the top corner of the paper. Murdered by the Nazis, he says, and he looks Josef Noth straight in the eye. Josef Noth returns to the apartment of St-John Perse and packs all of Perse's papers into a suitcase. He has made the decision to abandon his post. The next morning – his final day at work, though at that point known only to himself – Tab plays him an eerie recording. Listen to this, he says, and he plays him a recording known only as The Lovers. It's The Lovers, Tab says to him. These two are legendary. I found them last night. I was beginning to think it was an urban myth. But no, he says. Listen. Tab plays him a recording of two voices, a French woman and a German man, both with an odd robotic delivery. Chéri, viens, the French female voice says. Chéri, viens, it repeats. The male German voice replies with numbers, with a series of numbers that are different every time, Tab reveals. Drei. Fünf. Sieben. What does it mean? Josef Noth asks him. No one knows, Tab says, no one knows. The numbers are probably code numbers that, when deciphered, using a one-time-only sheet with a grid of letters on it, spell out certain sentences. Though no one has ever broken the code, or even worked out what side is broadcasting it, or from where, he adds. But to Josef Noth, right then, it feels like co-ordinates that read, sweetheart, come. Because everything is speaking.

162

Davey Brennan aka The Mole is sat in his car in a layby outside Burt. He is smoking with the window down. An ice-cream van pulls into the layby. Two men emerge from the ice-cream van and walk purposively towards Brennan's car. One of the pair removes a handgun from the inside of his bodywarmer and shoots Brennan in the head several times through the open window. They walk back to the van and speed off. Later the ice-cream van is found, burnt out, near Cloontagh.

163

Joyce and The Precious Gift return to their B&B in Carndonagh, near Trawbreaga Bay, and the barman tells him that there has been someone looking for him on the phone, someone called Mrs Crow has asked you to give her a call when you can, the barman says. Joyce heads upstairs to have a nap while The Precious Gift calls from a payphone in the lobby. The Mole is dead, Wise Crow tells him. Shot by suspected members of the Red Hand Commando. He was compromised, Wise Crow says. The Precious Gift holds his nerve. We compromised him, The Precious Gift says. And Wise Crow has to admit, we did. We may never get to the bottom of who killed Jim Monaghan, she admits. True,

The Precious Gift agrees. Is Joyce still with you? she asks him. What do you mean, still? The Precious Gift asks her. Of course she is, we're taking this trip together. Well, tell her 'The Mole is Dead'. Can't we wait till our trip is over? Why ruin a romantic getaway? But Wise Crow insists, tell her that 'The Mole is Dead', she insists. Use those words, she says. Upstairs Joyce is asleep on top of the bed. She is talking in her sleep. The Precious Gift whispers to her, what is that you're saying? She mutters something beneath her breath, something impossible to decipher. Then she says, I didn't say zilch. What? Then she goes back to mumbling incoherently again. Little bird, he says to her. Wake up, little bird, he says, and she puts her hand up to her eyes, as if she is looking off into the distance, staring straight into the sun, and she asks, who called you on the phone, and The Precious Gift says, it was a colleague of mine, part of the investigation, he says, and then he says, The Mole is Dead, and he cups her beautiful face in his hand, runs his thumb across her bottom lip, and slides a finger into her mouth. We may never know who killed your husband, he says, as he reaches round her to try to unzip her jeans. But she rolls away and says, no, I don't want to. Then she sits up on the bed and runs her hands through her long hair and says, wait, what did you just say? The Mole is Dead, The Precious Gift says to her. The Mole is Dead, she repeats. Then she looks at The Precious Gift with a look of infinite pity. Like a Catholic saint, she looks at him. Like a carving of a tragic Madonna in a cathedral. And then she says that she wants to get something to eat, and can they head down to the bar for dinner, immediately, because right now she really needs to eat, she says.

164

Luke G.B. Caird drives out to the airport to meet Tamar from her plane. Once more she is returning from New Zealand on the flight where they first met. He has made a handmade sign specially. It reads: 'Glasgow Welcomes Queen Tamar'. When she sees it, she drops her bags and runs towards him in tears. It is so beautiful, Mr Luke, she says. I am so moved. I love the book, Luke G.B. Caird says. I totally get it, he says. I knew you would, she says, and she calls him her king. My king, she says, as he takes her bags and leads them to the car park. It is so beautiful here, Tamar says, even as it is only motorway all around them and, in the distance, the hills. Isn't Georgia more beautiful than this? Luke G.B. Caird asks her, and she says, oh no, oh no. Georgia has a different kind of beauty. Like what? How would you compare them? Luke G.B. Caird asks her, and Tamar says, well, for a start it is more open here, she says, Georgia is a country of dark dells, is that the word? Dells? Dell, Luke G.B. Caird says, what is a dell? It is like a dark lonely valley, I think, Tamar says, and Luke G.B. Caird says, oh, I see, valleys and dales. You mean dales. I thought I said dales, Tamar says, and they both laugh. The north of England is like that, Luke G.B. Caird says. The north of England might be more like Georgia, he says. And Tamar says, my old boyfriend used to live in Penrith, she says. In the Eden Valley, she adds. In a dell there, she says, and they both laugh again but somehow Luke G.B. Caird is feeling weird about the mention of an old British boyfriend for the first time. And what did your old boyfriend do in Penrith? Luke G.B. Caird asks her, and Tamar says, he was a writer, of course. What did he write? Oh, love poetry, Tamar says. Epic poetry, she says. Love poetry. At which the car goes quiet, and they both stare out at the road in silence. Then

Tamar says, it was never so beautiful as this, just as they exit the Clyde Tunnel and, with the sun going down to their left, Luke G.B. Caird turns on the radio to that song by Jon & Vangelis, 'I'll Find My Way Home', that song he hates that is always on the fucking radio, with its words about the heart being at peace, whether the sun is coming up or going down.

165

Mekon and Alec Bolland take a walk over to the Hamiltons' place on the Old Manse Road, across from Sandyhills Church. First, they examine the scene of the crime. Check it out, Mekon says, there's still smashed glass here where the Hamilton boy was shot through the windscreen. Stealing horses, Alec Bolland says, and he marvels. What the fuck is that about? It's like the fucking Wild West, he says. There's Findlay, Mekon says, as he spots the brother working in the yard with some horses. You got your horses back? he shouts to Findlay, who is dragging bales of hay around the stables. Mekon, it's yourself, good to see you, he says. So, you heard, he says to the two of them. Brian got murdered, he says, and they stole our horses. These are new ones, he says, pointing to the two horses he's feeding. My cousin gave me two of theirs, he says, so we could still race them. I love my horses, he says. Where do you do your racing? Alec Bolland asks him, and Mekon says, this is my pal Alec, by the way. We just thought we would drop round and pay our condolences, Alec Bolland says. And to see if there was anything we could do to help. We race them in the streets, Findlay says. Mostly at night, he says, or in the early hours of the morning, he says. What are the police saying? No leads, no motive. And no witnesses to these horses running through the streets at night? Horses in the dead of night are invisible, Findlay says. That's how we get away with racing them, he says. Any threats made? Alec Bolland asks him. Any enemies? Who is this guy? Findlay asks Mekon, and Mekon says, it's OK, he's a godfather, and Findlay says, oh shit, sorry, sorry, I just wanted to make sure it was all cool, he says. I appreciate you looking in on us, Findlay says to Alec Bolland, and Alec Bolland says, no problem, no problem at all. Just trying to see if we can help you get to the bottom of this, because I'm guessing it's another family, another gypsy family, I mean, who rides horses through the night in Glasgow outside of us, he says, and Findlay says, true, true, and then Findlay says, any rumours, any word on the grapevine? And Alec Bolland says, no – he lies – he says there are no rumours doing the rounds and then he asks Findlay about his brother. Your brother was a bit of a scrapper, I hear from Mekon, and Findlay says, that's right. I hear he was a tough character, Alec Bolland says, and Findlay says, you could say that, and Alec Bolland says, did he ever give anyone a doing? As far as you know, did he ever give anyone a right pasting? Yeah, I mean, we sometimes got into scraps of an evening, Findlay says. Like what, Alec Bolland asks him, and he says, well, like, I've been thinking about this for a bit and a few weeks before he was killed, we got into an altercation with two guys outside of a nightclub and beat them nearly half to death. Who did? Me and Brian. We kicked the absolute shite out them. I think I took one of their eyes out, Findlay says, before we fled the scene. Could be we're looking for some cunt with one eye, Alec Bolland says, in that case. Or, better yet, an eyepatch.

166

Mindy Sparrow walks from the train station in Autun to Rue Jondeau and an apartment with a balcony overflowing with flowers and vegetables growing in containers that looks out over a tiny park with its old bikes tied up against railings in the late-afternoon sun. Her host waves down to her from the balcony, an older woman with a shock of black hair and huge beads and bright-red lipstick. Her name is Carina. It's the legendary Mindy, Carina says, and she says that she will buzz her in. In the hallway there is a stained-glass door leading up to Carina's apartment that features two birds in autumnal colours alighting on a branch. On the stairs there are terracotta pots with bulbs in them, some in full flower, white flowers with blousy heads and a smell like a summer of adventure. They hug as soon as Mindy gets through the door and Mindy says, everyone is calling me the legendary Mindy, you wouldn't believe it, it is so funny you said that, and Carina says, well, you are a legend, taking this trip all on your own, I wish I could have been as adventurous as a young girl, which is why I host my couch surfers, she explains, in the hope that I will meet my more adventurous self, she says, and Mindy says, you will never believe who I met on the train. Who? The Engrand widow! No! You know her husband was devoured by a lion?! I know, Mindy says. Or rather, I didn't know but now I do because she told me everything. Wow, Carina says. Was she drunk? Yes, Mindy says. She had just returned from scattering her husband's ashes in front of a reggae bar next to the Seine and she was mortal. There's a reggae bar next to the Seine in Paris? Carina says. That's exactly what I said, Mindy says. That's so weird. Her husband died a few years ago. I guess she only just got around to it, Carina says. And yes, she is a lush, Carina adds. She was drunk on TV in the wake of her husband's death. Her disgraced husband's death but also, now, well, then, also, for a moment, her almost redeemed husband, because no one could believe he had been so bold as to trust his fate to the lions, and not just once! And of course, Madeleine appeared drunk on this programme and caused a scene, although just as many people admired her, drunk or not, or maybe precisely because she was 'rat-arsed' (at this Carina makes the sign with her fingers for quotation marks), because she expressed admiration for her husband, even then, after all of it had happened to them. I haven't thought of her in years. I just presumed she had drunk herself to death. I have her phone number! Mindy announces. We can have her over and all three of us can talk about our crap partners and get 'rat-arsed' together, and Mindy makes the same sign of the quotation marks in the air right back at her.

167

Dan Ruff fucked up, Alec Bolland says to Mekon as soon as they leave the stables and make their way down the Old Manse Road. Remember the old rag-and-bone man that used to come down here? Mekon asks him. I do, Alec Bolland says, but then he returns to his point, which is that Dan Ruff fucked up and fucked up bad. Bringing his kid round with the one eye and the eyepatch. What a slip-up, Mekon agrees. What's his name again? Alec Bolland asks him. Scott, Scott Ruff, Mekon says. Scott Ruff killed Brian Hamilton, Alec Bolland says. Either that or Dan Ruff did it. Didn't think it was gonna be that easy to get to the bottom of this, he admits. You and me should get into the detective business, he says. Think about it, Alec Bolland says. Bolland & Brewster. That sounds more like a pair that hunts ghosts, Mekon says. What do you mean, hunts ghosts? Ghost hunters, Mekon says. Investigating hauntings and that kind of thing. Ah, I get you, Alec Bolland says. Poltergeists, you mean. Poltergeists and ghosts, yeah. What's the difference between a poltergeist and a ghost? Alec Bolland says to

Mekon and Mekon says it's down to how poltergeists are invisible and can throw things and move things around whereas ghosts can be seen but can't throw things or move things. It's one or the other, Mekon explains. Can they both walk through walls? Obviously. How close do you think you can get to a ghost? Alec Bolland asks Mekon. About three feet, he says. Right now, I feel close to the ghost of Brian Hamilton, Alec Bolland says. Tell me about it, Mekon says, and he goes into this voice, saying, 'Help me, Obi-Wan Kenobi, you're my only hope.' What's that about? Alec Bolland asks him. *Star Wars*, innit, Mekon says. Then they cut along the Shettleston Road and drop into the bookie's to put a line on.

168

So tell me, Tamar asks Luke G.B. Caird (they had been making love non-stop for six hours), how did you get into the detective business? Was it through a love of stories and adventure and of tragedy and romance and drama? Yes, Luke G.B. Caird says, what better vocation for a writer, he says. All of life is there, he says. All of life at its best and worst, Tamar says. Plus, you have to admit criminals are sexy, she says. What? Luke G.B. Caird says. He is already getting jealous of sexy criminals. Some of them are ugly, ugly on the inside and out, he tells her. Is there not beauty in ugliness, sometimes, do you think? Tamar asks him. That is a quote from Andy Warhol, she says. Do you like Andy Warhol? Luke G.B. Caird asks her, and Tamar says, I like *Electric Chair*, do you know that one? No, he says, what is that one? It is an electric chair, in colour, again and again, she says. Sounds amazing, Luke G.B. Caird says. What happens if you go into a gallery and look at a picture of an electric chair again and again, Tamar says, and Luke G.B.

Caird nods and says, yeah, I know what you mean. Wow, he says. No, Tamar says, I am asking you what you think happens if you go into a gallery and look at pictures of electric chairs in different colours again and again, she says. I have never done it, she says. I only saw a photograph. What do you think happens? she says. Knowing your love for sexy criminals, you probably get turned on, Luke G.B. Caird says, and inevitably they go back at it all over again.

169

The Precious Gift turns the shower on and looks at himself in the mirror. It's so strange, travelling back to the place where you lived another life completely. And in these circumstances. These circumstances of being watched over by angels, perhaps. And perhaps, also, demons. Is it true, he asks himself. Are angels real? Demons? He wipes the steam away and looks at himself. Is it possible? Are they onto me? Are they onto us? Was Jim Monaghan the only thing holding it off? His features are hardening. Those are hard smile lines fixed around his cheeks. Could be worse, he thinks. Could be hard frown lines. He pulls his skin tight with his fingers in order to lift his face. He can almost see the boy he once was. But not quite. Who is this old man, he asks himself, with death so all around? Right then he hears a voice from next door. Joyce is saying something. I'm just getting into the shower, darling, The Precious Gift says. Give me a minute, he says. In the shower he sings his favourite Undertones track, which is 'My Perfect Cousin'. He works the thickening shampoo into his scalp. It stings as it runs into his eyes. He gets out of the shower and dries off and then he stands there naked while he scrubs his teeth with smokers' powder, just like his father before him. He pulls on some clean underwear, even though he spots a small hole in them. He's at that age where he doesn't care about that sort of thing anymore. He splashes some Old Spice around his neck and dresses in a white vest under a white shirt with a pair of dark-blue slacks. His hair is still wet as he emerges from the bathroom. I don't mind a shower, but I will always prefer a bath, he says as he walks into the room, but Joyce is nowhere to be seen. She must have shouted through that she would see me downstairs, he thinks, but when he gets down there Joyce is nowhere to be seen. Have you seen Joyce? he asks Gerry the barman and Gerry says she walked past and went outside to the car park. But when The Precious Gift goes outside to check, Joyce is nowhere to be seen. For a moment he thinks of the cliffs, and the sea lapping, and the waves, but then he thinks, no, surely not, surely she hasn't thrown herself from the cliffs. He goes back inside to wait at their table. He's there an hour before he accepts that she is not coming back, though it would be more accurate to say that she has disappeared completely. He speaks to Gerry at the bar. She really said nothing, he asks him, she really didn't say anything as she passed? Gerry says, no, but that she seemed preoccupied. Like she was on a mission, he says. And The Precious Gift says, what was she talking to everyone about this afternoon, did she say anything that might have stood out, what was the topic of conversation? She was talking about you, Gerry says. Really? The Precious Gift is taken aback. She was talking about how she was bringing you back home, Gerry says. Although, come to think of it, she put it in a strange way, Gerry says. Like what? She said that the chicken was coming home to roost. The Precious Gift returns to their room, and spreads out a map, and combs the territory with his mind. Are there angels in these same skies? he is asking himself, as he looks down at this territory, beneath him, at these occasional figures in the landscape, moving this way and that, and yet no sign of Joyce, as The Precious Gift haunts the places of his past. It's as if she has been lifted up, into the very same sky that he now looks down from.

170

Josef Noth is leaving Paris. He has commandeered a motorcycle with a sidecar in which he stores his suitcase and a box containing the papers of St-John Perse. He passes through the great boulevards lined with swastikas. Versailles, too, has a swastika flying from its roof. He stops in Dreux to admire the Chapel Saint-Louis de Dreux. He sits on a bench outside and eats a sandwich and drinks hot soup from a flask. He is dressed in full uniform. He is approached by an old man dressed like a simple bum, his battered sandals, his trousers held up by a piece of string, his prodigious gut, his white vest, his drinker's nose. The old bum engages Josef Noth in conversation, in German. How do you think it will end? the old bum asks him, and Josef Noth says, how what will end? The war, the old bum says. How do you think the war will end? For me, the war has ended, Josef Noth says. How can you say that? the old bum says, and Josef Noth says, because I am absconding, he says. Because I am leaving the war. There is no escaping the war, the old bum says. Are you a fan of poetry? Josef Noth asks the old bum, an old bum who turns out to be a German by the name of Heinrich. Oh yes, Heinrich says. Oh yes, I am a fan of the Norse epics, he says. Also, *Gilgamesh*, he says. *Gilgamesh*? Josef Noth asks him. What is *Gilgamesh*? He was a hero in Mesopotamia, Heinrich says. He killed the bull of heaven and offered up its heart to the god of the sun. Why? Because the nature of the universe is sacrificial, Heinrich says. No, Josef Noth says. No. I used to think that, he says. I used to think that a sacrifice was required, just like the ancients believed, that without death the sun wouldn't rise in the sky. I no longer think that way, he says to Heinrich, who responds by saying, but look at all the dead. That is what I intend to do, Josef Noth says. I am on my way to visit the grave of my lover, he says, and then I intend to leave the war and travel to China. Why China? Heinrich asks him, and Josef Noth says, because there is a pagoda there from which you can see all of history. The poet St-John Perse wrote a poem called *The Anabasis* there. He was an old friend of mine. But what is an anabasis? Heinrich asks him. It is a journey, Josef Noth says. It is a journey into the interior, he says. And back again.

171

The problem for Andrew Lethal is that no one on the council actually likes him. He has long ago come to this conclusion. Sat at his desk looking out over the exquisite, romantic rose garden at Tollcross Park in the east end of Glasgow, he is thinking about the Aztec kings and how they were probably more feared than loved but also that somehow those two things can become confused. He thinks of how long he has worked for the council – twenty-three years – as the terrible hieroglyph on his own tomb. His writings too. His Mayan studies, in particular. What great man was ever, truly, liked? Great men are by their very nature unlikeable precisely because they are so great and therefore inspire resentment and jealousies in other, lesser men. What was it Nietzsche said about resentment? Exactly. But resentment, too, has a strange form of love in it, in that it longs to be everything that it claims to resent. So it is with anyone who holds power over you, he thinks to himself. And then he thinks of the photographs. The photographs that, should they ever be released, would surely spell an end to his council job and his reputation as a serious Mayanist. He thinks of the power of the past over the present and wonders if that's why we are more in love with it than we are with the moment. Because we wish to have the power of the past. Andrew Lethal certainly does. He wishes to have the power of the ancient Aztec kings over life and death. But not only that. To have power over life and death means direct access to the mechanic at the heart of the world. The phone goes. Andrew Lethal looks at it in fright. The past is calling. Hello, Andrew Lethal says. And the voice on the other end says, Lethal, where did an ineffective dweeb like you get the name Lethal, it says, and Andrew Lethal says, fuck you, fuck you, to the voice on the other end of the phone, and the voice says, calm down, pal, I hold your whole future in my hands, it says, so shut the fuck up. That's the one thing that no one has control over, Andrew Lethal says, and the voice says, not so, pal, not so. In this case, I do, it says. And, if you go along with our demands, so do you. You broke into my flat, Andrew Lethal says. You ransacked the place. And not just the photographs. You stole my video player, you stole my old bike and my watch, and you even made yourself a sandwich at the kitchen table while you were at it. Call the police, the voice says. In that case call the police and as soon as they turn up at the door, that is if they can fucking find us, these pictures will be everywhere. These salacious pictures, the voice says. These explicit pictures, it says. These straight-up fucking sleazy-as-fuck pictures, if you ask me, it says. And Andrew Lethal says, I told you before. I don't have that kind of money. You are making it impossible for me, he says. And the voice says to him, well, but that's precisely why I am calling. I'm going to offer you a one-time discount. Hear me out.

172

Dan Ruff has made up his mind. He says to Big Paul Vickers to take some time off the dodgems and join him in his caravan. They are blasting T. Rex all across the site through a pair of really shitty speakers. Tyrannosaurus Rex, eh? Big Paul Vickers says to him, and he nods back out towards the fairground. What?! Dan Ruff says. That's all we fucking need, he laughs, and he mock-punches Big Paul Vickers in the stomach. I need to talk to you about war, Dan Ruff says. I need to talk to you about the tactics and logic of war, he says. I'm all ears, Big Paul Vickers says, and they both laugh again, because, although it hasn't been pointed out previously, Big Paul Vickers has a massive pair of lugs on him. Let me ask you a question, he says to Big Paul. Why do you think some cunt from the council like your man Andrew Lethal might want to start an internecine conflict? Let me think, Big Paul says, and he takes a stool at the breakfast bar. Now they're playing OMD, 'Joan of Arc'. Because he wishes for one side to destroy the other, because they have become a problem for him, would be my opinion, he says. Exactly, my boy, Dan Ruff says to him. That's my boy, he says to Big Paul. Because they have something to fear from the other side. Because Andrew Lethal has something to fear from Alec Bolland, he says. Alec Bolland has something on him. This is my guess, Dan Ruff says. But here's what I'm concerned about, Dan Ruff admits. I'm concerned that we showed our hand, somehow, Dan Ruff says. Call it an intuition, call it some kind of sixth sense, he says, but it really seemed to me, or rather, seems to me, because I didn't fully clock it at the time, because, and I'm going to be honest here, I think Lethal played me like a fucking cuckoo. Like a fucking cuckoo? Yes, like a fucking canary, Dan Ruff says. Like a fucking budgerigar, he says, exaggeratedly enunciating every syllable as he does so. And I fucked up, Dan Ruff says. I fear I might have fucked up, and you being my lieutenant, I need to be completely honest with you. I feel that I might have exposed Scott to danger, he says. I should never have taken him with us. Why didn't I even think of it? That's the eye for an eye right there, Dan Ruff says, and Big Paul says, ah, fuck, I see what you're getting at. The motive, he says. And the thing is, fucking Alec Bolland, it seemed to me up until then, had barely given the murder a second thought. But now what if he puts two and two together, Big Paul says. Ah, fuck, he says again. What were youse all talking about while I was in there talking to Bolland? The boys, did they say anything about Scott's eyepatch? Dan Ruff asks him. Aye, they did, Big Paul says, but just to call him Captain Birdseye and shite like that, he says. Still, Dan Ruff says. They'll remember. They'll remember the fact he had his eye out. We're bollocksed.

173

Carina, Madeleine Engrand and Mindy Sparrow are sat around the table at Carina's apartment in Autun getting steadily 'rat-arsed'. Mindy called Madeleine on the phone and invited her to lunch at Carina's and now Mindy is explaining her mission in Europe to the two of them. That's what she calls it. My mission, she explains, is to visit all of the French churches that my lover loves so much. He passed me a note, she says, he passed me a note on the one and only night we met in Paris when I was on a date with someone else, an older man, she says. On the note it said, astonish me. I have come here to France so that I might secretly astonish him. My husband astonished me by taming lions, Madeleine says, and by putting his head in their mouths and by getting eaten alive by them, she says. Tell me,

Carina says to Mindy, as she opens a second bottle of white wine, do you intend to write up your experiences and send it to him by way of a diary? No, Mindy says, and she explains the nature of her project to them. I intend to photograph every cathedral and package the photographs of each cathedral in a hand-painted box with a drawing of the sun on the front and include alongside them the actual panties I wore when I visited the cathedral that day, she tells them. Wow! they both burst, and they have to laugh. Mindy, you are astonishing, Madeleine laughs, and Carina has to agree. But I have a question, Carina says. Why didn't you just use the money to go visit your love in Paris? Well, Mindy says, for one it is more astonishing, she says, and again the two older women marvel and have to agree, and for another, Mindy says, I have a feeling that we may never meet again. Or, should I say, that perhaps we should never meet again. Why is that? the widow Engrand asks her, and Mindy says, why, because it was perfect, she says, and what is perfect cannot be imitated or repeated, because of its perfection, and so it has to die, she says. But sending the gift of your panties alongside the pictures of the churches is surely the opposite of killing it? Carina says. That way he will always dream of me, Mindy says. To live in a dream is to cheat death, Madeleine agrees, who said that again? she asks them, I think it was a famous Jewish poet who said that to be alive in a dream inside of a dream was to cheat death, I think, she says. I think I was Jewish in a previous incarnation, Carina says. I have always been affected by the sad klezmer music of the Jews. I feel like a young bride every time I hear it, she says. All my life I have dreamt of the Balkans, even though we went there only once, she says. Now Carina has opened a red wine to go with the beef-shin ragù she has just produced from the oven, which she is serving with her own handmade gnocchi. Were you married, Carina? Madeleine asks her, and Carina says, yes, that she was married, and that in fact she is still married, she says, even after his death, she says, even after the death of my husband Silvio, I am still his bride, she says, and Mindy says, but that is beautiful, and she asks Carina, do you think that true loves are united in eternity, and before Carina can say anything Madeleine says, I hope so. I hope to God that's the case, she says. Because I have forgiven my dear husband everything and only long to be back in his arms once more.

174

The police arrive at the guesthouse in Carndonagh and they interview The Precious Gift under caution. Why under caution? The Precious Gift asks them. There are two police officers, Officer Shan and Officer McCullough. You admit you were one of the last people to see Joyce Monaghan alive, Officer Shan says. How do you know she is dead? The Precious Gift asks him. We don't, at the moment, have any proof that she is dead, Officer McCullough says, but did you know that her husband was murdered? Did you know that her husband was murdered in a frenzied attack? Yes, I did know that, actually, The Precious Gift says. And you were Joyce's new lover? Officer McCullough asks him. No, I was her friend, The Precious Gift says. A friend who shares her bed? Officer Shan says. You were booked into a double room together. We never made love, The Precious Gift says. But you were planning to? You were planning on seducing her on this romantic getaway, Officer Shan says, and he gestures round the room as if it were a secret love nest. I thought it might be on the cards, The Precious Gift admits. We were developing a relationship. And how did you come to know Joyce Monaghan? Officer McCullough asks The Precious Gift, and The Precious Gift says that he got to know Joyce through her husband, who he worked alongside. Worked alongside him doing what? Officer Shan asks him. We were both involved with a secret service project that I can't talk about, The Precious Gift says. The officers look at each other and then back at The Precious Gift. Give me a fucking break, Officer Shan says, and The Precious Gift says, I suggest you call your superiors, he says. And give them my name. Someone will be able to confirm my story. In fact, I was part of the investigation into Joyce's husband's death. And yet you're fraternising with his wife? Officer Shan says. Isn't there some kind of law or ethics against that? Are you arresting me? The Precious Gift asks them, and Officer McCullough says, no, we are simply questioning you in the hope that we can get some information that might help us locate the woman you reported missing, he says. And then he instructs The Precious Gift to wait there in the room while they make some calls. There's someone on the door, they tell him, just in case you are thinking of going anywhere. As soon as they leave, The Precious Gift sits down at the desk and in his mind he tries to scan the outside of the building, the car park, he tries to remote-view how many cops they have sent for him and whether anyone is actually performing a search right now, but it's like he can't, it's like someone has shut down the power, and that's when he has this vision of a castle, this vision of a fortress, in his mind, seen from above, a fortress that he seems to be hovering over, and as he attempts to zoom in, as he attempts to dive down towards this castle, like Peter Pan, he thinks, just then, the castle retreats, it retreats like it takes up fewer, or who the fuck knows right now, maybe even more, dimensions than he can access, he can feel a panic surging through him, and he gets a terrible sense of vertigo right then, as he opens his eyes and stands up and grips the table, as he walks over to the window and cracks it as far as it will go and leans out into the evening air, suddenly gasping for breath, and that's when he sees it, when he thinks he sees it, in the car park, across the way, a figure is stood next to a lamp-post with its head cocked, with its head cocked like a bird, like an awful upright bird, and as he looks closer, there can be no doubt, it is the same birdwoman from Derry, the same birdwoman that stood outside his hotel in the dark, returned, and of course he closes his eyes and tries to zoom in, but it's no use, it's all black, except for this fortress, except for this sealed fortress that has taken the place of everything in his imagination, and he opens the door of the room – there is no one guarding it after all – and runs down the stairs and bursts through the lounge, where the officers are stood behind the bar, talking on the phone, and he makes a break for the car park just as Officer McCullough shouts at him to freeze, get back here, he shouts, but The Precious Gift is already outside, and running towards the lamp-post which he can see, already, he can see that there is no one stood there, no birdwoman to be seen, and he comes to a gasping halt, bent over with his hands on his thighs, trying to catch his breath, just as Officer McCullough body-slams him and brings him to the ground. What the fuck are you thinking, the officer says to him, and The Precious Gift says, someone is watching us, someone is taunting us, someone is running the game, he says, just in time for Officer Shan to roll up and cuff him, and for the two of them to drag him back to the bar, and to tell him that, now, you can bet your fucking life we are arresting you now, secret service bullshit or not, they say, even as The Precious Gift insists on running his mouth about this birdwoman, this birdwoman that keeps following him, and about Project Deep Run. Call them, he keeps telling the officers, call them and confirm my story, he says. But when they do, they tell him that no one can confirm his story. That there is no Project Deep Run, whatever the fuck that is.

175

Josef Noth pulls out of Moon-sur-Elle on his motorbike with its sidecar piled high with suitcases and drives across the old stone bridge. Down below people are swimming and lying in the sun on towels and feeding ducks in the middle of a war. He turns left at the other side and follows the river along a meandering road. Now there is not a soul to be seen. He comes to the hamlet of Le Caperdu, just as The H had painted it. He sees the row of old houses set back from the sandy road and he parks up his motorbike. He approaches the third house, the one that has the name 'Ferme Rouge' on it, and walks round the side, to the back garden, where he finds the grave of his lover and her cousin marked with two simple crosses. X and X. Murdered by the Nazis.

176

Luke G.B. Caird is taking Tamar along to his first fiction workshop at The Warehouse in Springburn. She gasps at the tall flats across the way. Wow, she says. Imagine waking up there every morning, with that view over the whole of Glasgow. How delightful, she says. They both check in with Susan on the door. Hi Susan, Luke G.B. Caird says, and Susan says that it's lovely to see him and she asks him, who's your beautiful bride, and then she says, whoops, that was a sleight of the tongue, she says, although she means a slip of the tongue, and now she's even more flustered. Sorry, Susan says. I meant your beautiful companion, she says, and Tamar says, thank you very much, and Susan says to Luke G.B. Caird, keep shooting above your station, son, and she winks and points them down the corridor to the room where the workshop is taking place. What does 'shooting above your station' mean? Tamar asks him, and Luke G.B. Caird says, it just means doing well for yourself, he says, and Tamar says, what a beautiful thing to say. In the room there are desks set up like in a classroom. In fact, they are desks that were actually nicked from a classroom during the summer holidays. As is the blackboard that The Escapologist is standing at and already writing things on, graphics, shapes, but not actual words, at least not at this point. The Dragonfly waves from the corner when he sees Luke G.B. Caird. He appears to be attempting to fix an overhead projector. Luke G.B. Caird recognises someone, an older man sat at a desk, and Tamar suggests they take the desk next to him. Hi, she says, and the guy looks up and offers her his hand, hi, the guy says, I'm Andrew, he says, and Luke G.B. Caird realises that it is in fact Andrew Lethal, a councillor with a bit of a rep, though he pretends not to recognise him. I'm Luke, he says, and this is my friend Tamar, he says, and Tamar says, he means his girlfriend, and Luke G.B. Caird almost blushes. You're cute, Andrew Lethal says to Tamar, and she says, why, thank you. You both writers? Andrew Lethal asks them. Struggling writers? You could say that, Luke G.B. Caird says. Just here to hone my craft, know what I mean? What about you, Tamar? You a wannabe writer? Oh no, Tamar says. I'm just here to accompany my man, she says. I'm his big fan, she says. And then she says, I'm a reader, she says, not a writer. A lover not a fighter, eh? Andrew Lethal says, and Tamar says, yes, I am an air hostess. Really? Andrew Lethal says. I've always had a thing for air hostesses. Are you a member of the Mile High Club, by any chance, he says, and he winks at her. And before Luke G.B. Caird can say, now that is just a fucking impertinence, Tamar says, yes, of course. (What the fuck?). I'm fairly well travelled myself, Andrew Lethal says. Take flights all the time, he says. Luke G.B. Caird is stood there looking at Tamar like, what?! Mostly to Mexico, he says. Do you know Mexico? he asks Tamar, and she says, what is the ancient city, the ancient city near Mexico City? and Andrew Lethal says, Teotihuacán? With its pyramid of the moon and pyramid of the sun? Yes, that's right, Tamar says. I have visited there, once. With an old boyfriend, she says. This whole conversation is really starting to wind Luke G.B. Caird up but he's trying to remain cool. I'm a bit of an expert on the ancient Mayans, Andrew Lethal says. I've published quite a few articles about the Mayan glyphs, he says, and Tamar says, what is a glyph? It's an image that is a stand-in for a word or a number. So, it is a letter? Tamar asks him. No, he says. It is a graphic representation that can also be read. It is about the thing and representative of the thing at the same time, he explains. Isn't everything? Tamar asks him, and he has to laugh. Yes, in a way that is exactly right, that's why to me the Mayans were the closest to the way things are and have to be forever, he says, and Tamar says, right on! Right on, Luke G.B. Caird thinks, what the fuck. But, thankfully for Luke G.B. Caird, right then they are interrupted by The Escapologist, who goes straight into his workshop without any introduction. He looks like a military man, Luke G.B. Caird thinks to himself, when he gets his first good look at him. Sharp, neat. Tall. Short jet-black hair. Eyes of a killer. Eyes that say: I'm killing you, motherfucker. Lily-white hands. Lily-white hands made for slow strangulation. What is this, The Escapologist asks the crowd, which consists of about ten people, and he points to something that looks like a cylinder or a rolling pin that he has drawn on the blackboard. Can anyone tell me what the fuck this thing here is, he says, and he taps the blackboard repeatedly with his finger. Speak up, he says. Make something up, he says. You're all fucking writers, or so you think. So run wild, he says. Finally, someone says it: a rolling pin, some weedy guy sat at the front that looks like a junkie says it. A fucking rolling pin? The Escapologist says. Why the fuck would I be pointing to a rolling pin in a writers' workshop? Em, because it's all about flattening out and expanding your story, maybe, the wee junkie tries again. What the fuck are you talking about, of course it's not a fucking rolling pin, The Escapologist says. Fucking home economics is next door, pal, he says, and he jabs a thumb towards the door. Someone else, someone else tell me what the fuck this is on the blackboard here. Is it one of they galaxies? someone says. What?! Is it one of they weird-shaped galaxies, like the rolling pin galaxy? The fucking rolling pin galaxy?! What the fuck is it with you lot and fucking . . . pastry?! Of course it's not a fucking galaxy in the shape of a rolling pin. OK, alright, what's this? I'll make it easier for you, The Escapologist says, and next to this thing that to be honest looks exactly like a fucking rolling pin he draws what looks like an easel with a half-finished painting on it. Then he draws a line coming from the head or the handle of the rolling pin and moving towards the painting and the easel. OK, what is it now? Andrew Lethal puts his hand up. You don't need to put your hand up, The Escapologist says, we're not at school. It's an easel with a half-finished painting on it. Almost, The Escapologist says. Thank fuck we have a guy that can see with the eyes of a fucking artist in the room, he says, and he gives him a quick clap. Almost, he says. That is the first page of a novel, he says. And that, he says, pointing to the line coming from the handle of the rolling pin, is a pen or a pencil. Now put two and two together, he says. The room remains silent. What the fuck is going on here? Someone is writing a book, Tamar says, and The Escapologist says, correct-a-mundo, someone is indeed writing a book, he says. But how are they doing it? Look closer, what is going on here? That's when Luke G.B. Caird sees it. He's writing a book with a pen – or a pencil – in his mouth. He is writing using his mouth, Luke G.B. Caird says. Why? The Escapologist says. Because he is living inside an iron lung, Luke G.B. Caird says. This is the greatest writer who ever lived, The Escapologist says. Since he was a boy, he has lived inside an iron lung with only his head protruding and this young boy taught himself to write with a pencil in his mouth and a notepad on an easel. He wrote seven novels, one after the other, in pain and confusion, none of which were ever published. What was his name? Andrew Lethal asks him. What was his name, motherfucker? The Escapologist says. What was this motherfucker's name? His name is YOU, motherfucker, The Escapologist says. His name is you. And this is the first lesson. Write hopelessly, he says. That's the first fucking lesson, motherfucker, and he prods his finger against this mad fucking drawing that suddenly reveals itself as a young boy in an iron lung writing mad unpublishable novels with his fucking teeth.

177

There has been a major fuck-up. The police have only gone and dug up the dead horses in the allotment, and not only that. They also discovered a box of ammo – actual bullets – beneath the floor of the hut right next to them. Terry Johnstone, whose allotment it was, is on the phone to Dan Ruff. I gave up my plot, he's telling Dan Ruff. I meant to tell you. You meant to fucking tell me? Dan Ruff says to him. Now we are well and truly bollocksed, he says. What the fuck were you doing leaving ammunition there? I forgot, Terry says. I forgot I had stashed it there. Who the fuck did you stash it for? This cunt, Terry says. This fucking RHC cunt. Or UVF cunt, I don't know. I was helping him out. And where is this UDA cunt now? Fuck knows, Terry says. We lost touch, he says. But anyway, he says, the new cunt what took over my plot ripped up the floor of the hut and found the bullets and then they called the police and they taped off the entire plot and dug it up and that is when they found the bodies of the horses and now they are calling me a satanist. What?! A fucking satanist, that is what they are saying, every cunt in Acre is accusing me of doing the black magic. What did you tell the police? I telt them that I have no idea what the black magic even is, outside of sticking a pin in a doll. Why did you bring up sticking a pin in a doll? That shows you've got knowledge of the black magic right there. But I don't, I'm not lying, this has got fuck-all to do with the black magic. I says to them, sure, I'd no fucking idea these horses were buried in the ground, I says to them, it's fucking fertilisers, innit, fucking rotting horses are as good as dung, I says, probably, you would think, anyways, I says, and besides, I says, I've only had this plot for a year and so they were probably buried by the previous owner, who it turns out moved to Australia and is now dead anyway. They can do autopsies on horses, Dan Ruff says. They'll know how long they have been dead for. Plus, they'll find bullets in their skulls, and they'll put two and two together, he says. Then he says, let me think here. But Terry says, it gets worse. What?! It gets worse. I've had reporters outside my house all day, he says. It's gonna be all over the papers in the morning. Ah, we're bollocksed, Dan Ruff says, and he looks out the window at this fucking mad fucking Ferris wheel, turning.

178

Anne-Marie knocks on Andrew Lethal's door at the City Chambers. Have you heard about this? she says, as she drops a copy of today's *Evening Times* on his desk. The headline reads: 'Horses Discovered Buried Upright In Mass Grave In Maryhill'. Buried upright, Andrew Lethal says, that's some Mayan shit right there, he says. What do you mean? Anne-Marie says. Horses were buried upright as a sign of respect, he says. Plus that way they could go charging into the underworld. Gotta be your travellers, huh? Anne-Marie says. Respecting horses and shit, she adds. Then Andrew Lethal remembers the book that Dan Ruff recommended him, *The Art of Horsemanship*, by Xenophon. This could escalate, Andrew Lethal says. This could escalate into a turf war, he says, and he can't help but feel excited, even though his arse may be on the line. This is everything you read about in the books, he thinks to himself. This is the Maya right here, he thinks, and for the first time ever he thinks of the other meaning of the word 'maya': illusion. It has never occurred to me before, he says out loud. What has? Anne-Marie asks him. That the word 'maya' means illusion, he says. That maya is what we must wake up from, he says. Wow, he says. Fuck me, he says. Then he says, everything is speaking. What? It is like everything is speaking, he says. And then he says, can you excuse me, I have an appointment at The Warehouse in Springburn.

179

The Saint-Lazare Cathedral in Autun features the marvellous Romanesque sculptures of Gislebertus. To Mindy Sparrow it seems like a portal. There is something magical in its dimensions. She is wearing her specially chosen outfit for the day. A summer dress with no bra, a floppy sun hat and white lace panties that once belonged to her mum. As she photographs the wonderful sculptures on the capitals, so alive and carved with such warmth and love and good humour, she has a woozy sense of vertigo, as if the sculptures themselves are a form of ingress. Ingress to what? To whatever lies back of it. There is a secret cathedral, Mindy thinks to herself. Within the cathedral itself there is a secret cathedral. It has begun to reveal itself, she thinks. Why? Because of the ritual. She photographs *The Three Magi*, *God Questioning Cain*, *The Three-Headed Bird*. Then, *The Temptation of Eve*. Then: *The Final Judgement*. With Christ in the centre as *The Unreadable Boy*. Because he is the fact of boyhood. She will write all of this in a letter to Achilles Noth one day, she thinks. The astonishing acts that invite her in, not to understanding, but to wisdom, she thinks. The Signs of the Zodiac. Boyhood's mother, Mary. St Peter. All heaven and all hell. On the tympanum of the north facade are the words 'Gislebertus Hoc Fecit'. Gislebertus Made This. Mindy repeats the words under her breath. This is the certain gate of heaven, she tells herself, and she imagines stepping from this world, into the place of the saints, or the angels, or even the Virgin herself. And of taking that little boy Christ in her arms. Saint-Lazare, she thinks to herself. That is literally me.

180

At about the exact same time as Mindy is photographing the Saint-Lazare Cathedral in Autun, Achilles Noth is arriving at Benito Juáres International Airport in Mexico City for a conference on 'The Mesoamerican Morning: Beginnings and Endings in the Art and Civilisation of the Olmec and

Maya'. His ride is late. He steps outside, into the sweltering evening, and lights up a cigarette. Someone waves to him: mister, you need a ride? He declines. He has been warned not to take any taxis on his own, otherwise he might end up at the bottom of a ravine next to a dead dog. Someone famous has arrived behind him at the gate, as a crowd of young Mexican boys and girls mob a fat black man who looks like a rapper, dressed in a tracksuit and bucket hat. Achilles spots Felipe and his new girlfriend in the distance. Hey, brother, Felipe shouts, and he says, this is Lucía, introducing his girlfriend who has short black hair and dresses like a tomboy. Lovely to meet you, Lucía, Achilles says, and then he embraces Felipe. So good to see you, brother, he says. We need to walk to my car, Felipe says, and he asks Achilles how his flight was. Smooth, he says. Once they're in the car Felipe goes over his itinerary. A bunch of presentations and a panel discussion. But first, tomorrow night, you're playing a DJ set at a bar in Coyoacán, Felipe says. It's all set up, he says. All of the attendees have been invited but it's open to the public too, he says. Should be a vibe, Felipe says. Is that the right word? I know vibes, Achilles says, and he smiles. So, my brother is going to give you his flat while you are here, Felipe says. You know he is a filmmaker these days? He makes documentary films about the underbelly of Mexico City, Felipe says. Wait, Mexico City has an underbelly? Achilles jokes, and they all laugh. I can give you a tour of the underbelly while you are here, Lucía says, at which Achilles laughs again. What the fuck is she talking about? What would you like to do just now? Felipe asks him, and Achilles says that he would like to get a drink, and then some tacos. Lucía suggests a bar, what bar, Felipe says, that bar that shows the boxing, she says. Do you like Roberto Durán? Lucía asks him, and Achilles says, yes. I met him once, Lucía says. But she doesn't elaborate. As they pull off the motorway Achilles can see ghostly figures in the underpasses, cooking over hotplates. That looks like a good place for tacos, he says. But Felipe just laughs. You'd be taking your life in your hands, he jokes, not to say your asshole. It smells of shit at those taco stands, Lucía says. Of shit and of spice and of gasoline, she says. Sounds to me like the perfect taco, Achilles says. They pull up to a bar with an open front that stretches out onto the pavement. Inside they are showing amateur Mexican boxing on a TV sat on top of a fridge, next to a cat that is sleeping. Felipe speaks to the barman, but they are no longer serving food. We'll grab a drink here, Felipe says, and then I will take you to a good taco joint, he says. Would you like me to arrange any day trips for you? Lucía asks him, and Achilles says, no, this time I am more intent on exploring Mexico City. Do you like Octavio Paz? Lucía asks him, and Achilles says, yes, I do. I can give you a tour of the Mexico City of Octavio Paz, if you like, she offers. Is this in addition to the tour of the underbelly, he asks her, and she says, well, there is some crossover, before excusing herself to use 'the ladies' room'. She's crazy, Felipe says. I love her but she is crazy, he says. Look, he says, and he takes a photograph out of his pocket. It's of Lucía taking a photograph of herself in a mirror that she has smashed with a hammer. Read the back, he says, and he turns the photograph over to read the words 'you did this to me x x x'. Chicks are insane, mate, Felipe laughs, we know this, and he puts the photograph back in his wallet just in time for her return. Do you fight? Lucía asks Achilles. What do you mean? Do you do martial arts or boxing, she clarifies. Oh no, he says. I mean, I work out, he says. But I don't fight. I could tell, she says, and she turns towards the TV and drinks her cocktail with a straw. Anyway, Felipe says. The taco joint is walking distance. When they get there Achilles is disappointed to see that it's some cheap taco chain. This OK, mate? Felipe says and Achilles nods regardless. It's fine, he says. You want some pozole, mate? Felipe asks him, as he knows it's Achilles' favourite. Damn right I do, he says. You know me too well, he says. What kind of music do you intend to play tomorrow night? Lucía asks him. A mixture of punk and sixties and new wave, he says. The server brings them an extra-spicy salsa. Goes well with cold beers, he says. Afterwards Felipe drops him at his brother's place while Lucía waits in the car. Felipe introduces him to the security guard for the building, Ventura, and tells him that Achilles will be staying there for a week. The apartment is on the top floor, at the end of a long corridor like a hotel, like the Chelsea Hotel in New York, Achilles thinks, and it is split over two floors, with a messy living room and kitchen downstairs where every surface is piled high with books and an even messier bedroom upstairs with a bathroom off it where the water is heated by an old industrial boiler that Felipe warns him about. Be careful with that, he says. You have to light it with a match but be careful not to leave it on unless you are using it, he says. Otherwise what? Achilles says. Otherwise kaboom, Felipe says. So, he says. Do you intend to take Lucía up on her offer? he asks Achilles. What offer? Achilles says. Her offer of these tours, Felipe says. You can have her, if you want, he adds, conspiratorially. No, no, don't be silly, he says. But then he tempers it. She seems like a nice person, Achilles says. You think so? Felipe says. And then he says, we'll pick you up at lunchtime tomorrow. In the meantime, there is a good cafe nearby where you can get breakfast, he says, and he draws him a map. Also, he says, the neighbourhood is safe to walk around at night, just so you know. Then he leaves him to it. Achilles could do with a shower but he doesn't want to be dealing with this mad boiler on his own at night and so he just strips off and jumps into the unmade bed, which stinks of damp and of fungus. I'm back in Mexico, he says to himself. He lifts the curtain next to the bed and realises that it faces onto the window of the opposite apartment which is literally about six feet away. Some fat guy with no top on is writing on a typewriter at the window. He doesn't even notice Achilles looking at him. Achilles pulls the curtains back over, and switches out the light, and he has that same dream of his, that same dream that has come to him periodically across his life, is it an anxiety dream, this dream of being cast off in a basket into a river and then arriving at the sea.

181

There's a sound, a sudden scuffling, in the bushes at the side of the garden. Josef Noth cries out, who goes there? An older woman emerges with her hands in the air. It's OK, he says. I'm not a soldier. What? I'm not a soldier, he repeats. You are a soldier, the woman says. What, what do you mean? You are dressed as a soldier, she says. Josef Noth has completely forgotten that he is still in uniform. I'm sorry, he says. Put your hands down, he says. I'm sorry, I should have said, I am no longer a soldier. Why? the older woman says. I just left the war, he says. And the older woman says, you can never leave the war, and Josef Noth says, what is that, everyone keeps saying it to me, and the old woman says, the war is like a malady, it is the one to decide whether to leave, or whether to stay. He nods his head. This is my lover, he says, and he points to one of the Xs in the ground. Death? the older woman says. Death is your lover? There is no end to these Nazis, she thinks. No, he says. That is literally my lover whose body lies buried in the ground there. You knew the ballerina Thérèse Barnier? the older woman asks him. It is so strange to hear her referred to as that once again, only this time like a ghost out of history. Yes, he says. She gave birth to my son, he says. And the older woman gasps. You're Josef Noth? she asks him. I had your son, she says. I had your son, but he is gone. And now he is in the hands of the Resistance.

182

Fancy a night out tomorrow, mate? Luke G.B. Caird asks Mark C. Burl over lunch at a greasy spoon on the corner of Partick Station. This is the best bacon-and-egg roll known to man, Mark C. Burl marvels. What's the occasion? he asks Luke G.B. Caird. The yolk is getting all over his beard. Tamar has a few friends in town, Luke G.B. Caird says. Bunch of air hostesses in town for a few nights. Thought you might fancy joining us. I'd love to, Mark C. Burl says, but I need to meet The Gimp beforehand. I forgot about The Gimp, Luke G.B. Caird says. He still squealing? Dynamite, mate. Knows everything that is going on, he says. Feeding me some major shit, he says. Need to keep schtum for the moment, though, he says. Fair enough, Luke G.B. Caird says. Fucking air hostesses, mate, Mark C. Burl says. Still can't get over the fact you're banging one of them. You know I have a thing about air hostesses. All blokes do, Luke G.B. Caird shrugs. He is drinking his Coke through a straw like a dumb kid. Mile High Club, mate, Mark C. Burl says. Bet they're all in it. Well, I know Tamar is, Luke G.B. Caird says. She told you? Mark C. Burl asks him. No, she told some other bloke at the writing workshop. Wow, that's weird. I know, he asked her, and she said that, yup, she was in it. Yup, she has been banged by some guy on an aeroplane, just so everyone knows. Well, you've got to admit she was pretty forward with you, Mark C. Burl says. Think she's a bit of a pick-up artist? Who knows, Luke G.B. Caird confesses. I mean, she seems really genuine to me. Naïve, even. It's partly why I've fallen in love with her. You and how many others? Mark C. Burl says. Who knows, mate, who knows. How was the writing class? It was good, mate, it was insane actually, it wasn't what I was expecting at all, but I really enjoyed it. That mad councillor who went whoring in Mexico on the council's tab was there. Lethal? You talking about Andrew Lethal? Mark C. Burl says. Yeah, mate. What a mental name. I know. What was he saying? Anything of interest? No, mate, we were just talking writing. And if you think that's a mental name, mate, Luke G.B. Caird says, you should hear the name of the guy that was doing the lecture. Some ex-con. That reminds me, Mark C. Burl says, interrupting him. I didn't tell you, but Aaron Murray called us, says he wants us to look into some guy with a mad name. Sounds exactly like an ex-con, an ex-gangland guy with a mad nickname, would be my guess. What's the name? Luke G.B. Caird asks him. The Escapologist, he says. Ring any bells? Luke G.B. Caird freezes with the straw still in his mouth. No, he says. No, doesn't ring any bells with me, he says. What was the name of the guy you were going to say? Mark C. Burl asks him, and Luke G.B. Caird says, eh, The Dragonfly, this guy was called The Dragonfly, he lies. That's so funny, Mark C. Burl says. They could almost be related. Why does he want to find this Escapologist? Luke G.B. Caird asks him. He thinks he had something to do with the kidnapping of his brother, Mark C. Burl says.

183

4.45 p.m. on a Thursday afternoon in June. As Andrew Lethal leaves the City Chambers, Dan Ruff and Big Paul Vickers fall into step behind him. He crosses George Square and cuts along West George Street. Then he walks up to

Blythswood Square. This cunt is addicted to the prozzers, Big Paul Vickers says, but no, he cuts round Blythswood Square – a notorious red-light district with a seedy park in the centre that is always littered with condoms – and heads along Sauchiehall Street and through Charing Cross. He takes a right at Kelvingrove Street. He's headed for the park, Dan Ruff says. Might be a fruit merchant. But no, Andrew Lethal crosses a small garden to his left, overgrown with pampas grass, and knocks on the ground-floor door of a tenement which is opened by a portly blonde in a short white dress with blonde hair and smoking a fag. Fuck me, this cunt really is addicted to the prozzers, Big Paul Vickers says. That's a brothel. That's when Dan Ruff says it. Call me Xenophon, he says. But this is my take on what is happening. Your man Lethal is addicted to the prozzers. He's out of control and can't help himself. And someone has incriminating evidence that they are using to blackmail him. And that person is Alec Bolland. And so Lethal made up some story about us being implicated by Bolland in the killing of the kid and the stealing of the horses. And he hoped that, when we heard this, we would take out Bolland and his boys for him and save him one motherfucking headache. Except, as we all know, he was actually fucking right, and we are implicated in the death of the young boy and the theft – and subsequent execution and burial – of said horses. And now Alec Bolland knows it was us, even though I don't believe he had any knowledge of it before we brought it to his attention, because he saw my boy with his eye out. It's Lethal's fault, Big Paul Vickers says. If he hadn't started off this chain reaction, we wouldn't be here lurking outside a whorehouse next to Kelvingrove Park in the evening. Speak for yourself, Dan Ruff says.

184

Imagine there is another world after this, Donald Murray says to his son Aaron, sat on this bench in the past. Imagine you wake up from this and you have to say what you have seen. What do you mean, Dad, Aaron says. I don't understand. Imagine it's a dream, and in reality none of this has ever existed. Imagine the tales you would tell once you woke up from it. Of what? Of there being a thing called love, his dad says. That you could fall in and out of. Of men and women. And of a thing called the sun that rose every morning and went down at night, and of night and day, and how they happened. And how clouds would pass in the sky and birds would sing from the tops of trees. And that there was such a thing called smell, and you could smell things, like roses, and that things grew, and you could eat things that grew. And there was a thing called music and a thing called dancing. Not to mention parks, he says. Things called parks in the middle of cities where everyone lived, he says, gesturing all around him. And fathers and sons, Aaron says to his dad. Yes, his dad says to Aaron. Yes, and that there were fathers and . . . sons, he says. Imagine trying to describe all of this to someone who could never even dream of it. It is as if words are returning to Aaron's father. And in his dreams, perhaps, a little boy too.

185

The Precious Gift is no longer considered a suspect in the disappearance of Joyce Monaghan. He is released without charge in Derry and heads straight for Joyce's house, only when he gets to the curve of the cul-de-sac he can see that there are police stationed outside of it, so he turns around and hurries off. He checks back in to the same hotel, where – unbelievably – the same guy who was looking for a corkscrew the first time he arrived is drunk in reception once again. Alright, what are you doing back here? The Precious Gift says to the young man, but he just looks at him, blankly. Remember, he says to the young man, I was the guy who opened a bottle of white wine with my boot. Fuck you on about, pal? the young man says to him. Anyway, there's Michelle at the front desk. What can I do for you? she asks him. The TV is playing the same video of Ireland filmed from the skies set to traditional Irish music. Back again, he says. But Michelle makes no response. How long will you be staying with us? Michelle asks, and The Precious Gift says, a week, I'll be staying another week. She gives him his keys and tells him that breakfast is served from 7 a.m. in the room across the way. I know, I know, he says, and he takes the stairs up to the second floor, and to the same room that he stayed in before. And then he remembers the peregrine, the dead peregrine falcon that was in the window of the pub across the way. He looks out of the window but it's already too dark to see. He lies down on the bed, still in his clothes, and immediately falls asleep. Then he wakes with a start. It must be the middle of the night. He opens the curtains and gazes out into the street. And that's when he sees it. The birdwoman. The birdwoman come back across the way. The woman with the body of a bird is stood outside the abandoned bar at the other side of the road, beckoning to him. This time The Precious Gift puts on his jacket, walks down the stairs, unlocks the door of the hotel and crosses the road towards her. The birdwoman turns and leads the way. The Precious Gift follows, into flutter darkness.

186

Listen, Luke G.B. Caird says, as he is in the taxi with Tamar, if anyone brings up the writing workshop this evening, don't mention The Escapologist. Why not? Tamar says. Is it because you want to keep those precious writing tips to yourself? Ha ha, yes, in a way, he admits. There's a twist in the plot, put it that way. You writers, Tamar says. I love it. Always reading everything like a book. You're the hardest book to read, Luke G.B. Caird says to her. The taxi driver overhears him, and he says, good line, mate, that's a good line, mate, keep them coming, he says, without a hint of sarcasm. Why am I the hardest book? Tamar asks him. You make me sound like Dostoevsky, she says. Ha, he's certainly up there, in terms of the hardest book to read, Luke G.B. Caird says, and she asks him, well, what is the actual hardest book to read? Probably *Finnegans Wake* by James Joyce, the taxi driver chips in. I'd have to say that is probably the hardest book you could ever read because, believe me, I have tried. How far did you get? Luke G.B. Caird asks him, and he shrugs and looks at the two of them in the rear-view mirror and says, I don't know, a couple of sentences? Or maybe it was all just written in one long single sentence. In that case say about sixty words. And then I gave up. When I said the hardest book to read, though, I meant more the kind of book that teaches you a big lesson that maybe you weren't even ready for, Luke G.B. Caird says. Keep them coming, mate, the taxi driver says, that was a good one, he says. What books are those? Tamar asks him, and he says, Shakespeare. *King Lear*, he says. *Hamlet*. You would compare me to a play by Shakespeare? Tamar says, and her dark eyes glisten, and those little crow's feet that have Luke G.B. Caird's heart, and those eyebrows, like a bird's, he thinks, like a child's drawing of two birds taking flight, that's how heartbreaking it is right then, the pinch of her waist in her long skirt, her polka-dot top, and he says, yes, I would. But not *Romeo and Juliet*? she asks him, and the driver looks at them in the mirror and says, I was just going to say that. Now you're on the spot, mate, he says. It's deeper than that, Luke G.B. Caird says. Deeper than love? Tamar says, and Luke G.B. Caird says, I'm not sure that there is anything deeper than love, he says. I think, even when you get to the bottom of everything, even when stepping into some final darkness, even when encountering all that is lowest and most depraved in human nature, deeper, still, there is love, and that it is always starting over. That's been my experience, he says. In my line of business, he clarifies. Bravo, my man, the driver says. Here's to love, he says, and he beeps the horn out of an excess of high spirits. Tamar kisses Luke G.B. Caird on the cheek and she says, language is so sexy to me, I get so turned on by language, she says, and then she says, starting over, yes, here's to starting over, baby, she says, as she holds her slender fingers against Luke G.B. Caird's cheek – her long dark hair and her perfume – and sees that, behind his eyes, behind his dark eyes, it is true, there is love.

187

We knew the Germans were here, Thérèse Barnier's neighbour says to Josef Noth. We had seen a convoy pass just a few days earlier. France had surrendered. They had given us up. I knew they would, says the neighbour, whose name is Nicolette. France is a country still in thrall to sacrifice, she says. Unlike you Germans, she says. Then the soldiers came. I had been talking to Thérèse over the hedge, she had shown me Achilles in his little basket. Suddenly there were shouts in German, herauskommen,

herauskommen! Marceline entered the house, followed by Thérèse, who asked me to look after the baby, so I crossed into their garden and picked up Achilles in his basket, and then I heard a commotion outside, and I ran. I ran back to my garden, but I was too afraid to take the baby into the house. Then I heard gunshots. Terrible gunshots, oh Lord. Oh Lord, I thought. I took the baby into the summerhouse and drew the curtains, locked the door from the inside. Unbelievably, Achilles didn't cry. He simply woke and looked up at me in astonishment. Then I heard the soldiers come into the back garden. After a while, things went silent. I stayed in the summerhouse until it was dark, when I crept into the house to find the enemy gone. I sneaked out to the street, and there were no vehicles. And what did you do with Achilles? I have contacts, Nicolette says, contacts within the Resistance, a Resistance that sprung up soon after you invaded Poland. A Resistance that was convinced that France would fold in the face of the enemy of everything that it stood for. Such is France. I move in radical circles, Nicolette says. I left with Achilles right away and I arranged for the Resistance to smuggle him out of the country. Where were they taking him? Great Britain, Nicolette says. And did they succeed? I have no way of knowing, Nicolette says. They disappeared, that is how the Resistance works. I never heard from them again. What were their names? The people who smuggled Achilles? I'm not going to tell you their names, Nicolette says. I'm sorry, but I won't endanger them. I'm Achilles' father, Josef Noth says. I wouldn't do anything to endanger the people that rescued him. I'm sorry, but I don't trust you enough to tell you, Nicolette says. You're a German soldier, she says. How will I ever find my son again? he says. Are you insane? Nicolette asks him. You went to war against him. Tell me, Josef Noth says. Does he look like me? And Nicolette says, he is nothing like you.

188

On his first day in Mexico City, Achilles heads out to the coffee shop that Felipe recommended him. He asks the guy serving him whether there is a place round here where he can change money, and the server, who has a twirly moustache like a pirate, tells him that there is a place in a shopping centre about a twenty-minute walk away. Achilles orders some kind of bun confection thing and sits outside in the warmth of the morning and smells that smell of Mexico City, that smell that transports him every time, that smell of sweet grease, and of urine, and of gasoline. He lights a cigarette, and sits there, basking in it. Then he heads off in the direction that the server pointed him in, round the perimeter of this huge central park. He can smell the effluvia from the stinky rivers that skirt it. He passes a portable toilet on the street that has been turned into a barbershop with the addition of a chair and a mirror. A guy comes up to him and tries to sell him a boiled egg, already peeled. Achilles loves the Mexican street hustle. He stops to look at some plants for sale on a barrow in the street and looks down to see that some madman has literally crawled along the floor and is polishing his shoes for him. The man looks up at Achilles like a happy lunatic. Fucking Mexico City, man. He sees a wooden sign on the street for an 'English Language Bookshop' and he enters a shady old apartment complex and follows the signs to the second floor, where he can hear a young man with an American accent talking on the phone. He is speaking to his father. Yes, Dad, he says. I know, Dad, he says. Don't worry, Dad. Look, I need to go, he says, and he hangs up and says hi to Achilles. Looking for anything in particular? the clerk asks him, and Achilles says, no, just browsing. Achilles spots two beautiful editions of Melville in hardback on display.

Pierre; or, The Ambiguities and *Redburn: His First Voyage*. Next to them there is a lovely hardback collection of poetry by a poet he has never heard of. Achilles Noth picks it up. St-John Perse, a voice says behind him. It's the American clerk. *The Anabasis of St-John Perse*, he says. What is an anabasis? Achilles asks him, and the nameless clerk says, it is a journey, outwards, and back again. Right then Achilles has a mad feeling of déjà-vu. Of a dream recalled. It's pretty mind-blowing, the clerk says. I'll take it, Achilles says, and he pays him the equivalent of a week's wages in Mexico for it. He slips the book into his pocket and heads back out into the heat. He crosses at a wild junction with traffic roaring haphazardly left and right. The shopping centre is built in the shape of a pentagon. The entrance is on the other side of a bridge across a stinky stream. Down below he watches as a figure dressed in dirty white overalls walks along the bank of the stinky river. He has a wicker basket in his hand filled with trash and junk. It makes Achilles think of his dreams and he shudders. Something is working itself loose inside him. Inside the shopping centre it looks like it must be some kind of holiday, because nothing is open. All of the units are either shuttered or boarded up. Eventually Achilles finds two cleaning ladies and asks them where the money exchange is. It is closed, one says. It is gone, the other says. It's cool inside, though. Achilles opens a bottle of water and takes a seat on a white bench on the top floor, looking down on an inexplicably lush display of plants in deep white containers. In this boarded-up shopping centre, shaped like a pentagon, he takes out *The Anabasis of St-John Perse* from his pocket, and he starts to read.

189

Carina has Mindy working for her floral business this weekend. They are supplying flowers for a wedding reception that takes place in one of the secret walled gardens of Autun. Lilies and roses are the national flowers of love, Carina tells her, as if love were a separate nation. In the morning a man turns up with a horse and cart, on the back of which are piles of lilies – orange and white – and roses – pink and peach. The orange is for passion, Carina says, as they start to set up the reception area. The white for virginity, she says. The pink and peach, for the flowers of women. It's a shame to miss the wedding, isn't it? Mindy says. God no, the reception is always the best part of the wedding, Carina says. I mean, if you've seen one wedding you've seen them all. But a reception, a reception is where anything can happen and often does. What was your wedding reception like? Mindy asks her, and Carina says, I always remember that the photographer we hired wept, Carina says. She wept to see two people so in love, Carina says. That's so beautiful but sad too, isn't it, Mindy says. Maybe she had never known love, she says. Or maybe, Carina says, she had loved and lost. Is it really better to have loved and lost than to have never loved at all, do you think? Mindy asks Carina, and Carina says, to have never known love at all would mean you would never know what a precious gift true love is. Which would mean you could live in ignorant bliss without it. But to have loved, and lost, well, that is to be wounded. That is to be forever marked, in your heart. Each day is lived in remembrance of that. Are you remembering right now? Mindy asks her, and Carina says, these flowers, she says, these flowers already plucked, they are set to die, like love is, and Mindy says, you see, that's how I feel about my love for Achilles, she says. I intend to never pluck it, and that way perhaps it will come back forever. That's what you call a perennial, Carina says. Love is perennial, though, isn't it? Mindy says. It always comes back. Despite all of the mistakes and all of the regrets and all of the broken hearts, the summers of our love are always coming back. This wedding today, Carina says, and then she breaks off. This precious gift, she says.

190

What is this? The Escapologist asks the room. It's the second session of the creative writing workshop at The Warehouse in Springburn. Andrew Lethal puts up his hand. What did I tell you about that? The Escapologist says. Sorry, Andrew Lethal says, I keep forgetting. Someone is bent over, he says. Someone is trying to reach for something that is perpetually out of reach, he says. Maybe, he adds, and he shrugs. That's a good one, The Escapologist says. And what are these things above him here, in the sky? He points to a crude drawing of a bent-over stickman under a rain of balloons and small blooms that look like comets. He is bent towards a star figure, a five-pointed star on a stalk grown up from the ground. Is it falling stars? Andrew Lethal offers. The fucking nursery is next door mate, The Escapologist says, talk sense, and then he says, anyone else, and Tamar says, they are blimps, they are blimps and bombs in wartime raining down, she says. But he isn't even aware of them, The Escapologist says. Look, he says. He isn't even aware of them because he is The Lover. Because he is The Writer. And he isn't aware of them because something else has caught his eye, he says. Literature, The Escapologist announces, and he jabs his finger at the five-pointed star growing up from the ground, art, he says, is the sniffing of flowers, in the park, during wartime.

191

It starts with a firebomb through the letterbox. Terry Johnstone, whose allotment they found the buried horses in, gets a fucking firebomb stuffed through his letterbox in the middle of the night, only he's still up, just passed out on the couch in his pyjamas when it happens, and he hears this explosion, and his door is blown right the fuck off its hinges, and even so, like a madman – fearless – Terry leaps through the flames, like a fucking stuntman, like *The Fall Guy*, and he's off up the road in nothing but a pair of worse-for-wear pyjama bottoms and his slippers, in pursuit of these two figures in balaclavas. You can see all his mad tattoos on his arms and chest as he's running there, fucking 'No Surrender', fucking 'Red Hand of Ulster', fucking this and fucking that. Thing is, he's gaining on them. Against all the odds he is gaining on these two young fellas in the ballys. And then he reaches out, he reaches out and he grabs the first one by the arm of his snorkel jacket and he pulls the guy back – with almost superhuman strength – so that the young fella goes arse over tits and hits the ground with a thud. And he's knocked out. He's unconscious, lying on the ground there. His pal escapes in the confusion. When this cunt wakes up, he is going to be tied to a chair in Terry's half-burnt-out house with a massive blade to his throat, in a hostage situation.

192

Wait till you hear this, Andrew Lethal is telling Luke G.B. Caird at The Warehouse, where there is supposed to be a creative writing workshop taking place only so far The Escapologist is nowhere to be seen. You couldn't make it up, Andrew Lethal says. They found four horses, buried, standing up, in an allotment in Maryhill. Each one had a single bullet in its head. Underneath the greenhouse, they found a stash of bullets. I know, I heard about that, Luke G.B. Caird says. In Georgia there is a tradition of burying horses standing up, Tamar says. In order that they may canter into the afterlife, she says. Canter, Andrew Lethal says, that is such a good word. Tamar blushes. Andrew Lethal is starting to seriously get on Luke G.B. Caird's tits. Don't think it has quite the same historical tradition in Maryhill, Andrew Lethal says to Tamar, and Tamar laughs. Luke G.B. Caird just sits there. What is this mad rapport they have? That's when The Escapologist appears. He walks through the door wearing a trench coat and a bunnet. He is dressed like the Invisible Man, with gloves and with bandages wrapped all round his head. He ignores everyone's greetings. He walks straight down the middle of the room and then across the stage and out the back door and is never seen again that evening, even when the class just sit there for forty-five minutes in the hope of learning the meaning of tonight's lesson. What do you think that was all about? Andrew Lethal asks Tamar and Luke G.B. Caird as they finally get it together to leave. Reality will always outstrip fiction, Luke G.B. Caird says to the two of them. That has always been my experience, he says. In my line of work, he underlines, while looking at Tamar. And what is the lesson? Tamar asks him. Write like it's real, he says.

193

Luke G.B. Caird and Mark C. Burl meet up at the Pot Still on Hope Street for a few drams before they head over to meet the girls at the Hilton. Revisiting the scene of the crime, mate, Mark says to Luke, who rolls his eyes and laughs. Can't believe we're going to be hanging out with a bunch of air hostesses, mate, he says. Still can't believe I'm banging one, Luke says. Where's the catch? Ha ha, mate, angels are real, mate, Luke says, you're just going to have to accept it. How's The Gimp? he asks Mark. He's got so much shit on everyone, Mark says. He could bring down the entire council, he says. Like what? Oh, the usual, sex and drugs. Deviant behaviour. Et cetera. Must be some way to monetise that shit, Luke says, and Mark says, oh, he's on it, believe me. One for the road? Mark says, and they have a final whisky before heading down Hope Street on the kind of perfect summer evening that makes you think that maybe boyhood is just around the corner, that those two boys joking there, and excited about their night out, are the same two boys forever. Men rush past with their collars popped, and with hats on, and with newspapers tucked beneath their arms. At this point Glasgow is still a working man's city, and romantic like that. It's Friday night. Sudden blasts of music and singing erupt from the open doors of pubs as they cut down the side of Central Station, where revellers are spilling out onto the concourse. Beneath the bridge people are milling around and looking lost, like they just washed up in the city with no plans but to disappear forever. Some junkie is passed out on a bench with his trousers halfway down. That'll be me later tonight, Mark says. No joke. The girls are sat in the bar waiting for them; they're already on the cocktails. Mr Luke! And Mr Mark! Tamar shouts when she sees them, and she runs towards them, tottering on her high heels and in her minidress. Fuck me, Mark says, when he sees the air hostesses, these birds look like Miss World. Tamar introduces them both as crime writers, and neither of them objects. This is Bailey, she says, pointing to a small dark-haired woman with perfectly black pupils and a lopsided smile that is so sexy. And this is Tatiana, she is from Oaxaca, Tamar explains. Tatiana has her hair in a sharp dark bob and is wearing leather trousers and a black off-the-shoulder T-shirt so you can see her bra strap. So, where have you ladies flown in from, Mark asks them, and Tatiana says, from Brazil! Which is why the barman made us these crazy Carnival cocktails especially. Try some, Mr Mark, Tatiana says, and though he's not normally a cocktail man, he says, I'll get us all another round of Carnival, and the girls all cheer. They're pretty sauced already. Tell me, Bailey says to Mark, as a writer, where do you get your ideas? Uh, from real life mostly, he says. Glasgow is a great place for a writer, he says. There is so much mad energy on the streets, if you just listen to people's conversations you hear the maddest things. Like what? Tatiana says. Like, for instance, only the other day they found these horses buried standing up in an allotment in Maryhill, and they had all been shot in the head. Oh no! Tatiana says. Who would shoot a beautiful horse? What is an allotment? Bailey asks, and Luke explains it's a small garden you can rent to grow your own vegetables. Horses are so beautiful, Tamar says. Who needs men when you can have a beautiful horse, she says, and all three girls crack up laughing. Who was the god who made love to a woman disguised as a swan? Tatiana says, and Luke says, it was Zeus, Zeus made love to Leda in the guise of a swan. There is nothing sexier than being made love to by a swan, Bailey says, don't you think so, Mr Mark? Mark is back with more cocktails. I can think of a few things that are sexier, he says, and Bailey slides her pinkie into her mouth and bites down on it, just for a second. What, in your opinion, are the main causes of crime? Bailey asks Mark, and he says, wait, let me think, and then he says, probably having a dick, and everyone bursts out laughing all over again. I have a bottle of mezcal in my room, which I brought from Oaxaca, Tatiana says. Have you ever played strip poker?

194

Dan Ruff gets the call. Get your arse up here, Terry Johnstone says to him. I've captured one of them. What the actual fuck, who have you captured, you madman? One of Alec Bolland's boys. They tried to firebomb me out my own home. Plus, bring a door. What?! Bring a fucking door, my own door got blown off its hinges by the blast. Dan Ruff calls Big Paul Vickers. Get a spare door from out of storage, he says to him, and load it in the fucking van. Then he calls Scott and explains the situation. What would Xenophon do, Dan Ruff is thinking out loud as they drive over to Acre. Barter enemy combatants, Big Paul says. What? He would instruct us to barter hostages. For what? For silence, Big Paul says. They agree to drop any knowledge of the murder, as well as those horses what we were forced to shoot in the head. In return for sparing the life of one of their boys. Now you're talking, Dan Ruff says, though it isn't clear whether he's referring to Big Paul or to Xenophon. Sure enough, Terry Johnstone's door is charred black and hanging off its hinges when they pull up. Big Paul gets to work fitting him a new one and then he fucks off before he's implicated any further; what a wanker. Terry leads them through to the back kitchen where he has this boy tied to a chair with a pillowcase over his head. Plus, he's completely naked. Why did you strip him naked? Scott asks him, and Terry just says, weapons, that's all he says, and he shrugs. How about the big reveal, Dan says, and Terry slides the pillowcase off to expose the badly bruised, cut and swollen face of fucking Findlay fucking Hamilton. Fuck me, Scott says. What?! Fuck me, Scott says again. Then he reaches up and takes off his eyepatch so that you can see the wound, the sewn-up flesh like a horror show. Remember me, he says to Findlay

Hamilton, and no fucking joke, Findlay Hamilton pisses himself and starts crying, right there on the spot.

195

Get his trousers off! Tamar commands Bailey and Tatiana. Mark C. Burl is losing, badly, at strip poker, or perhaps it's deliberate. They're sat around a table in the bridal suite on the top floor of the Hilton. The girls always book the bridal suite, 'just in case', they joke. Bailey and Tatiana hold Mark's arms while Tamar slides his trousers down. A whole bunch of cash and some keys fall to the floor, but by this point both Mark and Luke are too drunk to notice. Mark is sat there in his underwear, almost cross-eyed with booze. Oh, I see you are pleased to see us, Mark, Tatiana says, and Tamar whispers to Luke, let's go, let's leave them to it and split back to yours, she says, and Luke stands up and says to Mark, I think this is the point where we leave you at the mercy of these two, but Mark can barely muster a response. Don't worry, baby, Bailey says to him, we will take care of you tonight, and Luke kisses the girls goodbye and winks to Mark on his way out who simply mouths back at him the words 'what-the-fuck'. In the taxi Tamar is sliding her hand beneath Luke's shirt. I want to make love to you in your office, she says, how hot would that be? Your wish is my command, Luke says, and he asks the driver to take them to Dumbarton Road. As soon as they get inside, Luke lifts Tamar onto a desk and starts to unzip her dress. My queen, he calls her, as he covers her with kisses. Wait, she says. Wait. I want to change into something special for you, she says. Go next door, she says, and I will let you out when I am ready. Luke goes next door to the meeting room, and Tamar locks him in. Now you are my prisoner, she mocks, and he hears her walk away on her heels. And then: silence.

Come on, baby, Luke says, eventually. I'm so horny, baby, he says. Let me out. But a response never comes. Half an hour later he decides to break the door down and Tamar is nowhere to be seen.

196

Felipe shows up at his brother's apartment to pick Achilles up for the DJ set, only but this time he has a buddy in tow. This is Chico, Felipe says. Chico is my brother, he says, and at first Achilles is confused until he works out that he means his spiritual brother and not Diego, his actual brother, who has loaned him this flat. Chico is wearing a Lou Reed T-shirt that says 'Legendary Hearts' on it. Chico has the darkest eyes Achilles has ever seen, the blackest glassiest eyes, and of course he will come to realise that's why Chico's nickname is The Black Pig, because he has the eyes of a wild Mexican pig stuffed and mounted in some museum somewhere. Chico has some poppers with him. Mate, mate, wanna do some poppers, mate, he says to Achilles. His English is basic. No, I'm OK, mate, Achilles says. Then Chico pulls out a sheet of LSD. I got us some LSD for the DJ set, he says. Felipe says he needs to call Lucía to come and pick them up and heads upstairs, leaving Achilles and Chico together. What tunes you gonna play tonight? Chico asks him, as he sticks a purple bottle of poppers up his nose and takes a great huff. Punk rock, Achilles says, mostly. New wave. Chico pulls up the sleeve of his cardigan to reveal a tattoo that says 'Hey! Ho! Let's Go!'. I saw the Ramones play The Rainbow in London on New Year's Eve in 1977, Achilles tells Chico. Fuck me, Chico says. The one where they recorded *It's Alive*? Yup, the very one, Achilles says. I grew up in London, before I moved to Paris, he says. What about The Undertones? Chico asks him, and Achilles says, yeah, I saw them in seventy-eight supporting The Rezillos, who sucked ass, he says. What do you mean?! Chico laughs. The Rezillos are legends. Then Chico says, I have tickets to see Billy Idol next month. Do you like the Billy Idol? he asks Achilles. Ha, that explains why you like The Rezillos, Achilles says, and though he is half laughing and rolling his eyes at Chico's naff taste, there is something in Chico's love for even the cheesiest of rock 'n' roll that seems pure and heartfelt, even as Chico is lying back on the couch amid stacks of tatty paperbacks, high as a kite, and singing to himself the words to 'True Confessions' by The Undertones. Felipe returns and says that they should head down, that Lucía will be here in ten minutes. They say hi to Ventura the doorman on their way past. Lucía's car has a smashed front window, though somehow it is still intact. Achilles jumps into the passenger seat and Chico and Felipe get in the back. Lucía is playing a cassette of some American guy talking over random bursts of abstract noise. Fucking Cage, fucking *Indeterminacy*, man, Chico says. What happened to your windscreen? Achilles asks Lucía, and Lucía says, what the fuck do you think happened? I have no idea, Achilles says, but Lucía just lights a cigarette and doesn't respond. Ignore her, my brother, Felipe says, and he pats Achilles on the shoulder. She was in a hit-and-run, he says. And now you don't want to talk about it, isn't that right, Lucía? Some fucking guy threw himself onto my windscreen as I was sat at some traffic lights, she corrects Felipe. And I fucking drove over him and left the scene of the crime, she says. And don't dare tell Achilles to ignore me, she says. When they get to the club, which is on the second floor of a building with an outdoor balcony all around it and a back yard with firepits and a guy with two hotplates flipping tortillas beneath a tree in the corner, it's already almost full. I told you, my brother, Felipe says to Achilles. They are all here to hear you play some underground shit, he says, and true enough the room is a mad mix of older professorial types and eccentric batshit women alongside a lot of cool-looking younger people. Achilles waves to a group of Mayanists that he recognises, sat around a round table, drinking beer and shots. Also, Felipe tells him, we have arranged for you to be interviewed by the press after your set, he says. I hope that is OK. It's all cool, Achilles says, and then he says, did you get me that bottle of mezcal I asked for, and Felipe says, oh shit, I forgot, let me get you one. In the meantime, Chico can help you set up. Chico and Achilles plug in the record decks and test the PA and with the first crackle of electricity the whole audience turn, as one, to look at Achilles, and then just stand there, expectantly, like they are at a gig, and he is the main attraction. You're a rock 'n' roll star, Chico laughs. This is Mexico, man, he says. These people are hungry, he says. Some girl passes Achilles a note, a beautiful girl in black leather trousers and with a dark bob and scarlet lipstick, she passes it to him across the low table where the decks are set up. It says on it: 'Please play Dire Straits', signed 'Ramona'. Achilles looks back at her and she smiles and nods and disappears into the crowd. He gets his first record ready. Chico gives him the thumbs-up that the PA is all set up and ready to go. Achilles' first track is 'Just Can't Get Enough' by Depeche Mode – there's the crackle of the original 7" vinyl and then that amazing crude synth line comes in – and as Felipe returns with a bottle of mezcal and passes it over the table with a grin, the entire room erupts.

197

Dan Ruff is on the blower to Alec Bolland. Alec, he says. It's Dan. Dan the man, Alec says. What can I trouble you for? You can hear him turn down that fucking TV that's always blaring so as you know it's serious. It's me that's troubling you, Dan Ruff says, but Alec Bolland just laughs. As if, he says. No, I am genuinely troubling you, Dan Ruff says. Ha ha, Alec Bolland says. That's a good one, Dan, he says. I have one of your boys here, Dan Ruff says. I have one of your boys here in a hostage situation after they tried to burn down my friend Terry's gaff in Acre. Is this about the horses? Alec Bolland asks him. Aye, Dan Ruff says, it's all about the horses. Thing is, Alec Bolland says, whoever you have there, he's nothing to do with me. Thing is, Dan Ruff says in return, it's Findlay Hamilton. Findlay Hamilton is nothing to do with me, pal, Alec Bolland says. Thing is, he says again, it occurs to me that you have made a very basic mistake, he says. And what would that be? You have opened a second front in this war. In this . . . internecine conflict. Hold on a second, he says, and he hacks up a filthy amount of phlegm into a hanky. Because that boy is of no value to me, he says when he returns. And yet, I know what you did. I saw your son with the fucking eyepatch, and I knew. And I continue to know, he says. Who continues to know? You either know something or you don't, Dan Ruff says. Sometimes you might forget, Alec Bolland says. Sometimes you can be encouraged to forget, he says. Which is the whole point of this phone call, I suspect. The point being, you were about to offer me the life of one of my boys in return for my forgetting, he continues. But this is nothing to do with me. Do what you want with the kid, he says. You might have to go ahead and kill him. If you have the balls, that is. What do I care. But fuck with me, or any of my boys, and you're a dead man, motherfucker, he says, and he slams the fucking phone down, like that.

198

The Precious Gift follows the birdwoman deeper into the darkness. Up ahead he can see the silhouette of a bird's head, leading him on. They cross through an estate in the dark. Then into a park. At the end of the park, there is an old tunnel. An old tunnel whose entrance has been fenced over. But someone has bent two of the bars so that it is possible to squeeze through. The birdwoman stops at the bars and points to them. They look like open brackets, The Precious Gift thinks to himself. Then she steps through the bars. Somewhere in the night there is an explosion, and the sound of gunfire. The Precious Gift looks behind him, and all he can see is flames. Everything is ending forever, he thinks to himself. Everything is ending as soon as it is begun, he thinks, as he steps through this gap, blind now, and feeling his way towards an ending.

199

All of Europe is in flames as Josef Noth makes his way across the continent. He is a civilian now, a German civilian, in hiding. He is dressed in the clothes of the late husband of Thérèse's cousin, the widow Marceline. He fancies it makes him look like an artist. A bum artist, an out-of-work artist, a homeless artist at the end of his tether, but an artist all the same. He uses French with the French and German with the Germans that he meets on the road, most of whom are dispossessed, like himself. There is a vast subterranea in Europe in the early 1940s, a whole continent of the stateless, wandering this way and that. He is joined on the way by nameless companions. Where are you headed, Josef, they ask him, and he says, China, I am headed to China so that I may see it all clearer, he says to them. I am searching for a vantage point, he says. And where are you off to, Josef asks his companions in return, his nameless companions now, his long-dead companions, himself in the clothes of a dead man. What were any of them in a past life? Ghosts, shades, gymnasts, scientists, doctors, artists, bums. Sons, daughters. And they mostly say, home, in search of home, or of family, or sometimes they say, anywhere, anywhere but here, they say. Josef Noth crosses back through the Ardennes. He is walking the reverse journey into the future. There is nowhere else to go but backwards, now. The whole world will never be the same, a bum says to him – we are all bums now – as they sit around a forest fire deep in the Ardennes after fishing for trout in the river and stealing some stale bread from a recently abandoned farmhouse. On the contrary, Josef Noth says. The world will always be the same. The world is always passing out of existence. Every single time, we burn it down, he says, and they eat the baked trout still ashy and burnt, with its crisp skin from the fire, and they picture shapes, they picture shapes in their minds that might resemble the shape of history, like the sign of infinity, a wonky circle, a number turned on its head. In the morning Josef Noth's companion stabs him through the hand in a scuffle and runs off with his backpack containing all the unpublished poems of St-John Perse.

200

Luke G.B. Caird is on the phone to Mark C. Burl. What the fuck happened last night? I can't remember, Mark says. I can't remember getting home, he says. Tamar locked me in the meeting room at the office and then ran off, Luke says. What?! I lost my keys, Mark says. I had to kick the fucking door of my flat in. I think. I woke up in my bed with the door off its hinges. Did you fuck Tatiana and Bailey? I can't remember, Mark says. I can remember them in their underwear, and me trying to get a condom on, but I don't think I could get hard, I don't think I could perform, I was too drunk. Fucking hell, the two best-looking birds of your life and you couldn't even get it up, Luke says. I phoned the Hilton, Luke says, and they have already checked out. They're gone. I'm not being funny, Mark says, but is there anything missing from the office? Did she steal anything? Not as far as I can see, Luke says, but you should get yourself over here and check. I need to wait for a locksmith, Mark says. Plus, I lost my office keys as well as the keys to the safe. Lucky I have a spare set, but it's starting to look a little shady. Do you think those girls played us? For what? Luke says. I don't know . . . Mark says, anyway, I'll be over in an hour. When Mark arrives, he checks the safe behind his desk. There's something missing. Everything OK? Luke asks him. Mark lies and says, sure, no problem, all perfectly intact. But a file is missing. A very important file. A potentially very lucrative file. And Luke says, this just makes the whole thing even more fucking inexplicable, even though Mark is starting to have a fair idea of just exactly what the fuck is going on.

201

The bride and groom enter the walled garden in Autun. Mindy and Carina's flower displays dazzle with their rapturous colour. The bride seems a little unsteady on her feet. Looks like someone has been hitting the wine early, Mindy jokes. The groom has his arm around her as he helps her up the three steps to the stone podium and everyone applauds as the groom – who looks like James Bond, a French James Bond, which is even more handsome – takes his speech from his inside pocket and unfolds it. He calls her his beautiful bride. Danielle, my beautiful bride, he says. Thank you, he says. Thank you for the happiness you have given me. The bride is now seated, which seems odd. The groom turns to address her. Then he starts addressing God. Thank you, God, he says, for the time you have given us. This short time, he adds. He turns to Danielle, who appears to be crying, softly. My Danielle, the groom says. Know that wherever you are, I will always find you. Not two people, he says, and instead he holds up one finger. One person, he says. Then he says, my heart is a crescent without you. He talks of Danielle's bravery, her perseverance in the face of her illness. Oh no, Mindy says to Carina. I can't take this, she says. Then he calls her his bride in eternity and says that the next six months will be months of joy and not sadness. And then we will begin again, my darling, he says. And then we will find each other all over again. Now most of the audience are in tears. Then he picks her up. He picks his beautiful bride up from her chair and the audience split like Moses and the Red Sea as he carries her in his arms all the way to the head dinner table, which now, inevitably, appears like the Last Supper. Did you know? Mindy asks Carina. No, Carina says, no, I had no idea, she says, as she dries her eyes. This is too much, Mindy says. And she thinks of Achilles, her wild night with Achilles, and of how much time there is to be thankful for. Even a moment, she thinks to herself. Even a moment, together, is the precious gift.

202

Someone has complained about the volume. A couple, an older woman and a man, have said that they simply cannot stand the music that loud and that it is damaging their hearing. A rumour reaches Achilles that it's the ageing Mayanist Tatiana Proskouriakoff who is complaining, but it turns out that it's actually Linda Schele. How loud does she think the Mayan death rituals were, with their conch-shell trumpets and turtle-shell drums, he thinks to himself, as he drops 'Sultans of Swing', as requested by Ramona. Then he lines up 'Ghost Rider' by Suicide. Afterwards he is interviewed in the back yard of the bar by a reporter from a Mexican newspaper. The reporter only wants to talk about music. What is your favourite record of all time? he asks Achilles, and Achilles says the first thing that comes to mind. *The Velvet Underground & Nico*, he says. How do you like Mexico? the reporter asks him, and Achilles says, it is my spiritual home. Here and France are my spiritual homes. I have visited Mexico many times over the years through my interest in the Maya, he says. Where were you born? the reporter asks him. I was born in France, in Paris, France, just before the occupation, he says. Then I moved to London, he says. He saw the Ramones at The Rainbow when they were recording *It's Alive*, Chico interrupts. I am so high, by the way, Chico says, and he runs his hand through his hair. Achilles can't be bothered with this interview. He is keen to get back to the bar and to search for Ramona. Chico, he says, do you know the girl called Ramona? Ramona? he says. Ramona Sánchez? Ramona with the dark hair and the red lipstick who passed me the note, Achilles says. Yeah, I know her, he says, but she is batshit crazy. She comes from a mad rich family, he says. A dangerous family, mate, Chico says. And now Achilles is even more intrigued. Tell her I'd like to buy her a drink, Achilles says. Tell her to hang around until I am finished with this interview, he tells him, and Chico heads off to find her. What is your favourite English band? the interviewer asks Achilles. Probably The Fall, Achilles says. And what is their greatest album, in your opinion? *Hex Enduction Hour*, Achilles says, and the reporter writes it down. What in your opinion is the greatest French band?

Heldon, Achilles says, and again the reporter writes it down. And what in your opinion is their greatest album I should listen to? *Electronique Guerilla*, Achilles says. And now, finally, who is the greatest French poet, in your opinion, the journalist asks him, and Achilles says the first thing that comes to mind: St-John Perse. St-John Perse is the greatest French poet, he says. And what do you recommend by him? *The Anabasis of St-John Perse*, Achilles says, and the interviewer asks him, what is an anabasis, and Achilles says, it is an ascent, followed by a descent, and then Chico appears, and he signals to Achilles, and Achilles says, look, I really need to go, is that enough? One more question, the journalist says. Do you like Rimbaud? I love Rimbaud, Achilles says. What is your reason for loving Rimbaud? And Achilles says, because he cured himself of poetry. Because he cured himself of poetry at an early age and walked out the other side of art, into life, he says, which, if you'll excuse me, is exactly what I intend to do, right now.

203

Deeper, into flutter darkness. There is a tree. There is a black tree in the tunnel. The birdwoman points to the tree, which is silhouetted in the darkness like crooked bones. There is something on the tree. There is something impaled on the tree. What is the obverse of Christ? The Precious Gift thinks to himself. The backside of Christ is a murdered boy. A bird is the dream of matter into nothing. Who said that? Now the birdwoman has alighted in his mind. A small boy leaves Firhill Stadium hand in hand with a shadow. It is like The Precious Gift is viewing the scene from up above. The shade leads the boy, with almost impossible speed, up Firhill Road, before cutting onto the canal. For a split second they disappear under a bridge, then reappear on the other side. At one point they pass in full view of the crowd in the stadium, past a group of young men watching the match for free from the towpath. Later, when questioned, none of them will remember the young boy, and the dark shade, passing. There is a final bird. Now they are high above Garscube Road. On their way home, is how it would appear, to passers-by. On their way home from the game. They pass the Highland Distilleries warehouse on Dawson Road. Beneath the pylons. They cut through the trees across from Speirs Wharf and into some shaded industrial wasteland where stones and debris and traffic cones and piping mark out the shape of Omega. And what takes place there at the centre. My brother, The Precious Gift says. What have you done?

204

Achilles Noth heads back to the party, where Chico is sat drinking at a table with Ramona Sánchez and an older Japanese man. Dude, Chico says, when he sees Achilles, here's Ramona, he says, and check this out, he says, pointing to the Japanese man, this guy's name is Hiro Shima. What? It's true, the Japanese guy says, and he offers Achilles his hand. My name is Hiro Shima, he says. I'm very much looking forward to your talk. Are you a Mayanist? Achilles asks him as he pulls up a seat, and Ramona says, he is an arboriculturist. A friend of yours? Achilles asks Ramona, and she says, a friend of the family. We have been talking about his project, she says. And what's that, Achilles asks them. Chico passes him a beer. Hiro researched every tree that was destroyed in the bombing of Hiroshima, Ramona says. Isn't that right, Hiro? That's right, Hiro nods. He is wearing black wraparound shades indoors and is smoking a roll-up. I took on the name Hiro Shima in order that I might restore the trees that were destroyed in the apocalypse, he says. What brings you to the conference, or were you just here to enjoy the tunes? Achilles asks him. I believe I have found the oldest tree in the world, Hiro Shima says. In the Yucatán Peninsula, he says. I believe I have found the original Tree of Life, in Mexico, he says, at the bottom of a crevice, in the middle of the jungle. How did you find it? Achilles asks him. It came to me in a dream, at first, he says. I saw it as if from above in a strange reverie, he says. Then, thanks to the funding I received from the Sánchez Foundation, I was able to take helicopter trips into the jungle and survey the landscape. That is when I saw the wound. The wound? The same wound in my dreams, the deep crevice, the ravine, he says. The ravine where, at the bottom, in the darkness, the oldest tree flourishes. In the darkness, he says again, wearing those wraparound shades as though he is speaking from this same darkness entirely.

205

From Autun, Mindy Sparrow travels to Lyon. She has treated herself to a hotel this time. The hotel is walking distance from the station and as she is wheeling her suitcase along the pavement she sees an old man begging. A hideously ugly man with a face like a terrible bird, with no chin and with a massively elongated forehead and strange googly yellow eyes, is stood there immobile with a cap in front of him on the pavement. No one seems to notice him as they pass but Mindy cannot take her eyes off him. She moves towards him, through the crowd, so that she might read the cardboard sign propped up behind the cap. In very basic French it explains that he was a soldier, during the war. And that now he has nothing. Even as she gets impossibly close to him, so close that anyone would react, the man remains motionless, stood staring into the distance. Is he blind? Mindy thinks to herself. She drops some money into his cap and walks off, troubled by this emaciated man. When she arrives at the hotel, she discovers it is an ancient gambling den and still has its own casino attached. Would you like me to book you a place at a table tonight? the receptionist asks her, another emaciated Frenchman who looks more like Bela Lugosi, and she says, sure, I've never played, but sure. What is the game where you throw dice onto a spinning wheel, she asks Lugosi, and he says, roulette, that would be roulette, and Mindy says, OK, book me a place at a roulette table this evening, please. She is amazed when she realises she can see the towers of the Saint-Jean-Baptiste de Lyon from her window. She changes into her special outfit and walks the few streets to the cathedral. Wooden chairs sit next to old rusty tables in shady side streets. Birds flit through the trees. From an open window someone is singing opera. This is Europe as it once was. Everywhere there are people on mopeds, going this way and that. What a delight to be a young girl on her own in Europe, the way it once was. Safe, in the past. She thinks of Achilles, of what he is up to right now, and of her special mission, her art project, and she feels astonishing.

206

Andrew Lethal is sat at his desk at home, in the early morning, refuting, refuting, refuting. Some clown published a paper saying that when the Jews were expelled from Egypt they arrived in Mexico via a tunnel that runs from North Africa to the Yucatán Peninsula and that Mexico is named after Messiah and that some mad explorer met some members of this lost tribe of Jews hundreds of years ago and that they lived on an island in the Yucatán and that each member of the tribe crossed the waters in a narrow canoe and repeated the same formula to him, reciting the 'Hear Israel' to him, and making gnomic comments on patriarchs who live in the middle of the sea and signalling with their fingers and predicting the arrival of a messiah whose name they said was Mexico. Now this clown is claiming that Mexican and Jewish cosmologies were essentially the same, that the Maya were monotheistic and that their saviour was sacrificed and that the great flood, the biblical deluge, happened in Mexico, where birds were sent out, across the waters, to look for dry land, and all they found were unassailable mountains upon mountains, completely submerged except for their tops. And that in Mayan art all of the cocks are circumcised. Andrew Lethal looks up from his typewriter, out across Tollcross Park, with its hierophantic rose. He sees a bird, a large bird, settle in the centre of the rose garden. What is that? He gets up to have a closer look. Some kind of raptor? It's huge. And then it rises up. It rises up from the roses in the shape of a woman, and it beckons to him. What?! This birdwoman is beckoning to Andrew Lethal from across impossible waters. And now everything is coming true.

207

Put a pillow over that cunt's head, Dan Ruff says to Terry Johnstone. I can't stand looking at this wee bastard's greetin' face, he says. You blinded my boy, he says. Give him a taste of the eternal darkness that awaits him, he says. Terry gets the pillowcase back on his head. He's sitting there naked with a pillowcase over his head and a pool of pish on the floor. Let's talk about the options, Dan Ruff says, and he winks at Terry and Scott. We could kneecap the cunt for starters, Terry says. Shoot him in the back of the knee so he can never walk straight again. Youse are going down for murder, Findlay Hamilton says, between tears and snotters. Double murder, Dan Ruff says, and there are more tears and more bogeys. Have you ever heard the phrase, an eye for an eye? Dan Ruff asks him. Of course I've fucking heard the phrase, Findlay says. Well, that's how the world operates, my friend, Dan Ruff says. You initiated this whole chain of events by attacking my boy for no reason whatsoever other than him being a fruit merchant. Dad, come on, Scott says. I'm not a fruit merchant. Whatever, Dan Ruff says, you took my boy's eye out because you thought he was gay and now look where it ends up. You lot murdered my brother, Findlay says. Youse are the ones that will do time, not me. You ever heard the phrase, better to be hung for sheep than a bam? Dan Ruff says to him. Now there's music playing. Terry Johnstone has stuck on some music. Just sticking that on to drown out the screams, he says. What screams? Findlay Hamilton says. The screams that will be forthcoming, Terry says. It's better to be hung for a sheep than a lamb, the phrase is, Scott Ruff corrects him. Either way, son, Dan Ruff says, you're the sheep I'm happy to be hung for, he says, patting Findlay on the head through the pillowcase. The music is the first Big Country album. The song is 'In a Big Country'. What a fucking track this is, Terry Johnstone says, and he picks up a hammer and hands it to Scott. You first, he says. Fuck this wee bastard up, he says. And Scott takes the hammer in his hand and steps up in front of this trembling kid covered in his own pish and shit who is now begging for his life, and that's when the phone rings. Is that the fucking phone ringing? Terry Johnstone says. Fuck me, it is. Answer it, Dan Ruff says, and Terry Johnstone turns the music down and answers the phone and it's only the fucking polis. It's only the fucking polis who are outside and have the place completely surrounded.

208

Andrew Lethal rushes down the stairs and crosses the road to the park where the birdwoman waits for him in the rose garden. It is Tamar. The birdwoman is Queen Tamar stood among the roses. Tamar, Andrew Lethal says, Tamar, what are you doing here? I thought you were a bird, I thought you were a tall bird, rising up from the flowers, when I first saw you, he says. I'm your guardian angel, Queen Tamar says. Easy to mistake for a bird, she says. Flight and consciousness, she says. Flight and consciousness are the same thing, she says. Wow, Andrew Lethal says. Exactly, he says. They are as far as we can go, he says. In terms of ingress, he says. It's normally one or the other, Queen Tamar says. Except in the case of angels, she says. Which means that I am always with you. And Andrew Lethal starts to cry, stood there, in the rose garden, at the revelation of his guardian angel. Here, she says. I have something for you. She hands Andrew Lethal a file with the word 'Welt' on it. Everything is forgiven, she says. In the end. And she puts her wings around her little boy, stood there, shaking, in Tollcross Park, in the rose garden, in the east end of Glasgow, on this bright new morning.

209

On the dark tree there are birds. Out of tiny seeds grow little birds. Their feathers are weighted this way and that. There is a sound like the tide coming in. Like the tide running across countless little stones in the dark. As the waters rise around his feet, The Precious Gift starts to climb the tree. The dark birds are wittering in many languages. Each bird sings a different letter in this book of death. Higher. There are bodies strung throughout this tree. There are nameless bodies, unrecognisable bodies, decomposing bodies, blown-apart bodies, shot-in-the-head bodies. Vampire, the birdwoman says, in a voice inside The Precious Gift's head. There is the body of Jim Monaghan. The stinking decomposed corpse of Jim Monaghan. If there be fear, let there be fear. If there be a black bird, let there be a black bird. Higher. There is the body of Davey Brennan. The Mole. The stinking decomposed corpse of Davey Brennan. Higher. There is the body of a boy. Nemo.

210

Everyone is heading back to Ramona Sánchez's place in Coyoacán: Achilles, Chico, Felipe, Lucía and Hiro Shima. Have you heard of the ginkgo tree? Hiro Shima asks Achilles in the cab. No, he has not. It is one of the oldest trees in the world, he says. It is thought to be the last living species of the Ginkgoales, Hiro Shima tells him. They arrived on earth 170 million years ago, he says. What do you mean, they arrived on earth? Achilles asks him. Well, Hiro Shima says, one moment they weren't here, and the next they were. Who knows where they were beforehand? he says. When they dropped the bomb on Hiroshima in 1945, six ginkgo trees survived, Hiro Shima tells him, some of the few living things that were not obliterated at the centre of the blast. Wow, Achilles says. But there is more, Hiro Shima tells him. I have located another survivor, he says. I have located another survivor here in Mexico, in the Yucatán. It seems to me that the ancient Mayans cultivated these same trees, these trees that have come to be known as 'the living fossil', 'the survivor' and 'the bearer of hope'. I collected a sample by hanging out of a helicopter, Hiro Shima says. It was the only way to get close. I had the pilot hover above it, in this impossible-to-reach ravine that I had seen in my mind, and I broke a sample off. I can show it to you, later, he says. And the incredible thing is, this tree had been struck by lightning and survived. This dark tree in an abyss of Mexico has defied lightning the way that the trees in Hiroshima defied the atomic bomb, he says. This dark tree of Mexico, he says, and he blows cigarette smoke out the window, still wearing these goddamn black wraparound shades in the night. Ramona Sánchez lives in some mad private complex with a security guard sat in a sentry box outside. Ventura, Ramona says to the guard. Ventura, I have had such a ventura, she says. Are all security guards in Mexico named Ventura, Achilles is thinking to himself. I always make that joke, Ramona says. So funny. She lives in a four-storey building built out of white brutalist concrete. Everywhere there are framed posters of Bob Dylan on the wall. I love Bob Dylan, she says. Do you love Bob Dylan? she asks Achilles and Hiro. Achilles nods. Hiro says, *Blood on the Tracks*. That's all he says. Chico and Felipe and Lucía have arrived ahead of them. Chico is already chopping out lines on the table. Bob Dylan can get fucked, Lucía says, and everyone laughs, though she's mad like she means it. All that shit about infinity going up on trial, she says. Give me a break. But this time no one laughs, and Hiro and Achilles look at each other, just for a second, but all the same. Chico passes round some lines on a dinner plate, and everyone does one, except for Lucía, who says it gives her the fear, fuck that. They head up to Ramona's rooftop garden. Achilles is trying to continue his conversation with Hiro, but Lucía keeps interrupting and offering them shots from her hip flask of mezcal and asking Achilles to dance with her to the music that Chico is playing on a boom box, a compilation he made specially for the 'afterparty'. 'You Can't Put Your Arms Around a Memory' by Johnny Thunders comes on, and Lucía grabs Achilles and starts grinding up on him and dancing away. You can have her if you want, Felipe says to him, again, holding a beer, talking in his ear. But before Achilles can say, no, don't be mad, what are you talking about, Ramona gets in between the two of them and folds her arms and stares at Achilles straight in the eyes and says, no, no, no, you are mine tonight, and before Lucía can even object, Ramona grabs Achilles and drags him downstairs, to a spare room with just a futon and a TV in it, and she pulls up her denim skirt and slides down her panties – she is wearing green panties, everything feels significant right then – and after giving him the greatest blow job of his life (© Ramona Sánchez) she climbs up on him and fucks him senseless, forcing her small tits into his mouth while she speaks in fast Spanish or maybe in tongues, Achilles can't be certain, but when she licks her lips when she comes, it is so sexy for sure.

211

Mindy gasps when she rounds the corner and gets her first glimpse of the Cathedral of Saint-Jean-Baptiste de Lyon. After all, it is one of the most beautiful cathedrals in the world. She steps delicately across the stone floor, her high heels echoing around the light-filled temple like she is sneaking up on herself. She takes out her camera and goes down on one knee in her stiletto heels so she can get a better shot of the famous astronomical clock. Achilles would love this, she thinks to herself. And I love it too. I can see this becoming a passion, she says to herself. Church-hopping, she imagines.

212

Deep in the forest of the Ardennes there is an uncanny fortress. The fortress is built of stone and has no windows or doors. Josef Noth has circled the fortress three times and still cannot locate any means of ingress. Everything is silent except for the songs of the birds. The stone too. Its silent battlements. Impregnable, is the word that comes to Josef Noth's mind. The impregnable fortress at the heart of the wood. The heart of the wood is the scene of tooth and claw. What did St-John Perse call it? A pagoda. A pagoda at the centre of the world from which you can see all of history. A pagoda is a tiered tower. That's when Josef Noth realises. The fortress towers above the trees of the forest and into the clouds. This blasted tower has no end, he thinks to himself. And no entrance, neither.

213

Tell them we have a hostage, Dan Ruff says to Terry Johnstone. Tell the police we have a hostage and that they better back the fuck off, he says. Terry tells the policeman on the phone that they have a hostage, only he calls it 'a hostage situation'. We have a hostage situation, he says, and the policeman says, what do you think this is, fucking *Taggart*? Tell them if they hold back no one will get hurt, Dan Ruff says, and Terry Johnstone tells the policeman, only this time he says that if he 'reins in his boys, no one will get hurt'. The policeman reminds him once more that this isn't fucking *Starsky & Hutch*. That's right, Terry says. This is the fucking *Terminator*, he says, and he slams the phone down, like that. It rings again immediately. Ignore it, Dan Ruff says. They'll smash through that fucking cheap door in seconds, he says to Terry Johnstone. Fucking get some wood and nail that door shut, he tells him. We're under siege. Then seal up all the windows, he says. Wait, he says, what is the back of this house facing onto? A railway line, Terry Johnstone says. Sure, it faces onto the railway line. So they can't come in the back, Dan Ruff says. Good. Scott, you help Terry nail up the windows and doors and I'll deal with this cunt, he says, nodding in the direction of Findlay Hamilton, bollock-naked and with a pillowcase over his head, who immediately starts whimpering, all over again. Then he gets a chair, and he runs up to the top of the stair and he places it on the landing, looking straight down at the front door which Scott and Terry have now nailed shut with bits of wood from out the shed. Then he takes the pillowcase off Findlay Hamilton's head, and he drags him naked up the stairs by the hair, bouncing him off every step as he goes, until he gets to the landing, and he ties him to the chair, facing the front door. If those cunts come through that door, he says to Findlay, you're the one what's getting shot, he says, and he ties Findlay's arms to the sides of the chair and his legs too, and toes him in the naked bollocks for the fuck of it.

214

At The Warehouse in Springburn, The Escapologist draws a picture of a tall figure leading a smaller figure towards what appears to be a sealed fortress. Above them, an angel hangs from the sky. What is the lesson?

215

The first talk at the conference on 'The Mesoamerican Morning: Beginnings and Endings in the Art and Civilisation of the Olmec and Maya' is about Chichén Itzá, in particular the bas-relief carvings in the Temple of the Warriors that feature figures with serpent headdresses covered with feathers. This is by the Mexican scholar Rulo Velásquez. What happened at Chichén Itzá? he asks the room, though it is a rhetorical question, in other words a question that facilitates an answer. They faced off an invasion, Rulo says, Rulo Velásquez, the Mexican scholar of some repute, without waiting for a response. They were invaded by a snake with feathers, who, up until that time, had been the object of their devotion, he says. I would argue, he says, that these glyphs, these emblazoned columns, are more akin to mirrors, he says. Black mirrors, he adds. Metaphysical mirrors, he elaborates. Not art. Achilles Noth whispers in Ramona's ear. Mezcal time, he says, and they slink out of the auditorium together, with all its talk of black and uncanny mirrors at the end of art. The second talk is titled 'Back of the Big Switch' and is about what the author Nicola René describes as 'pre-pictograms'. This is of more interest to Achilles. René talks about cup and ring markings on stones, about how the same signs have been found in Mexico, in Europe and in India. She talks about the knot-languages of the Peruvian quipus – different lengths of string knotted at precise intervals – as not some kind of abacus or counting machine but rather as 'language'. Of notched sticks tied together in angles by the miraculous Polynesian navigators as 'maps' (and here she makes the point that if sticks tied together could show man how to 'cross space' then couldn't they 'speak' of other things too, in lieu of 'language'?). Of the wampum belts, whose beads, sewn together at intervals, served as a musical score, by which singers remembered songs.

216

Mindy Sparrow arrives in Montpellier, where she is couch surfing with another burlesque dancer, Danita St-Simone. Danita is a goth and she has her dyed black hair all crimped up and a snake in an aquarium in the living room, right next to the couch that Mindy is going to be surfing on. You didn't tell me you had an anaconda, Mindy says to her. It's not an anaconda, Danita explains. It's a python. Do you want to feed it some live mice? she asks Mindy. God no, Mindy says. Please yourself, Danita shrugs. Do you like The Cure? Danita asks her. Yeah, I like The Cure, Mindy says, and Danita puts on a song about dancing at a funeral. I've got you on the bill, she tells Mindy. I'm handing over my crown, she says. It's the Miss Rockwear contest at Rouge Profond tonight. Did you bring your outfit? she asks Mindy. I did, she says. But it is more like a sexy Frida Kahlo than a rocker, she explains. Miss Rockwear just means sexy and cool, Danita says. You'll be fine. I've arranged for us to have drinks with some friends, some of whom are single, she says, and she winks. When they pull up at the bar there is a group sat round a table outside, mostly wearing black and everyone in make-up, including the guys. She is introduced to the Odorisio brothers, who have a goth group called Inseminated Insekt, as well as Danita's friends Serafina and Chiara who are smoking cigarettes in cigarette holders and having a conversation about a writer named Georges Bataille. He wrote a book about Gilles de Rais, Serafina tells Mindy, who notoriously murdered children. Why would he write a book about that? Mindy asks them. He saw de Rais as a libertine, one of the brothers, Riz, says. That's repulsive, Mindy says. But no, the other brother, Marcio says, no, that is sacred. What do you mean, murder is sacred? All that is taboo, Riz says – it is like they are a double act – all that is forbidden: sex, death, blood and entrails, he says, all that, is sacred. Well, I think churches are sacred, Mindy says. And beauty is sacred too, she says. The boys roll their eyes. And do you think paintings of angels with feathered wings rising up and sounding horns are sacred? Riz asks her. I do, she says. As a matter of fact, she says, I have been travelling round France photographing these angels for an art project I am working on. What kind of project? Chiara asks her, and Mindy says, I make art boxes where I paint the sun on the front and include all of my pictures of a single church and then I include the underwear that I was wearing the day I photographed it and then I send it to my boyfriend in Paris as a gift, she says. Wow, the girls say, what a mad idea, they say. Your boyfriend must love that, Chiara says, you all dolled up like an angel in a cathedral. Do you wash the panties before you send them to him? Marcio asks her. No, she says. I leave them as they are. Wow, Riz says. That is the sacred right there.

217

Then: after his third circumnavigation of the impassable tower, the sealed fortress, this castle of heaven, windowless, secreted in this secret forest of the Ardennes in 1942, in secret, Josef Noth spots it. There is a ladder.

218

Get in the car. A dark shade sits in the driver's seat. Get in the car. Jim Monaghan is smoking a bifter while taking a piss outside The Alcazar in Derry, in the beer garden of The Alcazar, what a joke, this beer garden is more like a fucking bomb crater, and Derry looks more like the moon at night, a sea of exploded concrete, and no sign of tranquillity in sight, as well as graffiti, endless fucking graffiti, when this car with no lights on pulls into the car park, pulls up to your man Jim Monaghan, and signals for him to get in. Sorry, lads, he says, zipping up his fly, with the snow coming down, but times being what they are I'm not about to get into an unmarked car and driven to my own execution, he says, cause he's a cool customer, your man Jim Monaghan. Get in the car, this dark figure, this shade in the driver's seat, says to him. Sure, it's for your own good, he says. Who are you? Jim Monaghan asks him. You're Jim Monaghan, it says. And you're in there drinking with that bad bastard The Precious Gift, it says. What's he ever done to you? Jim Monaghan asks this shadow, this shadow with a Belfast accent. Did you know The Precious Gift's brother was a jailbird? the shadow says. What's it to you? Jim Monaghan says, though it's true, he had no idea that The Precious Gift even had a brother, never mind that he had done time. The door of The Alcazar opens and it's your man from The Undertones, John O'Neill. He goes over to the boot of his car and takes an amplifier out and walks it into the club. Get in the car, the shadow says, and we'll explain everything. This is starting to look suspicious. That's cause it is fucking suspicious, Jim Monaghan says. It's suspicious as fuck. What are you doing driving around in the dark with no lights on? Subterfuge, the Belfast shade says. Your man The Precious Gift is not who he says he is, the voice says. Get in and I'll explain. Passenger side, it says, and inexplicably Jim Monaghan walks around the car, opens the door, and gets in. There are two silhouettes sat in the back. Here, the driver says, have another bifter, and in the glow of the lighter he catches his face for the first time. Fuck sake, Jim Monaghan says to him. What happened to you? Flew too close to the sun, he says. Mind you, you're one to talk, he says. Here, he says, take this, and he hands Jim Monaghan a folder with the word 'Welt' on it. What's this? Jim Monaghan asks him. It's a dossier, the Belfast ghost says. Who are you? Jim Monaghan asks them. We're The Precious Gift's worst fucking nightmare, this shade says, as they pull out onto the street, into the darkness.

219

At the conference on 'The Mesoamerican Morning: Beginnings and Endings in the Art and Civilisation of the Olmec and Maya', this conference that is taking place in Mexico City, the time has come for Achilles Noth to present his paper, 'The Sacrificial Universe'. The hall is packed. Everyone is there. Linda Schele. Tatiana Proskouriakoff. Chico, Ramona, Felipe. Plus Felipe's crazy girlfriend Lucía. Plus Hiro Shima, the arboriculturist. Plus some drunk guy who is sat in the middle of the front row drinking one bottle of beer after another from a plastic bag at his feet. Noth's thesis is that everything is dying for the sake of everything else. In a nutshell. That's how Ramona sums it up. I read it last night, while he was asleep, she tells Chico and Felipe and Lucía and Hiro Shima. After I fucked his brains out, she adds. How banal, Lucía says, and she makes a big deal of yawning and patting her mouth with her hand. Everyone's dying so that everyone can die. What an insight. No, Ramona corrects her, everyone is dying so that everyone can live, she says. And Hiro Shima says, and yet, there are things that are undying, he says. Things that defy death. Achilles deals with that, Ramona says. These are the demons that the Maya figured in stone. The demons that refuse to die. The demons that refuse to give up their place so that someone else can live. Evil is static, in the view of the Maya, is what Achilles argues, whereas life is what goes. Life is dynamic. And that the Mayan temples were centres of evil. Great centres of evil where the Maya performed the central ritual of sacrifice, of human sacrifice, in stone temples that stood like full stops against the future, is what he says, in so many words, Ramona says. And what he says is that Mayan civilisation didn't last long enough to realise that even stones too, even these stone temples that they believed were manifestations of evil, that were mocking demiurges, in a way, demiurges that had to be stormed by death, ritually assaulted by sacrifice, and murder, were subject to entropy, and endings, and death themselves. And yet they still stand, Hiro Shima says. And the Maya are long gone. And everyone experienced a weird internal shudder when he said that. Here he comes, Felipe says, breaking the frozen atmosphere, as Achilles Noth walks on stage.

220

Achilles Noth's father, Josef Noth, is stood on top of an impossible sealed fortress that towers above the treetops in the forest of the Ardennes, next to that unassailable fortification, the Maginot Line, that final line of defence, that has been sundered forever. And now he can see for miles.

221

Backstage at Rouge Profond in Montpellier, Mindy Sparrow is changing into her Frida Kahlo outfit for the Miss Rockwear competition. She is pinning a silk baby-blue turban to her long red hair, which she has curled up in a bun. Now make your eyes long and sexy with some liner, Danita says to her. Here, she says, do you want me to do your make-up for you? Mindy says that she would love that, and Danita extends her eye make-up into sweeping points that make her look like a cat, like an Egyptian cat, Danita says, and she lets out a purr, or what do you call it, the eye, the Egyptian eye. I don't know, what is the Egyptian eye, Mindy asks her, and she says, what do you call it, the eye, the Eye of Horus, that's what it is. When it opens and closes a whole new world is born, Danita says, and Mindy says, I can relate to that, I've been feeling reborn since I took this trip on my own. It's so daring, Danita says. I would never go travelling on my own. Why? Because of the danger, she says, and Mindy realises, perhaps for the first time, that she has never really considered the dangers, that she is travelling on faith alone, faith in the good nature of other people. You are naïve, girl, Danita says. You need to watch yourself. But Mindy says, nonsense, if you open your heart to the world then it opens its arms to you. Who said that? Danita asks her. Me, Mindy, Mindy says. I said that. I brought a box of records with me, Danita says, you can pick what music you want, and Mindy goes through the box – it's mostly goth and new wave – and comes across an LP by The Undertones, and she says, oh my god, this is perfect, I choose 'Teenage Kicks', she says. After all, she says, it's Miss Rockwear, isn't it? Now some bright-red lipstick, Danita says, on those beautiful lips of yours, and Mindy doesn't even tell her that she was a lipstick model in a former life. Because that's how it feels right now, like another life altogether. She thinks of everything she has left behind, everything but Achilles Noth, who she imagines as up ahead, now, waiting for her somewhere in the future, waiting to hear her fantastic stories of how brave she was in Europe and to see her photographs of the beautiful churches that he loves so much, and, best of all, to sniff her sexy panties.

222

The Precious Gift is ex-Red Hand Commando, The Precious Gift and his brother both, this shade with the Belfast accent is explaining to your man Jim Monaghan. They are in a safe house, is what you call it, in a secret location in Derry, near the famous Derry Walls, because let's not forget that Derry is a walled city, one of the last surviving examples of a city that was completely walled in for its own protection. We know what youse are up to, this Belfast shade is explaining to your man Jim Monaghan. We know that youse are attempting to use psychic powers in order to track paramilitaries. Psychic powers, Jim Monaghan says, what the fuck are youse on about? Remote viewing, the Belfast shade says, and the two heavies that were in the back of the car put their hands on Jim Monaghan's shoulders and press him down onto the couch, which is the only bit of furniture in this bare godforsaken dump, lit up by a single lightbulb. What's your success rate? he asks Jim Monaghan. What do you mean? Jim Monaghan says. I'm asking you how successful are these remote viewings at tracking paramilitary movements? I've no idea what you are talking about, Jim Monaghan says – despite it all, he stays true – and the Belfast shade says, break his fucking balls, and one of the heavies grabs Jim Monaghan from behind and holds him steady while the other takes a golf club from out of a bag propped up against the wall – it's a fucking nine-iron – and fucks him right between the legs with it. Let's start again, the Belfast shade says, as he kneels on top of him and punches him one in the fucking face. Start talking, sunshine, he says. Start talking about these mad fucking dark arts that youse are practising in there with that cunt The Precious Gift.

223

Andrew Lethal is outside the sealed-up house in Acre with a megaphone. Let him through, the police say, and they push through a crowd of gawkers and neighbours and ne'er-do-wells. I work with these communities, Andrew Lethal says. I know how to talk their language. He raises the megaphone to his mouth and a roar of feedback comes out. He presses a couple of buttons and tries again. Hello, he says. Hello, hello. Can you hear me? It's Andrew Lethal, he says. I'm here for you, he says. But we need to talk. The crowd are stood in silence as they wait for a response. It isn't long in coming. Fuck off, you fanny, a voice from inside the sealed-up house responds, and the crowd crack up and start cheering, even as the police are fighting to maintain order and Andrew Lethal can't look round for embarrassment.

224

A fly lands on Aaron's father's thigh as he is sat there in his good suit on a bench in the Botanics, looking like a little boy now. He swats it with a single move. Bam! Wow. Then he looks at Aaron. There are some things you never forget, he says. And now he is remembering that he has forgotten. Something happens to you, he says to Aaron, something happens to you when you lose your boy like that. My boy, he says, and it's heartbreaking. My boy, he repeats, to the birds, and the air. I know, Aaron tells him. I know, he says. Then: Dad, something happened to me too. Oh no, don't tell me, he says, oh no, and Aaron says, no, nothing like that, don't be silly, but something happened to me all the same, when Nemo was taken. I think it's a form of overcompensation, is the way I've come to understand it. I have the power to travel anywhere in my mind. I can move between the specifics of one person's story and the next. I have acquired a bird's-eye view, of all of it. And the thing is, my bearing witness is an inseparable part of the writing of it. Can we write our boy back to us? his father asks him. Dad, you will break my heart. But yes, I think so, I think we can write our boy back. Through force of sorrow, and trauma, he tells his dad, we have the power to bring him back home. And now he is crying there, Aaron's father is crying there on the bench at the thought of his boy, in a story, coming back to him. Who is writing the book, Dad? No one. Nemo. No one is writing this book from an impossible sealed fortress with no means of ingress.

225

This idea of sacrifice, this idea that only through propitiatory suffering can we end suffering altogether, or, worse, that ritual sacrifice affords access to the realm of the supernatural, is the greatest fallacy that humans have ever fallen into. This is Hiro Shima speaking, the arborist and the preserver of the ginkgo tree that survived a nuclear bomb. Everyone is sat around a table on the second floor of a taco joint in a square in Coyoacán, in Mexico City, looking out towards a rundown church and a grand fountain where children and dogs are leaping in and out. It's Old Aeon thinking, he explains. What do you mean? Achilles Noth asks him. Old Aeon, it's a mindset that human beings have been stuck in ever since the first morning, he says, which is what so interested me about this conference when Ramona told me about it, he says. I've heard this before, Ramona says, listen to this, this is pure genius. Chico is back from the bar with a full bottle of mezcal and a fistful of Coronas. Primitive man believed that when the sun went down at night, it died, Hiro Shima says, as Chico pours the shots.

And that, in order for it to be reborn each day, some kind of sacrifice, some kind of atonement, was necessary. For primitive man there was no such thing as eternal life, no such thing as the continuity of existence. But now we know, he says. Now we know that the sun doesn't die at night and get reborn in the morning, now we know that the scarab beetle doesn't roll the sun through the underworld like a ball of shit and return it to us each day. Although we cannot see it, the sun shines, always. And requires nothing in the way of sacrifice to maintain it. The Aeon of the Dying God, which was the Aeon of the Maya, is over, Hiro Shima says. Now, it is the Aeon of Childhood, the true first morning. And what comes after the Aeon of Childhood? Achilles Noth asks Hiro Shima, this mad arborist and the protector of the oldest tree in the world, which is the lightning-struck tree, the atomically rearranged tree, the tree with roots, and he says, why, the Aeon of Ma'at, he says, the Aeon of Peace and Justice, comes next. Who is Ma'at? Ma'at is the angel that weighs your heart at the end of your life, Hiro Shima says. If it is lighter than a feather, then eternal life is yours. What does it look like, this Ma'at? Lucía asks Hiro Shima. A beautiful young woman, marked by two feathers, or wings, he replies.

226

Inside the sealed house in Acre they are talking about Xenophon and the nature of sacrifice. Blood must be spilled, Terry Johnstone is insisting. There's like a cosmic ledger where everything has to balance out, he is maintaining. Scott Ruff is just stood there, listening. But where does it end? Dan Ruff is asking him. Right here, Terry Johnstone says, he is caught up in the madness of the moment, it fucking ends here, he is saying. Code of honour, he is insisting. The Dan Ruff of old wouldn't have thought twice, he is underlining. And then he says, listen, the police are going to storm the house either way and so . . . And that's when Andrew Lethal's voice comes straining through the barricaded walls. It's that fanny Lethal trying to talk us down, Dan says, and Terry Johnstone shouts, fuck off, you fanny, and he hears everyone laugh, sure, there's some crowd out there, he says to Dan Ruff, and Dan says, we need to escape via the railway line before they shut off the trains and come in the back way. Here, he says, Scott, would you get me a big fuck-off kitchen knife from the drawer. Sure, and some gaffer tape. Then we'll leave it in the lap of the gods. But something has clicked in the mind of Scott Ruff, something about the nature of sacrifice and the lack of regret and the duty of brothers, not to say the sanctity of boyhood, and now he's starting to think that there is, perhaps, another way out.

227

And now Josef Noth can see as far as the sun. What was once inside him has been taken from him. Wait, are there horses? Are there horses drawing the sun across the sky? And what's that inside the sun, Josef Noth? A skull. It appears there is the skull of a horse on the face of the sun as if risen up and uncovered by hot sands. And its mouth opens. The skull of the sun opens its mouth, and the teeth fall from it one by one – they make a plinking plonking sound like a wonky piano as they fall – and reveal themselves now as a staircase, a staircase made of tooth and bone that runs all the way up to the sun. And Josef Noth takes a first miraculous step, and then another, as he steps from the roof of this impossible fortress, and he can see his boy from up here, his boy Achilles who will go on to do so well in his life, lit up by the sun, as Thérèse Barnier stirs in her grave, with all of the grace that she had in real life, like some kind of final judgement, to be returned there, also, as the displaced make their way across Europe like the shadow on a lung, and they too rise up with the sun, and the war turns, also, the Russians turn towards Germany, as the pushback begins, and the Allies enter Europe and further still, on the horizon, a great mushroom cloud rises, at its base a blackened tree, as Josef Noth steps into the air, with nothing to hold him up but old bones, in order to disappear in the sun, and become, once more, the cause that was there before any of us. No one. Which is called Nemo.

228

Do you remember, Father? Do you remember how we sat Nemo on the horse, in the fields outside Rose Cottage? And do you remember how we let him go? How the horse charged off with Nemo on its back? And how we ran after it in a panic? And then the sea? How the sea tried to snatch him on the same holiday? The elements conspired in love to take him from us. The wild horses too. And now Aaron's father is remembering. On a bench somewhere in the past now, Aaron's father Donald is remembering the first time he ever saw Nemo, when they picked him up from the foster home. He was asleep in his cot and when Aaron's father bent over him, he woke – he never cried, not until years later, when he snapped his wrist with a rubber band – he woke with a look of joy, his perfect blue eyes, the google of his mouth, as Aaron's father bent over him, a brief sun now himself, and Nemo reached up, and hooked his tiny finger around his father's pinkie, and refused to let him go, as his father lifted him up towards him, become, now, a fisher of men.

229

Call us rebel angels, the Belfast shade says, as he fucks Jim Monaghan in the nuts one more time. Now, I'll ask you again, what was your success rate at Project Deep Run? How many deaths did The Precious Gift prevent? How many did you? And what kind of monsters did you protect? Jim Monaghan can barely speak. How am I supposed to reply if you keep breaking my balls with a fucking nine-iron, he says, curled up like a foetus down there on the ground, his precious balls cupped in his cut and bruised hands. Alright, boys, hoist him up, the shade says, and the two boys lift him up by his arms and drag him over to the single burst couch in this fucking pit of a room. We were monitoring the movements of paramilitaries, Jim Monaghan says. Sure, now we're talking, the shade says. Both sides, Jim Monaghan says. You're hedging your fucking bets, the shade says. It was Republican paramilitaries youse were monitoring, youse didn't give two shades about the movements of Loyalists. The Belfast shade is using the word 'shade' as a curse word now. And how do I know that? this shade asks Jim Monaghan. Because The Precious Gift ran teams for the Red Hand Commando. Some of the most successful teams the Red Hand Commando ever had. These boys had a fearsome reputation. And he protected killers. He protected child killers. Ever heard of the Vampire of Derry? The child murderer they could never catch? Does the name Jackie Semple mean anything to you? Nothing, Jim Monaghan says. That's The Precious Gift's brother. A feared man in the Red Hand Commando. And a paedophile. Did time for disseminating child pornography. Now let me ask you another question. How were youse monitoring these 'both sides', this shade asks him, and he puts his fingers up in the air like ironic speech marks. Remote viewing,

Jim Monaghan admits. We were using remote viewers. Like yourself? Yes. And how does that work, tell me? You pick a location, and you go there in your mind. Like, so, in other words, you imagine it? Yes, but not quite. How not quite? Cause you can see it. See what? See the landscape, the landscape down below. And can you see people? Can you zoom in on people? Sometimes, some people can, yes. Like The Precious Gift? Yes, like The Precious Gift. No wonder the Vampire of Derry was never caught, this shade says. I heard the rumours, that they had some kind of star child running things from behind the scenes. What kind of a fucking name is The Precious Gift anyway? It's like the second sight, The Precious Gift. What I want to know, says one of the shadowy henchmen stood behind the couch, is whether this Precious Gift is looking down on us right now. We're in a house somewhere, Jim Monaghan says. He's not looking down on us. You can't just take the fucking roof off. You have to come through the door, he says. What? the Belfast shade says, and the three lads all look towards the front door of the house. Make sure that fucking door is locked tight, the shade says, and the two lads check the door is bolted just in case, like. You mean they can teleport here like fucking ghosts, this shade asks him, and Jim Monaghan says, not quite, most can't, but some of these fellas, it was rumoured, could literally walk through walls, he says. There were rumours, he says, rumours of operatives that could get inside buildings. In their mind? In their mind. And once they catch a trail . . . Then what? Then they're all over the shop. Then they can move from one story to the next. What do you mean? Once they latch on to someone, they can latch on to everyone associated with that person, and track all these branches, running off. Through space, and time. The redeemers, they call them, Jim Monaghan says. The high-flyers. Apparently, he says. See, here's the thing, the Belfast shade says, as one of the heavies wraps his arm around Jim Monaghan's throat, but before he can reveal what the fuck the thing is, the fucking door comes flying off its hinges and four heavily armoured soldiers, dressed completely in black and with black visors and with heavy machine guns, come barrelling into the front room and blow all three of these lads to literal bloodied shades lying mangled on the floor there, while one of them grabs your man Jim Monaghan and takes him by the arm and leads him, quick as you like, out into the street, where a black armoured patrol car is waiting for them. As Jim Monaghan gets in, he pats the side of his jacket, just to make sure that he still has that folder secreted in the lining there, and he remembers the word 'Welt' written on the front. Who are you? Jim Monaghan asks his captors, as the car jets off into the night. The Feather of Ma'at, a voice says to him, from the passenger seat. What the fuck is The Feather of Ma'at? Jim Monaghan asks him. And the voice says, Department of Justice, and the special operative sat next to him fucks him over the head with a cosh, and he's out for the count, and that's the last thing Jim Monaghan remembers.

230

On stage at Rouge Profond, Inseminated Insekt are making an unholy racket. Danita's pal Serafina is on vocals, while the Odorisio brothers play synth-bass and keyboards. Marcio is wearing a T-shirt that says 'Alien Sex Fiend' on it. Serafina keeps repeating the same words, turn to flesh, turn to flesh. This is pure goth, Danita says, in admiration. Riz wears an oversize black jumper with skintight black denims and Doc Martens, his hair crimped and dyed black. Danita's pal Chiara is dancing, theatrically, down the front, in a billowing batwing top. Chiara went to England to study with

Kate Bush's choreographer, Danita says to Mindy. Said he had a dick on him like a truncheon. They play three songs, all completely submerged in chorus and flange, so that they sound exactly the same. Then Danita jumps on stage and introduces the evening. Welcome to Miss Rockwear France! she says, and everyone cheers. There must be a hundred people in the club, at least. We will be going on cheers alone, on the level and volume of your appreciation, so if you have a favourite, cheer loud, she instructs the crowd. All of the girls tonight have chosen their own music, she says, and we have competitors from all over France, from the goth scene and beyond, she says, including one competitor all the way from England! It's Scotland but whatever, Mindy shrugs to herself, as Danita points her out in the crowd, and everyone cheers. First up is a petite blonde named Sindy in a blue one-piece swimming costume and high gold heels who has studded belts wrapped around her and a dog collar with spikes around her neck. This is like Hot Gossip never happened, Mindy says to Danita, but Danita has no idea who Hot Gossip are. The new-wave blonde does an interpretive dance to the song 'A Forest' by The Cure that is so literal it is cute, parting foliage with her hands like a mime, staring up at dark phantom shadows and mock-running on the spot from the ghosts in the trees. Mindy goes backstage to check her make-up, and Chiara is there, getting ready to go on. Fancy a line? Chiara asks her, and Mindy says, why not, I'm feeling particularly astonishing, and they both snort coke from a hand mirror. Got a gangster boyfriend, Chiara winks, best shit ever, she says. I want a gangster boyfriend! Mindy mock-protests, and Chiara says, be careful what you wish for, honey, and kisses her on the cheek, leaving a big red lipstick mark, cause she is already high off her tits.

231

And that's when Scott Ruff hears Aaron's voice, as clear as a bell. It's like he's stood in this empty kitchen in Acre with him. And now there he is, unmistakably: Aaron has appeared at the far end of the kitchen. He has appeared in this sealed-up house, this impregnable fortress, because he knows what is about to take place. He holds out his arms to Scott. My brother, he calls him, and Scott crosses the kitchen to embrace this ghost, this ghost of his best friend, but how can you embrace a projection? You don't have to do this, Aaron says. But the fact that I'm here, now, says to me that you will. This way I get to rescue everyone, Scott says. This way you all get off Scott-free, he says, and they both laugh, though Aaron starts crying, and then Scott too. Do you remember when we got that Polaroid taken together at the Garden Festival? Scott asks Aaron. In the Clydesdale Bank Tower? Do you remember what I wrote on it? 'We're on our way.' Yes. Well, this is the way. Make no bones about it. But I'm not over any of this, Aaron says. You don't get to be, Scott says. Which is what makes us boys forever.

232

Jim Monaghan wakes up on a park bench in Derry. That goddamn sun, so bright there in the sky, bearing down on him, scorching his eyeballs. When did he become so sensitive to the sun? And how did he end up on this park bench? He is losing his memory. Where does he live? What did he even do before he was a bum asleep on a bench? He feels like a ghost. A ghost that has been tasked with remembering. He puts his hand in his pocket, feels around in there. He has cash, he has a bit of cash. Must have come from the begging. He rolls out of his sleeping bag and folds it up into his rucksack. It is like his mind is a fortress, a sealed fortress, with no means of ingress. He puts on his coat; his animal-hide coat made of fine feathers. His old coat, he thinks, at least he can remember that, right? Where are his shades? There they are, a big massive pair of black wraparound sunglasses. Martin Rev. Martin Rev of Suicide would wear glasses like these when they played at CBGB back in the day. How come he can remember that? Then Vaseline. He smears Vaseline over his face to protect him from the sun's rays, just as he has been doing his whole life. He thinks. Then he remembers something else. He thinks. The Precious Gift. What is The Precious Gift?

233

Now it's Mindy's turn. She looks like Frida Kahlo on acid. Those lips. Come on, Mindy! That riff comes in, that riff that is teenage forever, that riff that is about teenage dreams and how they can't be beat. And Mindy is there in slow motion. The way she moves, it is like she is holding back the song. It is like she is holding on to it for just a few seconds more than she is allowed and refuses to let go. The force of these dreams. She throws her long red hair over her shoulder and it is the trees of eternity. She unravels her scarf and runs it between her legs and it is Rouge Profond, the words flash in the window, Rouge Profond, as a young man grabs her scarf from out of the air and holds it to his nose and inhales her, it is pulsing, Rouge Profond, as she raises her eyebrows, just so, in confidence and in surprise over everything that is happening in this moment, this moment when the Eye of Horus opens and closes, one more time, because everyone in the club is dead and born again, to see this beautiful young woman at the peak of her powers. She is the little bird that everyone wants to hold. Their fast hearts. The warmth of their breasts. Their perfect legs on their stiletto pedestals. It's fair to say that it is a religious performance, this teenage. And now she is crowned Miss Rockwear, as the crowd erupts, and everyone punches the air and says, yes, this is what it is all about, yes, yes, yes! You know that moment when Bianca Jagger came into Studio 54 on the back of a horse? Yes!

234

On the final day of the creative writing programme at The Warehouse in Springburn, The Escapologist had talked about the notion of authorship. Well, not so much talked about it as demonstrated it, Andrew Lethal says to Luke G.B. Caird, and he has to agree. They are having lunch together afterwards. But what was his point? Luke asks him. His point, it seems to me, was that there is no such thing as authorship. Yes, Luke says. There is only bearing witness, he says. That's why he was sat there on stage saying nothing for an eternity, Andrew Lethal says. He was the author inside the brain. Watching. Listening. Or maybe he is not inside the brain, Luke suggests. Maybe the author themselves is out there, he says, and he pointed to the all around them as the presence of the author themselves. At this point, Andrew Lethal confesses, I'm willing to believe anything. By the way, where's Tamar? We split up, Luke confesses. That's a shame, Andrew says. She was a real catch, he says. She blew through my life like a hurricane, Luke confesses. And left me in ruins, he says. And now Luke G.B. Caird is tearing up out of nowhere. Andrew Lethal puts his arm around his shoulders. Better to have loved and lost, he says, than to have never loved at all. Is it, though? Luke asks him. And Andrew Lethal has to admit that he's not exactly sure himself. You know I'm a private investigator on the side? Luke asks him. No, you never told me what you did, Andrew says. Are you going to track down Tamar? he asks Luke. Ha, no, she never left a trail, Luke confesses. All I know is that she worked for Emirates as an air hostess. And then she disappeared. No, he goes on, I'm talking about The Escapologist. You know he was a jailbird? I thought most of the people at The Warehouse were ex-offenders, Andrew says. I thought that was the point. Yeah, but the nature of his offences is pretty shocking, Luke says. Like what? Disseminating child pornography. What?! Yeah, only he said it was art. Mail art. What's mail art? It's art that you send through the mail. Art that you make on envelopes and postcards so that everyone who delivers it can see it. Sounds like a form of exhibitionism. It is, exactly. Anyway, he went down for it. Thing is, he was involved with a notorious paramilitary group in Northern Ireland. The Red Hand Commando. Before he was arrested, there was a spate of missing children, kidnapped, disappeared, mostly in Derry, but across the North. The Vampire of Derry was the name they gave him, this unknown paedophile, who escaped every time, and who was never caught. Anyway, the point is, it all stopped when The Escapologist was in jail. And it started again once he was released. Only he seemed to have broadened his trail. Because boys started going missing in Glasgow too. He calls himself The Escapologist, Andrew Lethal says, and he has to marvel. Fuck me, he says. That's some bold shit. Or just a complete fucking psychopath, Luke G.B. Caird says. Listen, can I ask you something? Luke G.B. Caird says to Andrew Lethal. Do you believe that trauma can change a person? Do you believe that the body – or the mind – compensates for intense suffering with an expansion of the senses? That's when Andrew Lethal explains that he is in fact an expert on the Maya and that he has thought long and hard about the problem of suffering and the sacred. Yes, he says. Yes, I believe that there is a relationship between suffering and access to the sacred. I believe that the Maya made ritual use of this. I believe the Maya were seers who drew their powers from human sacrifice. In fact, I believe that suffering is the precious gift. Without it, barbarism. We call them angels, Luke G.B. Caird says. People who draw on their own wounds, in order to tend to others. We call them angels. Do you believe in angels, Andrew? I do, Luke, Andrew says. I have been visited by them. Me too, Luke says. Me too. When Luke gets back to the office, he tells Mark C. Burl what a good man Andrew Lethal is. He's a good man, Luke repeats, but Mark just goes about his business and says nothing. Then Luke G.B. Caird goes into the conference room, and calls Aaron Murray, and tells him all that he knows. A good man.

235

Mindy Sparrow arrives in Perpignan on the train. All along the route there were flamingos, flying. She had never seen a flamingo in real life. She makes her way to a back street off Rue Petite la Réal, where she has arranged to 'house-sit' while the owner is travelling. Perpignan is a city of dog shit. It is literally everywhere. The buildings look half-lived-in, semi-abandoned, and when she retrieves the key from the lockbox next to the door, two sullen kids stare at her from the dark entrance of a trashed-out apartment across the way. She locks the door behind her when she gets in, but it's beautiful inside, three storeys with a small rooftop garden. She unpacks her things and goes through the photographs she took in Autun. They look amazing. Tonight, she'll paint the first of her boxes for Achilles and post it to him from Perpignan. What a surprise he's going to get. In the meantime, she wants to see the ramparts and the star-shaped Gothic fortress that overlooks the city. And, of course, Perpignan Cathedral. She changes into her special outfit, straps her camera around her neck and puts on her special floppy hat for Europe in the summertime. The streets are deserted. She makes her way up the echoing stairwell to the palace, and it feels more like creeping through a cistern, or a Victorian sewage works. There's no one around as her empty footsteps echo back at her. When she comes out at the top she takes a photograph of the view – you can see the mountains in the distance – as well as a shot of a solitary black cat, sat there by the entranceway to the palace, which unfortunately is already closed for the day. She sees a sign for the cathedral and follows it through winding, medieval streets, with tall worn-down apartments. It is like a ghost town round here. She comes out on a square where there are men sat around reading newspapers and smoking and playing cards. There are no women at all. Mindy really stands out with her floppy hat and her expensive camera. She's starting to feel uneasy. This is the danger they all talked about, she thinks to herself, as she mutters under her breath not to panic, to act calmly and just keep walking. She passes a bar without a door where black women are lined up against the wall with huge afros while the men sit around tables and drink. She's starting to feel lost. Three young boys are screaming at an old woman and taunting her with sticks. She trips down a side street to avoid them. She spots another sign for the cathedral and follows it up a winding back street to the side entrance, where a young man is handing out guides and information. Do you speak English? she asks him, and when he explains that he does, she asks him if Perpignan is dangerous. That depends what part of the city you are talking about, the young man says, and when she tells him where she is staying and where she has come from, he confirms that, yes, it is a very dangerous part of the city, in fact it's the gypsy quarter and they don't even allow anyone to take photographs there. Mindy has to laugh at the oblivious way she wandered through there with her camera round her neck. Sometimes I think it's my complete dizziness that keeps me safe, she says, and they both laugh again. When she enters the cathedral itself, by a side door, she has to gasp. The sheer scale of the cathedral is overwhelming. Not only that: it's the darkest cathedral she has ever been in. There is something oppressive and bleak about it. Even the gold of the iconography feels dead and unreflective. In the corner there is a diorama of Christ's body as it was taken down from the cross. It is grotesque. The figures that surround Christ are broken and missing body parts. One officiant has no hands. Another has a syphilitic wound in its face where its nose has caved in and an eye, a missing eye. A man walks over to her and points to her hat and motions for her to take it off. She totally forgot she still had her hat on. This is the beginnings of Spanish Catholicism, she tells herself, dark and bloody and suffering. She takes some pictures, surreptitiously. She feels self-conscious and weird. It's so dark she doubts any of her pictures will come out, and then she has the sudden urge to flee, to escape this horrible, prophetic cathedral immediately, and she heads for the front door and keeps walking, all the way to the canal, where she spots a steakhouse where she orders beef tartare (why did she do that, once upon a time she couldn't even have a steak rare), and it tastes so good, with chopped capers, and a dark Belgian beer. She sits out on the patio and watches the people going past. Perpignan is a city of freaks, she decides. Everyone seems damaged or broken or insane or all of the above. An old woman with a massively deformed head sits at the table next to her, reading a crime novel with a handheld magnifying glass. A midget goes by on a skateboard. Mindy orders a second beer and she has to laugh. You're so far from home, Mindy, she says to herself. How did you get here? But you're going to be alright. She picks up a bottle of wine on her way back to the flat and spends the rest of the evening painting an archival box scarlet with a great golden sun on the front. She goes through her photographs from Autun – how full of life and thankful joy the carvings of Gislebertus are – and picks out her favourites, which she puts in the box beneath the white lace panties that she wore that day. She doesn't sign her name. Instead, she kisses the rear of one of the photos with her famous lips and leaves a great kiss mark there. Then she ties wrapping paper around the box and addresses it to Achilles Noth, in Paris. He will be so astonished, she thinks to herself, and she gets so horny that she masturbates in bed, just thinking about him. Then she falls asleep, looking out at the abandoned buildings all around her, feeling adult and brave. How could anyone ever find her?

236

OK, let's fucking split this joint, Dan Ruff says to Terry Johnstone in this sealed-up house in Acre. You fucking talking to yourself, he says to Scott, as they cut through the kitchen. Just singing a song to myself, Scott says. Fucking amazing, Terry Johnstone says. Talk about grace under fire, he says. Findlay is tied up at the top of the landing with a fucking blade taped to his hand. They'll think it's a booby trap. That'll keep them off our tails for a bit. We'll scale the fence and cut across the railway line, make our escape. Of course, we'll need to go into hiding, Dan Ruff says, but we'll deal with that when it comes. We're gypsies, mind, he says to Scott and Terry. We're used to living off the map. Here, he says to Scott, I'll give you a footsie up, and the three of them climb over the fence and make their way down the steep embankment to the railway line. But there's something in the shrubbery, on the other side of the tracks. Something is moving in there. Fucking hell, I thought that was the polis for a second, Terry says. I think it's some kind of big fuck-off bird, Dan says. A fucking heron or something, he says. Aaron. It's Aaron, Scott thinks. Come back as a bird. The time is now. Watch me, Scott says. What? Dan and Terry have already crossed the tracks. Quick, Dan says. Get a move on. There's a fucking train coming. Sure enough, from round the bend there is the sound of a train barrelling towards them. Watch me. Scott says it again. Then: everything is forgiven. And he takes a step forward, onto the tracks, in perfect time for the train to cut him down, and to destroy him completely.

237

Josef Noth checks into a hotel in Derry. It has taken him decades, but he has tracked down one of the killers of Thérèse Barnier, the mother of his son, Achilles, who, on the contrary, he has been completely unable to locate. The other one, the killer's accomplice, was long dead once he got to him. Fuck it. Half-revenge is better than no revenge at all. The killer's name is fucking Klaus Von Fucking Bullshit whatever. After the war he met an Irish woman and moved to Belfast, and when she died he inherited the family home in Derry. He's retired now, and lives there on his own, where he plays in a traditional folk trio at his local pub, the Golden Gate, at the Waterside, every Wednesday. Josef Noth, too, is at the end of his rope. He has never been the same since the accident, the accident on the farm he worked at after the war, outside Wuppertal, where he fell into a vat of hot slurry and burnt all of his hair off, and poisoned himself, and burnt some of his skin off too, and – inexplicably – turned his eyeballs yellow. That's what finished him with poetry. Spit-roasted like a hog in a trough of boiling shit. Well, it would, wouldn't it. Now, all he reads are books about the war, particularly guerilla warfare, particularly tales of the resistance, in Germany, in Poland, in France, and in Cambodia, and in Vietnam too. Booby traps. Deadly asphyxiating tunnels. Floating mines. Suicide bombers. Punji sticks coated in faeces and urine and animal blood and pus. Spiked bamboo whips. Snake pits. Tiger traps. The ingenuity of man's hatred for man, the absolute savagery of his revenge, never fails to impress him. And now, this final mission. To kill some frail old bastard who will have no idea why he was even murdered. Getting a handgun in Derry was easy. All you need to know is the right taxi driver. They'll even throw in a balaclava, gratis, free of charge, zip. Josef Noth arrives at the Golden Gate just as the band are setting up in the corner. He orders a pint of Guinness. Pint of Guinness for the Angel of Death. The barman looks into the face of the Angel of Death and doesn't flinch. Every night there are Angels of Death in here, drinking, puzzling, plotting, punishing. You've seen one face with the skin flayed off, you've seen them all. Klaus Von What The Fuck Ever has some kind of involuntary spasm that seems to only calm down when he plays the hand drum. This is like some kind of care-in-the-community bullshit, Josef Noth thinks to himself. Klaus Von What The Fuck Ever is an emaciated old cadaver now. The killer. What a joke. His friends in the band seem glad to see him, they're joking about how every fucking time he gets a pint of Guinness in his hands he fucking spills half of it down his fucking front before it gets anywhere near his fucking gob. Josef Noth orders a cheese toastie at the bar and listens to the music. They are singing songs about the ancient heroes of the olden days. That was you and me once, he thinks. Heroes, he spits. Only I kept my hatred sharp. He removes a photograph from his pocket, the photograph of him and Thérèse and The H and St-John Perse, stood there, in the Magic-City, in Paris, in the mouth of Leviathan, in the years before the war. What happened to us. The obliteration of the world. That is what happened to us. As he walks to the toilet, he notices a middle-aged man sat with two older women, talking conspiratorially. It's the guy from the hotel, Josef Noth realises, it's the guy that spoke to me at breakfast, he thinks to himself, and although he doesn't look up, there's something that makes him think of the poet St-John Perse, all those years ago. *In the flaming heart of the moment, man is immortal.* Two boys, for a moment there. And he thinks of the impossible fortress, that impregnable tower in the Ardennes from where he ascended into the sun, like a trapdoor fucking exit, and left the war behind. Josef Noth pulls a balaclava over his head and draws a handgun from the waistband of his trousers, amazed to be back in the war again. He walks into the bar and without a word or a warning or a single thought in his head he blows this cunt's fucking lights out, and then he walks out, calm as you like, and disappears in the sun. And now his name, once more, is Nemo. An old god.

238

I am your atoning angel, Aaron. This is The Precious Gift speaking now. In his flat on the eighth floor of the Wyndford Estate, from way up in the air there. It was only through the appointing of my own angel that I received The Precious Gift, he is telling Aaron. Which was the revelation of my own angelhood. I have watched over you ever since I came into your life, Aaron, he tells him. There is a second anabasis, he insists. Make no bones about it. But Aaron can see beyond all of this, now. That is the gift that *Boyhood*, and not The Precious Gift, has given him. Because now he knows that the angel of The Precious Gift was truly no angel at all. Because he has read it in the book. Still, everything is speaking. And the voices are, unmistakably, those of angels.

239

Lucía is taking Achilles Noth on her promised tour of the underbelly of Mexico City. But first they go to the Coyoacán Market to get some seafood cocktails with ketchup and a couple of shots of mezcal. Felipe is a homo, Lucía says, when they take a seat at a table outside in the sunshine. That's one thing you should know, she says. I'm fucking Chico on the side, she says. The Black Pig?! Achilles says, and Lucía says, gotta get it where you can. Besides, she says, I'm basically a lesbian. Anyway, she says. Do you like sleazy strip clubs and rock 'n' roll bars? I do, Achilles says. But I also like cathedrals and old ancient buildings too. Unfortunately, that's not my speciality, she says. But I can take you to the Metropolitan Cathedral if you like. But before that you must come to my favourite bar, the Exotic Dancer. My mother was a dancer, Achilles Noth says. An exotic dancer? A ballet dancer, a famous French ballet dancer. She knew Picasso, apparently. She was disappeared by the Nazis. Well, we'll need to be a little careful ourselves if we're not to be disappeared in Iztapalapa, Lucía says. Why? It's the most dangerous part of Mexico City. The Exotic Dancer is in El Hoyo, The Hole, in Iztapalapa, Lucía says. She doesn't even ask a thing about Achilles' mother or her fate at the hands of the Nazis. We'll get a taxi in and out, she says. Don't worry, they know me at the bar, she says, and sure enough, when they pull up at the Exotic Dancer (it is lit up there, in English) some guy with a moustache and greasy shoulder-length hair greets her in Spanish and when he sees Achilles he says to her, so, who is your victim tonight? I'm going to have to search you, the guy says, and he tells Achilles to put his arms out by his sides. Then this dude reaches out and cups Achilles' balls in his hand. Just in case you were hiding a bazooka in there, he says, and he laughs and waves them in. Ignore him, Lucía says. He is just fucking with you. But Achilles is a little freaked out and starting to feel weird. The bar is at the back of what looks like an abandoned used-car lot. On either side of the entrance there are old classic cars like T-Birds and Cadillacs all piled up on top of each other and rusted in the sun. There's that familiar Mexican bouquet of sweat and piss and gasoline and grease. In the doorway someone is flipping tortillas on a hotplate. Eat that and die, Lucía says, pointing at a greasy pile of cooked entrails. They pass through a curtain into the red light of the interior. On stage there is a man in drag wearing thigh-high boots, a one-piece bathing suit and a wig, singing Spanish disco in a cage. They get locked in there, Lucía says. An hour each. Can't even take a piss, she says. They take a couple of stools at the bar. All round the sides of the room there are women in short dresses and bikinis. At the tables there are groups of men in cowboy hats, some of them with women on their laps. Hey Frenchie, Lucía says. This is my pal Achilles, she says. What you having? Frenchie asks them, a fat woman who looks like an overgrown child. Two beers, Lucía says. And two mezcals. And some chapulines, she says. Have you ever eaten dried grasshoppers? Lucía asks Achilles. I actually love them, he says. Then Lucía says, do you think we are near the end of the world? What? Do you think that the end of days is imminent? Lucía asks him. I think it is always just before the end of the world, Achilles says. Or maybe always just after it. You think it's after the end of the world? Lucía asks him, and Achilles gestures around the room, bathed in this infernal red light and hot as hell. I think this is almost exactly what it would look like after the end of the world, he says. Well, we were just hanging out with a man called Hiro Shima, Lucía says. That would seem to be a portent that the world is already over. Listen, she says, we should get a room. What? You and I, we should get a room, Lucía repeats. They have back rooms here, you have to see them. The engine rooms. What? The very engine rooms of Mexico are beneath this bar, she says. The machinery of night, she says. Who said that? You're thinking of Allen Ginsberg, Achilles says, of the poet Allen Ginsberg, only he called it the dynamo of night. The dynamo of night is beneath the Exotic Dancer, Lucía says. She's drunk already. Anyway, we should get a room, you and I. You can fuck one of these women, she says. After the end of the world, she says. In the dynamo of night, she says. In Mexico, she says, and she raises her glass to the fat-child barwoman Frenchie and they both shout out, Mexico! Come on, she says. I can watch you fuck her, she says. Pick a girl for me, Achilles says. You choose. After all, he says, you are my guide to the underbelly. Do you like curves? Lucía asks him. I have no curves, she says. I am basically a boy. I like curves, Achilles says. And asses, big asses, and legs, he says, strong legs, he says. You want to be asphyxiated by a Colombian, in other words, Lucía says. Leave it to me.

240

Andrew Lethal gets a phone call at his office. It's Dangerous Dan Ruff. Dan the man, Lethal says. Where the fuck are you? I'm not going to fucking tell you that, am I? he says. I'm on the run, he says. Listen, he says. My boy is dead. The way he says it, his boy, it gets to Lethal, in this new world of angels and innocent children that he's living in. I heard, Lethal says. And I'm sick to death of it, he confesses. Of what? Dan Ruff asks him. Sacrifice, he says. Violence, he says. Revenge. I used to think it was a song. What? Dan Ruff asks him. All of it, he says. I thought it was just music. Just? Dan Ruff asks him, and he has to laugh. Sure, I'm sorry about your boy, Lethal says. But you know the police have closed the case on the murder of Brian Hamilton. When they rescued Findlay, he identified Scott as being the one who shot his brother. They think Scott killed himself through guilt and desperation. My boy is an angel now, Dan Ruff says. He was perfectly innocent, he says. You don't need to hide, Lethal says. You'll get a deferred sentence. You're not going to do time. You were a distraught father, that's all. I'll stand up for you. You know how I feel about your community. Listen, Lethal says, I have something for you. Can we meet? Can we meet one more time? I just want to pass something on that I think might help you. If you betray me, then I will be doing time for murder, Dan Ruff warns him. I'm loyal, Lethal says. Loyal to life, he says. These days.

241

The Precious Gift makes his way to The Warehouse, in Springburn. He has a final appointment, with his brother, The Escapologist. The revelation of Jim Monaghan's angelhood, of his watching-over of The Precious Gift, means that there is some kind of cosmic reckoning taking place. Finally. Otherwise, The Precious Gift is less than life. Together, the two brothers recall their boyhood together, its terrors and joys. Their father, and his father before him. They reminisce about their time as homeless bums in Krakow, all those years ago. Of the mail art scene, which they were both active in, back in the day. And the industrial music scene, which they both passed through. Their time, together, in the Red Hand Commando. And how it couldn't have been any other way. Do you believe in free will? The Escapologist asks The Precious Gift. I see no evidence of it anywhere, The Precious Gift says. Except once, maybe. Which is why I am here, finally. Still, you are a lover of liberty, The Escapologist says. Yes, The Precious Gift says. Within the confines of the game, he says. The game, The Escapologist says. You have to admit, he says. What a game. Yes, what a game, The Precious Gift says, and then he says, I know everything, Jack. He calls him Jack. Can The Escapologist really be called Jack? Again: I know everything. Make no bones about it. I've protected you for far too long. And now the game is up. Finally, The Escapologist (Jack?) says. Write it like it's real, he says. With a pencil in your mouth like a fucking paraplegic, he says. The fact that I am here, The Precious Gift says, means that it is written. And with that the pair get up, and embrace each other, one last time, as brothers, and The Precious Gift walks out, into the precious sunlight, and leaves The Escapologist to literature.

242

Aaron is sat on the bench with his father in the Botanic Gardens in the west end of Glasgow. Look, Dad, he says, and he draws a handgun from the waist of his trousers. That's a . . . machine, his dad Donald says. That's a machine for shooting, he says. Whatchamacallit. A chatsby. It's a gun, Aaron says. I believe I have found the man who kidnapped and murdered Nemo, he says. Your son, he adds, just in case, because you never know with Aaron's father at this stage. Are you going to blow his balls off? Donald asks him. Yes, Aaron says. And he has to laugh. I am going to blow his balls off and each of his limbs one by one so that he is left looking like a starfish, Aaron says. How do you know? Donald asks him. How did you find out about my boy? An angel told me, Aaron says.

243

The Precious Gift appears to Jim Monaghan in Derry. He looms over him on a park bench in Derry where Monaghan has been sleeping under newspapers to protect himself from the sun. Jim, he says. The Gift, Jim says. How do I know you, you're The Gift, he says. I am The Gift, Jim. I am The Precious Gift, he says. What is the vision of the fortress? Jim Monaghan asks The Precious Gift. I don't know, The Precious Gift replies. What is the vision of the fortress? Jim Monaghan is starting to remember. It is something unassailable, he says. It is an impossible density that lies at the centre of the world, he says. I have seen it, he says. With my own eyes. Your eyes are no more yours than this fortress at the centre of the world, The Precious Gift says. What else have you seen with these supposed eyes of yours? Murder, Jim Monaghan says. Kidnap and murder. And what did you do about it? Nothing, Jim Monaghan says. Who is this person that witnessed and who is this person who did nothing? The Precious Gift asks him. That is the vision of the fortress, Jim Monaghan says. Have you compromised us, Jim? Who's 'us'? Jim Monaghan says. I can't remember. In that case you're a dead man, The Precious Gift says. I'm sorry, Jim, but that's why I'm here. I'm the Angel of Death, he says. And Jim Monaghan says, who is this person who is dead? Nemo, The Precious Gift says. It is no one that is dead, he says. Then The Precious Gift takes Jim Monaghan by the arm, and leads him to his car, and they drive out to the Prehen Woods, to an impossible fortress, one of them never to return.

244

Mindy Sparrow heads off to the post office in Perpignan to send Achilles Noth the first of her astonishing art boxes. What a beautiful, fresh morning it is. The birds flit around the high apartments, pale-coloured in the sun beneath the blue sky. Afterwards she goes for a glass of wine and a cheeseboard, in a back street parallel to the canal. Everywhere around her young people are drinking and eating. No one seems to have a care in the world, except perhaps for how to extend this perfect moment forever. She has so many dreams. Perhaps she will be an artist in the world to come. After Europe. Or a singer, maybe. A singer in an art exhibition of all her photographs, where she will stand in the corner of the gallery and sing a song of pure longing and sex and affirmation and joy. It's unlikely she will have kids. What's wrong with a woman not having kids? What's wrong with living life on your own terms? These are the thoughts that Mindy Sparrow is having on the terrace of a bar in Perpignan, in her first daring summer of adventure. And of her and Achilles Noth marrying, and living in a tiny village in France, in peace but with culture, owning a stereo and cooking each night and occasionally going to a concert and dancing together. I'll look back at this trip as the beginning of my life, she thinks to herself, and she mutters under her breath, yes, forever, like a mantra or a prayer. Then she gets up and consults her map. There's a park near her apartment, and in the centre of the park, a pagoda. She decides to make her way there. When she arrives, she can see that the park is dilapidated and gone to seed. There are fenced-off pastures where animals used to be kept in an urban zoo, now completely deserted. Plus, there isn't a soul around. It's all over for this park, Mindy thinks, as she climbs a spiral path where all of the city opens up beneath her. Strange modernist flats, curving medieval terraces; in the distance, there, the mountains. Mindy thinks of flamingos, flying. Suddenly there's a voice out of nowhere. Someone is approaching her up the path. He shouts something in French, what? He wants her handbag. In this deserted park he wants the contents of Mindy Sparrow's handbag, which amounts to some make-up, a hand mirror, her accidentally pilfered copy of the collected short stories of Silvina Ocampo, and her bank card. He pulls out a knife. Vite, he says. Help! Mindy Sparrow screams, and she starts shouting from next to this deserted pagoda in this rundown park, as her assailant grabs her – one arm round her throat, the other a tight fist in her hair – and drags her into the bushes.

245

Here, Andrew Lethal says. I want to give you this. He's meeting up with Dan Ruff at an undisclosed location in Robroyston. Dangerous Dan Ruff. It's the Aztec obsidian scrying mirror that the magician John Dee used to communicate with angels. I had my mate The Janitor nick it from the British Museum and replace it with a fake, he says. But I've no need of it now. This is priceless shit, he says. Maybe you can talk to your boy with it, he says. Angels, he says it again. But Dan Ruff says, no. I've no need of it neither, he says. It's a beautiful gesture, Andrew, he says. And then he says, I got a tattoo to remember my Scott by, Dan Ruff says. It just came to me, he says. And he pulls up his shirt to reveal a pair of feathers, just beneath his left nipple.

246

Lucía comes back with a girl named Vedah. This is Vedah, she says. Statuesque Vedah, voluptuous Vedah, she says, and Vedah laughs, her long dark hair, her glittering eyes, her gold bikini top, her short black skirt, and she says, baby, do you want to tie me up and eat my asshole in a private room? And Lucía says, he wants you to smother him, then she corrects it and says, I want you to smother him, with your ass, she adds, just to be clear. Yes, Achilles says. Yes, I want to tie you to my face and eat you, he says. It is like he is tripping on drugs or something. Is it seafood poisoning from that fucking market? He's feeling woozy. You want to be smothered by her ass in the engine room of the night, Lucía says. Isn't it a shame, she says, that man is born from a pussy but can't crawl up a woman's asshole when he dies? Vedah says something to one of the bartenders and he leads them down a sloping corridor where the heat is infernal. It's like they are burrowing through an escape shaft into the earth. Finally they come to a door, a door in a long corridor of doors. It's like they are tunnels into the underworld itself, what a turn-on, Achilles is thinking, though at the same time it is confused, as if Lucía has spiked his drink and he is experiencing everything from above or outside of it. The bartender unlocks the door and beckons them inside. There is a bed made from a wide wooden board strewn with sheets with dubious stains on them beneath a single bare lightbulb. Do you want to wear a condom because bareback is extra, Vedah says, and Lucía interrupts to say, of course he doesn't want to wear a condom. This is a ritual, she says. We intend to give birth to something tonight. Tie her up like a starfish, Lucía commands Achilles, and Vedah lies face down on the wooden board while Achilles ties her hands and legs to the base of the bed. Then Lucía says: open the curtains. Achilles gets down on his knees at the foot of the bed and slides Vedah's skirt up round her waist and pulls her gold bikini bottoms to one side and spreads the starfish of her asshole. At first, he toys with her, sliding a single finger in and out, tapping and probing. But then he opens her cheeks – what a vista – and enters her with his face. His tongue is deep in the dark brown of her asshole. Open the curtains. Lucía commands it again. Achilles rises and there are curtains – red velvet curtains – hung on the wall next to them. The infinite folds of the rose. Open the curtains, Lucía commands Achilles, again, and Achilles gets up from where Vedah is spreadeagled – face down, her skirt up round her waist, her bikini bottoms pulled back – and parts the red velvet curtains that have appeared next to them. Behind the curtains there is a featureless wall. Knock on the door, Lucía commands. What door? Knock on the door, she repeats, and Achilles shrugs and knocks on the wall, three times, like that: doom, doom, doom. And then a door opens. A door opens in this sealed, featureless wall, and Achilles steps inside. It is a nest. Inside it is a corridor lined with feathers and scraps and wool and grass and mud and soil and blood and mucus and yes, ~~memory~~ excrement. There is a fluttering of wings on the furthest horizon of consciousness, which is caked red, now, like a gauzy sunset, or a smouldering sunrise. Deeper, into flutter darkness, and there is a tree. The lightning-struck tree. The atomically rearranged tree. The tree with roots. Impaled on the tree is a series of corpses, rising up. One of which is a young girl. A young girl is pinned to the tree in the scarlet darkness. Hot, like metal boiling. Black, like ashen trees. And what takes place there at the centre.

AND WHAT TAKES PLACE THERE AT THE CENTRE

This is Nemo at three months old. He could recognise voices and follow moving objects quite well. He seems to have an amiable nature, and he seldom cries.

In the garden during a spell of sunny weather. Nemo's screwed-up little face shows what he thought of the sun. Date: 13.7.74. Hair: Blond. Weight: 15lbs 3½ oz. Eyes: Blue.

A 'real swinger'. Nemo still has a happy nature which shows in the smile which now can turn into a genuine giggle.

Now six months old, able to sit up by himself – with the occasional tumble. His face is fattening and his features forming. Date: 20lbs on 18.10.74. Still no teeth and a little more hair!

Nemo's Timetable: Wakened: 9 a.m. Bath & Breakfast: 9.30 a.m. Lunch: 1.30 p.m. Tea: 5.30 p.m. Supper: 9.30 p.m. Bedtime: 10.30 p.m. (or anybody's guess). Nemo is a sleepyhead by morning and alert and wakeful by evening.

First tooth! 21.11.74.

Nemo's first Christmas: What a lot he got! Horses. Teddy Bears. Panda. Rupert Bear. Building Cups. Pyjamas.

Trousers. Jumpers. Racing Track. Reins. Plastic Bib. Stuffed Toys. Cot Rattle. Chocolate. Bell. Suit. Plastic Pants. Bubble Bath. Jumpsuit. Mobile. Money. Drinking Cup. Dungaree Trousers. Sweets. Vests. Rubber Building Toys. Hot-Water Bottle.

1975: Resumé. Weight: 24lbs. Teeth: 6. Age: 8½ Months. Skills: several sounds, recognition of object names, swift movements on back, can reverse baby-walker. Likes: picture books, car rides, tearing paper. Dislikes: crowds, going to bed.

Between 10–12 months: complete control of baby-walker now, for speed and manoeuvring. But despite ability to stand, still no attempts to make walking movements. Losing the baby look! Getting the cheeky look!

Nemo's First Birthday: speaking only a very few words. Gabbling but not English. Understands well enough. A little more at ease with strangers and interested now in other children. Walking steadily, managing obstacles with better balance. Feeds himself efficiently but messily. Still has a four-course breakfast! Bedtime is still very unpopular but getting better – usually 9 p.m. Still an avid reader with quite a library of books. Probably will need reading specs by age two. Certainly has lost that early placid nature. More self-willed.

July 1975: Nemo accepted our visitors pretty quickly. Now very active and has the run of the house but it does not seem to tire him any more quickly nor make bedtime any more attractive. Allowed out in the back garden alone now but doesn't like amusing himself for very long.

December 1976: First word! Car. Nemo seems to have discovered speech all of a sudden and has acquired a good vocabulary in a short time.

Steady enough on his feet now to play outdoors but has discovered his ability to climb stairs. Nemo has only just learnt to stand up and sit down without help. Now he can't be immobilised!

The always-smiling look has now been replaced by the occasional drawn brows and dour disapproval. Nemo's way of asserting his newfound self-will! Can stand quite firmly and walk with a steadying hand. Definitely a 'man's man' who waits all day for the return of Donald. Walks outside with his dad are now in great demand. The chair has gone out of favour somewhat since Nemo found he could take steps. He now walks and runs in it rather than side-stepping.

Nemo and Aaron co-exist fairly well, though Aaron's tendency to destroy any constructive game can make him unpopular. Favourite co-operative game at the minute is 'chasing' i.e. frantic dashing from room to room. Favourite shared activities: leaping (from sofa). Leaping (from washing basket). Leaping (from chairs). Tramping (through the wettest, muddiest parts of the plot). Result: bumped heads, sodden clothes, frayed nerves. A change noted in Nemo's play – more creative with building materials, more imaginative in his use of cars, models, etc. He loves his model fortress, and he plays with it daily. He plays very well alone but prefers inside when it's cold. Affectionate, talkative, needs lavish praise, helpful/cheeky, articulate, sensitive, sometimes aggravating.

Nemo started school enthusiastically and without fuss. His teacher is Mrs Simpson. He has taken to schoolwork very easily and seems to learn quickly. Nemo goes to school by car because it's rather far away.

Advances noted. Drawing: better controlled, can now really depict objects. In figures draws head/body/limbs. Imagination: plays 'shops', 'mummies and daddies', 'soldiers' and 'monsters'.

Holiday at Rose Cottage: Nemo really enjoyed his first holiday, especially having constant company. Nemo slept and ate well but can be affected by too much sun. Now he is no longer afraid of horses. Or of the sea.

POSTSCRIPT

Achilles Noth arrives back at his apartment on Rue Lepic in Paris after his visit to Mexico. He waters his plants, then goes through all the mail that has arrived. Journals. Some vinyl. A few books. And an inexplicable box with a postmark from Perpignan. Achilles doesn't know anyone from Perpignan. He cuts through the wrapping with a small knife, revealing a sealed red box, battered from the post, with a crude painting of the sun on top. He breaks the seal and removes the lid. There's a pair of white lace panties in there. What? Beneath the panties, which are obviously used, are individual photographs of some cathedral somewhere. On the back of one of the photographs there is a lipstick kiss. No other details. Who knows what the hell that is about, Achilles Noth thinks to himself, and he tosses the box to one side, where it slides along the floor and ends up lost, and forgotten, behind the floor-length curtains, from where it is retrieved a few weeks later, by Achilles Noth's cleaner, and deposited in the bin.

Anabasis.

QUOTED MATERIAL

p. ix: Dickinson, E. 'Split the lark and you'll find music'/'Loyalty' in *Poems by Emily Dickinson: Third Series* (ed. M. Loomis Todd). Boston: Roberts Brothers. 1896.

p. ix: 'The Four Legends of St Mungo', in *Vita Kentigerni* (comm. Bishop Jocelin of Glasgow). 1175.

p. 3: 'Sixty Eight Guns' by The Alarm (I.R.S. Records). Written by Mike Peters and Eddie MacDonald. 1983.

p. 4: 'Hot Legs' by Rod Stewart (Warner Brothers). Written by Gary Grainger and Rod Stewart. 1978.

p. 6: Perse, St-John. *The Anabasis* (trans. T.S. Eliot). London: Faber & Faber. 1930.

p. 7: Xenophon, *On Horsemanship (The Art of Horsemanship)* (trans. H.G. Dakyns). Project Gutenberg, 2013.

p. 7: Feather, Leonard G. *The Encyclopedia of Jazz*. Boston: Da Capo Press Inc. 1984.

p. 8: *Trout Mask Replica* by Captain Beefheart & His Magic Band (Straight). 1969.

p. 8: *Hex Education Hour* by The Fall (Kamera). 1982.

p. 8: *Marquee Moon* by Television (Elektra). 1977.

p. 8: *Fun House* by The Stooges (Elektra). 1970.

p. 8: *The Modern Dance* by Pere Ubu (Blank). 1978.

p. 8: *The Modern Lovers* by The Modern Lovers (Beserkley). 1976.

p. 8: 'Live in Sheffield, 1966', *The 1966 Live Recordings* by Bob Dylan (Columbia). 2016.

p. 8: *Suicide* by Suicide (Red Star). 1977.

p. 8: *Sounds of a Tropical Rainforest in America* by Smithsonian Folkways (Folkways Records). 1952.

p. 9: *Andy Warhol's Velvet Underground Featuring Nico* by The Velvet Underground (MGM Records). 1971.

p. 10: *Electric Warrior* by T. Rex (Fly Records/ Reprise Records). 1971.

p. 10: *Dandy in the Underworld* by T. Rex (EMI). 1977.

p. 10: 'Ride a White Swan' by T. Rex. (Fly Records). Written by Marc Bolan. 1970.

p. 11: French, Marilyn. *The Women's Room*. New York: Summit Books. 1977.

p. 11: 'Cosmic Dancer' by T. Rex (Fly Records/ Reprise Records). Written by Marc Bolan. 1971.

p.16: *Declaration* by The Alarm (I.R.S. Records). 1984.
p. 19: Kipling, Rudyard. 'If' in *Rewards and Fairies*. London: Doubleday, 1910.

p. 25: *The Anabasis*.

p. 25: *The Elephant Man* [film]. Screenplay by Christopher De Vore, Eric Bergen and David Lynch (dir.), Brooksfilms / Columbia–EMI–Warner Distributors. 1980.

p. 26: Dalí, Salvador. *Christ of Saint John of the Cross,* 1951. Oil on canvas. Kelvingrove Art Gallery and Museum.

p. 26: *The Anabasis*.

p. 31: *Songs the Lord Taught Us* by The Cramps (I.R.S. Records/ Illegal/ Zonophone). 1980.

p. 33: *Songs the Lord Taught Us*.

p. 34: Eliot, T.S. *The Waste Land*. London: Hogarth Press, 1923.

p. 34: *The Anabasis*.

p. 44: *The Anabasis.*

p. 46–7: Benjamin, Walter, *The Arcades Project* (trans. Howard Eiland and Kevin McLaughlin). Massachusetts: Harvard University Press. 1999.

p. 50: *The Anabasis.*

p. 51: 'The Floral Dance' by Terry Wogan (Philips Records, 1978). Written by Kate Emily Barkley Moss. 1911.

p. 52: 'Red Red Wine' by UB40 (DEP International/ Virgin). Written by Neil Diamond. 1983.

p. 53: *The Anabasis.*

p. 54: 'Being Boiled' by The Human League (Fast Project). Written by Philip Oakey, Martyn Ware and Ian Craig Marsh. 1978.

p. 56: *The Anabasis.*

p. 58: Rilke, Rainer Maria. 'The Rose-Window' in *New Poems* (trans. Stephen Cohn). Manchester: Carcanet Poetry. 1997.

p. 58: Cendrars, Blaise. *Moravagine* (trans. Alan Brown). London: Peter Owen. 1968.

p. 58: Apollinaire, Guillaume. 'L'Adieu' in *Alcools* (trans. Donald Revell). Massachusetts: Wesleyan University Press. 1995.

p. 58: De Nerval, Gérard. *Aurélia* (trans. Geoffrey Wagner). New York: Grove Press. 1959.

p. 58: Keats, John. 'Ode to a Nightingale' in *The Poetical Works of John Keats* (ed. H.B. Forman). London: Reeves & Turner. 1884.

p. 58: Rimbaud, Arthur. *Illuminations* (trans. John Ashbery). New York: W. W. Norton. 2011.

p. 62: 'Sixty Eight Guns'.

p. 68: *The Elephant Man.*

p. 73: 'Hero' by Neu! (Brain, United Artists). Written by Michael Rother and Klaus Dinger. 1975.

p. 74: Shakespeare, William. *Hamlet.* London: Edward Blount, William and Isaac Jaggard. 1623.

p. 76: 'I Won't Let You Down' by Ph.D. (WEA). Written by Jim Diamond and Tony Hymas. 1981.

p. 80: Shaw, Bob. *Other Days, Other Eyes.* London: Macmillan. 1974.

p. 83: *V* [television series]. Created by Kenneth Johnson. Kenneth Johnson Productions / Warner Bros. Television. 1983.

p. 86: Da Vinci, Leonardo. *Mona Lisa*, 1503. Oil on poplar panel. Louvre.

p. 86: *Venus de Milo.* Parian Marble. Louvre.

p. 87: Géricault, Théodore. *The Raft of Medusa*, 1819. Oil on canvas. Louvre.

p. 87: Delacroix, Eugène. *Liberty Leading the People*, 1830. Oil on canvas. Louvre.

p. 92: *Guinness Book of Records.* London: Guinness World Records Ltd.

p. 93: 'I Feel Love' by Donna Summer (Casablanca). Written by Donna Summer, Giorgio Moroder and Pete Bellotte. 1977.

p. 95: *The Anabasis.*

p. 99: 'Forever Young' by Bob Dylan (Asylum). Written by Bob Dylan. 1974.

p. 104: 'Teenage Kicks' by The Undertones (Good Vibrations / Sire Records). Written by John Joseph O'Neill (© West Bank Songs Ltd.) 1978.

p. 104: 'Forever Young'.

p. 106: 'Eleanor Rigby' by The Beatles (EMI). Written by Lennon-McCartney. 1966.

p. 107: *This is Our Music* by Ornette Coleman Quartet (Atlantic). 1961.

p. 107: Byron, Lord. 'Dark Lochnagar' in *The Works of Lord Byron*. London: John Murray. 1819.

p. 116: Gide, André. *The Immoralist*. New York: Alfred A. Knopf. 1930.

p. 116: Gide, André. *The Return of the Prodigal Son*. London: Secker and Warburg. 1953.

p. 116: Gide, André. *The Counterfeiters*. New York: Alfred A. Knopf. 1927.

p. 116: Gide, André. *The Fruits of the Earth*. New York: Alfred A. Knopf. 1949.

p. 116: Gide, André. *The Attempt at Love*. London: Secker and Warburg. 1953.

p. 117: 'The Magnificent Dance' by The Clash (CBS). Written by Joe Strummer, Mick Jones, Topper Headon, Norman Watt-Roy, Mickey Gallagher. 1980.

p. 117: 'You're the One For Me' by D. Train (Prelude). Written by James Williams and Hubert Eaves III. 1981.

p. 119–21: *On Horsemanship*.

p. 120: 'Fat Bottomed Girls' by Queen (EMI). Written by Brian May. 1978.

p. 124: *Radio City* by Big Star (Ardent). 1974.

p. 124: *Like Flies on Sherbet* by Alex Chilton (Peabody). 1979.

p. 124: *Collision Drive* by Alan Vega (Celluloid). 1981.

p. 124: *The Idiot* by Iggy Pop (RCA Victor). 1977.

p. 124: 'When the Moon is Strong' by Toerag (Onset/Offset). Written by Steven Tobeck. 1985.

p. 124: *River Falling Love* by Wreck Small Speakers on Expensive Stereos (Ajax Records). 1993.

p. 124: *Bewitched* by Look Blue Go Purple (Flying Nun). 1985.

p. 125: Rustaveli, Shota, *The Knight in the Panther's Skin* (trans. Marjory Wardrop). London: The Royal Asiatic Society. 1912.

p. 129: *On Horsemanship.*

p. 135: *Taxi Driver* [film]. Screenplay by Paul Schrader. Dir. Martin Scorcese. Bill / Phillips Productions / Italo-Judeo Productions. 1976.

p. 135: Verne, Jules. *Twenty Thousand Leagues Under the Seas* (trans. Anthony Bonner). London: Bantam. 1962.

p. 135: Wells, H.G. *The Time Machine.* London: William Heinemann. 1895.

p. 135: Stoker, Bram. *Dracula.* London: Archibald Constable and Company. 1897.

p. 137: *Picture Book* by Simply Red (Elektra). 1985.

p. 139: Nietzsche, Friedrich. *Beyond Good and Evil* (trans. Helen Zimmern). Edinburgh: T.N. Foulis. 1906.

p. 141: 'Truth Is Marching In' by Albert Ayler (Base Records / DIW / ESP-Disk). Written by Albert Ayler. 1966.

p.143–4: *The Knight in the Panther's Skin.*

p. 150: Eleazar of Worms, *Three Tracts.* California: Tree. 1975.

p. 151: *Reader's Digest Atlas of the World.* New York: The Reader's Digest Association. 1963.

p. 154: Xenophon, *The Cavalry Commander (The Cavalry General)* (trans. H.G. Dakyns). Project Gutenberg. 2013.

p. 159: 'Never Gonna Give You Up' by Rick Astley (RCA, PWL, BMG). Written by Stock Aitken Waterman. 1987.

p. 162: Michelangelo, *Sistine Chapel Ceiling*, 1512. Fresco. Sistine Chapel.

p. 162: *Death in Venice (Original Motion Picture Soundtrack)* by Various Artists (Varèse Sarabande). 1971.

p. 168–9: *The Knight in the Panther's Skin.*

p. 171: *On Horsemanship.*

p. 171–2: *Neighbours* [television series]. Created by Reg Watson. Grundy Television / Fremantle Australia / Amazon MGM Studios. 1985–2025.

p. 174: *Happy Birthday* by Altered Images (Epic/ Portrait). 1981.

p. 177: 'Eleanor Rigby'.

p. 179: *Live in Japan* by John Coltrane (Impulse!). 1973.

p. 179–80: *Annie Hall* [film]. Screenplay by Marshall Brickman and Woody Allen (dir.), Jack Rollins and Charles H. Joffe Productions. 1977.

p. 183: *The Knight in the Panther's Skin.*

p. 187: *Cheers* [television series]. Created by Glen Charles, Les Charles and James Burrows. Charles / Burrows / Charles Productions / Paramount Television. 1982–1993.

p. 188: *It Came from Outer Space* [film]. Screenplay by Harry Essex. Dir. Jack Arnold. Universal Pictures. 1953.

p. 190: 'Teenage Kicks'.

p. 190–1: 'I am sitting in a room' by Alvin Lucier (Lovely Music). Written by Alvin Lucier. 1969.

p. 191: Ocampo, Silvina. *Thus Were Their Faces: The Selected Short Stories of Silvina Ocampo* (trans. Daniel Balderston). New York: New York Review Books. 2015.

p. 197: *Reporting Scotland* [television series]. BBC News / BBC Scotland. 1968–Present.

p. 198: *Blankety Blank* [television series]. Created by Frank Wayne. BBC / Fremantle. 1975–Present.

p. 198: 'To All the Girls I've Loved Before' by Julio Iglesias and Willie Nelson (Columbia). Written by Hal David and Albert Hammond. 1984.

p. 202: Kafka, Franz. *Kafka's Diaries*. New York: Schocken Books. 1964.

p. 202: *Harvest* by Neil Young (Reprise). 1972.

p. 209: 'Smooth Operator' by Sade (Epic). Written by Sade Adu and Ray St John. 1984.

p. 220: 'I'll Find My Way Home' by Jon and Vangelis (Polydor). Written by Jon Anderson and Vangelis. 1981.

p. 224: *Star Wars: Episode IV – A New Hope* [film]. Screenplay by George Lucas (dir.), Lucasfilm Ltd. / Twentieth Century Fox. 1977.

p. 224: Warhol, Andy. *Electric Chair*, 1967. Silk screen ink on synthetic polymer paint on canvas. Froehlich Collection.

p. 225: 'My Perfect Cousin' by The Undertones (Sire Records). Written by Damian O'Neill and Michael Bradley. 1980.

p. 227: *The Epic of Gilgamesh (Gilgamesh)* (trans. Stephen Langdon). Project Gutenberg. 2006.

p. 228: *The Anabasis*.

p. 230: 'Joan of Arc' by OMD (Dindisc). Written by Andy McCluskey. 1981.

p. 242: *On Horsemanship*.

p. 245: Paz, Octavio. *The Labyrinth of Solitude* (trans. Lysander Kemp). London: Allen Lane. 1967.

p. 253: Dostoevsky, Fyodor. *The Idiot* (trans. Constance Garnett). London: William Heinemann. 1913.

p. 253: Joyce, James. *Finnegan's Wake*. London: Faber. 1939.

p. 253: Shakespeare, William. *King Lear.* London: Edward Blount, William and Isaac Jaggard. 1623.

p. 253: *Hamlet.*

p. 254: Shakespeare, William. *Romeo and Juliet.* London: Edward Blount, William and Isaac Jaggard. 1623.

p. 257: Melville, Herman. *Pierre; or, The Ambiguities.* New York: Harper & Brothers. 1852.

p. 257: Melville, Herman. *Redburn: His First Voyage.* New York: Harper & Brothers. 1849.

p. 257: *The Anabasis.*

p. 260: *The Fall Guy* [television series]. Created by Glen A. Larson. Glen A. Larson Productions / 20th Century Fox Television. 1981–1985.

p. 266: *It's Alive* by The Ramones (Sire). 1979.

p. 267: 'True Confessions' by The Undertones (Good Vibrations / Sire Records). Written by John Joseph O'Neill, Michael Bradley and Damian O'Neill. 1979.

p. 267: *Indeterminacy* by John Cage (Folkways Records). 1959.

p. 268: 'Just Can't Get Enough' by Depeche Mode (Mute Records). Written by Vince Clarke. 1981.

p. 273: Da Vinci, Leonardo. *The Last Supper*, 1498. Tempera on gesso, pitch, and mastic. Santa Maria delle Grazie.

p. 274: 'Sultans of Swing' by Dire Straits (Vertigo). Written by Mark Knopfler. 1978.

p. 274: 'Ghost Rider' by Suicide (Red Star). Written by Martin Rev and Alan Vega. 1977.

p. 274: *Andy Warhol's Velvet Underground Featuring Nico.*

p. 274: *It's Alive.*

p. 274: *Hex Education Hour.*

p. 275: *Electronique Guerilla* by Heldon (Ursus Records). 1974.

p. 275: *The Anabasis.*

p. 280: *The Crossing* by Big Country (Mercury). 1983.

p. 283: *Blood on the Tracks* by Bob Dylan (Columbia). 1975.

p. 283: 'You Can't Put Your Arms Around a Memory' by Johnny Thunders (Real Records ARE3). Written by Johnny Thunders. 1978.

p. 285: *Taggart* [television series]. Created by Glenn Chandler. Scottish Television / STV Studios. 1985–2010.

p. 285: *Starsky &Hutch* [television series]. Created by William Binn. Spelling-Goldberg Productions / Columbia Pictures Television. 1975–79.

p. 285: *The Terminator* [film]. Screenplay by James Cameron (dir.) and Gale Anne Hurd. Hemdale/ Pacific Western Productions/ Cinema '84. 1984.

p. 288: 'The Funeral Party' by The Cure. Written by Simon Gallup, Robert Smith, Lol Tolhurst. 1981.

p. 293: 'Teenage Kicks'.

p. 303: 'A Forest' by The Cure (Fiction Records). Written by Simon Gallup, Robert Smith, Matthieu Hartley, Lol Tolhurst. 1980.

p. 314: *The Anabasis.*

p. 317: Ginsberg, Allen, 'Howl', *Howl and Other Poems.* San Francisco: City Lights Books, 1956.

p. 322: *Thus Were Their Faces.*

CREDITS

White Rabbit would like to thank everyone at Orion who worked on the publication of *Boyhood*.

Agent
Clare Conville,
Conville & Walsh

Editor
Lee Brackstone

Copy-editor
Silvia Crompton

Proofreader
Kim Bishop

Editorial Management
Susie Bertinshaw
Ciara Mongey
Lily McIlwain
Alistair Thompson
Jane Hughes
Charlie Panayiotou
Lucy Bilton
Patrice Nelson

Audio
Paul Stark
Louise Richardson
Georgina Cutler-Ross

Contracts
Rachel Monte
Ellie Bowker
Phoebe Miller

Design
Steve Marking
Nick Shah
Deborah Francois
Helen Ewing

Photo Shoots & Image Research
Natalie Dawkins

Finance
Nick Gibson
Jasdip Nandra
Sue Baker
Tom Costello

Inventory
Jo Jacobs
Erika Andrejuskinaite

Production
Sarah Cook
Michael Peters
Katie Horrocks

Marketing
Tom Noble

Publicity
Aoife Datta

Sales
Dave Murphy
Victoria Laws
Sammy Luton
Group Sales teams across Digital, Field, International and Non-Trade

Operations
Group Sales Operations team

Rights
Rebecca Folland
Tara Hiatt
Ben Fowler
Maddie Stephenson
Ruth Blakemore
Marie Matuschka